Desert Dwellers Born By Fire

The First Book in the Paintbrush Saga

Desert Dwellers Born By Fire

The First Book in the Paintbrush Saga

Sarah Bergstrom

LODESTONE BOOKS

Winchester, UK
Washington, USA

First published by Lodestone Books, 2015
Lodestone Books is an imprint of John Hunt Publishing Ltd., Laurel House, Station Approach,
Alresford, Hants, SO24 9JH, UK
office1@jhpbooks.net
www.johnhuntpublishing.com

For distributor details and how to order please visit the 'Ordering' section on our website.

Text copyright: Sarah Bergstrom 2014

ISBN: 978 1 78279 587 2

A CIP catalogue record for this book is available from the British Library.

Design: Stuart Davies

Printed in the USA by Edwards Brothers Malloy

We operate a distinctive and ethical publishing philosophy in all
areas of our business, from our global network of authors to
production and worldwide distribution.

CONTENTS

To my son, Jordan, for his hand in designing this book, for my son, Jesse, whose insight is always valuable to me, and to Rachel, whose encouragement and writing critique shaped the final script.

Acknowledgments

Thank you first of all to my husband, for financially supporting this endeavor so that I was not a poor, starving artist, and for his encouragement. Also, thanks to my parents and brother for being the first readers, and my mother and father-in-law, whose continual support means so much. My mentor, Krystina Kellingley, and her cunning eye, for helping me improve as a writer, the rest of the team and John Hunt Publishing for taking a chance on me. My writing group led by Roxanne Sadovsky, who pushed me to rewrite and then supported me through the process, and to Issac, who, wanted to read the manuscript and meet to discuss it.

Finally, thank you to the youth in my life who first inspired the characters: my nieces, nephew, cousins and young friends. You are the salt of the earth.

"And think not within yourselves, We have Abraham to (as) our father: for I say unto you, God is able of these stones to raise up children unto Abraham."
(Matthew 3.9 King James Bible)

Preface

My eldest son, Jordan, coauthored this book on many levels over the past five years but he does not wish his name to appear as an author. This book is essentially plagiarized from his mind. The world, the creatures and the events are all designed by him. Jordan gave me assignments for each chapter and we developed a system. I'd write a chapter, we'd read through it together and he'd offer feedback, then I'd rewrite and reread the chapter before getting my assignment for the next one. It was a rewarding experience and I'm grateful to him for his patience, his enthusiasm and his perseverance through this process.

Jordan has always been interested in geography and during seventh grade was one of only a hundred students in all of Minnesota, grades five through eight, to attend the State National Geographic Bee. He's poured over atlases and articles on different regions and people living around the world.

While I did the writing, character formation and plot, he extensively researched all plants for each climate and drew a map of the world with its various regions. The story and place are fictional, but the geography is fairly realistic. See if you can figure out what is real and what isn't. You might be surprised at what you find.

This aside, the book is not meant to educate, but to entertain, so sit back, relax and enjoy the ride. If you like this book, as I'm sure you will, I hope you'll explore some of these places for yourself and create your own adventure, as I try to do with every hike and camping trip, taking joy in being outside, understanding how to live as we were designed to live, as part of the created world, still being created.

Please visit me at www.desertdwellersbergstrom.com

Prologue

Clara's blue eyes widened with surprise as the door opened and a glowing figure entered, blocking the shadowed hallway beyond. Her face and hair emitted a halo of bright orange and yellow light, as if she were encased in fire. Long black hair draped over her shoulders like strands of fine silk, framing a delicate face. Clara ducked behind her father's robe as her surprise gave way to apprehension. She looked up into her parents' faces — it was time.

"Lourdes, you made it! Were you seen?" Clara's father asked, his forehead layered with wrinkles.

"No," the woman reassured him. "I came in just down the hall and checked for guards first. But you know I can hide in plain sight if I need to."

Einar breathed a sigh of relief, the stranger's answer appearing to satisfy him.

Lourdes gave Clara's parents a troubled look. "I wish I could convince you to come with me."

Einar adamantly shook his head. "They'd find us. The king needs us, but he doesn't need Clara, and he won't go out of his way to find her." He shot Clara's mother a glance and his face relaxed as he saw the approval in his wife's expression.

Alexis was small next to her towering husband and her face was youthful. Strands of silver hair cascaded around her shoulders and shimmered in the sunlight streaming in through the window of the small, sparsely furnished room. She turned back to the woman. "Tell the others not to trust the king, and don't send any more of your sick to the palace for treatment."

"What happened?" Lourdes asked, dismay filling her voice. "The king assured us—"

"Yes, I know, but he lied," Einar said flatly. "His gestures of friendship are a farce. I know that's hard for you to understand, but he's bent on destroying you. He's never had any intention of helping. He's used your sick for …"

"For his experiments. He's trying to make weapons, living weapons," Alexis finished. "He's betrayed us, too, using our research to kill instead of heal. He plans to use these weapons on you," her voice faltered but she regained control. "You all need to leave and go into hiding. You can't stay there. He knows where you are!"

"You know that we'd never leave Orchid Pond." Lourdes shook her head. "It's our oracle, the Spirit resides there. Leaving is not an option. We'd die to protect it!"

"If you want to protect it then leave! The king doesn't care about the pond, only you," Alexis said, grabbing Lourdes's arm.

"We won't leave. I'll relay what you've told me, but it'll never happen," Lourdes replied, giving Alexis a firm look, clearly communicating that the discussion was over.

Clara saw her mother bow her head and bite her lower lip, reigning in her frustration.

Lourdes turned to Clara. "Don't worry, you'll be with people like yourself."

Clara bowed her head like her mother had, avoiding the woman's gaze and picking at a spot of oatmeal on her cloak. Her stomach clenched as she realized that the breakfast they'd just eaten was the last meal she'd share with her parents for a very long time. What did, 'people like yourself' mean anyway? She could feel their eyes cutting into her like lasers, exposing the fear inside, and wished they'd keep talking and forget what was supposed to happen next. Her stomach churned as if something was whipping her breakfast into pancake batter.

"Thank you for believing us. We didn't know how the king was using our research. We've stopped working for him, that's how we've ended up in this prison. He left us alone for a while but now he wants more from us. We can resist, as long as—" Alexis's eyes rested on her daughter. "Thank you for taking her."

"Clara, you'll be in good hands," her dad said. He choked up, swallowed, and forced a smile.

"Why does the king hate us?" Lourdes asked, and Clara heard the stranger's steady voice crack. "We're peaceful."

"You're powerful and that's all he sees," Einar said. "You're a threat to humans, in his eyes. There's nothing you can do to change him."

"I don't understand?"

"There's nothing to understand — it's reckless jealousy. Listen to my warning and pass it on to the others. He talks about Old Earth a lot. We believe he wants to recreate the way things were back there."

"What does that mean?"

Einar searched the woman's face in disbelief. He rubbed his hand across his chin. "You don't know? There's no time to explain. I wish I could but you need to go before the guards come back," he said, gently urging them towards the door.

"Will I ever see you again?" Clara asked, staring at her father's brown, fuzzy curls, not wanting to see doubt in his expression. She wanted to be strong for her parents, but who could be strong when they were being forced to leave their home forever?

Einar silently held out a travel cloak that Clara obediently slipped her arms into. He lifted her pale curls free to tumble down her back. Alexis handed Lourdes a cloth bag which she stuffed into her backpack. Clara thrust her chin out to force a courage she did not feel but she couldn't conceal her quivering lower lip. She was nine years old, forced to flee a home she'd never before left, because of a battle that made no sense to her.

"We will see each other again, Clara," her mother said with determination. "And you'll be safe there. They'll take good care of you. You're not safe here and though it breaks my heart, that's why you have to go."

"But that means that you're not safe either!" Clara fought back the tears flooding her eyes but they rolled, uninvited, down her cheeks.

Her mother stroked her hair. "Quiet, Clara! As we told your guardian, we won't be harmed as long as we stay here. Going with you would endanger all of us and we need to know that you're safe."

Both her parents hugged her before relinquishing her to the mysterious woman. "Please," Alexis whispered.

The woman nodded, gently taking Clara's hand and stepping quickly into the rock hallway. Clara glanced each way, checking for the familiar sight of the prison guards, burly giants who looked like normal people in every other respect, but were many times the size of her parents and teachers. They had always been good to her; even sneaking her treats and toys on occasion.

"Clara, stop!" One of the giants ordered as he rounded a corner and saw them.

Clara turned, halting in her tracks, considering what to do, while her guardian tugged her the other way. It felt strange to be escaping the people who'd cared for her with someone she didn't even know. It felt wrong to disobey them but when she glanced back at her parents, panic had whitewashed their faces.

"Run!" Her dad's voice faltered even as he called out to her. Clara stared, the guards were charging towards her, the once gentle giants' features twisted into furious creatures she hardly recognized.

Lourdes tightened her grip on Clara's hand and yanked her along the hall so fast her feet hardly touched the ground. Clara didn't dare to look back but she could hear the pounding grow louder as the guards lumbered closer.

Suddenly, Clara was hoisted towards the ceiling. There was a hole in the solid rock above and Lourdes threw her up into it. Clara clung to the ledge and climbed into a dark space, swiftly scrambling out of the way to make room for her companion. Her guardian leapt up to grasp the edge of the opening, levering herself up until she could lift her legs inside. One of the giants reached for her ankle but his fist closed on empty air.

Lourdes placed her hands over a pile of speckled rock near the hole they'd just climbed through. Her hands glowed red hot, like flaming steel pokers shaping liquid glass; melting the rock until it was soft enough to smooth over the passage. The soft rock sank into the opening, quickly solidifying upon meeting the cool air. Lourdes continued spreading more liquefied rock over the sinkhole in a manner that reminded Clara of someone icing a cake. The surface would look undisturbed if not for swirls and ridges that appeared out of place amid the layered granite surrounding it. Once her hands extinguished their light and the rock cooled, having sealed them inside, it was dark as midnight.

"We're safe for the moment," Lourdes whispered, "but they know where we are now. This hallway won't be abandoned for long. Hurry!"

So that's what it was, a hallway, just like the one below, Clara thought to herself as she ran behind her guardian in the pitch black. They traveled for what, to Clara, felt like hours before finally stopping. Once again the woman's hands glowed red as she placed them on the wall to the right of them and conjured intense heat to melt the rock.

"I hear something!" Clara exclaimed. "They're coming from the other direction, ahead of us." Lights bounced up and down, growing larger as they closed in on them.

Lourdes shoved the magma putty outside to reveal another dark tunnel. "Clara, now!" she hissed urgently. Clara slipped her legs through the hole and jumped down. Her feet and hands landed on more rock. The blackness around her was so thick it seemed as if she should be able to touch it.

"We're underground," Lourdes said as she slipped through the opening to join Clara. "This tunnel will take us to the surface. Run, I'll catch up!"

"But, it's dark. I can't see!"

"Just go!" Lourdes ordered as she turned around to replace

the putty.

Clara had taken a few hesitant steps when she heard a scuffle. She glanced back to see a giant hand firmly grasp Lourdes's forearm, steering her hot hand away from its huge bulk while pulling her inside the palace walls. Lourdes struggled against him, trying desperately to pry her arm away, but the guard was too strong.

Clara paused. She had to help Lourdes — but how? "Run! Run! Go!" Lourdes decided for her.

Clara ran, stumbling along the tunnel a short distance before a scream from behind brought her to a stop. Turning around, she saw flame converge onto Lourdes's free hand, erupting from her fingertips, igniting the guard's wrist like a candlewick. The giant broke its grip on Clara's guardian and pulled back, nursing the injured limb, while Lourdes fell to the ground. There came another terrifyingly loud scream from within the rock fortress, resounding with pain and anger. There was no time to seal the hole. Lourdes scrambled up off the ground. Another guard squeezed his large body through as she bolted towards Clara.

Clara was about to resume running when she saw more flames blaze out, but this time, the fire streamed from behind her guardian like a rocket. Automatically, she braced for impact as Lourdes swiped her off the ground. They sped forward at light-ening speed, Clara clinging to Lourdes, who held her tight with one arm while extending the other as a kind of torch. The light pouring from her guardian's hand provided a semicircle of vision ahead of them. Dirt walls and snarled roots rushed past as they raced along the lengthy incline to the surface.

"I see a patch of sunlight," Lourdes said at last. "We're almost at the surface."

Clara's spirits lifted slightly as she turned her head and saw a bright circle, growing larger as they approached. Within seconds the oppressive dirt walls opened into a forest of evergreen trees, sparse enough to let the light shine its full strength on them as they burst forth out of the ground.

However, Clara's joy was to be short lived as over Lourdes's shoulder she spotted a horde of guards in hovercrafts, descending on them like flies on a rat carcass.

"Hold tight!" Lourdes ordered, swinging around and plowing through the forest, setting a random, zig-zagging course in a frantic effort to throw off the league of giants rapidly gaining on them. While the hovercrafts were fast, they were not able to maneuver between trees with the same finesse as her guardian. Nevertheless, they were merely inches away at every turn.

"Lourdes!" Clara screamed as one of the craft swooped alongside of them. Long arms swung over and yanked her away from her guardian. In the instant Lourdes took to perceive what had happened, the craft sped away. Clara stared back despairingly.

Undaunted, Lourdes, blazing hands held out in front of her, as fearsome as any flame breathing dragon, raced towards the guard who'd taken Clara, plunging fire deep into his chest cavity, teaching a fatal lesson to any who would snatch her charge. Pausing only long enough to make sure Clara was secured to her, Lourdes leapt into the air again. Clara's arms and legs clenched around Lourdes as her guardian once more tightened her one armed grip.

Glancing back, Clara could see that many of the giants had continued the chase but Lourdes's speed and skill outmaneuvered the hovercrafts. The two pulled further and further ahead and sped alongside the mountain range. Finally, after losing their pursuers, Lourdes found a secure place to set down.

"We walk over the ridge," she told Clara. "Flying will draw too much attention. But we need to keep our eyes open. Let me know if you see anything suspicious."

Clara nodded obediently, keeping her thoughts to herself; her guardian was the most suspicious character she'd ever seen.

After a while Lourdes said, "Why does the king hate us so

much?" Her voice sounded weak to Clara's ears.

"I figured the king hated everybody," Clara said, matter of fact.

To her surprise, Lourdes chuckled. "I suppose you're right, I shouldn't take it too personally."

Cold air nipped at Clara's chin and nose and she shivered as they walked. Finally, she succumbed and voiced the question that had been eating at her since the start of their escape. "So, how do you make fire come out of your body?"

"I'm one of the fire reaume. That's what we do."

"I've heard of reaume, in school, but everyone considered them — well, bad. I don't know why. We weren't allowed to talk about them. The teacher told us it was inappropriate."

"Inappropriate?" Lourdes asked and shook her head. "Unbelievable."

Clara shrugged. "So how can you live outside of the dome? My teachers say that no one can survive outside."

"Your teachers say a lot of strange things, I think. We prefer living outside to being confined in a dome."

"But the dome protects us. There are so many dangers out here, like, cold and wild animals and dark." Clara's eyes were wide. She held her forearms glued together in front of her shivering body, an inadequate shield against the unpredictable wind gusting randomly around her. Her shoulders slumped forward.

Lourdes paused and slipped an arm around her and she sank against her guide's robe, peering around the wilderness.

"I assume that's what your teachers would have you believe," she said. But what do your parents say?"

"They say that's not true, but I don't really know what to think. I know you probably don't like them, but my teachers are really smart."

"I'm sure they are, but let me assure you that your parents are as smart as people can get." Lourdes paused, she knelt down, bringing herself level with Clara, her eyes shifting randomly around, as if searching for the right words to magically appear in the trees. She placed a hand on Clara's shoulder. "Listen, I won't tell you there are no dangers out here because there are, but sometimes it's more risky to hide from something than to face it. There are times when you *must* hide because it's the only thing you can do, but shutting out the world is like backing yourself into a corner with no way out. I know that you'll miss your parents, but living outside the dome will be good for you, Clara — you might even find it fun. Your parents know that, and they want that for you. Listen, I have a son your age and he would not, for one minute, trade his life outside the dome for life inside."

Somehow, the idea that Lourdes had a son made Clara feel better. "What's his name?"

"His name is Aedan," Lourdes told her as she rose to her full height and continued walking. "And he can't wait to finish his daily chores so that he can play."

Clara studied her guide as they marched along. Lourdes was very pretty, one of the prettiest women Clara had ever seen, with smooth skin the color of the golden caramel candies the giants used to sneak in for her.

A biting breeze blew through Clara's cloak and she shivered even more as they ascended a dirt path her guide called a logging road. Grasping her hood she pulled it up to cover her hair, cinching it underneath her chin with a clasp. "It's cold. How can it be cold when the sun is so bright? I thought the sun was supposed to be hot?"

"Well, the sun is very hot, but it's also far away."

At school, Clara had learned that the sun's rays showered plants with food, warmed the planet and melted snow, so she had naturally assumed that being in it would feel like a hot bath, only without water. It occurred to her now that a lot of things would be different to what she'd imagined.

A short distance further along the track brought them to a line of trampled grass that cut through the woods. "This is a wildlife trail," Lourdes said. "Animals traverse the same territory humans do and create paths just like we do. We'll need to follow this trail in case the guards search the road."

"What if we run into wild animals? Will they hurt us?" Clara strained to peer deep into the woods but her guardian gently nudged her forward.

"Wild animals are very shy. They'll avoid you if at all possible. The only time they attack is if they're scared or protecting their babies. Anyhow, we don't taste good to them, and you're too skinny. If they're that famished, they'd rather have me."

Clara whipped her head around in alarm and saw Lourdes smiling playfully at her.

"Don't worry," Lourdes added, "I'll look out for you."

Ahead lay a clearing in the mass of trees dotting the mountainside. The top of the climb appeared to be a ridge, nestled between white-capped peaks. Clara had seen these mountains often from her window in the palace prison, but always through glass. She used to imagine their dark, jagged edges cutting the sky open and the stars falling to the ground.

She lifted her mitten covered hand to her face, using her exposed wrist to warm her frozen nose and cheeks. "Lourdes, I can't feel my face."

"Do you need another wrap to keep you warm?" Lourdes asked, but Clara shook her head no. She was already too hot and sweaty from climbing and couldn't see how another wrap would help her cheeks anyway. She gulped air as if it was in short supply. Above all, she wanted so much to rest but her parents had said survival depended on getting away quickly.

Mom and Dad will be all right, Clara told herself. They had said they were too important to the king to have any harm come to them. But the thought of them made her eyes ache and she forced her attention back to the rocky switchback up the mountain.

Finally, they reached the top of the ridge. Clara gasping for breath, almost undone by the sight of white peaks on either side of them, equally as tall as the path they'd just ascended.

"Don't worry." Lourdes smiled, apparently reading her mind. "We're not climbing the peaks. It'll be easier going now that we've reached the ridge, and safer, because we'll no longer be visible to anyone from the palace who might be searching for us."

The grass grew thicker as they descended the other side and Clara saw water glistening ahead. A field of purple tufts on tiny green stalks lined her steps.

"Clover," her guide explained.

Everything outside was so strange, much different to anything she'd imagined. "I've never been outside before," she confided.

Sadness flitted across Lourdes's face. "No, I suppose not. Now you'll see what you've been missing."

Clara came to an abrupt halt, staring at a yellow and black winged creature, buzzing wildly in circles, as if doing a dance. She'd seen something like it in books, back home, but in the books it was somewhat smaller, the size of her thumb. This one was at least four times as big. "It looks — strange," she told her companion.

"What you see is a giant bee, and where there's one, there are many. If they feel threatened they can sting. Why don't you come closer to me, just in case?"

Clara obeyed and the two of them watched the insect dance. Soon, more of the creatures had amassed, coming from the spread of clover, while others flew in from a tree nearby. Clara ducked low to watch. A swarm of the creatures had formed. Then the one who'd started the dance flew down the hill and the others followed.

Without a thought for her guide, she bolted along the trail after them. "Wait!" she cried. "Wait! Where are you going?" Lost in the moment, she wanted to fly with them but she couldn't keep up for long and the buzzing cloud drew further and further from her.

Tears streamed down her face and into her mouth as she watched the creatures speed away. The next instant, she almost choked with the shock as streams of sand wound around like ropes getting ready to clench her, but instead spread into a blizzard. The blizzard of sand soon melted into a glass globe that enclosed her, like the fishbowl that housed her guppies back home. It grazed the tips of tall seeded grasses as she was lifted a few meters off the ground and found herself sailing down the hill, trailing the large insects. When she glanced up, she saw Lourdes, encased in fire once again, towing the glass globe, making them both soar through the air. They entered the tree line that skirted the meadow and darted through the forest.

"Are they the sort of bees that make honey?"

"Oh yes!" Lourdes answered with what sounded like a multitude of voices. They're bigger than the ones in your books, so they make all the more honey. It also means their sting is deadly, so we'll keep our distance."

As they raced after the bees, they emerged from the trees into another meadow and bright sunshine stung Clara's unaccustomed eyes. The swarm flew down a hillside covered in every hue of red and orange; as if the land had blossomed into the loveliest fire she had ever seen. Lourdes swooped low to the ground as they tailed the mass of bees and Clara managed to catch a closer look at one of the flowers. It resembled red fire blazing on a green stem. The sight gave her a surge of energy.

"Look at those flowers!" she exclaimed. "They're so pretty! What are they?"

"Paintbrush." Lourdes smiled. "Paintbrush are tools of the Spirit — these are the flowers that painted our world."

YEARS LATER

PART 1

DESERT

Chapter 1

Salt House

It was not one of her better moments, but then again, she did have a point.

"Why won't you let me compete in the race? Everybody else who wants to race gets to. Why not me?" Qeriya glared at her mother, dark eyes determined. She was usually an obedient daughter. She did what she was told, for the most part, and didn't argue much, but her parents' insistence that she and her brothers were not to race was ludicrous. They didn't even have a good reason. She knew they cared about her, but their care, these days, was smothering.

"You know why not," her mother, Ruth, answered, strain sharpening her voice as she set a basket of sweet mesquite pods on an elevated table towards the back of their house. Both the table and the house were made from bricks pressed entirely out of salt. The only light was the evening sun, filtering through loose bear-grass curtains on the open windows and door.

Qeriya watched her mother bend her tall, slender frame gracefully over another basket filled with material: cholla spines for sewing and the hand carved knitting needles her dad made from the woody branches of a creosote shrub. She finally retrieved a large rock and flat, stone slab from the bottom. The baskets were some of many that sat upon salt brick shelves lining one complete wall of their house. Qeriya found it difficult to reach the topmost ones. She'd always assumed she would reach her mother's height, but she hadn't grown in two years and was giving up hope of ever passing her present five feet three inches. In her eyes this was most unfair, if her hips were the size of her mother's, her height may as well be too. She frequently wished she took after her mom instead of her dad.

"You're so lucky. If only I was as pretty as you, Ruth," she'd cried last year, during a crisis at school. Her class was one of many, located on raised plateaus jutting out from a canyon wall west of her village. The classes were attended by students of all ages. During class, boys were assigned to sit on one side and girls sat on the other. There was one particular boy she thought was very cute. He was a serious student with an amazing smile that gave her chills to think about. She'd just got up the nerve to sit across the aisle from him, when he immediately rose and moved to the front of the class. She'd assumed it must be because of her. "You can't possibly know what it's like to be me," she told her mother later that day. "I'm shaped like that deformed tomato Khalid found the other day. You know, the one with the large growth?"

"You are not shaped like a deformed tomato, Qeriya." Her mom's lips had trembled trying to suppress a smile, but she'd been unable to hold back a giggle, swiftly clearing her throat to hide her mistake. "Your body's changing. You're becoming a woman. Those hips may carry children someday. And my name is Mom, to you, not Ruth."

"I don't want maternal hips," Qeriya wailed. "I want to be proportional."

"Proportional? What's that? Where do you come up with this stuff, honey?"

"I don't know," Qeriya said and shrugged.

"Your friends are talking, aren't they?"

"Does it really matter? All that matters is, I'm misshapen."

"For what it's worth, you're one of the most beautiful women I know, Qeriya."

"You would say that. You're my mother."

"I said ... for what it's worth. You obviously don't believe me. Nevertheless, I'm being honest. You don't realize your own beauty. Your body's just gone through some changes and you're not used to them yet. Your brown hair is soft and shiny; your eyes are like obsidian stones. Your skin—"

"Is full of acne," Qeriya interrupted.

"— looks like gold when it shines in the light," her mother added.

Qeriya groaned theatrically. "This sounds like a serenade. Next you'll be telling me my nose is like the Wadi, always running." The Wadi was a stream that ran from east to west. It lay to the south of her village and was the town's only source of water, but the water flow was steadily thinning every year.

Ruth had squared her shoulders and stood directly in front of her daughter. "You know, some people get acne a lot worse than you. I certainly did when I was your age. Maybe you don't deserve to be beautiful if you have this attitude. You really should be more grateful and not waste time on trivial things like vanity. All your schoolmates probably feel exactly the same way. And some kids have more difficult issues to deal with. Rather than blinding yourself with self-pity, why don't you reach out and make others feel better about themselves?"

Her mother always made sense, even when Qeriya didn't want to admit it. She was so wise in every way, except now, when it came to letting Qeriya run. She wasn't asking for that much. The race beckoned her. She wanted to run more than she'd ever wanted anything, even breasts.

Ruth returned to the baskets lining the tiny abode, reached in one and took out a serrated knife. "The race is too dangerous, Qeriya. Kids get hurt in those competitions. They don't police them well enough."

"I can take care of myself," Qeriya argued, pacing back and forth and fiddling with her head cover, tightly woven from shredded mesquite bark. Mesquite used to grow in abundance beside the stream and its bark also made up some of her other clothes. Her nicest dress was made from bison hide, but she rarely wore the soft gown now since it was irreplaceable. It wasn't as if bison would ever wander into the desert.

"Haven't I shown you how responsible I am? I get water from the Wadi every morning without complaint, carrying that giant red clay pot on my head a mile each way, and don't tell me that can't be dangerous. There are a lot of people who would rather steal mine than get their own. It's speed that saves me. Even carrying a jug on my head, I'm still faster than any of them."

Ruth extended a hand, but seemed to change her mind and pulled back. "I'm sorry, honey. Yes, you do a great job of taking care of yourself and our family, but we don't have a choice in sending you to get water. We need you to do that, just as we need your brothers to tend the garden and preserve the food. Your dad and I work long hours on the salt flats, just like everyone else."

"Yes, I know — but why? What's the point? What do you all get for your work? Why do we go to school if we're only going to end up working on the salt flats like everyone else?"

"We don't work because we want to. We work to build and repair houses, to pay teachers, to buy food and for access to the Wadi."

"I know a lot of it's used to build homes like ours, but not all of it. Where does the rest go? Don't you wonder sometimes?"

"It takes a lot of salt to compress into bricks."

"I know that, but come on, it's not all going to make village homes. And it's a dangerous job. We hear about people getting swallowed by the sludge underneath and I always worry that some day — I just don't understand why you have to work there for almost nothing."

Ruth shifted uncomfortably as she spoke. "Believe me, Qeriya, I'd change everything if I could. I wish I could get the water for you." Her eyes filled with tears and she quickly looked away. "But I can't, and this is different."

"First of all," Qeriya said, unmoved. "No tears. It's not fair. You know I don't want to hurt you, but this race is important to me. And you're turning my words around. I'm not asking you to excuse me from my chores. I'm asking permission to race. I can't see how that's any more dangerous than getting water. How do you explain the difference?"

Her mother looked at the floor without answering.

Qeriya threw up her hands in exasperation. They always did this. Whenever she made a reasonable request, her parents made it sound as if she was asking for something else. Well, it wouldn't work this time. Her eldest brother had given up arguing for permission long ago, but she was determined.

Her dad ducked into the bear-grass doorway of their one room home and circled left, around turkey feather bedding and cattail pillows piled on top of sleeping mats her mother had made by plaiting the long, skinny leaves of a sotol plant. He approached his wife from behind as she prepared to grind sweet mesquite pods and dried corn.

"Did you make pinole?" he asked and smiled when she nodded, moving closer to wrap his arms around her waist from behind. "Delicious. That's my favorite." He stood a few inches shorter than her mother, but his frame was thick with muscle. When the nights drew in, they often lit candles to do their work by, candles Qeriya made from the pulp of prickly pear fruits, but their door faced west and tonight the evening sunlight poured through the weave of the loosely woven curtain, illuminating the tiny, rectangular abode. The floor space measured about five of her aligned head to foot one way, and three the other, there was just enough room for everyone to stand inside.

"What's wrong?" he asked, sensing the tension in his wife's rigid frame.

"The race—" was all Ruth said, but it was enough.

"Your mother's right, Qeriya, it's too dangerous. And given your well expressed views, young lady, there's no explanation that could possibly satisfy you."

Qeriya was not giving up. "That's just an excuse not to give me a reason. I'm fourteen years old. I'm not a child anymore!"

"Yes, you are a child, as long as you live under this roof!" Her dad's eyes flamed and his dark skin reddened as he loomed over her. It was his authoritarian way of pulling a trump card, but it didn't work. Qeriya knew his bark was much worse than his bite.

"You'll listen to your parents when we give you instructions. You may not like what we say, but there comes a time when enough is enough!"

"What did that mean, enough is enough?" Qeriya wondered. What could it possibly mean other than, 'shut up'? It answered nothing about why her parents refused to give a reason for excluding them from the desert games, when every other parent in the village encouraged their kids to participate. Nor did it tell her why her parents treated her as if she was on the verge of exploding. She was mad now, yes, but most of the time she kept her emotions hidden. It sometimes felt as if her mom was almost afraid of her, of what she might do.

Ruth moved to place a hand on her husband's thickly muscled forearm, her eyes closing to block out the escalating scene. "Jeremiah, it's all right ... I'll handle this."

"She needs to listen!"

"I know ... but this isn't helping. It's just making her angrier. I don't want her to ... to do something rash," she whispered in his ear.

Qeriya could hear her anyway. "There you go again, telling secrets!" she said. "There's no need to whisper. I can hear you." Deep down she knew that they didn't want her to run at all, in the race or otherwise. They were afraid when she ran for some reason, but she couldn't muster the courage to confront that, as if even the thought was taboo. They saw something happen when she ran, and she felt it too, but the message she got was always ... hush, be afraid of it.

She remembered scorpion hunting, years ago, with her dad. Qeriya had been hot, sticky and tired. They were approaching a shady canyon lined with ledges, where they'd rested for a moment, but they still had a way to go. A hot breeze blew from behind her and she relaxed into it, letting it carry her forward, her feet barely touching the ground. Within moments her dad had grabbed her shoulders and lowered her until she set her feet down.

"Never do that again!" he'd whispered fiercely in her ear before letting go.

Qeriya had stared at him, waiting for some explanation, some acknowledgement of what she'd done, but there was nothing.

"I can't believe running in a race is even an issue," she continued. "You asked Doctor Michael what he thought when we were having dinner at his house, and even he agreed with me. Why would you ask him and then not take his advice?"

Doctor Michael was a close friend of her parents and had spent a great deal of time with them over the past two years, Qeriya knew they trusted his opinion. He was usually rather aloof and stiff, so Qeriya didn't pay much attention to him, but when her parents asked him about the competition, surprisingly, he had taken her side.

"Of course she should compete," he had insisted. "They all should. How else will they learn to manage themselves when they're grown, if you don't give them some freedom now?"

Doctor Michael was her best ammunition. He silenced her parents then, and even the mention of him silenced them now. They would at least have to consider her argument. It was too bad they couldn't just trust her to compete in the race.

"You two have got to be the strictest parents on the planet!" She'd made her point and now it had to simmer. She bolted out of the room, ripping the grass curtain in the process, but what did she care about a curtain at a time like this? She looked up at the sky, pink with streaks of apricot, and dug her feet into the soft sand. Surrounding her were remnants of a dying ocotillo plant, portions of which were rerouted and cultivated around her home forming a living fence. The hem of her woven, grass dress stirred patterns in the dust as she sat before the fire pit. Stars emerged, growing brighter by the minute. One moon was making an appearance and the other would become visible soon. Qeriya thought for a moment of the stories her dad used to tell when she was young. His stories were all about life back on Old Earth, back in ancient times. They were strange legends, where people moved fast over land, and even through the air, in large metal vehicles. What she wouldn't do to travel and see the rest of New Earth. But the only metal here was the tools people had and she still wasn't sure where those tools originated, nor would anyone tell her.

She squinted towards neighboring homes and their likewise deteriorating borders, each spanning at least fifty feet. The web of houses lay on a vast, flat plateau, fronting a series of plateaus to the northwest and butted up against the Wadi to the south. On the other side of the plateaus to the north was the Playa, the flat where her parents harvested salt. However, out past all of the surrounding features, in every direction minus one, lay endless crescent sand dunes that stretched beyond anyone's guess. Those who attempted to traverse the dunes in any direction came home with voices rusty from dehydration, or else never returned. One man only, among all of them, claimed to have traveled south to the end of the dunes, and declared that he had come to an ocean. He said the water was cold and salty. He had collected some to take home, but used it instead to douse his clothes in the hot sun. He was very strong and had carried all the drinking water he could when he set off on his journey. Even so, it had been barely enough. He was severely dehydrated when he arrived home. Some said his claim to have seen the ocean was just delusion brought about from the trauma of it all.

East of the village, at the mouth of the Wadi, a date palm oasis flourished. But no one was allowed to approach it by law. Qeriya didn't know why, and whenever she asked, her question was deflected. Beyond the oasis was more sand and then rose an impassable border of jagged mountains. The few who had tried illegally to approach the fountainhead and traverse the mountains could not even manage to find a route, much less make any real attempt.

The village plateau lifted only a little above the soft sand around it and was essentially a flat mass of sandstone covered in a layer of loose golden grains. The closest canyon to the west side of the village served as their school. It shaded them for most of the day and the walls offered a surface on which they could write with rocks. Some canyons ran deep in the ground, while others, like their school, were formed between raised sandstone hills and a higher plateau to the west.

Qeriya watched the landscape become dotted with orange lights as people lit fires to cook their evening meal. Most of them would eat food from Murphy's agave: a hedgehog or prickly pear cactus, and purple mahonia berries, if they were lucky, or maybe some Christmas cholla fruit. But since their garden did so well, Qeriya and her family would have garden vegetables also. Qeriya sometimes made vau, a strained prickly pear juice, to go with dinner, but she was not in a helping mood tonight. The flat rock her mother used to grind foodstuffs lay outside, holding a stack of blue meal cakes made from corn maize. They were ready to be cooked over the fire. Her mother and father darted in and out of the house, carrying food and supplies. Once her brothers returned home they would eat dinner.

Qeriya frowned, where were her brothers? They were usually home by now. Lately, Khalid, her eldest brother, had taken to disappearing in the late afternoon and Qeriya was tempted to follow him. He never stayed to play ball games or to shoot targets with cliff rose arrows like he used to anymore, and Qeriya was determined to find out why. Tomorrow, Qeriya suddenly decided, she would do just that. She wouldn't wade through the crowds to exit school as usual. She'd climb up the rock wall and sprint to the entrance to find Khalid as soon as he emerged from the mouth of the canyon. She'd have to move quickly, but speed was her talent.

Nothing compared with running. Nothing gave her the same sense of freedom. If only her parents knew how she felt. She was careful not to give in to that taboo power she seemed to have, but even without it, she loved the exhilaration of seeing the world whizz by as she ran.

Hearing a noise behind her, Qeriya turned to see her dad lift the torn curtain. Candlelight glowed inside the house. Qeriya's stomach lurched as she prepared for another confrontation, but it did not come. Instead her mom and dad came to join her where she sat, shoulders slumped. Her mother's eyes were red and swollen.

Qeriya and her mother sat in silence as her father steadily rubbed a small bow back and forth across a hardwood drill. She watched as the base of the drill spun in a fireboard cradle below, tinder placed carefully around the fireboard in hopes of catching a spark. She was not sure where the hardwood drill or fireboard came from. It didn't look like the ironwood they used for fuel and it wasn't acacia, joshua, date palm, or any other wood she was familiar with. And yet, as with so many things, Qeriya never felt at liberty to ask about it. She had been taught to spark a fire, but it was difficult. Her dad could spark one in a few minutes. Soon an ember grew and he steadily blew on it, feeding it more tinder and larger sticks until it was ready for an ironwood log.

"Where did we get that bow drill?" she finally dared to ask, overcome with curiosity.

"It was given to us," her dad said. Her mother said nothing at all. Qeriya sighed. That was all she ever got, half answers, to any question she asked.

"Listen, Qeriya," Jeremiah said. "We're all subject to someone, and sometimes we have to obey, even when we don't under-stand. Your mom and I have to obey the king, whether or not we agree with what he decrees — we don't get to ask questions. You're subject to us for now, and you have to obey us — whether or not you agree with our decisions and whether or not we explain our reasons."

Her mom skewered vegetables for roasting onto wooden sticks that were soaking in a tub of water. She stabbed large chunks of peppers and onions, some of the vegetables her eldest brother, Khalid, grew in his garden. He carefully cultivated them in the harsh climate, composting the soil: protecting and creating more over time, dripping water onto each plant by hand so none would be wasted. He had a way with vegetable plants. His garden consistently produced more than any other family in the settlement. But while most people sold any extra produce, Khalid and their parents gave extras away to those whose crop was poor. Qeriya was proud of her parents, even if she didn't always agree with them.

A mouthwatering fragrance wafted towards her. Her mom cooked vegetables so the bitter char balanced perfectly with crunchy sweetness. Obstinate as she felt, it was not enough to affect her appetite. They had better not wait for the boys before saying a blessing over the food tonight, as they had every day this week, Qeriya grumbled to herself. Let them go hungry if they insisted on being late. That would give them a reason to be on time.

"There they are. Khalid! Lahcen!" Ruth called. "I was wondering when you'd get home."

Coming from the southwest in the waning light, Khalid and Lahcen approached the barren sandstone from a woody garden of desert plants. Behind them, a line of acacia trees stood in the distance, flanking a massive area all along the Wadi. The trees provided stability for other shrubs, cacti and grasses. The boys' long woven pants dragged along the ground as they walked. They were deep in discussion, but Qeriya could not catch what they said. Khalid stood tall and slender, like their mother, and his speckled eyes appeared like blue ornaments set on his high cheekbones. He took long strides and moved with gentle grace.

In contrast, Lahcen was stocky and muscular like their father, with brown eyes resembling her own, but shrouded in dark skin that made him look like a shadow in the pale light. Thick curls surrounded his face. His movements were assertive and brusque. The three of them were so unlike each other that most people were surprised to learn that they were related.

"Where've you been?" Qeriya demanded as they approached.

"We were just exploring," Khalid explained calmly.

"Exploring? Why?" There was an edge to Ruth's voice.

"Why not?"

"Because it's dinner time."

Khalid held his mother's gaze. "Mom, do you ever wonder why no one leaves the village? Other than the hunting trips we took with Dad, circling around the area, we've never seen what's beyond."

"That's because there's nothing there but sand."

"No, there's still territory all around the canyons, before the dunes. I've seen for myself. There's still so much to explore."

"That's not a good idea — there are dangerous creatures out there. It's not safe."

"There are no creatures out there, much less dangerous ones. They've all vanished," Lahcen said, wading into the conversation. "The Wadi's getting scrawnier by the minute."

Jeremiah, who had been silently contemplating his calloused hands, looked up. "Where did you go?"

"We went downstream, to the end of the Wadi," Lahcen answered.

"That's not a safe place to go without your dad," Ruth insisted. "You must stay around the village. Why don't you join in with the other boys? Don't a bunch of them go target shooting after school?"

"And … somehow wielding bow and arrows with a bunch of reckless teenage boys is safer than trailing the Wadi downstream?" Khalid challenged.

"Yes, as a matter of fact, it is."

"Come on, Mom, I'll be eighteen next year. Don't you realize? At this point in time, not venturing out of here is unsafe. The Wadi isn't going to last another generation. We have to figure out an alternative water supply if we want to survive.

"What are you afraid of, anyway?" Khalid asked, genuinely curious.

"There are venomous snakes … and … poisonous scorpions," she said turning away from his probing gaze.

"You mean the kind I hunt for food?"

"And … well … other creatures that'll eat you … " her voice trailed off. "Just promise me you'll stick around here."

"I'm sorry, Mom, I can't do that," Khalid spoke gently, but gave her a hard, long stare. "You both are hiding something from me, from us. The answer is out there, and I intend to find out where."

Ruth fumbled with the skewers only to have them fall into the smoldering embers. Scrambling shakily to her feet, she ran back into the house, avoiding the scrutiny of her eldest son. Qeriya scurried to rescue the scrumptious morsels while her brother stood still, his mouth ajar.

"Now look what you've done!" Jeremiah said in frustration as he darted inside to join his wife.

Lahcen kept his head down. "I can't believe you talked to Mom like that, Khalid."

"You do it all the time," Khalid retorted.

"I know I do, but you never talk back, and you didn't just talk back, Khalid, you accused her and Dad of lying to us."

Khalid sighed, scrubbing his hand through his fine flaxen hair. "I don't want to, but they're withholding something from us. Obviously they think it's for our own good, I don't question their motives. Anyway, last week, I found a cave … you have to see it. There wasn't enough time to show you today, but tomorrow marks the weekend. I can't make Mom a promise I've no intention of keeping. And I don't want to lie to our parents, even if they're lying to us. Lying's worse."

"I prefer to think of it not so much as lying, but rather sparing the bad news," Lahcen reasoned.

"That appears to be what they think," Khalid declared.

"Where's this cave?" Qeriya asked.

"Downstream — south. Beyond this canyon, where we used to hunt, are more, a cluster of canyons that run east to west. One of them in particular has a cave."

"That's pretty far. You've been stockpiling water."

"I have." Khalid nodded.

"Can I come?" Qeriya asked.

"No way," Khalid said.

"Why not?"

"First of all, it's too dangerous and you're too young. Anyhow, you saw how much trouble I got into just now for going there in the first place. Just think what they'd do if I took you along."

Qeriya's lips curled into a snarl. A few minutes later her parents reemerged, coming to stand close to the fire, holding hands in solidarity.

"We discussed what you said earlier about racing, Qeriya," Jeremiah began.

Qeriya looked at them with guarded interest.

"I know that you've been wanting to compete as well, Khalid." Jeremiah paused, drawing out the moment. "We've decided to let you all compete in the games," he announced to their amazement. "But you have to promise us one thing — you will never venture beyond the village again."

Following her first day of school, Clara walked slowly towards her new home on the outskirts of the village, staring at the magnitude of plant life around her. She'd only arrived yesterday and was heartsick at leaving her parents. She allowed herself a small sigh. She had a new home, a new family, a new school and a whole new life to get used to. Suddenly a loud explosion boomed overhead. Startled, Clara gazed around herself trying to see what had made the noise, but the tree canopy hid the sky from view. Nervously, she realized that the dull forest light was steadily becoming darker. Soon she felt something wet, like water, pouring down from the sky. It covered everything.

Clara ran as fast as she could in the direction of home, and straight through the doorway, squealing in panic. What was this poison covering everything in sight? Were they being attacked? Had the king discovered her location? She tried to brush the stuff from her arms and legs with a soft blanket draped over a chair.

A husky man with short black hair and brown wrinkled skin peered in, her new guardian, Carlos. "What is it? What's wrong?" he asked, stepping inside. "I saw you running home as if a wild boar was snapping at your heels."

Clara stared at him, her eyes big and round. She couldn't under-stand why he was just standing there, calm. How could he not know?

"I think the king's attacking us!" she stammered. "Didn't you hear the explosion? Now he's dumping stuff from the sky! I think it's poison! What do we do?" she pleaded.

"Poison? What? Clara! Settle down, it's all right." He tried to put his arm around her to reassure her, but she brushed him away.

"Didn't you hear me?" she sobbed. "They're trying to kill everyone! They're looking for me!"

"Clara, what do you mean by poison? What poison?"

"This!" she exclaimed, and squeezed some out of her hair. "Didn't you hear the explosion in the sky?"

"Oh! You mean the thunder? I heard thunder in the sky." He smiled and again gently placed a loose arm around her shoulders to comfort her. "It's all right, Clara," he repeated. "There's nothing to be afraid of.

The explosion you heard was thunder, and this 'poison' you refer to is just water. It's rain, Clara, it's just rain. It rains almost every day here."

"Rain?" she said, her voice full of wonder and disbelief. "I've seen rain from my window at the palace, but I've never heard the explosions."

"It's just thunder, Clara. You wouldn't be able to hear thunder from inside the palace. The structure's too thick. Don't worry, Clara, you're safe. The king doesn't know you're here. Come, sit down." He looked at her kindly. "You've had a difficult few days. Sit down and I'll make you some cocoa tea."

Chapter 2

Fire Reaume

"I thought we weren't supposed to go off like this," Lahcen said to his brother after school the next day. Their school met on a series of ledges lining steep canyon walls along a dry wash. Each period they climbed the steps built into large mounds of sand to sit at the feet of their teachers and learn about Old Earth.

Khalid wasn't listening; he dragged Lahcen by the arm toward the mouth of the canyon. "I'm supposed to be the troublemaker, not you," Lahcen added.

"Fine," Khalid said as they crossed a line of shadow that sliced one canyon wall. "You can take the blame if we get caught."

Even though Lahcen would push boundaries with his parents by staying out past curfew or getting up at the last possible second before leaving for school, he did not relish the idea of disobeying a direct order.

"Listen, Lahcen, trouble or not, you have to see this, it's important. Mom and Dad are keeping something from us, everyone is, and whatever they're hiding, it's in that cave, I know it. I just don't understand why it has to be a secret. Maybe we'll find the answer to that when we find what's in there," he muttered, half to himself.

Along with the rest of the students, they passed from the mouth of the canyon into a blaze of sunshine. "What do you mean, secret? Why would they keep secrets from us?" Lahcen asked.

"Probably because, in their minds, they're protecting us from something."

"Like ..."

"I don't know. But I'm ready for answers. I mean, why do we learn about all these different places like rainforests, oceans and

32

mountains, but we never see them?" Khalid asked, raising his hand to shade his eyes.

"Who could afford a trip like that? The water weight a person would have to carry to get out of here would be enormous. Also, no one knows how far away those places really are. People have tried leaving, only to come back on the edge of death. We're land locked."

"You could." Khalid shot his brother a knowing look and Lahcen felt his face grow hot. He turned his head to scope the area and see if anyone might be listening but couldn't see anything aside from the bushes and an occasional tree bordering the Wadi. This was the first time anyone had openly acknowledged his ... ability.

"How do you know about—?" Lahcen stopped, but his brother gently tugged on his arm, signaling him to keep trudging towards the stream.

"Don't worry," Khalid said, as they made their way through a thick patch of sand. "I won't tell anyone, not even Mom and Dad. But I've seen it. Don't you think it's odd that you rarely drink? You're never thirsty are you? It's as if water just comes to you."

Having reached the Wadi they turned west and followed alongside the bank. After a few moments silence, Lahcen glanced at his brother. "It does come to me. I don't know how or why. It's always been, well, embarrassing. I mean, everyone else has to work so hard to get water, but not me. It's like I breathe it."

"I know, but there's no need to be embarrassed," Khalid said. "Watch this."

Lahcen eyed him carefully as he squatted down on a rock and leapt an unnatural distance through the hot, desert air before landing gracefully on the sand bank lining the wash. Having watched his arc, Lahcen ran to catch up.

"So that's it?" Lahcen teased. "You jump like a frog? Gee, wow."

Khalid punched him in the arm and Lahcen, still grinning,

rubbed the pain away — it was worth it for the chance to poke fun at his big brother. "All right," he admitted. "It's pretty impressive. Still, I'm more impressed with your climbing." Every time they scaled the sandstone cliffs, Lahcen only managed a few feet in the time it took his brother to gain the top. It was as if Khalid was a spider, running effortlessly up the sheer face, instead of clinging to it, white knuckled, feet scrabbling for toe holds, like any normal person would.

"Actually, climbing's part of it, too. I'll show you more in a bit, when we get to the cave," Khalid said as they passed a mass of black brush.

They walked a ways in companionable silence, watching the trickle of water meander along the wash as if it were a long snake. Khalid stopped to pluck some pale green sage leaves to complement dinner that evening and stuffed them in his backpack before continuing on.

As Lahcen looked back towards his brother, he thought he saw something disappear behind the thick brush edging the Wadi, a long way upstream. He squinted.

"What is it?" Khalid asked.

"Probably nothing," Lahcen told him, with a slight shake of the head. Further ahead the cattails that lined the Wadi disappeared as the trickle was reduced to deadly quicksand. Lahcen remembered years ago, back when there were animals in the desert, he had been hunting with his father when he sank in quicksand up to his chest. Fortunately he'd managed to drag himself through the thick sludge, close enough to the edge that his dad could reach in and pull him out.

Suddenly, Khalid dived for Lahcen's knees, collapsing them both onto the ground. Luckily, Lahcen's hands hit the sand before his teeth could. "This is hardly the time to wrestle!" he protested.

"Move forward!" Khalid ordered. "Move, move! But stay down."

"Why? What—"

"That's why!" Khalid pointed to a knife tangled in the last of the cattails, just above where they crouched. They didn't dare reach for it, lest there were others to follow.

"We're at the end of the brush! There's nowhere to go!"

"Over there!" Khalid pointed to a narrow passage heading south into a shallow canyon, on the other side of the stream.

Without another word, Lahcen sprinted the short distance to the passage following Khalid and dove behind the bank of a tributary that had dried up long ago. Another knife thudded into the other side of the bank but again it was too exposed for them to reach for the weapon.

"This way," Khalid instructed, and they scrambled off as fast as Lahcen could manage.

"We're not allowed to go south," Lahcen called.

Khalid shot him an uncomprehending look. "We're not allowed to be here at all, remember? Anyhow, we're being chased by a madman with a knife, and you're worried about getting in trouble?"

Lahcen shook his head. "It's not a man, it's a woman."

"How do you know?" Khalid asked as they both ran along the wash, Lahcen panting alongside his unaffected brother.

"Don't know for sure," Lahcen managed to answer between breaths. "Caught a glimpse as I crossed the Wadi, looked female, spikes on her head … white stuff on her face. She's close."

This couldn't be real, but it was. He pushed harder than ever, looking back despite himself to see what was coming: nothing yet. As they plunged ahead, the banks grew taller, into rock walls once again, cutting off the afternoon sun. They pushed on until a fork appeared that led to two narrow canyons and then veered right. Before long they reached another fork and darted left, running as fast as Lahcen could move.

Khalid covered the distance effortlessly but he could see Lahcen was tiring.

"If whoever it was followed the bank onto the rock wall above us, then we should be safe. There's no way to get across." Lahcen slowed down, panting. "And there's no way they can tell which fork we took."

"Keep it up, Lahcen," Khalid urged.

Finally, the canyon opened up and they traversed bare sand once again. There was no one in sight, behind them or otherwise, and they had traveled, what seemed to Lahcen like several good sized deserts of soft, wearying, ground. Between the heat and his exhaustion, Lahcen had started to think he was in some circle of hell especially reserved for disobedient teenagers. Eventually, as he was on the point of giving up and insisting they turn back to face the lurking enemy head on, the mounds of sand transformed into tall canyon walls. They progressed down the canyon as it began to steadily narrow and the light dimmed to a dull grey.

"How do we get through there? I don't think even my head would fit," Lahcen grumbled, pointing to where the walls compressed to form a narrow passage.

"We don't," Khalid answered. "We go up."

Lahcen's mouth gaped open in disbelief. "You're kidding. These walls are smooth as a baby's butt!"

"We don't climb, we shinny. Keep an eye out while I go up, then it's your turn. If we still have a follower, this'll throw them off," Khalid said. He placed his feet against one side of the canyon while his hands pushed against the other in a horizontal position. Alternating hands and feet, he rose upward without a hint of sweat.

"Yeah right, that's all we have to do," Lahcen mocked. "Not all of us are mega-man with superhuman strength." But there was nothing else to do and Lahcen was forced to follow suit, muttering, "Stupid," at intervals as he ascended. Sweat covered him as he tried to keep his large frame taut and his butt in the air to avoid plunging to his death below. Two thirds of the way up, the rock walls widened slightly and he groaned. He couldn't last much longer.

Within seconds he saw a foot dangling beside him and heard Khalid call to him, "Lahcen, grab on!"

Lahcen couldn't breathe, much less answer, and terrified as he was, the thought of taking one hand off the rock was even more frightening. His muscles were tired and he shook uncontrollably. There was no way he could climb down, much less ascend any further. He had no choice, with his last ounce of energy he pushed off the wall with his arms and grasped his brother's ankle.

Khalid's leg swung him back and forth along the canyon like a pendulum, gaining more and more momentum with each swing, until Lahcen was thrust into the air and over the edge of the precipice, landing shoulder first on gritty sandstone. He was bruised and scraped, but alive.

As soon as Lahcen gained his wits, he hurried to help his brother, but to his surprise, Khalid simply hoisted his trunk onto the ledge with his hands and threw a leg over, pulling forward until he was clear from the edge.

Lahcen's eyes almost popped out of his face. "How did you do that? I wasn't anywhere near the top, and you just plucked me up as if I were a piece of grass! Were you just holding on with your fingers?"

"Maybe," Khalid tried to suppress a conceited smile, surveying the canyon below. "It's part of my gift, I guess."

"Part? Superhuman strength is *part* of your gift? Why can't I have your talents?" Lahcen complained, joining his brother in searching for whoever hunted them.

"Look, there!" Khalid exclaimed. "Somebody just darted into one of the rocky coves on this side of the canyon."

"I wouldn't worry. There's no way anyone could get up here but you, and me, with your help."

They made their way further up a gently sloped field of curved sandstone, marbled with shades of pink, tan and orange. It was the tallest point they knew in their vast desert home, aside from the top of the Grand Arch. Beyond them lay a steep drop down the other side.

Lahcen pondered the relationship he had with water, his 'gift,' as Khalid called it. His connection with water didn't seem that great a gift compared to his brother's iron muscles. But even so, why was he so ashamed of it? Now that he knew Khalid knew, it didn't seem like such a big deal, and, in fact, it even seemed like a good thing. He tried to remember when it was he'd first realized he could manipulate water, or at least to cast his mind back to a time before he thought there was something wrong with him. But as far back as he could recall, he had carried his secret within him. It felt good to have his brother know and not judge him.

They stopped to rest on a flat topped boulder and Khalid finished the remaining water. Lahcen gazed at the view and sighed. Even with a persistent killer on their tail, for the first time, he suddenly realized, he was at peace. Besides, there was no way anyone could top that canyon, so here, with just Khalid for company, he could relax and be himself. He had no need to be afraid that someone would see what he could do. "Remember when I used to gather water from the Wadi, like Qeriya does now?" he asked.

Khalid nodded. "Yes, I remember. You slammed the pot down on my foot once and I could barely walk for weeks."

"Oh, yeah, sorry. Anyhow it was never very heavy for me to carry. I'd get home in a flash and set it down in front of our house."

"Yes?"

"Well, then I'd sit and play with it, but not with my hands. I'd stir the water with my mind. I willed it to move."

"Go on," Khalid encouraged.

"One morning Mom came out and saw me lifting water out of the container, spinning it in a circle around my head." Lahcen began to tremble uncontrollably. Khalid gently put a hand on his brother's shoulder. "She — she screamed like a banshee, telling me to stop. I panicked!"

Khalid nodded in agreement.

"The water spilled onto the ground and she grabbed at it, even though it'd soaked into the sand. I didn't know what was wrong, why she was acting so crazy. All I knew was that Mom never reacted like that, so I must've done something really, really bad. I waited until she went inside, drew the water out of the sand with my mind and put it back in the container.

"She came out again later, looked at the dry ground and the water back in the pot, and acted as if nothing had happened. After that they made Qeriya take over water duty. They never let me near water again. Somehow I knew not to ask, not to speak of it. I've been ashamed of what I can do ever since."

Khalid extended his arm around his brother. "Lahcen, listen to me. You didn't do anything wrong. Don't you see? You aren't the problem. What you have is a gift. Spirit created you this way. The problem is all the secrecy."

"But how do you know that?"

Khalid gave him a searching look. "I came here last week — you remember I told you I found some markings in a cave?"

Lahcen nodded. He longed to be convinced, to be able to stop looking at himself as some kind of freak, but what could some markings in a cave have to do with any of it?

"Well, that's not all I found," Khalid said, his eyes gleaming with suppressed excitement. "There's a mass of papers in there, full of information, history and stories. It's nothing like we've ever seen before. You have to see it for yourself. I wanted us to get far away from town before telling you, so no one would overhear."

"You say there's a lot of paper? Paper's valuable. Maybe we could sell it."

"No, Lahcen. This paper is worth too much to even think of selling it. There's so much information in those papers about the outside world, answers to questions we've never been allowed to ask."

Lahcen stared at his brother, thinking. Obviously Khalid had learned a lot in just one evening.

Khalid handed him the water skins, gesturing for him to fill them.

Lahcen pondered what to do with the skins in his hands. Even though they were out in the middle of nowhere, even though there was no one to witness it, he felt decidedly uncomfortable. Sighing deeply, he put the feeling aside and concentrated. Within moments, water materialized into threads, coaxed out of the very air itself. Neither of them knew where it came from, but as they watched, the threads gathered to form a stream in midair, pouring steadily, filling the containers.

"How did you do that?" A high-pitched yell came from atop the canyon wall they'd just ascended and turning they saw their sister's bronze face peering from behind a nearby rock. Lahcen flinched at her sudden appearance.

"You followed us! How, on all that's holy, did you manage it with that killer on our tail?" Lahcen asked, his voice shrill, his dark face draining to a dull grey."

"Killer? What killer? I didn't see any killer! Did you think I was a killer coming after you?" Qeriya laughed, emerging from her hiding place.

Khalid and Lahcen glanced at one another to see what the other would say, but neither spoke. They decided to let it slide. No sense in scaring her now.

"I was pretty far behind you at first," she explained. "I saw your footsteps in the damp sand where you crossed over the water, that's how I knew which direction you went. After that I just ran fast and caught up to you before you reached the fork. You almost spotted me a couple of times in the desert, but I flattened myself and blended with the sand."

"But," Lahcen began, scratching his head in wonderment.

"How did you get up the canyon wall? I couldn't have done it without Khalid to pull me up."

"I jumped," she said, moving closer to her brothers.

"You jumped?" Lahcen asked in disbelief, but then again, stranger things were happening all around him.

"Don't worry," she said, "I won't tell Mom and Dad, or anyone else. I promise."

"Gee, thanks," Lahcen said, scowling as he finished filling the skins. "As if that's even on our list of concerns right now."

"It's on my list. Why are you here?" Khalid demanded with his hands on his hips like an angry mother.

"I was hoping to ask you the same question, but I realized I could probably find out more by following you. There's no way you would share all of this," she glanced at the water skins, "with your puny little sister."

"Who said anything about puny?" Lahcen teased, glancing at Khalid. "Sneaky perhaps, but puny?"

Qeriya punched his arm.

"You can't be here," Khalid said. "Mom and Dad will kill me."

"I can't be here or Mom and Dad will kill you. Send me back and I'll tell!"

"You wouldn't!" Khalid glared at her, in contrast to his usual gentle nature.

"Try me." Qeriya met his hostile gaze with her own, cool one.

"Oh well, she's here now," Lahcen interjected, tugging on Khalid's arm. "There's nothing we can do but take her with us. She knows this much — and why shouldn't she come? Mom and Dad may kill us, but it's worth it to us, and it's obviously worth it to her."

Qeriya looked at Lahcen with the kind of deep gratitude not often bestowed on a sibling.

Khalid broke his gaze. "All right, you can come. But you follow my orders, understood?" he commanded, shaking his index finger at his sister.

"Understood," Qeriya repeated.

They hiked across and down the steep, sloped, canyon wall that branched west. On reaching the bottom, they followed Khalid down the new canyon a short distance, until they reached the entrance to a cave facing west. Surprisingly, purple lupine and even some poppies surrounded the entrance.

"They're beautiful!" Qeriya exclaimed.

"Where did the water come from to give life to these desert gems?" Lahcen asked. "It usually needs to rain to get flowers like these."

"I think there's some ground water deep in the cave," Khalid said. "It feels almost dank in there."

South, beyond the cave entrance, Lahcen knew the plant life waned. One Joshua tree and a handful of woody shrubs were all that dotted the red dirt spanning for miles beyond the cave entrance.

"This was once carved by water, back when there was some. Hmm. The sun's just right. We timed this well," Khalid mused as the other two exchanged a look of mutual curiosity. They followed Khalid as he led them deep inside, where only a handful of persistent sunrays could penetrate. A precisely placed reflective mirror captured the light from the setting sun and deflected it onto others strategically positioned around the cave. The many mirrors were hung high, creating a web of bright light that bounced off the rust colored walls below to cast a warm glow. Everywhere they looked lay stacks of paper in haphazard piles. Lahcen could scarcely believe it. He picked up a few, examining their contents, but could not make sense of them.

"Here," Khalid said, motioning to them. "There're a few important and revealing things I stumbled on last week when I was here. I barely had a chance to look at them before it was time to go home."

He opened a book, the papers of which were held together by metal rings. It was titled: Fire Reaume. Khalid slowly flipped through the pages, stopping only briefly to study certain pictures. Fire appeared to burst from a boy standing in a nest of trees and plants, but he did not seem to be harmed by it. The flames were clustered around his hands and he appeared to be molding the fire, as if it were pottery clay or stiff maize dough for ashcakes. Emanating from all over his body was a bright glow, almost like a halo. As Khalid was about to flip to another page, Lahcen stopped him, staring at the picture. He tried to pry the book away to get a closer look.

"Not yet, in a minute. There's more," Khalid said. The pictures were full of detail, as if a professional artist had drawn them. "Look at this," Khalid said, "but without grabbing this time." He pointed to a group of figures, similar to the boy whose picture they had just been looking at. The group was spread out, interspersed among a wealth of trees, their hands poised to catch something. One in the group had his arm back, about to throw a ball of fire.

"Who — what — are reaume?" Lahcen asked as he closed the cover to see the title again.

"Fire reaume," he muttered. "They look human from the pictures. They seem to be humans who can create and mold fire. I wonder if this book is supposed to tell their story," he said, flipping through the pages in Khalid's hands. "There's no writing on any of the papers, just pictures." He grabbed the book once again, and rather than fight back, Khalid let it slide through his fingers this time.

Lahcen studied the pictures intently. "It's like a fairy tale world. It seems too fantastic to be true."

"And I would agree, if not for the fact that everything else I've found in here has been teaching material, and that— " he broke off as Qeriya lifted her hands into the air, breathing deeply. She pulled the air about her as if it were solid and lifted herself off the ground, moving rhythmically up and down as if she were a ship sailing the ocean waves. Carefree and smiling widely, she began spinning and dipping.

"You're flying!" Lahcen said, shocked, while Khalid laughed loud and long.

"We're not alone — there are others out there like us!" she exclaimed happily, spinning in wild, fast circles. "This feels so good, as if a tight coil holding me down has let loose. Not even the rocks Mom weaves into my dress can hold me down now!"

"Well, speaking of, if you're going to fly, I think a change of fashion is in order," Lahcen said. "It's men's clothes for you from now on."

Letting gravity take over, Qeriya dropped low in an attempt to knock down her brother, who by now was laughing uncontrollably.

"It's not a problem now," Lahcen choked out between gales of laughter. "Hey, don't kill the messenger!" he said, gently holding her away from him.

Qeriya sent him an evil look but from then on she stuck to bouncing vertically along stone outcroppings.

Khalid nimbly climbed the cave wall until there were no more footholds. He allowed his feet to let go of the rock wall and used his hands to grasp tiny nooks and crannies in the ceiling.

"You're walking across the ceiling with your hands. Amazing!" Lahcen said. In that moment he found the courage to let go of all his own inhibitions. Concentrating, he drew water from deep within the cave to fill their now empty skins, and watched the liquid move and twist, grabbing the puddle as it rose, letting it tow him around the cave. He wrestled the water beneath his feet and stood up, struggling to balance, tipping here and there until he sensed some equilibrium. He rode the water close to the ground, stumbling on occasion, but climbing back on the next minute.

Lahcen and his siblings quietly explored their powers and hours felt like minutes. Why, they asked each other, did their parents not let them express themselves, why did they have to pretend to be something other than who they were, why all the secrecy?

"I think we're related to those fire people somehow," Lahcen said as he landed gracefully on the ground, letting the water dissipate. Suddenly he heard a noise. The three turned in alarm toward the mouth of the cave. Someone was standing there.

"Clara, come on, come and join us, the water's safe. Don't be afraid," her guardian, Carlos, said, holding his wife's hand. Laura let go of his hand and brushed long strands of curly hair off her face. She looked like a daughter of the ocean, layered in jewelry made of seashells, each piece intricately created by her.

Laura waved for Clara to join them. Clara obediently grasped their hands and they both walked her out into the waves. She was nervous at first as they sliced through the breakers and as she felt the tug of water pulling back to sea, but she rapidly got used to it. The swimming lessons she had been given at the palace came back to her easily and from a decidedly shaky beginning, it ended up that she was the only one left in the water.

Suddenly, she saw something in the distance. Something broke the surface. It must be a dolphin, Clara decided. She had heard there were plenty of them that passed near the shore. There it was, only this time closer, and it was definitely not a dolphin, nor was it a shark, or a seal. It appeared to be human, and yet, there was no way that was possible, everyone was on shore and there were no other people around. But … there it was again! Not only did the creature appear human, it resembled a boy. Was she seeing things?

Chapter 3

Warning

"How did you find us here, Doctor Michael?" Lahcen asked, hastily dancing around a few stalagmites as he made his way over to him.

"I followed Qeriya part of the way," the doctor said, seating himself on a boulder that jutted up from the ground just outside the mouth of the cave, like a cavity pocked tooth from some mammoth beast.

"And the rest of the way? How did you know we'd be here?" Khalid pressed for an answer, his eyes narrowing to slits.

Doctor Michael wiped sweat off his forehead with the back of his wrinkled hand. "I tried to catch up, but you were too fast. Now I know why." He gave a harsh laugh before lapsing into a strained silence. His eyes roved over them as though he was considering his words carefully. Then he said, "I have to admit, I've been watching you all for quite a while now. I know you've been exploring the area, Khalid, and I wondered if perhaps you'd found this place."

"How did you know about it, and why didn't we?" Khalid demanded.

Lahcen and Qeriya watched with interest, Qeriya still hovering, dumbfounded, in the air, Lahcen standing beside his floating puddle of water.

"All I can tell you is that I just know and you aren't supposed to. You need to forget what you've seen here."

Khalid shook his head. "We can't do that."

The doctor glared at Khalid, his posture rigid. It was the closest Qeriya had ever seen him to being angry. The silence stretched and, deciding that there was no way the standoff would yield any more answers, Qeriya tried at last for a dignified descent, but only succeeded in landing awkwardly on her rump.

"I guess you need some landing practice." Lahcen chuckled, having recovered from the shock of seeing the doctor.

Qeriya scowled at her brother's smug expression and picked herself up from the dusty cavern floor, brushing dirt off her woven grass robe. She moved towards Lahcen's floating puddle to get a drink, but he moved it away at the last minute. Qeriya tried again, but each time, just as she was about to drink, Lahcen moved it out of reach.

"Hey, I'm thirsty!" she yelled and Lahcen finally relented, shaping the water into a manageable stream and letting her drink as if from a bottle. When she had taken her fill and began to pull away he allowed the remaining water to splatter onto her face.

Qeriya blinked water from her eyes. "That's so wasteful!" she muttered, throwing her brother a look of complete disdain.

"I'm just trying to keep you cool," Lahcen said, grinning.

Qeriya turned her attention to Doctor Michael. "Why were you following me in the first place?"

His manner suddenly became grave. "Because I'm afraid you may be in danger."

"But what kind of danger?" Qeriya asked.

"Being here. Doing this," he said quietly. "I promise you, that's all I can say."

Qeriya was unconvinced. "Dangerous? I don't see anybody or anything that's going to harm us. As for the flying, I — can't help it — there's just something wrong with me." For an instant a look that was half pride and half shame flashed across her face. "And I never let it happen when anyone else is around. But sometimes," she said, a note of pleading in her voice. "Sometimes it just wants to burst out of me."

Doctor Michael sighed. "Well don't let it burst out of you. There are dangers here that you don't know about."

Frustration rose up in Qeriya in a hot, angry, tide. She was tired of her parents, and now Doctor Michael expressing vague fears of unnamed dangers. "Yeah," she said, not even trying to conceal her irritation. "We've heard all that before. But can't you just give us a straight answer?"

"Wait," Lahcen interrupted, "how did you two get this far without water? Khalid had to bring a lot."

"I brought some." Qeriya held up the meager sized skin she took to school every day, avoiding her brothers' gaze, which she knew must read something like, 'How can you be that stupid?'

"So did I," Doctor Michael began, "but certainly not enough — and I took a double allotment. I drank every last drop on the way here." He turned his open and empty canteen upside down for them to see.

"You took a double allotment? That's not fair! Why would you take so much water when others barely have enough?" Qeriya demanded. "There's not enough in the Wadi as it is, and it's still shrinking."

"Qeriya, you're being rude," Lahcen said quietly, teeth clenched. "He's a family friend."

"Well it's true, Lahcen." Qeriya didn't bother to drop her voice.

"Qeriya," Khalid, always the more rational of her two brothers, said calmly. "Be quiet, please."

For a moment Qeriya was tempted to say, 'Yes, your majesty' but she bit the remark back. Instead, she folded her arms and stared at Khalid, obedient, but resistant.

"You're not being fair to Doctor Michael," Lahcen added, walking over to align with the accused. "He wasn't trying to steal water — and you're treating him like he was raiding our supply. I'm sure he had good reason to take extra." Lahcen looked at the doctor. "Isn't that right?"

"I took more because I'm a doctor and I need to carry extra water to care for my patients. Today I needed it to tail you three.

"We should really be getting back, don't you think?" he

suggested.

The reminder was like being awoken from a particularly good dream. It immediately dowsed their high spirits, leaving them oddly resentful. Reluctantly, they followed the doctor's lead and made their way out of the shade cast by the canyon wall.

Qeriya plodded behind Doctor Michael as he turned to travel east, away from the setting sun.

It was later than she had thought. Her parents didn't like her brothers coming in late, but they would be as angry as a diamond back rattler, caught by its tail, if she came home late. It was very unfair, but that was just the way it was, and she couldn't afford to make them any more upset, especially after she'd promised them she wouldn't leave the village.

"You're younger," her parents had said when she stayed out late one night. She'd been playing tag with friends in the twilight, on the sandstone slopes bordering the canyons northwest of the village. She'd lost track of how dark it was getting and had ended up in trouble. She'd pointed out the unfairness of her brothers being allowed to do more when they were her age than she could.

"But, you're a girl," they'd said, as if that made any sense at all.

"And that's important ... why? The last I checked there were more boys dying around here than girls," she'd said, snatching the final word. She'd considered herself the winner of that argument, in her mind at least. Boys died from accidents in greater numbers than girls. It was epidemic really. Though the fact never seemed to change the adults' preconceived attitudes to what boys could do that girl's couldn't. Her parents, along with many others, persisted in believing that girls needed more protection than boys. But, frustrated as she got, Qeriya knew her parents acted out of love, and some of her friends were envious that they cared enough to give her a curfew.

The four of them waded through thick sand in the waning sun, Qeriya resentfully abstaining from using her power. Lahcen carried a stick, batting any stray rocks he saw out of his way to ward off boredom.

"I suppose you'll be telling our parents?" she called to Doctor Michael.

"Oh, not necessarily," he said. "I'll tell them you were with me."

Qeriya's spirits rose. Maybe they wouldn't be in as much trouble if their parents thought they were with Doctor Michael. Just maybe, she would still be able to run in the race.

"Hey," Khalid said to Doctor Michael. "You didn't see anybody else on your way here, did you?"

"No — Well, I thought I might have seen someone else. But then I figured it must just be Qeriya. Why do you ask?"

"Oh, no reason, it's nothing."

Odd as that was, Qeriya thought she'd better wait until the doctor was gone to ask about it further. For some reason, Khalid obviously didn't want to discuss it with him there.

"You lived at the palace before you came here, didn't you?" Lahcen asked, changing the subject.

"Yes, yes I did. I was a doctor there," he told them, as they continued to meander a dry wash that ran parallel to the Wadi. They appeared to be looping around instead of backtracking, in which case they'd have to cross the Wadi further ahead. To do that was highly illegal. Perhaps, Qeriya reasoned, Doctor Michael had special permission.

"Were you a doctor to the king?" she asked.

The doctor laughed. "Oh no, not to the king. The palace is a massive city, enclosed in a rock dome, with thick, clear ceilings, to let in light. It's almost like a planet within a planet. I was just one of many doctors there."

Try as she might, Qeriya found it impossible to picture. "That sounds so strange," she said, still puzzling at it. "Did they have these … reaume people there? We saw information on them in the cave," she added in response to the startled look the doctor gave her.

"They're not people, they're reaume."

The siblings stared at him in astonishment. "Not people? They look like people," Khalid said.

"I know, but they're not human. They have a human-like body, but they're another species altogether," he explained.

There was a stunned silence as the three of them digested this information. Then Lahcen said, "Where are they from?"

"They're from New Earth, this planet."

"We learned all about Old Earth in school," Lahcen said as he searched the sky, seeking his ancient home in the stars. "But we haven't learned as much about the history of this planet, and we aren't allowed to ask too much."

Doctor Michael nodded his head in agreement, but said nothing.

"So how is it we've never heard of these reaume before? Nobody I know has ever seen or spoken about such creatures—" Qeriya broke off as an idea, so enormous, so exciting, and so frightening hit her that for an instant it blocked out every other thought in her head. "Is that what we are?" she said. Receiving no reply she ran around in front of him, barring his path. The sun was nesting behind her and she saw the once blue sky behind Doctor Michael change to a soft mauve.

The doctor rubbed at his eyes with his fingers as he worked out how best to answer. "Let's just say, I'm not at liberty to speak on this subject. Your parents could probably answer these questions for you some day, but not now. Keep these abilities you have a secret." He looked pointedly at Qeriya. "I know you're tired of secrets, consider this a warning, some secrets are necessary right now. You just need to trust me."

"Yeah, Mom and Dad are always talking about trusting them, too," Qeriya said. "And it's becoming an echo in my head. Because the more I hear 'trust me,' the more I don't." Her brothers glared at her disapprovingly but Qeriya didn't care. She was sick and tired of charades. She turned on her heel, marching ahead.

"What she means to say," Khalid added, attempting to smooth over his sister's brusque response, determinedly ignoring her taking out her frustration by kicking random rocks, along with sand, into the air, "is that we want to find out more and aren't sure why we're not allowed to ask questions. I'm sure there's a good reason, but—"

Lahcen inadvertently blundered into the small sand storm Qeriya had created. He spit, arming sand out of his mouth and eyes with his forearm, glaring at his sister, nostrils flaring. Qeriya quickly slowed her pace, moving to place Doctor Michael between them.

The doctor paused in his stride, pulling in a deep breath. "As you've seen from all the canyons and washes, more water used to pass through here, but now there's less and less every year." He gestured vaguely at the surrounding land. "There were buttercups all over here, and mallows and a variety of wildflowers," he said softly, coming back to himself.

Qeriya tried to imagine the desert dotted with flowers and other plant life. It was almost beyond her comprehension.

You'll have to find a way to leave eventually, if your generation wants to survive."

"That's what I keep trying to tell my parents," Khalid said. The sleepy sun was morphing to twilight and Khalid began to accelerate his pace as he spoke, suddenly aware of how late it was becoming. The others sped up to match. "They think they're protecting us by keeping us in the village, but unless we discover some other options, there's no way any of us will survive.

"I'm sure there's so much more you could explain," Qeriya said, starving for more information.

Doctor Michael stopped to draw a few deep breaths. "Yes, but, as it is, I've said too much on the subject already. The competition is tomorrow. It'll be a long day." He halted momentarily and the three turned to see what was wrong. "I'm afraid for you, your coming here today, this experimenting with your powers — it's not good."

They walked on in silence and Qeriya kept her eyes peeled to spot diamond back rattlesnakes in the residual light.

Lahcen noticed her scanning the area nervously and grabbed her arm. She jumped in alarm and whammed his head with her other fist.

"Ouch!" Lahcen exclaimed, rubbing his head.

"Oh, knock it off, Lahcen. Serves you right," Khalid said. "You won't see any snakes, Qeriya, if that's what you're worried about."

"There used to be wild turkeys that came around the village," Lahcen recalled.

"Yeah, I remember hearing about them," Qeriya said. "That was when people ate meat. And there were coyotes as well."

"That's right," Khalid added. "There were coyotes, and wild dogs, and even an occasional bobcat."

Qeriya remembered being terrified of mountain lions and dogs when she was little, but they'd all vanished now. Scared as she might be of snakes, she thought she could live with her fear if it meant the Wadi were returning to normal.

Her tongue was so dry and sticky it felt like a foreign object wedged in her mouth. But there was still a ways to go and she was much too proud to ask her brother for any more water. She'd wait until her tongue fell out before she'd stoop to beg anything off of Lahcen.

"Ha!" Doctor Michael called suddenly, making them jump.

"What is it?" Khalid asked.

"Water!" the doctor exclaimed, going over to a cactus plant.

Qeriya had seen barrel cacti before. She'd watched her father burn the spines and slice the barrel in half, sprinkling salt on top. Her mother had prepared the seeds for dinner. On the rare occasions they found honey *and* a barrel cactus, her mother would prepare delicious sweets.

They watched as Doctor Michael pulled a knife out of his robe pocket. "I won't be able to burn the spines," he said. "I'll just have to cut them off."

Once the cactus was smooth enough to handle, Doctor Michael harvested the plant and cut it in half, splitting his half with her and giving Khalid the other. They mashed the white pulp in their fingers the best they could. It tasted bitter and disgusting without proper preparation but Qeriya was so thirsty it didn't matter; she swallowed it down as fast as possible. "Slower, it's acidic," Doctor Michael said. "You'll throw up."

"I know, but I can't help it," she said.

"I'm just sorry we had to waste it like that," Lahcen said. "There are so many good ways to prepare it."

"Drinking isn't exactly wasteful," Khalid said.

"Yes it is," Lahcen argued.

Khalid punched him in the shoulder. "You could have made it easier on us and pulled the water out."

"I could've, but I really wanted to watch Doctor Michael use a knife," Lahcen teased.

Qeriya said nothing. She understood what Lahcen was really saying. He might talk about the knife, but she knew it would take a while for them to get used to feeling comfortable using their powers at all, much less around anyone else. They finished eating and walked north, until, finally, they approached the tree lined Wadi. The sun had fully descended and it was completely dark. Doctor Michael kept watch while they took turns crossing the water. It was illegal to even approach the stream, other than to fill a ration-sized container, but nobody seemed to notice them.

They walked out of the tree cover on the other side and headed directly for home. All was quiet as most people had already finished their late evening meal and extinguished their fires. The closer the small group came to home, the more their sense of trepidation grew. All of them, even the doctor, were expecting to be greeted by a few, still warm, cooking coals and some very angry parents.

Qeriya had been too distracted by what they had found in the cave to think clearly before, but now that she was home, guilt blasted her like a hot sand storm. She'd been careless taking off like that, and may have ruined her chances of participating in the race tomorrow, even if Doctor Michael stood up for them. Yet she couldn't truly regret her actions; she'd learned so much in this one afternoon about herself and her brothers. For the first time, she didn't feel quite so alone in the world. As they neared the house Qeriya braced herself.

It took a long moment for them to realize that all was in darkness and the fire extinguished. "Huh, I wonder where they are?" Lahcen said, running his strong fingers through his thick black hair until it stuck straight up on top of his head.

"Maybe they went to bed," Qeriya said, brushing his hair back down. "I mean, we don't really deserve dinner."

"True, they might've if it was just us," Lahcen said, batting her hand away. "But you're their princess. They wouldn't sleep while Princess was missing."

"Shut up! I'm not a princess. If I were, I'd have you beheaded," she said, swiping his hair back on end before he could brush her hand away again.

"Doctor Michael," Khalid said, "you can go on home. We'll be fine. I'm sure our parents are out looking for us and will be back soon."

"I'm sure you're right," Doctor Michael said, following them to the curtained doorway, "but I'll feel better if I see you connect with them. Perhaps we should check inside. Could they be sleeping?"

"It's not likely, but we can check," Lahcen said, peering into the darkened house. "Mom? Dad?" he called softly. "Are you asleep already?" There was no response.

Khalid dragged a few baskets out from within the doorway and dumped them on the ground. He found the giant block of hardwood, grabbed some lightwood and began rubbing them together. Qeriya and Lahcen felt around for the candles that were stored in the baskets. As soon as a flame was ignited, they lit the candles and entered the house.

Qeriya gasped. In the soft glow of candlelight she saw her parents, lying side-by-side on their bedding, as if taking a nap. There was no evidence of dinner or any signs of the other chores that normally occupied their evenings. Fear, like an iron fist squeezed her heart. "Something's wrong. Something's really wrong!"

Doctor Michael leaned over Ruth and Jeremiah, doing his best to examine them in the dim candlelight, while Qeriya and her brothers watched and waited without a word. Seeing her mother and father lying helpless on the ground conjured in Qeriya a feeling of utter responsibility, as if arguing with them that morning, their agreement to let her race, her absence tonight, were the sole reasons for what had befallen them. It didn't make sense and she knew it, but nevertheless, that's how it felt. She tore her eyes away from her parents' inert bodies and looked to see how her brothers were doing.

"What is it? What's happened?" Lahcen begged Doctor Michael to explain, but the doctor ignored the plea and continued his examination.

Khalid stood quietly staring, barely breathing so as not to interrupt the doctor, waiting for an answer.

After what felt like hours, though she knew it must only be minutes, Doctor Michael paused. He wiped his brow with the sleeve of his robe and raised his eyes. "I'm afraid I'll need to do some tests. A mouth swab will probably be enough." He took a flat stick from the folds of his robe and swabbed their parents' mouths, using first one end and then the other, before wrapping it in cloth.

Qeriya's felt her stomach somersault inside of her. She watched numbly as Doctor Michael turned them onto their sides. Their mouths hung open slackly; drool leaking from her father, leaving a string of saliva in its wake. The doctor fished in his robe again, bringing out an instrument the likes of which they'd never seen before. Behind a clear barrier, something that looked almost like a small fire projected forth from a slim tube. He pointed it into each parents' eyes. "I've positioned them this way so they can breathe and any saliva will drain out," he explained. "Don't worry, they don't feel any pain. I've adapted their brain state so that they're in hibernation.

"What's hibernation and what's that light?" Qeriya asked.

"Hibernation slows down their bodily functions so that they can go for a long time without eating or drinking. They experience it as a deep form of sleep. It's almost as if time has stopped for them. They'll be just fine until I can figure out how to help them. Shining that light into their pupils is the means of inducing this state."

Qeriya stared, dumbfound, along with her brothers. The shock of her parents' unconsciousness and the amount of new information her mind had absorbed today was making it increasingly difficult for her to take on board what was happening. None of this seemed real, and the doctor's words were fast becoming random noise in her ears.

Khalid felt his father's chest for a heartbeat. If not for their parents' slowly pulsing blood and the subtle warmth from their bodies, they could easily have been taken for dead.

"I know you want to stay with them," Doctor Michael said hesitantly. "But I don't know if what they have is contagious. You should stay at my house tonight."

"No!" Qeriya exclaimed. "We can't leave them like this. What if they die?"

"They won't die, Qeriya," Doctor Michael reassured. "They're just in hibernation, remember? We don't know what they have, but once I figure it out, it's just a matter of finding the right treatment. The palace has treatments for just about every ailment. No, I'm not worried about *finding* a treatment, the main problem is that medicine from the palace costs a lot of money, money that you and I don't have right now."

Khalid wrapped his arm around his sister, his own face registering shock, while Lahcen stared at the limp bodies.

"They're breathing," Lahcen noted. "I can see their chests move."

Doctor Michael nodded. "They're just sick, but you all might catch whatever they have if you stay. It almost reminds me of the sleeping flu, very contagious, but I'm not sure if that's it. You should come with me."

"No, thank you," Khalid said shortly. "We'll sleep outside."

The doctor looked as if he might argue further, but changed his mind. "All right, sleep outside then," he said, exasperation plain in his voice. "I should be going. I need to determine what this is."

"We'll see you tomorrow then?" Khalid said, glancing at Qeriya, who was shivering, despite the fact the evening had not yet turned cold.

"Yes, I'll be here early tomorrow — I'll help you get ready for the competition.

"Doctor Michael," Khalid said, "our parents are very sick. I hardly think we'll be competing tomorrow."

"Oh no, you must compete! You had a choice before, even though your parents wanted to protect you. But there are no options now, you don't have any money, and I don't have enough to give you. The reward for the competition is money, and you're going to need a lot of it if you want to find a cure for your parents. Each of you must compete, and each of you must win."

"So, are you fish or boy, Aedan?" Clara asked, treading water on one of her monthly trips to the ocean.

"What kind of question is that?" he asked in return, likewise treading water, but without the same degree of effort.

"Well, you look just like a regular boy and breathe air like one on land, but in the water you get webby things on your hands and feet, and you even get gills, like a fish. I don't get it. Are you a person or a fish?"

"I'm neither," he said, annoyed. "I'm ocean reaume." He began swiping at the water, making it splash.

"Well, I know that, silly!" Clara dismissed his obvious irritation. "But what is a reaume? Are you human?"

"Of course I'm not human!" He turned away, splashing the water harder and faster.

Clara sighed. "Oh come on! You say that as if my even saying it is an insult. I'm just asking!"

"It is an insult!" He turned back around to face her, his nostrils flaring. "Humans are mean! They hurt each other — and everything else. I wouldn't be human even if I could eat coconut candy every day for the rest of my life!"

"Hey, I'm human!" Clara exclaimed and splashed the water with her own fist. "If you hate humans so much then why are you here, playing with me?"

"Because you're different, you're my best friend." Aedan's voice softened and he looked away as he spoke.

"I am?" she asked, and she saw the back of his head nod. "Well, you're my best friend, too. Let's always be friends."

"Okay. Hey, want a ride?" he asked excitedly.

Clara's face lit up like a candle. "Yeah!" she exclaimed, grabbing a firm hold onto his shoulders. "Go faster than you've ever gone in your entire life!"

Chapter 4

Ticket to Freedom

Doctor Michael took down a book from his salt brick shelf. The tome was weathered and worn, with deep creases, much like the skin on his face. It sat beside the many classics on philosophy and travel he had accumulated over the years. He'd read and re-read those works many times, allowing the words to become a scaffold for his mind. The print reflected the real story of his life; in contrast to the silent lie he lived now. His fingers traced over the brown leather with its shiny patina as tenderly as any lover would stroke his sweetheart's cheek. It had been a long time since he'd handled this particular one, and he relished the smooth feel of it as he walked to his giant leather chair and sank into its cushioned depths beside the cast iron, wood stove, an ancient ivory pipe dangling from his mouth. Though it pained him to think of parting with this special book for any amount of time, he had no other choice. He had to give it to Khalid tomorrow. It was the only way.

He ran a finger absent-mindedly across the ornate carving on his pipe, a product of one of his archaeological digs from when the planet was first settled. Back on earth, ivory had been harvested from elephant tusks. It was considered so valuable that elephants died en mass because of its trade. So when elephants were genetically engineered for New Earth, they were recreated without tusks. Some ancient ivory objects however, found their way to the new world and lay buried amid layers of life and death that had slowly accumulated over the years. While ivory was once considered a rare treasure, its worth was beyond measure now, irreplaceable. Smoke from the restored pipe trailed a winding path toward the thatched, bear grass ceiling and then dissipated in a smoky haze, very much resembling his jumbled thoughts. This was the time to act, now that they'd fully discovered their powers. Two years he'd been here, but it was worth it. He'd finally found them. He'd lived here all that time, planning, and waiting for it all to be over.

The pungent smell of tobacco mingled with the aromatic scent of the braided sweet grass set high on another bookshelf. He breathed in deeply through his prominent nose. The smell reminded him of mountain ventures back when life was carefree. His father had worked during their travels, while he played and enjoyed life in all its forms. Beside the sweet grass, his bookshelf held many various sized pottery containers. He kept hop bush to treat aches and pains, jojoba salve to soothe burns, creosote, cliff rose and a variety of other herbs, as well as imported medicines and tools.

A shrill noise grew into a whistle and he stirred himself to remove a metal kettle from the wood stove, wrapping the handle in a thick woven cloth and walking it over a series of floor mats, woven from lechuguilla leaves, that formed a covering for his dirt floor. He took his largest pottery mug, decorated with geometric patterns in shades of red and purple, and filled it with the steaming water, adding a small palmful of mint leaves. The mug was a hand thrown gift from a time long past, and a life now long dead. He could hardly stand to look at it, carrying as it did tormented memories of the life he'd had to give up. He sighed. It did keep his tea hot a lot longer than any mug he'd found since however, and there was no sense in wasting such a perfectly made cup. He took a sip of the flavorful tea.

This was far from the existence he'd hoped for himself at this age, and every day he wished for his prestigious past. But his father had sacrificed for him, and now it was his turn to suffer. If he'd learned anything from his father, it was that sacrifice defined a man. You did what had to be done to protect those you loved, whether or not they knew it.

He took the tea over to his chair and snuggled down once

more, surrounded by the warm glow of the candles that illuminated the pages as he turned them, tracing his finger slowly
along a prescribed route. He remembered the eve of his
eighteenth birthday, when his father first bestowed the journal
upon him.

"There are secrets in here," his father had said, his voice
grave. "A path is detailed for when you travel the world." His
father had gripped his shoulder. "It's your turn to journey now,
my son. Learn all you can from what's out there. Add your
knowledge and experience to these pages. Then pass it on to the
next generation."

And he'd taken that journey … in part. He'd traveled to the
snowcapped mountains and seen their myriad of wildflowers.
He'd met a shy baby mountain goat face to face while on a steep
climb up Sacajawea Peak. He'd journeyed the plains, where he
had eaten bison stew and rainbow trout, not realizing at the time
that would be one of the highlights of his life.

He'd enjoyed visiting other forests besides those around the
mountains. The rainforest, however, was just outside of his
reach. Its bounty was always his favorite back when he lived at
the palace — juicy pineapple, bananas, grapefruit, coconut
water, breadfruit, and the spices, rich and diverse, adding
unrivaled taste to dishes. Now he wanted to see the trees that
produced these fruits and spices. Fortunately, he'd learned the
art of salsa making and how to prepare meal cakes and cactus
dishes here in the desert, but still, the sameness of it day in and
day out grew tiresome.

What he wouldn't do for some guayusa and cocoa tea from
the rainforest. He liked the dark, bitter flavor and creamy after-
taste of cocoa tea in the morning almost as much as coffee, while
guayusa was a refreshing and energizing afternoon tea. Not that
anyone would know what these were in this wasteland.

Studying the rainforest portion of the journal, he found the
old human settlement where his father once stayed. His father

had relayed his adventures there, stories of capturing a massive python from stagnant water, and learning to drum on skins stretched tight over hollowed out gourds. The wooden structures they had built for shelter had been adorned with intricate carvings. His father had sketched some examples in the margins of the journal. People there lived in bamboo homes with one or more walls left open to the elements, covered only by mosquito netting, and yet they stayed dry and comfortable. It had been his father's favorite place to visit. How disappointing that this village had to disappear. But someday it would return, in all of its glory, and he would be there when it did.

His finger traveled the journal's route toward the vast savannah. Yes, this would be the best way to send them, by the western border crossing. He picked up the bit of charcoal lying on a carved side table made of ironwood and darkened the line that the path took. The description had to be perfect. It must be legible and easy to decipher. There could be no mistakes. He would need to know where they were at all times, and Khalid would need to know where to lead his brother and sister when they left.

As he traced and dreamed, he saw movement out of the corner of his eye. Something rustled his bedcovers. Most people didn't have furniture as he did, and certainly not books. Being in charge always had its privileges.

He quietly watched as the movement continued, then one of his slippers fell from the bed. Rising to investigate, he picked up the animated slipper carefully, holding it away from his body, and peered inside to see a small, armored, creature with pincers. A scorpion, and this one was poisonous. Moving slowly, he grabbed a sharp kitchen knife, lifted the slipper over a cutting board and dumped the creature onto it. Quickly he slammed the knife down, severing the stinger from the rest of the animal with near perfect aim. Scorpion was rather tasty — deadly — but tasty. Despite having eaten dinner, he took a pan from its hook on the wall and placed it on the stove, ready to cook his tiny catch. It didn't take long; there was only meat sufficient for one bite, enough to give him a morsel of protein. He gnawed tasty bits with his teeth, teasing them into his mouth. If only he had curry to make a dip, or some peanut satay for those unlikely moments when a scorpion wandered into his slippers.

His impromptu meal finished, he resumed studying his father's journal. His attention wandering east this time, to the mountain border and the rainforest beyond that. The mountains rose sharply after the oasis. Their jagged cliffs were impossible to scale and infinitely high. But further east arose faint signs of life, tiny stiff plants and lichen on rocks. Further down grew white pine krummholz, oddly molded into beastlike forms from high winds. The mountains then gave way to a thick rainforest. Rain clouds consistently dumped their load here as air was forced upward into the heights before sinking into the heat beyond the mountains. Thus there was little moisture left for the barren land that was the desert. Nevertheless, there was a tiny crevasse, formed by avalanches of snow, that had carved a small basin for the run off, and water meandered into the desert oasis below, or at least it once had, until most of it was siphoned away.

When he thought about it, which he did often, he imagined that moving east, into the rainforest, must feel like entering a sauna and he longed for the time everything was over so he could see it. At the far end of the rainforest stood the mound of a volcano. Beyond that, the land rose sharply in elevation and eventually leveled. The climb transformed the landscape to an evergreen forest with very different flora. He'd visited that region once with his father. The people there were known for their hunting and he remembered feasting on fresh venison and pheasant, keeping warm by a wood fire on a cold night, already snug beneath his covering of beaver pelts. The next day they'd made the trek to the ancient palace. Never, if he lived to be a hundred, would he forget the majesty, the sheer breath-taking splendor of it.

He couldn't hold back a sigh — so many pleasant memories, back before the threat had grown strong. His father had contended with the looming unease, and was the first to see what was happening. However, his father could never have imagined how bad things would get. It was up to him now; he had to navigate a way out of this bind. He smiled, remembering the other night, when Qeriya had begged him to intercede for her about the race. How she'd pleaded with him to make her parents see reason. She wanted so much to compete in the desert games this year, and of course her parents were afraid, terrified of what would happen if she were exposed.

He surveyed the journal once again; his ticket to freedom. The map showed that beyond the old palace lay a massive ocean. He'd traversed this ocean by air, but never by watercraft. How he longed to visit beaches of white sand, bathed in sunlight, and to be able to explore the reef. Soon, everything would change. He would be free. It was time.

Clara pushed wet hair back from her face, smiling broadly as she armed salty drops of water from her eyes and listened to the seductive roar of the surf. If only they lived a little closer to the ocean, she could come every day instead of once a month. During her eight years living in the rainforest, Clara had come to appreciate the wealth of plant and animal life, but the ocean visits with her foster family were the highlight of her existence. She dived into a rolling wave and came up the other side, swimming further and further into the deep. Her guardians, getting nervous, began calling for her to come back but she pretended she didn't hear and lingered under water longer and longer after each breath. The water was tepid and sticky on her skin, as if she was bathing in liquid salt, buoying her up onto its surface. Everyone was afraid to go this deep, but somehow she wasn't. She never felt alone out here, even after everyone went back to shore.

Clara let herself float. She was thinking, as she so often did when she swam, of her ocean friend, Aedan. She could picture him so clearly, plunging about in the water around her; her best friend, who swam like a dolphin. But these last few years he hadn't come to swim with her like he used to. There was a sharp stab of pain as she remembered their carefree joy in among the waves. She wished he were here with her now.

Suddenly, she felt herself being swept away by a fast current, taking her deeper into the ocean and down shore from her group. She struggled to free herself, but nothing was working. Panic inched its way up her throat and into her mind; Clara realized she had moments left before it consumed her but determinedly, she resisted its grip. Relax, she told herself, over and over, don't fight it ... let it carry you ... swim sideways, not against it.

In that instant, she felt hands on her back, lifting her above the water. The hands supported and guided her steadily to a barren beach, miles down from where her family sat. Strong arms carried and set her gently on the ground. Clara stared at her rescuer as he knelt down to see if she was all right. He was beautiful, deep brown skin gleaming in the sunlight, water dripping from his tiny black curls.

"Aedan," she whispered, "you came back."

Chapter 5

The Woman with Steel-Grey Eyes

Qeriya's eyes swept over the swollen crowd and she tried to absorb their energy. Her heart was pounding so hard she felt it might sprout legs and bolt right out of her chest. It was almost evening. The sun would go down before long, but for now it was insufferably hot.

Aside from being her first competition in the annual Desert Games, this was also the first Desert Games to host royalty, or the prince anyway. How he'd arrived she couldn't begin to guess. She'd heard of the royal family, the king, his queen and their son, Prince Liam. But they'd seemed distant to her, as if in a fairy tale, and she figured her desert home must be forgotten, since no member of royalty had ever set foot on their dry, acrid soil. No one spoke much of the king, and, the little Qeriya had heard left her with a distinct sense that he was not well liked. But maybe, she thought, the prince would be different. Most of the other girls competing had run the course before. Unlike her parents, other families encouraged their children to compete. Qeriya drew in a deep, steadying breath. She had hiked most of the course while hunting with her father, she would just have to hope that would be enough.

"They'll be clapping for me at the finish," she muttered, trying hard to convince herself as she ran in place to warm up for the five kilometer race.

"I wouldn't bet on it," a voice sneered from the mass of runners stretching their limbs. "They'll be mourning you in the end."

Qeriya flinched, consumed by her worries and fears she was unaware that she'd spoken loud enough to be overheard. She searched for the person that went with the voice but couldn't pinpoint her location. The snide comment was little more than a momentary intrusion. Even her worries about the race were nothing compared to the image that constantly beat at her mind and tormented her heart. Though she knew she could not allow it to distract her, Qeriya could not stop picturing the awful sight of her parents, lying unconscious and helpless, at home. The thought that they would die unless Doctor Michael found a cure was like an iron fist, squeezing her insides, making it hard to breathe, much less concentrate on the course. And yet, that was exactly what she must do. It was vital she win this race. Doctor Michael could find all the cures under the sun, but they would be less than worthless if they lacked the money to purchase them. When she had first seen her parents like that, she had assumed it was something genetic, as so many of the conditions people died from in the village. She remembered her science teacher telling her class that, long ago, people had been able to select genes for their children, much as they now shopped for food from the market. Somehow, Qeriya wasn't exactly sure how, this gene shopping had messed everyone up. But Doctor Michael had ruled any such illness out. Anomalies, he'd told them, were rarely this sudden, and unlikely to affect two people at the same time.

"Prince Liam will say a few words before we begin the last event." The announcer's voice boomed from atop the canyon wall that edged the sandy wash where she and other anxious racers paced, above throngs of people lining the course. The prince rose and she saw that he was dressed in a smooth, unblemished robe, quite unlike the quilted old skins, turkey feathers and woven grass that everyone else wore.

From where she was it was difficult to see him in detail but his straight black hair draped down both sides of his chest. Standing beside the announcer, with an entourage of giants she supposed were his guards, he was encased by a clear box crowning the cliff.

"Desert dwellers," the prince called from his steep perch. "Thank you for your generous welcome and for giving me a seat at your annual competition. I've heard so much about your talent and am privileged to see it firsthand here today.

"In gratitude for your gracious hospitality, I've brought a palace feast to share with you after the games, a gift from the royal household. I'm hoping this will be the first of many visits." Everyone gasped and the crowd roared with approval.

While Qeriya appreciated the gesture, she wished he'd announced it after the race, as the clapping extended for what felt like years.

"Racers, to your marks," the announcer said and the applause waned.

Qeriya positioned herself to start. It was about time. Within seconds, she'd joined the stampede of barefoot young women wearing matching headscarves, clad in light woven dresses belted in the middle with braided grass. The clothes chaffed and slowed them, but it was better than running bare skinned in the sun. The boys wore short sleeves and no head covers. Their face and arms would endure painful burns by the end of the day — a mark of manhood no doubt.

The girl up front, head above the others, was the one to beat. Qeriya kept her eyes trained on the long legged girl sailing easily ahead of the other runners. No wonder she was three-time champion with legs like that! Her own instinct was to speed up but she kept herself in check, she needed to hang back a bit at first. Doctor Michael had given her instructions before the race.

It was not long before the pack thinned. Exhausted racers were left behind like weeds in a harvest and those injured in the aggressive front wave were quickly cleared off the course. Qeriya remained in the middle until the chaotic start settled down and each runner found the pace she hoped was best suited to carry her through to the finish. That was when Qeriya revved up her own momentum, pushing ahead, while keeping a careful watch for particularly fierce racers, making a silent note to pass them at a distance. The course began a ways from the village, east of the settlement, amid canyon cliffs that traveled east and west. The runners sprinted west; parallel to the dry wash that she had traversed yesterday, but further south.

"Hey!" Qeriya yelled and darted to the right as a woman she didn't know threw out her arm to knock her off the coveted path of stones and patches of scrub grass, cool and firm islands in a sea of baking sand. Idiot woman! Lucky for her she didn't have time to deal with her, Qeriya thought. She ran on the sand to avoid further conflict but, even so, another racer tried to trip her as she sped past. Qeriya dodged just in time and slapped the aggressor's chest; hurling the stunned girl to the ground. She would have to watch even more carefully for other desperate runners. Nothing was going to stop her winning this race — her parents' lives depended on it.

She wondered how Lahcen did on his run, an endurance race to see who could run the furthest distance without water. He wasn't crazy about competing, preferring a shorter race, but while there was some doubt as to his speed, there was no question he could outlast anyone without water. If only she could drink from the air like Lahcen, she thought, as her mouth quickly grew as dry as the ground her feet pounded over. How could she have forgotten water of all things? Fortunately, Doctor Michael had given her a bowl full to drink before she lined up, but it was clearly not going to be enough.

Her strides grew long and her body yearned to lift off and sail the air currents but Qeriya grimly fought the urge and concentrated on keeping herself on the ground. The dry wash circled north, soon joining the remains of the meager Wadi and the mass of wet sand felt like balm on her feet.

A girl a few paces ahead sank down to her ankle in quicksand and Qeriya pulled aside just in time to avoid her own feet sinking into the imprisoning muck. Glancing back she saw the girl tugging her foot free and breathed a little easier, realizing she would be all right. As she passed some more racers, she saw a rare wisp of columbine gracing a rock wall nearby. Time to move up, she decided, remembering Doctor Michael's hurried coaching. By now the initial, thick knot of other runners had thinned to a straggly line. Having crossed the Wadi's end, Qeriya merged with the path she and her father used to take hunting. Here she entered a wide, shady canyon, west of her school. She sped up slightly, picking off runners one at a time as the course meandered through a cluster of sandstone pillars.

Before long the canyon opened out and the wash expanded into a river of sand. The sun pierced her clothing and she felt its heat dig deep into her skin, but the discomfort was nothing compared to the sting of burning sand on the soles of her feet. Though the pain was intense, not so much as a whimper crossed her lips. Like all the runners, she bore her hurt stoically and, like the others, ran as fast as her lungs allowed. The urge to lift off the ground, to float on the slight breeze, was overwhelming and it took all that she had not to rise as blisters supplanted the hardened calluses on her feet.

An image of Khalid's timed, unharnessed, early morning climb flashed into her mind. The contestants, tightly packed, swarmed the rock face, resembling nothing more than a colony of ants. Qeriya had watched Khalid quickly scaling the cliff when, suddenly, a guy above him kicked a stone loose, deliberately aiming it at Khalid's forehead. She saw her brother falter momentarily as the stone unbalanced him, but he hugged the wall, clinging tight, despite the blood streaming down his face. The mystery climber stayed where he was, waiting for Khalid to catch up and, as soon as he was within reach, began to kick at him, hoping to dislodge him. Qeriya's stomach had roiled, sick with a poisonous mixture of fear and helplessness, but Khalid, edging carefully over to the left, managed to get past the murderous figure. Steadily, he'd persevered to the top, finding footholds in shallow distortions of the rock face, clinging to slivers of stone with his fingers, inching his lean body upward like a lizard climbing a wall. She had never seen anyone make climbing look as easy as crawling before.

"Finally!" she gasped, as a number of large stones, balanced precariously on top of one another, hove into view. The cairn! She had almost reached the Grand Arch."

Qeriya ascended a gently sloping rock face that lifted from the sand to a plateau above. She ran along the rising cliff, so close to the edge that no one dared to join her. The move enabled her to pass a slew of runners, but the sustained hard pace beneath the burning desert sun was taking its toll and again she berated herself for forgetting that most essential survival tool — water. Just beyond the cliff lay the most beautiful segment of the route and Qeriya wished she had the strength left to enjoy it. Her dad had sometimes brought her to that very place to watch the sun set. Qeriya swallowed painfully in a dust-dry throat. She mustn't think about that now. Her heart was working too hard to allow itself space to ache. Gritting her teeth, she narrowed her focus to the slap, slap, slap of her feet against sandstone as she ran.

The fiery ball of the sun settled nearer to the horizon, and the arch gleamed a magnificent orange. Deep shadows met shades of pink, purple and soft browns on its surface.

"Majestic!" Qeriya whispered softly.

Distracted, she failed to see the pale-faced girl with steel-grey eyes and spikes for hair until she was upon her, thrusting out her arm to push Qeriya off the cliff.

Qeriya fell: head first, down the canyon, a plunge that could easily snap her neck. Yet, instead of slamming against the rock below, the air thickened, like the foam mattress Doctor Michael owned. She sank into the cushion of air that had appeared out of nowhere, carrying her to a smooth stop a few inches above the rock. Stunned, but not hurt, Qeriya quickly rebounded, springing back to her feet and immediately thrusting one leg in front of the other. Now it was fear that dried her mouth. There was a lot of ground to make up and she could not afford to fail in her task. She scurried to join the other racers, running uphill once again, as if on Hermes' wings. She passed many runners, including the one who'd sent her plunging. Her aggressor was now in third place, but Qeriya kept her distance and focused only on the finish.

She passed under the arch, ran past the village and then south to the Wadi. Before long she descended the sand bank that once marked the edge of a roaring wash, sprinted across the village plateau and jumped across the water. This race was the only time that anyone was allowed to cross, except by means of the bridge, but she was too tired and too tense to enjoy it.

The stream was the last landmark before a short stretch of flat ground that would take her back to the starting line, which also doubled as the finish line. Qeriya spared a quick glance over her shoulder, just in time to see the same aggressive runner with steel-grey eyes who had pushed her off the cliff. This time, she was coming fast, and brandishing a knife. The girl lunged, slicing the arm of Qeriya's robe and drawing blood. It didn't matter. Nothing could be allowed to matter, except winning the race and getting the money Doctor Michael needed to make her parents well again. Qeriya picked up her pace, pushing hard now, covering more ground than seemed humanly possible as her fear of failing outweighed caution.

Ahead of her was the champion but the distance that separated them was far from great. Her mind blanked, as, finally giving in to instinct, she allowed herself to push the boundaries of normal running, slicing through the space between her and the champion like an arrow. Instead of feeling exhausted, she was invigorated, bounding toward her rival. Qeriya stormed the finish line watched by an almost silent crowd. Coming to a halt, she surveyed the onlookers. No one clapped.

"We have a winner!" The announcement resounded over the

heads of the stunned crowd. A low murmur started, rising steadily as, slowly, as if awakening from a dream, people began to applaud their unexpected champion.

Runners were now pouring across the finish line behind her, while others still struggled to complete the race. The girl with the knife came in second place, glaring at Qeriya with a look of intense hatred, and, in that moment, Qeriya knew that it wasn't over yet: that this girl was out for her blood. Who was she? Qeriya didn't recognize her from school, or from anywhere else for that matter.

"Oh! Doctor Michael, thank you!" Qeriya exclaimed gratefully as he emerged from the crowd, holding a large pottery bowl full of water. A shock of long black hair crept down the chest of his fiber robe while bluish grey eyes gleamed from the shadows under its billowing hood. He had always been a good family friend and now he had come through for them in the hour of their most desperate need. Qeriya was overcome by guilt at all the times she had taken his solid presence for granted, thinking him stiff and boring.

Gratefully sipping the water, it came to her that she felt even more energized than before the race. While other runners, even now, were leaning on their knees, straining for breath, she had only pretended that she needed to do so. "Doctor Michael," she began, "did you see that girl who came at me with a knife?" Her eyes flicked to where the girl had stood only seconds ago, but she had disappeared.

Doctor Michael's gaze was drawn to her arm, where blood oozed through her robe. His eyebrows knotted with concern. "I see what you mean." He examined the cut. "Let me fix that," he said calmly, digging his hand into a fiber bag and pulling out a pinch of dried plants and a bandage. He lifted her sleeve. Qeriya winced as the coarse material brushed against the wound on her tricep. Doctor Michael poured a small trickle of water over the bloody gash and stuffed a wad of dried creosote over the wound before she could so much as register what was happening.

"Ow!" Qeriya jumped, but it was already done and he was gently wrapping her arm with the bandage.

"That should help," he said. He frowned. "Who did this? I didn't see anything."

"I don't know." Qeriya scanned the crowd in the vain hope that she might see her assailant, but there was no trace of the other girl. She turned back to Doctor Michael. "I was hoping you could tell me. Her skin was pale, and her eyes were like metal."

"I've never seen anyone of that description," he said, frowning. He shook his head. "I was afraid this would happen, but I didn't expect it to be so soon." He surveyed the bustling, jostling crowds before returning his attention to Qeriya and forcing a smile.

"Anyway, let's not worry about that just now. The important thing is that you won. Now you have enough for any medication your parents may need."

Qeriya stared at him. "What d'you mean — you were afraid this would—" Her words abruptly turned into a scream as Lahcen ambushed her from behind, lifting and spinning her with hoots and hollers.

"Watch out for my arm!"

Lahcen instantly released her. "I just wanted to congratulate you!"

"Thanks, but couldn't you just congratulate me with a gentle pat on the back?" she said crossly, gazing at her brother. His dark hair lay in sweaty curls around his face. "Did you finish?"

"Of course I finished!" he smirked. "Once we got past twenty different shades of sand it didn't seem so bad. There were loads of canyons, and sand, and some funky cairns, and sand. And, by the way, did I mention all the sand? They had us running in circles — after the third lap I thought I might keel over with boredom."

It was all she could do to stop herself planting a big, smacking, kiss on his cheek. She contented herself with beaming at him instead. "I'm proud of you."

"Proud?" Lahcen tittered. "You're such a little mother." He paused. "I won too."

"You did?" Qeriya whooped. "That's great, Lahcen."

"Well don't look so surprised," he said, grinning. "And I won with some maniac trying to stab me the entire time!"

"Humph, that sounds familiar," Qeriya muttered showing him her bandaged arm.

"What is it with the competition this year?" Lahcen asked.

"Desperate comes to mind," Khalid said, joining them.

"I don't know," Qeriya said. "I've never seen my attacker before today, and believe me, the way she looks, she isn't someone I would forget. Anyhow," she added, making a determined effort to shake off her nagging unease. "Khalid, you were amazing! I saw you climb right before I was called to line up. The whole crowd was glued to you." She smiled. "And I'm glad to see your head no longer looks like it was pounded in a mortar."

"Well, aren't you going to tell us? How did it go?"

Khalid's hazel eyes sparkled. "I won — like you two. Great job by the way!" Khalid patted her back, flashing his brother a warm grin.

Qeriya eyed the crowd, keenly aware of suspicious looks being directed their way. They might be unable to marshal their sense of something off kilter, but they knew that something was odd.

"It is time for the champions to join the prince." The announcer's voice rolled around the canyon again.

Doctor Michael ushered them into line with the other winners waiting for an audience, but then stepped away from them.

"What are you doing? Where are you going, Doctor Michael? Aren't you coming with us?" Qeriya's face plainly showed that his place was with them but the doctor waved them on. "This is your moment," he said. "And well deserved. Go — enjoy yourselves, just—" he paused, placing his hands on Khalid's shoulders. "Promise me you'll return here, to me, as soon as you're able. I'll be waiting. There's something I need to show you. I have something important to tell you about your parents, there isn't time to explain right now. Go — enjoy your victory, you've earned it.

The winners hiked steadily up a switchback trail to the top of the canyon in order to join the prince within his clear enclosure. Most of them heaved their way up with shaky legs. Lahcen was obviously sore by the way he waddled uphill, puffing and blowing, but Qeriya felt largely unaffected by her exertions, and, judging from the way Khalid moved, he was also fine.

As the athletes reached the top, the prince moved to greet them. As expected, he had a strong physique, clad in a tanned deer hide robe, adorned with intricate glass beads that wound in patterns so complex, so satisfying, she wanted to extend her hand and follow them with her finger. Instead, she took a small step back, recoiling from the thought in alarm. His dark skin, straight black hair and prominent nose had lent him a distinguished air as he had made his way towards them, so Qeriya was taken by surprise when he looked down at her with youthful green eyes; the most beautiful eyes she had ever seen. Suddenly the fascination of the beads was all forgotten and her knees nearly buckled.

Clara waded into the ocean with her foster parents. She was half-hoping to see Aedan. He had told her that his reaume family had found out he was playing in the ocean with humans and had forbidden him from carrying on. But he'd come back anyway, just in time to save her. Maybe he would come again? She stared out across the sparkling waves, stifling a sigh. Since their last meeting she'd been left with more than only her previous eagerness to see him; now it was a constant ache, something more akin to longing.

"Do you see him, your boyfriend?" Carlos asked.

Clara froze, thoroughly embarrassed that he appeared to have read her mind.

"Carlos!" Laura scolded. "Don't tease her!"

"Oh, I didn't mean to tease you — well, then again, maybe I did." He snickered. "Oh, but don't worry. I can tease you because it's not even possible. Dating a reaume would be like dating a talking dog."

"There he is, I see him, at least I think that's him," Carlos said, scanning the distance.

Clara's heart beat faster as she saw him, closer now, skimming along the surface of the water. She threw herself forward, into the breaking waves, before anyone could see her reaction.

Chapter 6

Infatuation

"Please sit down." The prince spoke to everyone, but his eyes drifted in Qeriya's direction. He extended his hand, gesturing to seats hewn into the rock face. Khalid and Lahcen descended steps leading to the first floor, followed by Qeriya, and the prince close behind her. The air felt cool, as if it was evening. Qeriya exchanged puzzled glances with her brothers; the afternoon sun still shone from the west, painting a streak of light onto the floor before the full length, south facing window. What magic were the prince and his retinue using to combat the heat of those rays? Nor was that the only puzzle, Qeriya thought, surveying the area where they sat. How could anyone have carved all of this rock in such a short time without being noticed? The prince's giants must have created the enclosure, but with what, their bare hands?

She saw throngs of people below, gathered in the thick sand at the bottom of the canyon wall. Straight across from them lay an immense desert flat. Qeriya could not see the myriad of canyons weaving their way in and through that space, but she knew they were there, narrow vessels, fractured into capillaries that trickled into the thirsty sand. They were once carved by water, but that was back before she existed, back when more people died from drowning than dehydration. These days, flashfloods were simply welcome swells in the Wadi.

"Are you comfortable?" the prince asked, his eyebrows rising in his concern for her wellbeing.

Qeriya glanced over her shoulder, she was having trouble believing that the prince was speaking to her. "Yes," she said in a small voice, dropping her gaze meekly, unnaturally coy in the presence of royalty and doing her best to shrink into her seat. "Thank you."

"Something wrong, Qe?" Lahcen said in her ear, amused. "You sound sick."

Qeriya turned to her right, ready to threaten him, but all she could come up with was a stern mono brow and a clenched fist held close to his chin. He snickered in return.

Looking out of the window, she saw again the mass of gathered people stirring the sand, moving about as if actors at a large amphitheater. They reminded her of the plays she had occasionally seen with her family, though not from chiseled steps. They were held on a sandstone plateau west of the village, directly under the Grand Arch. People gathered on the sand below the platform to watch performers act out old legends of places and times past, stories that paralleled those told by her father. There they'd sit, family and friends, bathed in pink warmth as the sun set. A bonfire was lit and stoked with ironwood logs which smoldered deep into the night.

"Rolph," the prince called to one of his giants, the snap of his voice interrupting Qeriya's reverie. "Would you come here, please?"

Along the perimeter of the enclosure was a line-up of guards standing unnaturally still, legs spread apart, holding instruments resembling the bows her brothers used when shooting targets, only gargantuan in size. The guards were at least five times her height, but appeared human in every other respect. Except for their brawny physique, their features and body proportions reflected those of ordinary people, Qeriya could have passed for one, if somehow she were magnified in size. They wore uniforms in colors that matched their varying shades of skin. Their hair was long and pulled taut in a bun behind their heads. Upon close examination it appeared that they were a mix of men and women, but they resembled one another to such a degree it was difficult to tell sometimes which was which. A handful of the giants wore special adornments on their uniforms.

One of them, strung with a plethora of medals along his right breast, walked to the prince's side from the perimeter of the room. He towered over them without a smile.

"What can I do for you, sire?" Rolph's low voice rumbled out of his mouth like a rockslide echoing along the canyon walls.

Qeriya had heard of the giants. There was a rumor when she was young that they were tamed monsters from another planet, brought here to serve the king. But her parents had refuted that. "Giants are certainly real," her mom had explained. "They're just as human as anyone else around here, and like all humans, some are good and others are not. Nevertheless, if you ever see them, for heaven's sake, keep your distance." So much for keeping her distance! Here she was, drinking with an army of them, in an enclosed space with one, well-guarded door. Maybe it was just as well her parents weren't here to see this.

"Bring my guest one of my bowls and fetch water for the other athletes. Then you may all take some for yourselves," the prince ordered. Rolph took a few massive strides up the stone stairway to a pottery bowl the size of Qeriya's water container at home. The bowl was set on a pedestal hovering over the seats. It was etched with geometric patterns and painted deep yellow. Carved onto the outside and facing her, was a circle nearly the size of the bowl itself. Inside the circle was either a flame or a flower, she couldn't exactly tell which. The flame, or perhaps it was a flower, was painted as a seamless swirl of bright red, brighter than any red she could have imagined, with streaks of orange and every shade in-between. It was the most magnificent creation she'd ever seen.

"Paintbrush," the prince said, noticing her rapt attention. "It's a flower that grows in the mountains. There was a time it grew around here as well. It's a beautiful and hearty little flower — my mother's favorite."

Qeriya and each of her siblings received small, blue, pottery bowls filled with water. They cupped them in their hands with reverence, reciting a silent prayer of thanksgiving before drinking, as was their custom, marveling at the giants who lined up to carelessly scoop water with their bowls, gulping like the runners had gulped air not moments before, letting drops splatter on the floor and drip from their lips. Soon the guards finished and returned to line up in formation, as still as statues.

The prince, however, amazed Qeriya, as, following her example, he handled his water bowl as a treasure, pausing to savor every sip, purposefully, as she did.

"So, how does it feel to win?" he asked.

Qeriya noticed that his tone was far different to his formal speaking voice, far more mellow and musical.

"Well—" She struggled to think of some witty rejoinder that would leave him impressed. But her mind was a complete blank, caught up with the nearness of him: captivated by his strength, dazed by the dark mane of his hair and the warmth of his green eyes. Qeriya took a deep breath, pulling herself together. "I guess I feel — relieved."

"Really? he said, incredulous. Just relieved?"

"Yes," she said flatly, twisting her hands into a tight ball in front of her, keeping her gaze on the floor. "I ran for the money."

The prince leaned towards her. "And how will you spend your prize money?" He gave her a wide, disarming smile.

Qeriya shook her head. "My parents are sick," she managed, her voice cracking with emotion. "They're dying. Any cure the doctor can secure will cost a lot of money. I just want them back..."

His self-satisfied smile vanished at once. Setting his drink gently on the floor in front of him, he reached over to take her hands in his own, "I'm so—" but he didn't have time to finish.

Qeriya tore her hands away and sprang to her feet in terror, her bowl of water shattering on the floor. "What are you doing?" she asked, her voice trembling. Strange boys did not grab girls' hands uninvited. It simply wasn't done, unless he had something else on his mind.

The prince leaned back, holding his hands out, palms upturned in a gesture of peace. Glancing around she saw her brothers, as well as everyone else, staring at her uncomprehendingly.

The next thing she saw was the blur as Rolph, in one swift, flowing movement pounced on her from above. He clasped her wrist, twisting it into a painful kink behind her back.

"I'm sorry!" Prince Liam rushed to clear any misunderstanding, waving his hands in front of their faces and yelling as if they were miles away. "Rolph, stop, let her go! This is my fault, I should have known — I just forgot. I only wanted to say how sorry I was to hear about your parents. That's all, I promise. It's customary where I'm from to offer a hand to express condolence. Holding hands is not suggestive of anything inappropriate."

Qeriya could feel everyone's eyes on her. She stared down at the floor, her face flooding with hot blood. What an idiot! She should have realized! What was she thinking? He could have any woman he wanted! Why would he be interested in her? She was further humbled by his kindness in quickly moving to assuming blame, to spare her any more discomfort. Her gaze darted about searching for a rock she could crawl under.

Glancing toward her brothers, she saw the pallor in their faces. In the absence of any large enough rocks to hide behind, Qeriya sank down into her own seat with a small, despairing groan. Lahcen and Khalid were always calling her brash, and she was sure they would be calling her something *much* worse right now. She forced herself to meet the prince's gaze. "I'm sorry," she apologized, cheeks still flaming. "I should have known better. It's … just, I'm a little jumpy." Her mouth snapped shut. The prince smiled, revealing perfect teeth, as if he wasn't gorgeous enough already.

"It's all right," he said. "You've livened up the afternoon." He shot her another glorious smile. "Besides," he said seriously. "It can't have been easy running the race knowing so much depended on the outcome." He reached out his hand towards her own where it rested in her lap, remembered himself and swiftly pulled it back.

"You're very brave, Qeriya, and a formidable opponent, I'm sure," he said, his eyes traveling over her in admiration.

His warm appraisal awakened a swirl of untamed emotion that swelled up from the pit of her stomach. Qeriya sat straighter, her eyes fluttering. "Thank you, by the way," she said, "for your concern, I mean … for my parents. I appreciate it."

Prince Liam gave her a long look. "A man would have to be a fool to be without understanding in such a—" he paused, "grave situation."

Qeriya fixed her gaze on the horizon. She was keenly aware of the prince's presence beside her. The colors in the evening sky deepened and morphed into vibrant shades: pink to hot pink, orange to coral, purple to indigo, as the sun slowly settled into the horizon.

Prince Liam cleared his throat. "I imagine the weather is like this every evening?"

Qeriya thought there was a hint of nervousness in his voice. Perhaps, she thought, he was as unnerved as she was? The idea relaxed her a little, so that when she smiled at him it was her normal, open, sunny smile. She nodded. "Yeah, we don't get much else here. When it rains, the salt flats reflect the sky and the clouds. It's beautiful." She laughed. "Everyone tries to see their reflection in the water," she said, recalling how the children hunched over the water, swinging their heads and arms, poking one another's reflections, letting it all turn into a game of chase.

"Do you have mirrors?"

Qeriya shook her head. "No."

"Have you never seen yourself in a mirror?" he asked, staring at her.

Qeriya looked away. "No. I've heard of them, but we don't have mirrors. No one has time to figure out how to make them I guess." She shrugged content to leave it at that.

"You should really have a mirror," he said, fumbling over his words. "Just — just so you could see how lovely you are." That said, the prince moved as far away from her as his chair allowed. The poor man was probably unsure how she would react, Qeriya thought glumly. All in all, it was a wise move, since *she* didn't know how she'd react either; if he only knew the conflict boiling inside of her.

"Thank you," Qeriya murmured, stunned, flattered and increasingly self-conscious. Did the man not see her large hips and that annoying zit on her cheek? Granted, it was on the other side and nearly healed now, but still, he had to have seen it. Maybe he would change his mind when he did?

She pointed out of the window to the distant expanse of land in front of them, redirecting his attention, which was once again all for her. "The flat parts of the desert out there get massive dust storms, but here, we're surrounded by canyons and trees beside the Wadi that block the worst winds. Wind is all the weather related excitement we get."

"I never know if it'll be ninety degrees and sunny or thirty and snowing. It can drop that far in a few hours near the mountains," Prince Liam told her.

"I've heard of snow," Qeriya's voice was wistful. "I can't begin to guess what it's really like though."

"It's quite beautiful," Prince Liam said, staring at her again. Then, as if recalling himself, he turned his gaze towards the window.

"I like to go outside, but most people never go out."

"Why's that?" Qeriya tried to imagine not being outside, but even her home wasn't fully enclosed.

"People at the palace believe that venturing out is dangerous."

"How can they avoid going outside? It's everywhere." She pictured her family squished inside their little house, afraid to go out of their front door.

The prince laughed, his eyes full of affection and his smile warm and genuine. "The palace is actually a humongous dome with a roof of indestructible glass. We call it a palace, like those on Old Earth where royalty used to live, but it's not the same. Many millions of people live there. It's so big, I could never see all of it. Living there feels like inhabiting a planet within a planet."

"We've studied all about Old Earth. In fact, that's all we've studied as far as learning about the world."

"You've only studied Old Earth? I wonder why?" His expression became stern as he spoke softly to the glass in front of him. Obviously his questions weren't meant for her.

"It certainly does get hot here," he said, changing the subject, his voice growing animated once again. "It's comfortable now that the temperature's going down, but earlier I was afraid I might melt. Fortunately we brought a portable air conditioning unit to cool things down." He pointed to a series of slats on the ceiling towards the back of the room. Behind them, Qeriya could see an open mouth of black, exhaling its cool breath on them all.

She stared at the prince in wonder. "That's why it's so cold. I've heard of air conditioning in school, but it takes electricity, and we don't have it here." Qeriya rubbed at her arms.

"Are you cold? I'll turn it down. I should have known that you wouldn't be used to—" He was already getting to his feet.

"No, please," Qeriya interrupted. "There's no need to turn it down on my account. It feels good to be cold. It's usually cold at night anyway." She glanced at the unit again. "I can think of times when I would've given my last tomato to have one of those things blowing at me." She shook her head. "But we'd need some way to power it first."

The prince nodded. "This unit is powered by the sun."

An incredulous laugh burst from Qeriya, startling even herself and drawing the attention of everyone in the room once again. Mortified, she clapped her hand to her mouth. The prince cocked his head to the side.

"What? What did I say?" He opened empty hands to the ceiling.

"It uses the sun to make the room cold ... seriously?" Qeriya struggled to restrain her laughter, but she may as well try to stop breathing.

Her mirth must have been infectious because she saw the prince was grinning widely. "When you phrase it that way, it is rather ironic. I'd never thought about it like that before."

Qeriya relaxed. "So how did you get it out here anyway?" she asked, abandoning any remaining attempt at appearing reserved. "It's massive, and so is everything else — the pottery and this ... thing." She knocked on the clear wall. "Not to mention you and your giants."

"We used hovercraft," he announced, as if it should be obvious.

"Of course," she mimicked sarcastically. "What's a hover-craft?"

"You don't know what a hovercraft is?" His gaze drifted to the window again. "I didn't understand what life was really like here." He wrinkled his forehead, presumably wrestling with the ramifications of what it was like to survive on New Earth without the conveniences he was used to, whatever they might be.

"Well, it's the only life I know. But I like the desert. If only we had more water." Qeriya frowned. "The Wadi's shrinking. If you look at it, you'll notice that the wash is much larger than the stream, and the stream is getting smaller every year. Anyone who tries to leave either never comes back, or returns severely dehydrated. We're land locked."

"That's a problem," he murmured. He stared south out of the enclosure, beyond the tops of the canyon walls, lost in thought, his eyes distant. "Do you want to leave?"

"Well, yes. Not forever, but I want to be able to find better access to water. And travel a bit eventually, see how other people live." She smiled at him. "See what I'm missing." The prince smiled back and Qeriya was suddenly amazed at her own ease. Here she was, chatting with the prince as if she were catching up with an old friend. "You're not what I expected," she ventured.

"I didn't know you were expecting me to be here at all," he said, flashing a smile that gave her heart palpitations.

"I wasn't — oh, you know what I mean. I mean that you sounded just like a prince when you spoke to everyone, but in person you're really fun and easy to talk to."

"Thank you. I practice fun on a daily basis. It's part of my royal curriculum. The study of fun is a top priority in my education," he said in a formal voice.

Qeriya laughed.

At that moment the tallest of the giant giants approached, waiting respectfully.

"Qeriya, you've already seen Rolph. He's my first in command," the prince said, and the guard nodded curtly.

Qeriya, a little apprehensively, returned the nod. The image of his monstrous hands twisting her wrist, as if breaking off a thin branch for kindling, was still fresh in her mind.

The prince turned back to his guard. "Go ahead. What is it?"

"The craft is approaching, sire," Rolph said. "It should be here in half an hour. It's time for the awards ceremony."

Immediately Prince Liam rose, the handsome, fun-loving youth transformed before Qeriya's eyes as he spoke with the confident authority of a grown man. His speech was somehow amplified to the throng below and they hung on his every word as he thanked the contestants for participating, stressing that all athletes were valuable and that the competition could not take place without them. He was so charismatic, especially for someone who she knew was only as young as herself.

Rolph stepped forward, handing the prince a scroll that he unrolled. Reading off the names of the winners, he called each one forward in turn. The people below went wild, loud applause, whistles and calls carried up to them as he presented each winner with a bag of money. Inside her own bag, Qeriya could feel a satisfying pile of metal coins: enough to bury her hand in. Best of all, she and her brothers each had a bag. For the first time since finding her parents lying insensible inside their tent, something loosened inside Qeriya. Hope was reborn and quickly solidified into a comforting presence in her heart. With all this money, Doctor Michael would surely be able to save her mother and father.

Prince Liam was still speaking. "Now that the awards have been given, let the festivities begin!" he finished to a swell of applause. Qeriya scanned around looking for some hint as to where this secret feast for thousands of people might be. Meanwhile the prince remained standing.

"What's that noise?" Khalid asked at last as he got to his feet and approached the window.

Qeriya quickly followed him over. "It's growing louder."

"It's coming from over there," Khalid said as Lahcen joined them. As they watched, a giant vehicle appeared, riding towards them on a layer of air. It came from the east, the only side free of canyon walls. "What is it?" Khalid asked incredulously.

"It looks like a huge, floating rock slab," Lahcen said.

"I think it's made of metal," Khalid contradicted.

Glancing down, Qeriya saw some of the people below staring curiously at the strange craft. Others could be seen hurrying into the canyons in fear. The large object moved closer to the patch of sand where the competition had begun earlier in the day. A collective gasp went up as it lowered itself onto the desert floor.

"Metal?" Qeriya said absently, putting her hand on the clear barrier as if to reach through and touch the craft. "You mean like Dad's tools? Where does metal come from?"

"The ground," Khalid answered. "But not around here. I've never seen that much before, certainly not in one place."

Neither had Qeriya. But then why be surprised? She didn't

understand her own abilities, much less the saucer shaped floating *thing*, right now setting itself on the ground, it's buffer of air seeping out from underneath, its smooth metallic surface gleaming purple in the diminishing light.

The vehicle's roof lifted, dividing into four equal sections, like the wings of a giant insect unfolding, expanding outward into four circular modules rimmed with stairs. Now that the thing was open, she could see four voluminous bowls filled with what appeared to be tea on each section. Tables lined with unfamiliar food and towers of stacked pottery bowls and plates lay beside the vessels of tea on the craft floor. Giants manned each station. This was unlike anything the village had ever seen and everyone murmured in wonder. People were directed to line up at each station and receive refreshment.

"What is that?" Khalid hissed through his teeth.

"Oh," Qeriya said, offering her brothers a smug smile. "That — that's a hovercraft." She had just enough time to savor the perplexed expressions on their faces before she heard the prince's voice coming from immediately behind her.

"That's a very large hovercraft," he said. He looked at Qeriya. "As I'm sure you've realized. The rest of us came on smaller ones."

"It's unbelievable," she breathed, awed. "There must be so much I can't even begin to imagine beyond this desert." Yet despite her fascination, not even a floating lump of metal could distract from the dynamic man beside her. She hoped the giant craft would keep her brothers occupied for a while, leaving her free to spend some more time with him.

"Well, from now on, things will be different. I promise," he said. Qeriya pretended to fiddle with her dress. She was wondering just what he meant by that. Did he plan on coming back? Would she see him again? Oh, now she really was being ridiculous. What was wrong with her? He'd barely said a few kind words. It came to her that she didn't know the first thing about him, or the royal family. Her parents refused to speak of the king. They bristled if so much as his name was mentioned. And yet his son seemed so warm and generous. Of course, Qeriya admitted to herself, his attractiveness might be affecting her judgment.

"Why did you decide to come here?" she asked, eyeing him curiously. "Royalty has never attended the competition before."

"I've never been here before," he said simply, surveying the landscape. "People call it a wasteland. There's so little water, but even so, it's beautiful. The rock formations are amazing and the colors are breathtaking. As you said earlier, Qeriya, water must have coursed through here at some point to have carved these canyons and washes."

"Thanks," Qeriya said, beaming with pride. "It is a beautiful place. Unfortunately, the Wadi's drying up faster than we can figure out a solution. I can count the times it's rained in my lifetime, certainly no more than once a year, and when it does it erodes everything. We try to collect as much of it as we can, but it's either feast or famine."

"Since water is so scarce, how do you have enough to drink?" he asked, "and how do you clean yourselves or your clothes? I use water for so many things. I can't begin to conceive of life without it."

"Clean?" Qeriya said, unable to picture what it would be like to clean with water. It seemed so wasteful. "Well, we clean ourselves and dishes with sand, and we lay our clothes and bedding in the sun when they get dirty. Otherwise, there isn't much to clean."

"Interesting ... and what do you eat? How do you get your food? It must be difficult to grow anything with such poor soil and so little water."

Qeriya nodded. "The water's rationed, so I go to the Wadi every morning and fill a container about this big." She spread her hands. "That's how much we're allowed — then I trek home. We have just enough to feed our vegetable garden, prepare our food and for us to drink.

The prince's jaw dropped as she explained her routine. "How far away from the Wadi do you live?

"About a mile or so." Qeriya shrugged.

"You carry a day's worth of water a mile to your house?" he asked, astonished. "That's unbelievable."

"Are you saying you don't believe me?"

"No, I believe you, it's just that walking to get water is an archaic way to live." He shook his head in disbelief. "I'm amazed you survive!"

Qeriya couldn't help being annoyed at his comments, no matter how handsome he might be. She liked him better when he spoke about the beauty of her desert home. But now he was speaking about it as if there was something wrong with life here, as if her life was some sort of hardship. But this was all she had ever known, and it didn't feel as if she was lacking anything. Just as long as the Wadi didn't get any drier, and her parents recovered, all would be well. The prince's attitude reminded her of the times her parents complained about living in a barren prison, forgetting that their prison was her home.

The prince, reading the scowl forming on her face, quickly changed track, saying smoothly, "Let me rephrase that. I'm impressed with the beauty of this place and the fortitude of the people who live here. Anyone can see the strength of your people in the desert games. The competitions here are considered to be the most challenging worldwide, even though every location has them, even the palace, so it's an honor to be here to watch your games in person."

Qeriya recovered her good graces, sending him a sunny smile. "Really? I don't remember anyone coming to them ever before — how do other people know about us?"

He tilted his head to the side. "We watch them on a virtual screen. Most people have them, not just people in the palace.

Hm. It's hard to describe what that is if you haven't seen one ... Everything looks real. It's as if we're seeing it all in person, only from many different angles. The competitions here have a huge following, more so than any other athletic competition, because the athletes are so well trained."

"On screen, you mean like, film, or television? We don't have television here. We've never even seen one, but— "

"You learned about it in school," he finished. They both laughed and Qeriya relaxed into her seat. Still smiling broadly the prince said, "Well, I've watched them every year." His face turned thoughtful. "It must be frustrating to learn about the world and never see it."

Qeriya glanced away. "Mostly I hate that I don't really know very much about our planet. Like I said, we're only taught about Old Earth. Every time anyone asks a question about what's beyond the desert, we get a stony silence in response or else the teacher changes the subject. Although, this past year Doctor Michael has taught my brothers and me quite a bit about the world. He was trained as a scientist and a doctor. He knows a lot about genetics and all that kind of stuff. He even took a sample of our blood and showed us how he studies it on his equipment. His lab is like nothing else you can see in the desert. I've no idea how any of it got here. He also loves plants and geography—"

Qeriya broke off as she saw the prince's expression go from attentive to alarmed.

"Doctor Michael you say?" He leaned forward, his forearms on his knees, brooding, staring at the ground. "I know a Doctor Michael, a geneticist."

Qeriya wasn't sure what to say, if anything. His expression seemed so out of character from what she knew of him so far.

"I'll have to make sure to meet him," he said.

Qeriya couldn't tell what it was about his voice that caused her concern, was he suspicious, or simply confused? But just as she was contemplating this sudden shift in his demeanor, he shook his head, as if waking himself from a dream.

"I loved watching you race, by the way. Watching you was like watching the wind in female form." His eyes fastened on her admiringly.

Qeriya summoned a smile. If only he knew, she thought.

Beside her, Lahcen muttered, "You, the wind? Isn't that the truth? I can't think of anyone more full of hot air."

"Thank you, I love to run," Qeriya managed, hearing Lahcen's choked off gasp as Khalid elbowed him in the side. What would her parents say if they saw her now? Her brothers were bad enough. In Khalid's eyes she was still an innocent six-year-old whose favorite color was pink, and she was certain that Lahcen thought she would run off with the first attractive man that paid her any attention.

"Well, running seems to love you, too," the prince said, interrupting her thoughts. "How do you move so fast?"

Qeriya saw the way he was looking at her, hanging on her answer. All at once she was nervous, she had the distinct feeling that the prince was aware that her winning the race had more to it than talent.

"I ... don't know." She smiled. The prince did not smile back. Abruptly he seemed something very different than either the formal, or the relaxed, easy going prince she had experienced thus far. He didn't believe her — that much was clear.

He leaned closer, his gaze holding her own. "You do know," he whispered. "No human runs like that."

Qeriya stiffened, her throat constricting. He knew! He knew her secret! She realized she was shaking; what would he do, this prince with a room full of giants at his disposal? But nothing happened. After a moment he simply turned towards the window.

Gradually, her fear lessened. Maybe she was overreacting? It wouldn't exactly be the first time. Anyhow, how could he possibly know? She had been careful — surely she hadn't allowed it to be that obvious? No, it didn't make sense. She was being irrational.

Prince Liam had turned back to her and was regarding her closely. He smiled playfully, as if nothing odd had been said, and leaned away from her.

Qeriya relaxed somewhat, though shreds of anxiety still lingered. It didn't appear that he was going to do anything.

"Tell me," he began cautiously, "would you consider being my guest at the festival? Please don't think me forward," he hurried on, "but it's customary for me to bring a date to festivals. I — ah — don't connect well with the girls at the palace. They're too interested in being princesses, if you know what I mean."

"Is it getting hotter in here, or is it just me sitting next to these two?"

Qeriya heard Lahcen's stage whisper to Khalid. It dawned on her that she hadn't blinked in a while. Was she being asked to go out with the prince? Her parents would not approve! For an instant she was lost, wishing they were here to advise her, or maybe grant permission. But of course they wouldn't. They didn't trust the king, but, she wondered, how bad could he be with a son like this?

Preparations were underway. Giants moved about lighting candles in holders, carved into the walls like relief sculptures. Below them, others placed large stick torches into the sand around the perimeter of the crowd. The soft light accented Prince Liam's amber skin and sparkled in the depths of his emerald eyes. She would have to be stone to resist. Besides, one evening couldn't hurt. Her parents were not here to ask, there was no authority but her own to observe, and yet — Qeriya bit her lip, considering. "Thank you." She smiled warmly. "I'd love to go with you, but, I should ask my brothers." She paused. "I should really ask Doctor Michael too, I suppose. He's down in the crowd waiting for us."

The prince glanced at her sharply. "Yes, let's go meet him.

Your Doctor Michael sounds a lot like the one I know … I haven't seen him for years. However there's little chance it is the same one."

"This Doctor Michael is originally from the palace. I think his last name is Thoreau, or something like that."

"Doctor Michael Thoreau?" the prince echoed. "It is him! It's got to be! But why would he be here?" He frowned. "How do you know him?"

"He's been our village doctor for a couple of years now," Qeriya volunteered, "and a good friend of my parents. When Mom and Dad fell ill he stepped in and helped us, before and after the races."

Prince Liam inclined his head. "Come, Qeriya," he said. "Let's ask permission from your brothers and go meet the doctor."

Khalid and Lahcen looked astounded at being asked. Under normal circumstances she would never have deferred to them.

"How do we say no to the prince?" Lahcen whispered to his brother. "Isn't that a death penalty?"

"Please?" Qeriya pleaded.

Khalid weakened. "Certainly you can go."

"Wonderful!" Prince Liam exclaimed. Automatically, he reached for her hand before quickly snatching his arm back. "So, um — can I, uh, take your hand, so we don't get lost in the crowd?" he asked gingerly.

Smiling, Qeriya slipped her hand into his. The touch of his skin was magical, his strong, long fingers, warm against her own, opened up feelings in her she had never before experienced. This doesn't mean anything to him, she reminded herself.

They made their way down the long switchback on the rock face, snatches of her brothers' conversation drifting to their ears from behind.

"She's too young for this. You know Mom and Dad would—"

"What happened to the death penalty?" Khalid countered.

"I was joking! I didn't think you'd actually take me seriously."

"Of course I took you seriously! She asked you too, didn't she?" There was a small silence, then, "Listen, nothing bad will happen. He's a prince, he can't exactly drag her away somewhere unnoticed."

"As long as we stay with her, she'll be fine. Anyway, he seems nice enough."

"*She* seems to think so," Lahcen commented. "Now if he only had a sister … or two."

Reaching the ground they scanned the crowds in search of Doctor Michael.

"What happened to him?" Qeriya said, puzzled. "He said he'd be right here, waiting."

"I don't know." Khalid shrugged. "Let's just keep going, maybe he went on ahead."

Qeriya doubted that but there was little else she could do.

The crowd swelled and the hum of voices grew louder as people eyed the prince and his choice of a date for the evening. Within seconds her brothers had disappeared into the throng. Ahead stood the enormous hovercraft with its treasure of gifts for her people. Who could have imagined a flying ship full of tea and food emerging out of nowhere? Her parents used to remind her that a person had to work for what they got in life. "Do you expect water to appear out of nowhere?" her dad had scolded many a sleepy morning when she was late collecting it from the Wadi. What would they have said to the sight of this bounty?

Her desire to know what the world was like beyond the desert border grew stronger with every passing moment, every new discovery. She had studied science and technology at school, but considering their supplies consisted of clay tablets, sharp rocks, and an unlimited supply of sand, their learning was limited to facts and theories. Plus, it turned out that there were many things about the world that were, as of yet, untaught. The prince had said she would find out what lay beyond the border, whatever that meant. Qeriya couldn't help wondering why the interest in her desert? There were so many unanswered questions, but she had learned, as had all those who grew up in the desert, that certain questions were taboo.

She caught sight of her brothers, doing their best to reach her, constantly beaten back by the surge of the crowd. She tugged gently on the prince's hand as he led her towards the food, bringing him to a halt until Lahcen and Khalid managed to make their way through.

"Qeriya!" Khalid shouted over the buzz of the exuberant horde. "Qeriya, we found Doctor Michael. He says to hurry, something about Mom and Dad. We have to go now!"

Qeriya scanned the direction they had appeared from but Doctor Michael was nowhere in sight. The people thronged around her, insulating her like a blanket. For an instant Qeriya wanted just to lose herself in them, to let them carry her away from her sudden worry and uncertainty, to bury her fears in their noise.

"He must've gone to the house!" Khalid yelled, tugging at her hand.

Qeriya glanced longingly at Prince Liam. There was no time for explanation, and it was too loud to make herself heard even if there was. Nor could she pull him away from the feast. Tugging free of the prince's hand, she followed her brothers, the hungry swarm immediately swallowing her up.

"Where d'you come from?" Aedan asked, rolling over to float on his back after giving Clara a fast ride through the water.

Clara kept her gaze guarded. "Why d'you ask? You can see my family up there on the shore."

"Yeah." Aedan shot her a quick glance. "But you don't look anything like them. You're so much taller and your skin's pale. If you say that's your family then, okay, it is. I just figured you might have a story, that's all," he said, spinning around in the water, his head poking up through the surface.

"A story," Clara said cautiously. "Well, yes, I guess I do have a ... story, as you say. But I'm not allowed to share it with anyone." As she said the words, Clara's heart emptied. Not even Aedan's charm could keep up her spirits. She realized just how much she wanted to be able to share it all. "Maybe," she hesitated for a moment before rushing on. "If you promise not to tell anyone, and if you promise to stop spinning, I just might tell you." She splashed water at him and forced the corners of her mouth into a smile. "Watching you is making me dizzy."

"I promise," he said, abruptly serious.

Clara took a deep breath. Suddenly it was as if all the years between then and now had been wiped away. Once again the pain of losing her parents was fresh and as bitter as horseradish. She waited until she thought her voice would be steady enough before saying, "I–I come from the palace. My parents are scientists and prisoners. The king makes them work for him." Hot tears were on her face now, running in a fast flowing stream. Her voice had choked up but she forced herself to keep going "They do just enough for him to keep them alive. But he wants more. They — they were scared he'd use me to force their hand, so they had someone sneak me out.

Clara stared at Aedan with undisguised misery. "That's why you can't tell anyone. I was brought here to live with Carlos and Laura."

"I'm sorry, Clara. I wish it was different for you," Aedan said, gently touching her hand with his own, his eyes soft with sympathy.

They were silent for a while and then Aedan said, "My family doesn't trust humans." He shrugged apologetically. "Do you mind if I *ask what it is the king wants that your parents aren't giving him?"*

Clara sniffed hard. "My parents discovered a way to mix robots with people, and animals, and even dirt or rocks."

"Why would they do that?"

"Say a person or reaume lost a leg or has a genetic disorder. They designed a repair program to tell the body how to fix itself — fix its own problem. They wanted to help people. But the king used their research to experiment with making weapons." Clara screwed up her face in disgust. "He does these experiments with animals and reaume, putting them together in weird ways, and giving them weird powers. All the reaume die — but the animals, well, they've become his new weapons."

Chapter 7

Infected

"Where's Doctor Michael?" Qeriya asked her brothers once they'd made their way to the perimeter of the crowd and she could hear, but they were equally mystified. She followed as they circled around the canyon wall and journeyed north. Nothing lay between Qeriya and her home but waves of sand and the splintered wooden bridge across the tree-lined Wadi. It was the only place to legally cross the water, so there'd be a long line of people wanting to get home later that night, but for now it was empty.

"We don't know where he is," Khalid said at last, speaking to the air in front of him. Apparently he assumed she had superior hearing, so she ran up beside him as he spoke. "I thought he'd be waiting somewhere around here, but he must've gone back. He sounded urgent. I've never seen him that insistent about anything. I just hope he's waiting for us at the house." Khalid gave her a sideways squint. "It sure took you long enough to come with us."

"There was a huge crowd!" Qeriya defended, taken aback, and shot up a few feet in alarm before slamming herself back down on the ground, glancing around to make sure no one was watching. "I couldn't tell the prince where I was going because it was too loud. It was rude of me to leave without telling him anything, but I did, and I think that's reason enough to hesitate for the whole of five seconds."

The sun was down and they traveled by the light of a full moon. Most people would have torches to illuminate their way home, but that morning all Qeriya and her brothers could think about was their parents' sickness and their desperate need to win the games. Qeriya was less cautious in the growing darkness, skipping longer distances with each step, careful to hover close to the ground. Although her hurry was fueled by concern for her mom and dad, at the same time it felt so liberating to peddle through air and feel nearly imperceptible currents around her ebb and flow. She stretched, moving onto her stomach, feeling the air pressure lift her higher, flipping somersaults on an invisible fulcrum, teetering back and forth as if on a seesaw, then spinning forward in horizontal circles.

Like her, Khalid was finding wings of a different sort. He leaped high and long between sparse patches of scrub grass and rock which cradled each foot, springing him forward, and he sailed further with each jump. She glanced back to see Lahcen struggling to keep up and imagined the scowl that must be etched on his face. He was already exhausted from an entire day of running; now he was being forced to endure into the night as well. Minutes felt like hours before she reached the familiar fire pit.

"Doctor Michael must be inside," Lahcen said. They ducked into their salt-brick house, lit up inside with candles.

Sure enough, Doctor Michael was waiting for them in a cloud of dust, pacing the sandstone floor of the living area. His hood, thrown back now, revealed straight, dark hair, pulled taut behind his head, secured with twine, and a patchwork complexion of sun damage and tanned skin. Baskets lining the edges of the room overflowed with an assortment of blankets, slate tablets, cooking utensils and clay dishes. A backpack and some woven bags were set beside the door. To one side, her parents lay upon turkey feather bedding.

"I think I know what's wrong," Doctor Michael said, pausing and wagging his finger as if to scold them.

Their father lay disheveled; his covers kicked off and oddly bunched. "What is it?" Qeriya asked and rearranged her dad into a more comfortable position, straightening his bedding and propping his head on a feather pillow.

"I searched my more obscure medical books and found the

illness. I don't know how they got it. I barely know how to pronounce it. It's a type of sleeping sickness, but not the one I thought it would be. I'd heard of the sleeping flu, a viral disease that makes people sleep for weeks at a time, but this illness is not a virus, it's a bacteria, and that means it can be killed with the right kind of antibiotic." He paused as if to let the importance of this fact sink into their minds.

"You found a cure? How much is it? The prize money's here!" Qeriya held up her bag inches from Doctor Michael's face. "Where do we get the cure?"

"That's the problem," the doctor answered and pushed the bag to the side. "I've found the cure in my book, but it's not here. Not even the palace has it. The disease is so rare, there's no prepared antidote."

"Well then, what's the cure? How do we prepare it? What do we need?" Lahcen asked, standing with hands on hips, glistening with sweat and breathing heavily but primed to mobilize nevertheless.

"The remedy is a type of mold that only grows on a particular flower. It's called Paintbrush and it can be found in a mountain range near the palace," Doctor Michael explained, having resumed pacing back and forth.

"A flower can cure this disease?" Qeriya asked in disbelief. The idea of a flower having the power to heal her parents sounded nothing short of preposterous. Granted, most medicines came from plants, but flowers?

"This particular mold is the only known cure," Doctor Michael told her. "Your parents won't survive without it. You have to leave the desert as soon as you can."

"Leave!" Khalid exclaimed. He'd been listening quietly, his head down, thinking, but he looked up at the suggestion. "It's a death sentence to even approach the border. Anyhow, I can't drag my sister out there. She's too young to survive a world we don't know anything about."

"Don't use me as an excuse!" Qeriya exclaimed, sticking out her chin in protest. "But even if we were to leave, what if we didn't make it back in time, who would care for Mom and Dad? We can't leave them to die alone."

Lahcen's gaze flipped between her, Khalid and Doctor Michael, a look both undecided and surprised, unsure what to think and amazed at everyone else's apparent certainty.

Qeriya might have looked certain about what to do, but that was far from the truth. It was pretty clear to her that her parents would die either way if there was no one to protect them.

"Listen," Doctor Michael stopped pacing to bestow a gentle regard on the three. "I know it's a lot to absorb, but this flower is their only hope. I can watch over them, Qeriya, since I'll be here. But you three are the most equipped to go on this journey, and more capable together than you realize. You can make it." He gazed knowingly at each of them as if referencing their powers, but not voicing them, assuming the familiar taboo.

"Doctor Michael, if it were just me I would drop out of school and go in a heartbeat," Khalid explained. "But our parents would want me to think about my sister and brother."

"Some of us can think for ourselves, thank you very much!" Lahcen insisted, pointing at his chest.

"The trip's too dangerous," Khalid said and shook his head. "We don't know anyone outside the desert. I just need time to think … maybe if I go alone …"

"No! You need each other for this to be successful," Doctor Michael insisted, shaking his head emphatically. "And now that you have money, you'll be able to find food and lodging on your travels."

"You need to get off your high and mighty kick, Khalid," Lahcen confronted, moving directly in front of him and jabbing a finger into Khalid's chest. "I'm only a year younger than you. I don't want to be fodder for your martyr complex. How do you know what our parents would want? Maybe they'd want us to work together instead of you making decisions for everyone!"

"You're sixteen, I'm seventeen, and a year makes a big difference," Khalid retorted. Making a visible effort to swallow his anger he carried on, "Anyhow, just think about it, we have Qeriya to consider. I'm not saying we shouldn't go. I'm not even saying that I should make the decision. I'm just saying, we shouldn't be too impulsive."

Just then they heard the rustle of their grass curtain. "What was that?" Qeriya asked in alarm, almost tripping over her parents in her hurry to find out. Someone she didn't recognize, an older gentleman with wrinkled skin sagging around his bones and disheveled hair, tumbled into the room, panting heavily. He was clad in a robe with a red belt cinched at the waist, signifying that he was one of the medics. His eyes searched wildly across the small group before settling on the doctor.

"Doctor Michael! There's been an emergency! You need to come immediately! I know you said only to bother you if it's of the utmost—"

"What's happened, Omar?" Doctor Michael asked. "Who's hurt?"

"Who? Everyone!" he said, clearly panic-stricken, leaning against the wall for support as he caught his breath. "The entire village is sick — people are dying down there!"

"What! Where! Get a grip man!" Doctor Michael hissed.

"The–the race site."

"How?" Khalid asked, his face blank with shock.

"I don't know! But … I'm not sick and the only difference is … I haven't had anything to eat or drink. I thought I'd let the others get theirs first."

"And the prince — his giants, are they sick, too?" Doctor Michael asked, pacing the floor once again.

"No. No, they're not." The man's voice raised an octave. "It's just our people."

"The tea," Lahcen guessed.

Qeriya clutched a painful knot forming in her stomach.

Lahcen stared at them, his eyes wide. "The prince served tea and food to everyone."

"That must be it," Doctor Michael agreed. "The prince must've poisoned the tea."

Clara glanced around to make sure she wasn't being followed before leaving the foggy beach and entering the forest. Just prior to the tree line, on the sandy shore, lay an upturned, rusted metal boat. There, where the shore met the forest was the place Aedan had said he would meet her. She felt guilty stealing away from her guardians. They were fine people and so good to her, and trusting. But Aedan had wanted to meet away from the others this time.

"Aedan?" she called softly through the haze. Rays of light were beginning to peek through the heavy canopy from the ocean shore, wending their way around branches and leaves, reaching as far as they could possibly go. The fog had lifted. She walked to the end of the light and stopped.

"Aedan—"

"I'm here," he said, his voice coming from directly behind her. Clara whipped around, stumbling on a branch as she did so. Aedan caught her before she fell.

She had never before seen him away from the ocean. His dark skin blended with the shadows of the forest. He was no longer the bold and beautiful figure she knew from the water, with webbing and gills. Now he appeared to her as a mysterious, hauntingly handsome man.

Suddenly his lips brushed hers. He pulled back, searching her face. Whatever it was he was looking for he must have found, because, this time when their lips met, it was in a deep, passionate caress; his arms were firm around her back, pulling her close, his hand sliding through her hair, guiding their mouths. As unexpectedly as it had started, it finished, and Aedan backed away, leaving her hungry for more.

"I've wanted to do that for so long," he whispered hoarsely.

Clara's whole body tingled, her eyes fluttered open. The way he was looking at her made her want to melt into his arms again.

"Clara," he said, his voice shaking. "I asked you here today because I–I wanted to ask if you would … marry me."

Clara stared at him unable to believe her ears.

"You — you can take some time to think about it," he finished stiffly, as if afraid he had made a mistake and was offering her a graceful way *out.*

When she could speak, Clara said, "That's not fair." A smile burst across her face. "After a kiss like that…" She stepped closer to him, her eyes locked on his. "How could I possibly say no?"

He was about to respond when she placed her fingers to his lips. "Aedan," she said. "I would love to marry you — more than anything else in this whole wide world. There is nothing I could ever want more." Then, before he could say anything, she embraced his broad shoulders, meeting his lips with hers."

Chapter 8

Doubt

"They're as good as dead if you stay," Doctor Michael said, after a long period of thoughtful silence. The medic, having received his instructions had slipped away.

Lahcen knelt down to better observe the man and woman lying limp on the floor. Qeriya spread woven blankets over their bodies to keep them warm in the encroaching chill.

"This can't be coincidence ... our parents ... now this epidemic." Lahcen stood up. He felt the sap of bitterness course through his veins. What he wanted, more than anything at this minute, was to punch something. "What better way to exterminate a crowd? Butter them up and give them a death-day tea."

He saw his sister shudder. How cruel the prince was, and how perverse to let Qeriya think he was warm and generous, while all the time he was hell bent on genocide. The thought of him leading Qeriya by the hand made him itch to be able to get his own hands on him. They didn't know much about the royal family. Grownups didn't talk about them, and now he understood why. If he ever saw the prince again, he'd wrench every limb from his body.

"Go, now! There's nothing left for you here, and you have a chance to help your parents," Doctor Michael insisted, waving his arms towards the door, having lost all patience, but the others ignored him.

"We should listen to Doctor Michael," Lahcen announced. "The flower sounds like our only hope right now."

"Like I said before, we need to think one step at a time," Khalid reasoned, repetitively running his hand through his hair. "We should take a few days to think this through before rushing off."

"But there's no time!" Doctor Michael's voice was approaching panic. He clenched his hands tight behind his head, as if keeping it from rolling off his neck. "Your parents are dying, everyone's dying! I'm afraid for you..." his voice faltered mid sentence.

"What exactly are you afraid of?" Qeriya, who'd been crying, quickly reached to collect the tears from her cheeks and lick them off her finger as she spoke. It was a familiar practice; people, other than Lahcen, who'd rather play with it than drink it, didn't waste water in the desert.

Doctor Michael ignored her question. "You have to trust me! You must go!" He struggled again to regain his composure.

Lahcen was perplexed by his drastic change in manner.

"Like I said before, I'll be here. I promise to look after them for you."

Lahcen put his arm around his sister's shoulders. The thought of leaving felt wrong, even if he realized they needed to go. He watched his mother's long, pale hair spill softly down her shoulder as her head cover drooped to the ground. Her hair had always been such a comfort to him when he was young. Abruptly, memories crowded in on him — he was five, and his mother whispered in his ear, telling him what she wouldn't do to send him to a better place, where he could grow up with plenty of water and food and be safe. When he'd turned to feel her hair, it was wet with tears. It had frightened him to hear his mother talk this way, to waste her tears and speak of sending him away. He wasn't thirsty. They had enough food. Sure, it would be nice to have more, but what good was more of anything without Mommy's soft hair? He couldn't live without that. He had pulled her hair around him like a blanket.

"Khalid, you need to trust me. You're seventeen, but you're still young. This is too much for you to handle on your own. Your parents would want you to listen to me," Doctor Michael said and took off his glasses to rub his tired eyes.

Lahcen imagined that Doctor Michael must be living in a state of perpetual déjà vu, the bearer of bad news and the brunt of people's anger wherever he went, reminding Lahcen of Galileo — trying to convince people that the world was not the center of the universe — that there was no magic medicine to fix their loved ones.

"All right, Lahcen thinks we should go. What do you think, Qeriya?" Khalid asked gently.

Qeriya stiffened. "I suppose ... we should go if that's our only way to help Mom and Dad, and Doctor Michael's willing to care for them."

"All right then, if that's the consensus then we'll go," Khalid decided, obviously unconvinced, but resolute nonetheless. Having made a decision, both brothers gathered their robes and slipped them over sunburned skin, cinching the ties around their waists.

"Good!" Doctor Michael sighed with relief. "You're making the right decision, and yes, I'll watch over your parents."

"Then who'll care for you, Doctor?" Qeriya asked.

Doctor Michael stepped back, surprised by her concern. "Oh, me? Oh ... I'll–I'll be fine," he stuttered, flustered. He dug into his bag and pulled out a worn leather book. "Here, this is the only possession worth anything to me, but I'm giving it to you. It's a journal that belonged to my father, there's a map of his travels. It marks each land region that makes up the world. It'll guide you," he said, thrusting it into Khalid's hands.

Khalid flipped through the pages, skimming the pictures while Lahcen peered over his shoulder. Like Doctor Michael said, it was full of maps and diagrams detailing the world beyond their desert borders.

"Study it," Doctor Michael ordered, emphasizing each word. "I've mapped a route for you. Head downstream and continue straight to the western border. Be wise with your money. Like I said, you'll need it in the villages for lodging and food. Places to stay are listed in the journal as well."

"Got it," Khalid said abruptly.

"Good, good," Doctor Michael said, patting Khalid's shoulder. "The western border is the most straightforward place to begin your journey."

"Doctor Michael, before we leave, why did the prince poison our village, and why are you rushing us to leave instead of wanting us to help you tend our friends?" Lahcen demanded, barring the door. "I think you know more than you're saying."

Doctor Michael's coal black eyes glared at Lahcen intensely, aflame with urgency. He started to brush past him. "I need to get busy and you need to go."

Khalid placed his hand on the doctor's shoulder to stop him. "We need answers, Doctor Michael. We won't go without them," he pressed. "What else do you know?"

"The time—" Doctor Michael began, but the brothers held their ground. Creases etched deeper into the doctor's face, while sweat puddled in drops on his bushy eyebrows despite the cold.

Was the doctor afraid to tell them something? Qeriya wondered to herself.

"We're alone here, Doctor Michael. There's nobody for miles around," Khalid said, trying to allay what he perceived to be an unspoken concern.

"All right," Doctor Michael said reluctantly. "I can see you're not going to let this go." He sighed. "As you discovered in the cave, your powers come from life forms called reaume. You saw that — yes?"

"Yes, we remember, go on," Khalid said.

"It's because you have reaume powers that you're all targets. That's why your parents tried to suppress your abilities, why no one speaks of them. But the prince is more desperate than you might realize, and is no doubt following orders from his father, the king. I believe that the giants poisoned the entire village, with the sole purpose of exterminating you. They're willing to kill everyone, just to get you three. That's how much of a threat you are."

"No!" Qeriya trembled with denial. Khalid moved to embrace his sister. Lahcen stared as he listened, feeling only numb.

Doctor Michael nodded. "Anyone stirring out of city limits will be killed. They're distracted now, with the chaos, but they'll be coming very soon when they don't find you with the others. That's why you need to go now." He tapped the journal in Khalid's hand. "Take the western border route out. It's the safest way. And avoid the reaume. They have their own agenda and have certain … powers; they'll distract you from your mission. After this is all over, you can seek out your heritage." He moved to the doorway, grabbing a backpack that belonged to Khalid and thrusting it into Khalid's other hand.

"You have to find that flower. When you do, either scrape off the mold or else pulverize the petals and mix them with water, then force-feed the mixture to your parents. They'll be able to swallow. I designed the stasis so that when you treat the illness, it will lift. Don't worry about your mom and dad. Once you're gone the giants will go after you and not bother with your parents. In any case, they can't hurt them as long as they're in stasis.

"There's one more thing," the doctor added as he covered his head with the robe of his hood. "This desert we live in used to be a vibrant community, but now it's … Oh, there's no time to explain! "You must be careful when you approach the border. Go to the west entrance. There's an eastern entrance, but it's embedded in the mountains and will be heavily guarded. Beyond the mountains is a rainforest, so most people try to escape that way. The western entrance simply leads to an impassable barren desert so it's less guarded. But you'll be able to cross without a problem. Follow the Wadi downstream and straight west after that. After the desert, you'll hit a grassy savannah. There's a town close by. It's detailed in the journal. Now, I must get to my patients."

"But—" Qeriya pleaded.

"No! No more, it's time!" he said, a paroxysm of fear washing over his face.

They stared as he turned on his heels and hurried away. The night was black as Lahcen's hair but the stars glowed bright. The full moon would lend them more light than usual by which to travel. Quickly, each gathered a small collection of necessities to place in Khalid's bag.

Khalid shoved the journal into the backpack, followed by supplies, their prize money and food. "I guess I don't need to bring water do I?"

"Nah, you can just drink my sweat." Lahcen smirked as he tossed some roasted olneya tesota seeds, saguaro seeds and dried wolfberries to his brother. "Here, Khalid, take these. Anything else will spoil."

Qeriya stood by her unconscious parents: hand outstretched, creating a swirl of air current that circled above them. She breathed into the air to warm it, and then spread the warmed air upon them like another blanket to protect them from the night-time cold.

"This should keep you comfortable, Mom and Dad. We'll be back soon," she promised and the siblings bowed their heads in silent prayer before slipping through the curtain and out into the night.

They walked quickly, in single file, to the Wadi; silent silhouettes gliding through the darkness. Once they neared the water, Lahcen turned back to see lights flickering in the distance, behind their house. Ahead, trees lined the Wadi like black-spindle shadows and moonlit water showed through in patches. As they walked closer to the stream it appeared to expand.

"It swells for you, Lahcen," Qeriya commented, pausing to examine it more closely.

Suddenly Lahcen heard a slight whir and without thinking,

instinctively tackled Qeriya to the ground. The whir was followed by a thump. Something hit a small tree near to where his sister had stood by the bank. Glimmering in the faint light was the tuft of an arrow. "Duck!" Lahcen whispered and yanked Khalid down to the ground as well. They crawled a few feet further under tree cover until Khalid turned upstream.

"What are you doing?" Lahcen asked. "Doctor Michael specifically told us to go due west and you're traveling east."

"I know he did," Khalid answered, "but … just come with me and I'll explain." Lahcen and Qeriya obeyed and they scurried upstream, staying low to the ground.

"Look," Khalid said. "I want to trust the doctor as much as our parents did. He's been good to us. But it doesn't change the fact that—" he fumbled his words for a moment as they tripped over each other on the way out of his mouth. "The first and only time we used our powers was in the cave. Yet, by race time, we were already targets for murder. It only makes sense that we were discovered in the cave, and the only one who saw us there was Doctor Michael."

Clara felt as if she were nine-years-old once again — watching fire come out of a woman's hands. Only this time there were many of them emitting fire from their hands, and none of them smiled reassuringly. Flames soon swallowed the figures as they streaked into the forest.

"Don't worry," Aedan said, seeing concern on her face. "They're wary of all humans at first, not just you. It's from having to survive years of attack from the king." He squeezed her hand comfortingly. "I'm related to the fire reaume on my mom's side. Her name's Lourdes."

Clara gasped and her pale face grew white. She reached for a nearby branch to steady herself. "Did you say, Lourdes?" she asked. "Really?" She watched him nod. "She's the one who brought me here from the palace! She told me she had a son. It's never occurred to me it could be you. Your gift is water and she's fire reaume."

Aedan gave a brief shake of his head. "I can't believe you know my mother! How strange, what are the chances of that?"

"It must be providence," Clara said.

"No, not providence. It's a work of the Spirit." Aedan smiled, slipping his arm around Clara's slim waist, guiding her forward.

Chapter 9

Secrets Revealed

Lahcen froze, while a barely audible gasp escaped Qeriya. As awful as it felt to admit it, Khalid was right; Doctor Michael was the only person who could have alerted anyone. And yet ... he just had to be wrong. The idea that he might be right in his suspicions was too terrible to accept.

Lahcen checked the surrounding shadows before slowly drawing himself up to his full height. The other two followed suit. "Maybe we should just trust Doctor Michael," he said. "Maybe we just don't know the whole story. He couldn't get us out of there fast enough. Wouldn't he have tried to keep us there if he wanted us dead?"

Khalid let his breath out through his nose in a long, frustrated rush. "Look, I hear what you're saying, and yes, you're right, his hurrying us away is a good sign that I'm mistaken, but we can't afford to take chances. We can't just blindly put our trust in anyone anymore, not now, not here. We're alone. It could be that I'm wrong and Doctor Michael's our friend, but we have to consider what we know and be cautious."

"But ... what about Mom and Dad?" Qeriya's voice was troubled. "What's going to happen to them if Doctor Michael means us harm?" She shook her head. "Not that I think he does — just for the record, I don't really believe that for one second."

"I'm thinking about what Mom and Dad would want me to do, and they'd want me to get you out alive," Khalid said. "Right now I can't get you and them out at the same time, especially if Doctor Michael's working against us. Also, carrying Mom and Dad would handicap us. And if we go back for them, there'll be swarms of giants on our tail."

"We're not leaving without Mom and Dad if there's even a

remote possibility that Doctor Michael isn't on our side, although, again, I can't believe he isn't." Qeriya glared at Khalid as if he were the enemy. "And if we aren't going back for Mom and Dad then we should follow the doctor's orders and go the other way!" She and Lahcen turned around to head back, but as they did, a flood of giants gathered where the arrow had hit and they both pulled back, crouching down and peeking through a cluster of brush. The giants were all facing west. Among them Lahcen saw a young woman, who briefly spun around to scan the area to the east, a woman whose face, lit by the moon and torchlight, gleamed with steel grey eyes. Qeriya gasped and Lahcen covered her mouth. She began to pull away, dragging Lahcen with her. "That's her!" she whispered. "That's the woman who tried to kill me in the race!"

As they retreated, Lahcen backed into Khalid. "The giants— " he began.

"I'm sure they have Mom and Dad already," Khalid said harshly. "We can't go back. And I'm sorry to say, but it seems they're looking due west, the direction Doctor Michael told us to go."

"I just don't understand, we've been friends with him for so long, and he helped us," Qeriya said as they crept upstream once again. "I can't believe it's true. There's just something we don't know, some misunderstanding. We need to go west like he told us to do."

"There's no way to know for sure if he's on our side," Lahcen said, placing an encouraging hand on her shoulder. "Khalid's right. We should be cautious and travel east since they're searching the western route. It doesn't mean we're condemning him, we're just being careful. We can still hold out hope."

"I don't need to 'hold out hope'. I think we should go west." Qeriya halted, crossing her arms in defiance.

"Well you're overruled, Qeriya!" Khalid hissed, grabbing a hold of her wrist and pulling her along. "Now let's move!"

Trees flanking the Wadi thickened as they progressed further east, keeping them in complete shadow, as well as masking Qeriya's scowl. But Lahcen knew it was there. Fortunately, the thought of being pursued by giants seemed to spur her forward, as it did him. After they'd traveled a ways, Lahcen caught a moonlit glimpse of small white, or maybe purple, flowers and narrow leaves.

Qeriya saw them, too. "Don't we get berries from this type of plant?" she asked. "It looks like the same plant, but I don't remember seeing it bloom before."

"It's night-blooming cereus, the name says it all. Yes, we harvest its berries," Khalid said.

"But as we're not allowed to be out after dark, we've never seen it bloom."

"Come on," Lahcen insisted, waving her forward. "You'll never live to see it bloom again if we don't hurry."

Having succeeded in getting Qeriya moving, he pressed onward in silence, trying hard to suppress a tapestry of possible things that could go wrong from forming in his head. It was overwhelming and there was no way to prepare for, much less predict, what might happen. The road to their destination point was long; danger lay ahead and behind at every step and he couldn't afford to let his mind wander. He had to be fully aware, in the moment.

As the hours passed, they gradually allowed themselves to relax a little, but still Lahcen kept his ears and eyes peeled for any sound, any shadow, that was out of place in the desert night. Finally, they reached the source of the Wadi; a large spring surrounded by date-palm trees; a place that was forbidden to them. It was difficult for Lahcen to see much other than a pool of black water and trees decorated with the shimmering light of the full moons. They wormed through a cluster of palms lining the water's edge, reaching the fountainhead.

"I wonder how far the border is from here?" Lahcen asked.

They drank their fill and replenished their water skins then Lahcen scooped a head sized bubble of water from the pool with his hands. "I don't see how I'm going to make it to the border without any more water than this. I can ride it only so far before you guys will have to drink it, and I won't be able to pull any from the sand.

"Hey! What are you doing?" Lahcen felt a pair of strong arms slide around his chest from behind, pushing him down into a squat. Khalid leapt into the air, carrying both of them upward on an arc that spanned at least fifty meters.

"Oh, Khalid, I feel so safe in your arms," Lahcen mocked in a high voice.

"You should, you're light as a turkey feather."

"I'm not a turkey feather!" Lahcen snarled.

"You know," Khalid said, "better use that water as a landing pad."

"You mean *your* drinking water?"

"Yeah, that. Landings are still a bit tricky for me."

Lahcen didn't have time to obey, the next instant he was smashed into the sand with all the finesse of someone shattering misshapen pottery. He lay, sprawled face first, on the desert floor until he had to breathe, and then he slowly turned his neck, waiting for the pain to hit.

"Are you okay, Lahcen?" Qeriya asked, descending by his side.

"Yeah, are you okay?" Khalid timidly peeked over Qeriya's shoulder.

Lahcen groaned. He just knew it was going to cost him a great effort to speak. Luckily his fury supplied the necessary motivation. "No, I'm not! Tricky! Landings are a bit tricky? How about deadly!" Lahcen fought his way onto his hands and knees, inching upright to confront his brother, who slowly backed away. "Why didn't you speak up before? I could've broken my neck. I would've gladly risked dehydration instead. I prefer a slow and painful death of my doing to a quick one that's your fault."

"That may be, but then you'd certainly be dead, water magnet or not. It's pretty dry out here — no plants. At least you have a chance with me."

Lahcen growled and muttered to himself, brushing the remnants of sand off his face.

Qeriya lifted off the ground first, stretching her frame to float on air currents. A soft light swelled into existence as they moved but the space before them remained an eerie, hollow black. The sun was rising. They were prepared to travel for hours, so they were very surprised when only minutes later they nearly collided with a metal fence that blended into the vague pall in front of them. The fence extended horizontally each way as far as they could see in the twilight. It fused with a steadily rising sandstone slope that curved into vertical walls, reaching to a great height. This wall of rock was the dark void in front of them that cut off half the stars in the sky.

Lahcen paused. It was getting lighter. He began to see that the sandstone wall before them was only a front to gigantic rock peaks that appeared to penetrate the atmosphere. The entire scene soon glowed in pink and purple patches as the sun reached tiny arms out of its sandy crib.

"These must be mountains," he said, craning his neck to follow the peaks to their pinnacle.

"Boy are they tall! And behind them is supposed to be a rainforest, whatever that is," Qeriya added.

Khalid reached into his pack and pulled out the journal Doctor Michael had given them. He flipped to a map of their region and studied the eastern border. Lahcen spied the map over his brother's shoulder. Sure enough, mountains rose beyond the fence, followed by a rainforest. "Rainforest," Lahcen said quietly, savoring the sound of the word and what it implied. It seemed like a magical place, a place too good to be true.

"Well, Doctor Michael was right about this anyway," Lahcen said, nodding at their predicament.

There was a strange noise, a kind of low hum, coming from the barrier, which for some reason made Khalid uneasy. Picking up a clump of grass, he threw it at the fence and was disconcerted to see it sizzle. "Now what?" he asked his equally puzzled brother.

"Ask me something I can answer," Lahcen complained, slumping next to Khalid. "Digging's out of the question for sure. The thing's welded to the bedrock."

Suddenly, without a word of warning, Qeriya thrust her arms upward and swung them down, swimming into the air. She grabbed her brothers by the hand and rose straight up towards the sky, dangling them on either side of her.

Lahcen struggled to free himself, until he peered at the ground and realized how high they were. "What're you doing?" he cried, at a loss to understand how her small frame could carry their enormous weight.

Qeriya ignored his question and ascended towards the top of the fence bordering their land.

"Take us back down! Let's discuss this first!" Khalid ordered as they rose higher and higher.

The mountains, which they had only glimpsed before, were now revealed in all their grandeur and the brothers were momentarily struck silent with awe.

"This is crazy!" Khalid yelled. "But as long as you've dragged us up here, we need to get over these mountains. Can you fly us that high?"

"What do you think I'm doing? Taking you on a joyride?" Qeriya snapped.

Just as they reached the top of the fence and attempted to fly over, they bumped into an invisible wall. There was an instant of complete disorientation, but somehow Qeriya managed to hold on to her brothers as she recovered her wits. Below them, there was movement on the ground.

A lump of fear swelled in Lahcen's throat as miniature black figures, that he knew must be the giants, shot arrows in their direction.

"Watch out!" he yelled, bracing for impact, but the arrows whizzed harmlessly past them at the last second.

"That was close!" he called. "Did you do that, Khalid?"

"No."

"I did," Qeriya said. "I blasted wind at their arrows."

Every instinct urged Lahcen to retreat but Qeriya was in charge up here. He was just a limp mouse dangling hundreds of feet in the air. And he had absolutely no intention of irritating his sister with any well-placed advice. He clamped his mouth firmly closed.

Qeriya abruptly recoiled, falling as if hit.

"I'm going to be sick," Khalid husked as they plummeted.

"I think we're going to die," Lahcen croaked.

"Not now, we're not. Pull your legs up," Qeriya ordered, pulling her own knees up to her chin.

Lahcen and Khalid desperately followed suit. Inches from the ground, they bounced, caught in a net of air.

"Stay low," Qeriya said, bringing them gently down the rest of the way to the ground.

Lahcen had visions of giants storming towards them, ready to take them prisoner. He wondered what Qeriya was thinking. He could tell from her determined face that she wasn't done yet. Glancing over, he thought he saw Khalid pinching himself. It was hard to be an older brother and not be the one in charge.

Then he found himself yanked into a horizontal position as Qeriya bolted forward. They sailed above the rocky ground, as close to the surface as possible. Lahcen had disturbing visions of nasty scrapes on the sandstone and scratches from the woody plants inches below. He'd had his share of those climbing with his brother and well remembered the disproportionate pain that they gave. But the scrapes never came. Any thorny branches or sharp protruding rocks grazed a mass of thick air that had surrounded them instead, as if they were encased in rubber.

Soon they found themselves in a maze of cottonwood trees, and Lahcen was even more thankful for their air shield. While he couldn't see what was happening, he knew shooting at them must have taken the giants away from their normal positions. "Good thinking, Sis," he said, smiling at her ingenuity. But Khalid maintained a solid scowl. Soon though, Lahcen knew, the giants would discover that they were not dead.

After a while of edging northward, along the border, they came upon an abrupt lift as a mass of grainy rock protruded, like a large cyst on the mountain face over which the fence climbed. They moved to circle around the rock, but once in front of it, they encountered an entryway. Qeriya stopped abruptly and Lahcen and Khalid hit the ground a few feet below.

Lahcen rolled to the side, pausing to recover. Then he stood up to examine the place more closely. It appeared to be an under-ground house built into the mouth of a cave. "This must be a guard outpost. I wonder if there's a way to cross the border through—" he began, but was interrupted as Khalid rose to his feet and towered over their sister, who was seated on the ground, struggling to catch her breath.

"Qeriya, from now on, I'm in charge here. It was only good fortune that you saw the arrows in time. We nearly died. Next time you have an idea, share it or ditch it."

Qeriya hung her head, gulping air. When she had enough breath she faced Khalid. "You know, you're a real jerk sometimes!"

"She's right you know," Lahcen echoed as Khalid stormed towards the house. "No one elected you in charge!"

"Don't let him get to you," Lahcen said to his sister. He smiled encouragingly. "He's just jealous he didn't think of it. I thought it was pretty clever."

Qeriya managed a weak smile, her lashes damp with angry tears.

Lahcen extended his hand to help her up. As they joined Khalid near the doorway, Lahcen felt ill equipped. His brother and sister had been gifted with good, useful powers. He could do something with water, but there was never enough of it to do anything much.

They peered into the windows of a house built into a cave, full of furniture, but empty of life. It was proportioned to fit normal sized people, but was large enough to accommodate giants as well. "They wouldn't completely abandon this place, would they?" Lahcen asked.

"I would think not," Khalid replied. "That would be stupid, but who knows, maybe they are stupid."

Before Lahcen could elicit a response, he felt massive hands clench his neck from behind, yanking him away from the house: ambushed from the very trees that had protected them moments before. His youthful strength was no match.

"Khalid! Qeriya!" he squeaked, aiming a flurry of kicks at his attacker's legs, but the grip on his neck only tightened. His vison had narrowed to a light glowing, despite the daylight emerging from over the trees, at the entrance of the house. Then that was extinguished. In his panic, he couldn't tell whether it was his eyes that had failed him or if the light itself had gone out. His lungs were demanding air but he forced his body to continue to thrust at the stone-solid killer behind him, in the hopes of somehow breaking his strangle hold. He could feel himself growing weaker and knew he had only moments left before his body let go of the struggle. He felt it happen, the way his brain just seemed to give up control. A dark maw opened up, rushing towards him, and for an instant Lahcen teetered on the edge of collapse. Suddenly, the grip on his neck loosened, changing into something cold and wet.

"No!" A deep voice gurgled behind him as the gargantuan body transformed, dropping the folds of a cape and armor in a heap and leaving a floating puddle where the giant had once stood. Water had shed his cells and lifted into the air, abandoning his body to formless ash and bone. Lahcen stared motionless and pale faced. The water in the man's body was somehow at his allegiance.

More guards appeared. Rousing himself, Lahcen split the water at his command, throwing each puddle like a ball, watching it as it reached its target, splashing over the noses and mouths of the giants and sticking there as if it were a solid substance. The giants tugged and scraped at the liquid that now plugged their mouths and noses in vain; their fingers slicing through the mass without altering its airtight suction.

Behind him, he was conscious of Khalid and Qeriya, freed from enormous hands, gasping for breath, as their felled opponents lay twitching and struggling uselessly until, one after the other, they finally fainted. A part of Lahcen wanted to let the aqueous masks linger and suck the life out of them, just as they'd planned to kill him and his siblings, but he didn't. Fear stopped him, fear of what he was capable of doing.

"Quickly," he gasped in a hoarse voice, "into the house!"

Khalid and Qeriya, coughing, stumbled towards a round stone that covered the cave entrance. Khalid pushed the heavy boulder until it rolled out of the way. Lahcen followed on behind, keeping his eyes on the murky wood, searching for more guards. He backed in to the house, still trembling.

"You search, I'll watch," he ordered, glancing around for some means of blocking the entrance. Catching sight of a large metal crank to the right of the door, positioned high on the wall and appearing to follow a circular trajectory, instinctively he heaved it down towards himself. As he pulled, he heard the entrance stone move, sliding closed, eclipsing the new morning light. Instead of finding himself plunged into the darkness he had been expecting, he was surprised to find substantial light around him. Looking for its source, he found not one but many sources, like miniature suns positioned all over the house.

"Artificial lights," Khalid answered his unspoken question.

"Too bad we don't have time to explore this place." He frowned, his eyes scanning the room. "The crossing has to be inside here somewhere, and we need to find it fast. The fencing outside is nothing but electrified metal, with no sign of a door."

The border house resembled Doctor Michael's home in some ways, Lahcen thought, except it was even more luxurious. There were many rooms, not just one. The initial room they had found themselves in was full of plush cushions. There were more poufs than Lahcen had ever seen in his life. He went to sink his hand into one and it swallowed his forearm.

"Look at this!" Qeriya exclaimed from an adjoining room.

Khalid and Lahcen watched her pull on the handle of a metallic door.

Qeriya grinned at their amazed expressions. "It's a giant box filled with cold food. And see, the compartment above it is so cold it keeps everything hard as a rock. I've heard of freezing, but I could never imagine what it was really like." She touched the inside of the upper section and hurriedly pulled her finger away. "Ouch, it pinches, almost like touching fire."

Lahcen couldn't resist, he grabbed the door to the freezer and looked inside, taking a lump of white ice from the upper box and putting his mouth on it. "It's stuck to wy liph!" He yanked the ice off, taking some skin with it. As he held it, the cold lump began to melt in his hand.

"Hey, it's water, it's frozen water! This must be ice." He concentrated on the melting chunk in his hand, willing it to freeze once again. This was the first time he had attempted to control the temperature of water. He quickly discovered limits to what he was able to achieve. He could melt the ice in his hand, but he couldn't heat up the whole freezer. His hand ached from the cold as the stuff stuck to his skin but he was too enthralled to care and simply channeled his energy once again to make the ice melt.

"Look, there are lights everywhere. Even in this bottom cold box. And there's a lot of furniture," Qeriya observed. "Doctor Michael has a bed and a chair, but there's furniture everywhere here. Where does it all come from? How did they get the materials to make all of this?"

"They must have access to just about anything they want across the border," Khalid said.

"I could use one of these," Lahcen called from another room further down the hall.

Qeriya and Khalid, following the sound of his voice, found him standing beside a giant pad.

He grinned at them and, as they watched, pushed down on it. "It's springy. Doctor Michael has one, a mattress bed. Don't you remember seeing it when we had dinner at his house? He said he sleeps on it, but I've always wanted to jump on it." He climbed atop the elevated pad and bounced.

"I remember learning about some of this stuff in social studies," Qeriya said and then pointed at a tiny lever on the wall. "Hey, what does this do? I wonder if it opens a secret passage, you know how that crank you pulled controlled the door?" She flicked the little switch down.

"It's pitch black in here!" Lahcen yelled and the next second Qeriya heard a loud thump on the floor. She pushed the lever up and the light came back on.

Lahcen was propped into a sitting position, rubbing the side of his head. "So much for your secret passage," he said.

Khalid, who had wandered out into the narrow, dimly lit space that bridged the rooms together, appeared back in the doorway. "What was that?" he asked anxiously, looking at Lahcen, who was nurturing a swelling lump on his forehead.

"I fell off," Lahcen muttered irritably.

"I thought you were supposed to be on watch?"

"Oh, yeah, I got a little distracted."

"Well, get back on track. Forget keeping watch. Just help me look for a passage of some sort. They'll figure out what's happened soon enough, and then they'll hit us like a ton of bricks." Qeriya followed Khalid back out into the dimly lit space, a hallway, if she remembered her studies correctly.

Lahcen was on his way out to join them when he spotted the faint lines of another door on the far wall.

Going to investigate, he pulled a recessed lever tucked into the corner and the door folded open to expose a room full of material. "A whole room full of nothing but clothes. A lot of people must live here," he said to anyone who might be listening. Just then he heard his sister gasp and shot out of the door, in the direction the sound had come from. A few steps took him to her. She had opened another door, leading into a white room. There was glass on the wall. Lahcen moved to touch it, but as he did so, a hand met his and, startled, he pulled his own hand away. The other hand also disappeared. Lahcen brought his arm up again and waved at the glass and, immediately, the other hand returned. It was a reflection, Lahcen realized, just like you saw in the water on the salt flats after a rain.

Beside him, he heard Qeriya draw in a sharp breath. "Water!" she exclaimed. "They have a huge bowl of fresh water!" Sure enough there was an oval shaped basin with a raised lip, and it was partially filled with clear water.

"Qeriya, look at this weird glass," Lahcen urged. I think it's a mirror. You can see your reflection even more clearly than in the pools on the salt flats."

But Qeriya was completely captivated by the basin of water. She cupped her hands, ready to scoop some up to drink. At that moment, Khalid stuck his head in the door.

"Enough, Qeriya. We don't have time for that right now. They could be back at any moment. We have to find our way out of here."

"But ..." Qeriya pleaded. "All that fresh water."

Lahcen privately thought there wouldn't be any harm in Qeriya having a drink, but he didn't want to aggravate Khalid any more. They couldn't afford the time to argue.

"Come on, guys, back to work. You say you want us to work together, but you guys hop on any old trail that catches your attention. We've got to get out of here!" Khalid insisted.

Tempting as it was to stay, Lahcen did not want a repeat of what had happened with the giants. He was very grateful to be alive, but the fact that he had killed in order to survive sat more than a little uneasily on his shoulders.

After opening many doors and finding numerous switches that seemed to flick lights on and off, they finally discovered an immense cavern filled with what appeared to be narrow, raised beds. The space extended far back into the cave.

As Lahcen walked deeper into the room, past the beds, he saw rows of empty desks with lighted pictures protruding from a watery surface. The pictures looked real, as if he could touch them, but when he tried to do so, his fingers entered a film of water that merely rustled the image.

"More lights," Khalid said. "What are they?"

"Three-dimensional images that project moving scenes," Lahcen explained. "We learned about them in school. There's a bunch of them here. If we look closer, we should get a better view. They're moving pictures that pop out. Doctor Michael has photos in his house. Remember the one of the mountain range on his wall?"

"Yeah, I remember, but his don't move," Khalid said. "These are in motion?"

They crowded around one of the desks that displayed an image of a stream of water, lined with trees on either bank. "It's the place where we get our water, at the Wadi!" Qeriya exclaimed. "This is unreal. How can they see this?"

After a few seconds, each of the screens changed to an entirely different image, some of which were families asleep in their homes, the light of dawn creeping through their windows.

"These pictures show everything, even obscure places like that one." Lahcen pointed to another screen, this one depicting the canyon Qeriya had run through after crossing the Wadi's end during the race. The others hastened to the screen where Lahcen was standing. It soon switched to another home.

"Isn't that our science teacher?" Qeriya asked, looking at the figure of a sleeping man.

"Yeah, it is," Lahcen answered. "He should be waking up soon."

"They can see everything, even in the dark," Khalid observed.

Lahcen examined the moving pictures with rapt attention. The realization of what transpired felt to him like a large, thick curtain pulling back to reveal some great evil, an evil whose tentacles had invaded his entire life and the core of his relationship with his parents. He didn't know what was real anymore.

"This is why Mom and Dad used to call our home a prison. They knew about this surveillance." Lahcen waved his hand around the room they stood in. "They knew we were being watched."

"My mother's queen of the fire reaume and my dad's king," Aedan explained. *"But my dad's half water reaume. I take after that half. We're the odd ones in the pack. Reaume never intermarry as a rule."*

"Never? They never intermarry?"

"The only ones to ever intermarry are my parents, and both sets of my grandparents. My sister and I are related to all four reaume, water, fire, earth and air. So I've been under a microscope my whole life. You're human and that's even more radical. It's taken a long time for them to let me bring you here, and there are some who don't think it's a good idea. But that doesn't mean they don't like you," he hurried on. *"They just don't trust humans as a rule, other than a few exceptions. I hope you understand,"* he said, searching her face anxiously.

Clara reached for his hand, taking it in both of hers. *"Of course I understand. The king's hateful. He's the reason I had to leave my family. I just hope they can understand that I'm a victim of his hatred the same way they are. Being human doesn't mean we're all violent."* She gave him a tight little smile. *"When I was a child, I burned myself on a pot. I screamed at all pots after that, as if cooking pots were out to get me."*

Aedan chortled at the description.

It took a long time for my parents to convince me that it wasn't the pots that were dangerous, but the lit stove that heated the pot." She gave him another small, strained smile. *"I suppose that prejudice is like that in some ways, a basic survival instinct that isn't always right, and you have to unlearn it. I can help them unlearn it."* This time when she smiled there was nothing strained about it. She squeezed his hand gingerly.

Aedan breathed a sigh of relief. He didn't blame her for being anxious but the way she was dealing with it filled him with pride. His hand strayed to her hair and he grasped a handful, gently guiding her closer to touch his lips to hers.

Reluctantly, he pulled away. *"But, since you know my mother,"* he said, *"and they accepted my dad, then they'll certainly come to accept you. How can they not, as they come to know you as I do? Anyhow, tonight they're preparing a feast for you. We can walk slowly back and allow them time to get it ready."*

"A feast, just for me?" She halted in surprise.

"Yes, my love." He traced her cheek with his thumb, smiling gently. "You're the special guest tonight!"

"That's very kind of them." Clara linked her arm through his, snuggling close. "They must really love you and trust your judgment to give me such a welcome." As they walked along together, under the stars, Aedan, for the first time in his life, knew what love really was.

Chapter 10

Blind Escape

"Did they do all of this just to find us?" Qeriya asked, her lips curled.

"According to what Doctor Michael said, maybe so," Lahcen answered.

"Don't flatter yourselves guys," Khalid said, fiddling with an object beside one of the screens. "They were probably monitoring for signs of rebellion."

"I wonder where our home is?" Qeriya asked, sweeping her gaze over the numerous screens. "It's hopeless."

Lahcen copied his brother and fingered two spongy pads held together by an arched bridge. He lifted it up and heard a faint noise coming from the round pads. Putting them to his ears, the arched bridge surrounded his head. But as soon as he let go, the mechanism lifted away, hovering close to his ears so that he heard water trickling. The sound matched the image on the screen exactly. He regarded Khalid who did the same, and both were still as stone as they listened.

"Not only are we being watched, all of our conversations can be heard!" Lahcen ripped the bridge off his head and threw the thing on the table. "How long have they been doing this?"

The sound of a door slamming interrupted them. Muted voices rumbled outside.

Everything else momentarily forgotten, they glanced frantically around, thinking furiously. How could they do the impossible and find a way out of a room with apparently seamless walls, other than through the door they came in?

Khalid spotted something and hurried deeper into the cavernous room. Lahcen, squinting, could see an outline carved into the back wall. His eyes tracked left and he could just make out a levered handle. His breath came out in a ragged hiss. It was a door, leading deeper into the mountain. Hopefully this was the passage that would take them through the mountain border.

Armed with the terrifying confidence of a killer, he turned to face the imminent danger, as his brother and sister tried desperately to work the lever, finally wresting open the thick metal door.

"Come on!" Khalid urged and Lahcen, sparing a last glance in the direction of the approaching voices, dashed after them, finding himself inside a musty cave. Within moments they had heaved the heavy door closed and were buried in pitch black.

"I wonder if this is a hideout of some sort?" Qeriya asked.

Lahcen stretched out his hand, his fingers touching cool, damp earth, much different to the gritty sandstone of their familiar desert caves. He sensed cool moisture in the air that might have felt refreshing if it wasn't so stale. He ran his hand over the wall again. How strange to find wet ground so close to a dry desert.

"Let's move," Khalid said tersely.

They shuffled slowly deeper, feeling their way along and waiting for their eyes to adjust more to the gloom.

"If it's a hideout, then it's a long one," Lahcen offered. "The walls are narrow and I've yet to feel the end." He would have given a week's water ration right now for some of those lights they had seen in the house; instead, like blind moles, they navigated the passageway with their hands. Before long, Lahcen bumped into a wall of dirt. The soft grunts of the others confirmed what he already knew. They had reached a dead end. "Pull back," he commanded. Tension crackled in the air as they reversed direction.

"Feel around this time, in case we missed a turn off," Khalid ordered Qeriya, who was in the front as they backtracked. They retraced their steps into the unknown, hoping there were no scorpions down in these depths. Sweat poured from their faces.

A sudden noise brought them to a halt and they stared in horror as the heavy door was rolled open, allowing shards of blinding light to blast into the dark space.

The guards were heavily armed with bow and arrows: the same arrows that had almost knocked them out of the sky earlier. Just one of those fired into the tunnel would slice through its target easily, effectively separating them from their life force.

"Take a shot." One of the giants ordered another and Lahcen watched apprehensively as the guard strung his bow and aimed.

"I can get the female," he said.

Immediately Khalid leapt in front of Qeriya, while Lahcen pulled her to the ground, feeling her body jerk as her arms swung. He heard a thump as the arrow missed Khalid, deflecting into the ground behind them.

"Why did you do that, Lahcen? I had everything under control," Qeriya complained.

Lahcen ignored her. Grasping one of Khalid's hands, he dragged him and his sister a short distance along the dirt before turning into a passage on the right.

"Another tunnel," Khalid said.

They could hear the sound of the giants getting closer. "Run!" Khalid ordered, leading the way. Lahcen and Qeriya obeyed without question, Lahcen running, and Qeriya flying, as fast as possible in the dark.

"You were going to take that arrow meant for me," Qeriya's voice trembled.

Khalid just kept running.

"I guess you're not really a jerk, like I said before."

"You guess? That's your conclusion — after he saved your skin?" Lahcen challenged. "That's not even a descent apology, forget a thank you."

Lahcen, bringing up the tail, was running with his arms outstretched to avoid hitting Qeriya, but within seconds his hands plowed into her back and the rest of him followed, slamming into her despite his precautions. "What happened?" he asked.

There was silence, and then. "I ran into the corner of a wall," Khalid's voice was strained.

"A wall!"

"The path's a Y," Khalid managed to say.

"Qeriya, get up." Lahcen pulled his sister up by her arm. "Khalid—"

"I'm up, I'm up. We'll go left," Khalid ordered, already on the move.

Glancing behind him, Lahcen could see the faint glow of light, alerting him to the fact that the giants had gained the passageway. An arrow whirred through the air and thumped into the wall a short distance from his right ear. "Thank the maker Khalid took us this way," he whispered to Qeriya.

"They went the other way!" One of the guards yelled. "That means they'll reach the—"

"Shut up! They'll hear you!" Another voice grated.

"Reach the what?" Lahcen asked himself. "Khalid," he said urgently. "Something's coming up. I don't know what."

The next moment, he had rammed against his sister again. Qeriya merely grunted, refusing to waste breath on cries of pain.

"What now?" Lahcen asked in exasperation.

"Hah!" Khalid exclaimed. "I feel something. It moves."

"What?"

"Just grab hold of me. We're going for a ride."

Lahcen could see nothing, but held tight to his brother as instructed. Khalid plucked him from the ground like a garden weed and dropped him into a rectangular metal container next to Qeriya. Lahcen caught hold of the edges, pulling himself up to a squatting position with his hands. He guessed the walls of the box stood about waist high, though he didn't have time to stand up to find out because the container began to move. Khalid leapt inside to join them, landing on Lahcen's lap. Lahcen felt a tug as his brother reached a hand out of the box and pushed along the wall to speed them up, continuing until the wheels rumbled with the sound of friction as the number of rotations accumulated per second. The next thing he knew, they were hurtling along a track, with the cart vibrating so hard his tongue tickled. Judging by the noise, they were moving fast.

"Hold on tight to the edge of this cart," Khalid said. "We're going downhill."

"Are the giants behind us?" Qeriya asked.

"I'm sure they are," Khalid's voice was grim. "This was the only cart I felt, but then again I couldn't see."

"Yes, they're back there," Lahcen said, pointing pointlessly, as no one could see him anyway. "I see a light shining in our direction. Stay down." The bright beam flooded the space between them with light, and, judging by its unchanging size, it was keeping pace with them.

"They must be in one of these carts, too," Lahcen said. "How are we ever going to lose them? We're not even sure how to get out of here when this thing stops." He saw the blurred outline as his brother climbed to his feet, facing the cart behind them.

"Khalid, get down!" Lahcen and Qeriya hissed at the same time, yanking on his hairy legs.

"What are you trying to do?" Lahcen spluttered. "They've got weapons!"

"I know, just bear with me. It's a chance, perhaps our best one." Khalid lifted his right arm, running his hand along the dirt wall as high as he could reach. "I'm hoping we're nearly on the other side of the mountains, in which case … Hah, I found a tree root," he said and pulled hard. The cart slowed to a stop as Khalid held steady and Lahcen bit his lip. Sure enough, the root fell towards them, ripping the earth open above their heads, raining moist dirt and stray rocks down on them.

"Are you insane?" Lahcen gasped. "Are you trying to get us killed?"

"Trust me," Khalid said, continuing to pull hard on the root until what started as a shower of dirt became an avalanche of earth and rock. Just as the light behind them was growing bigger and brighter, the bulk of dirt and rocks crashed down between the carts: snuffing out the brightness that had been about to consume them.

"How did you do that?" he asked Khalid. "I know you're super strong, but that was beyond believable."

"I don't exactly know what happened," Khalid admitted, as he rustled around the cart for a moment.

Lahcen again felt the tug and vibration of a cart in motion and assumed Khalid must be pulling at the walls to make them pick up speed.

"I don't really know how I thought of looking for roots in the first place, but somehow I sensed the trees were there. It wasn't my strength that loosened the root. The tree wanted to help me somehow. I can't explain, really. Anyhow, the earth's unstable. It'll cave in soon. We have to move fast."

Just as Khalid had predicted, stray pieces of earth descended on their heads as they sped onward. It was difficult to perceive the passing of time accurately, but before long they popped out of the mountain and the cart steadily rolled to a stop on flat ground.

Lahcen peered around at the new world into which he'd been birthed. They were free at last, embedded in a grassy meadow, surrounded by lush forest at the foothills of jagged peaks, bathed in early morning sun, and he could not find the strength to put a finger outside of the cart.

Khalid swung himself to the ground first. Turning back to the cart, he helped Qeriya down beside him, then aided Lahcen in joining them. Together they slowly walked towards tree cover.

"I can't get over it, from no water to this. How did that happen? What a glorious name — rainforest. Do you really think it rains here every day?" Lahcen asked, feeling chatty now that he was up and moving in air thick with humidity. "I used to dream of being in a rainforest. I'd hide my head when Mom woke me up in the morning, so I could hang on to it for a bit longer. You know when you wake up and you really want to remember your dream, but the more you try the less you remember?"

"It's like trying to catch a crumb in sifting sand," Qeriya added, collapsing under a tree. She leaned her head against a grassy mound, leaping back up again seconds later as ants accosted her ears and cheeks.

"I guess you do know," Lahcen said, ignoring her plight.

"My dreams were always of flying," she said, cringing and brushing off the last few tiny invaders.

"I can believe that." Lahcen felt gaseous moisture envelope him. It appeared that water was everywhere here, even in the air itself. It was too magical to imagine, coming from a place where water was worth its weight in gold.

"Giants or not," Khalid said, interrupting Lahcen's reverie, "those bows and arrows were unlike anything we have at home. The arrows they used flew unnaturally high." He found himself a comfortable place to set down, leaning back on his pack with a contented sigh.

Qeriya followed suit. Ants or not, she was exhausted. "And that house was nothing like I've ever seen," she said, throwing an arm over her eyes.

"Even rich people like Doctor Michael don't have houses like that," Lahcen added, pacing among his drained siblings with renewed vigor. The moisture was like nothing he'd ever experienced and he felt fully alive, energetic.

"The giants were from the prince's army," Khalid said, finding himself a seat. "The prince is probably staying in that house while he's here."

"Now, why would the royal army guard the border so cautiously?" Lahcen asked. "Why be concerned about rebellion in a region with no water and no way to get out?"

"We did," Khalid said and Lahcen cocked his head in

agreement.

Qeriya abruptly sat up, staring around herself, her head swiveling from side to side. "I've just had an awful thought," she said. "Maybe there are others patrolling this side of the mountain."

"She's right," Khalid acknowledged reluctantly.

"Won't they think we're buried in that cave?" Lahcen speculated.

"Perhaps," Qeriya said. But even so, they'll find out soon enough that we're not."

Lahcen agreed. They would very likely be spotted if they lingered here, he realized. He turned to Khalid in expectation of further instructions, and at that moment, it came to him that, while he might resent his brother's authority, for some reason he couldn't help appealing to it.

"We move on," Khalid said and reached upward. The branch of a nearby Kapok tree extended as if to shake his hand of its own accord. Khalid pulled on the branch and it flung him forward to catch another, and another.

Lahcen sensed a mist swirling around him. It hovered just under the top layer of the forest air, so close it was like a second skin, filling up his senses, and he could tell, somehow, that it was as aware of him as he was of it. He opened himself to it and it came to him as if following unspoken orders, condensing into streams that floated in midair, blasting him from every direction until he was submerged in a giant liquid bubble. He wrestled it as he had the guard who choked him, feeling currents and directing their flow, savoring the pressure and sound of being immersed. He vaguely heard his brother and sister arguing a few feet away, they looked warped and misshapen through the water, but he found that he could hear their muffled voices.

Qeriya flew to pluck Lahcen from the watery grave, but Khalid grasped her ankle and they tumbled onto the ground.

"No! Qeriya let him be. He's learning," Lahcen heard Khalid

say.

"Learning to do what, drown himself?" Qeriya said, rubbing the arm she had banged as Khalid pulled her down.

"I love drowning," Lahcen said to himself inside his watery space. He flipped and turned his body in all directions, feeling the water's response to his every move. For the first time in his life, he felt free. No longer was he enduring his fate, now he controlled it. He concentrated the water and drained it down his body, letting it run down under his feet, where it converged to form an elongated wave that cruised along the ground below him as he surfed the surface.

"See?" Khalid said to his sister, as they got to their feet, brushing the dirt off their clothes.

"How did you know what was happening?"

"I guessed." He grinned and she punched him on the arm.

"Lucky for you it was a good guess."

"No kidding," Khalid chuckled as he launched himself into the trees.

Lahcen rode the water beneath his brother, constantly drawing moisture from the air to spin a path in front of him. He steered clear of low branches, and jumped rocks, always landing on the gathering path. Each time he passed over the water, it at once returned to mist and dissipated.

He watched Qeriya dive into the air. She glided as if she had wings, catching a lift on one wind current and bouncing onto another. She passed over his head, a reckless bird soaring through the trees, navigating branches by steering around them, unlike Khalid, who targeted them.

Suddenly Lahcen heard a vehement hiss and turned to look at where Khalid hung, dangling from a tree.

"Sorry," Khalid apologized, quickly letting go of whatever he was holding to grasp for a nearby branch instead. He shrugged, smiling. "I guess trees and snakes all look alike when you're not paying attention."

"Well pay attention!" Lahcen said. "We're in a hurry to save our lives, not find new and better ways to lose them."

They flew, surfed and jumped until Lahcen could no longer feel his feet and he signaled for them to stop. It had been one endurance race after another for two days and he was done. The other two did not take much convincing. The tree cover was thickening and the air was a comfortable temperature. They found a bare patch of ground on which to camp for the rapidly approaching night.

Lahcen stared up at the thick tree cover, no longer able to see even a patch of sky. His heart gradually settled down and stopped pounding hard enough to escape his chest, in seconds he was sound asleep.

"Wake up," Qeriya called.

Lahcen dragged his eyes open, what felt like only minutes later, to murky grey, barely twilight. Whether it was morning or evening he couldn't tell, he'd slept so soundly. Sitting up, he made out the vague outlines of plant life around him, and then his sister pointed east.

"What's that?"

Lahcen rubbed the sleep from his eyes and joined Khalid in following the invisible line determined by her pointing finger. There was a soft glow in the distance that, as they watched, expanded in their direction, slowly growing into two balls of fire. Within moments, tentacles of sand streamed from the balls of fire to surround the three of them. The sand quickly spreading out, thin and burning hot, cooling rapidly into a glass dome, trapping them where they stood.

"There's no use fighting. You won't get free," a host of female voices called in unison, through the curved wall of glass. "Who are you and what are you doing here?"

"I'm Khalid, this is my brother, Lahcen, and the girl with us is our sister, Qeriya. We come from the desert. Please, our parents are sick and our town is dying. We're on a quest to find medicine.

We don't mean harm to anyone," Khalid pleaded.

As suddenly as the globe had encircled them, it sifted away, the clear glass giving way to streams of sand that retreated back into scarf pouches the strangers wore at their sides. To their surprise, the host of voices was only two young girls, floating on air, a jet of fire emitting from the empty space below their feet; a space that surrounded them entirely and glowed like an aura. The two girls carried glass bubbles full of flame in their hands, and their faces were bright with unexpected smiles.

"They must be fire reaume," Lahcen said. "They look like the pictures we saw in the cave."

"Cousins," the girls called to them. "You've come home!"

PART II
FOREST

The old queen squatted, a thin, weathered body curved around bent legs, hunched beside Orchid Pond in the twilight, moving her finger over the water as if drawing a picture on black glass. It seemed almost as if she had held that position for years.

"I hope I'm not bothering you, Sara," Clara said quietly, so as not to alarm her.

Sara turned her head; a royal crown of woven flowers rested upon it. "No, please come. I know what you want."

Clara approached the water, kneeling respectfully beside her.

"We see so little of people other than in battle, when the human giants decimate us. I doubt I've ever spoken to one since I met your father, many years ago, such a kind man." She lifted her face, etched with the pattern of her life in the crisscross laughter-lines at the corners of her eyes and the worry lines stamped upon her forehead "You're not just 'one of them' any more than I'm just one of my kind."

"No, I'm not like the humans you've fought," Clara said. "I love this place ... your reaume."

"My reaume, you say?" Sara glanced up at Clara before once more resuming her drawing. Images appeared in the water, but Clara could not understand what they were. "Do you love them so much you're willing to make them your reaume?" Her sharp black eyes fixed on Clara. "Because that's what your children will be when you marry my grandson."

A wave of heat swept through her as the woman stared, scrutinizing her. There was no way a human and a reaume could conceive a child. It was impossible, and she had understood that reality when accepting Aedan's proposal of marriage. Now Aedan's grandmother, the wise queen mother, not only assumed it possible, but declared it would be — with such certainty! While Clara doubted her foretelling, one thing was sure, the fire reaume would be her family.

"Yes, I'm willing. I love your clan as my own, and I promise to protect them," she affirmed, surprised by her own confidence as she heard herself say the words.

The old woman nodded approval and continued with her work. "I believe you," she said. "You have my blessing. You'll make a good queen."

Chapter 11

A Brush with Fire

Khalid stared at the smiling girls in astonishment. Their faces were framed in reddish brown curls, the rest of their abundant hair plaited in small braids. The eldest wore a soft, cream colored tunic, decorated with vines, and cropped pants, while the youngest wore the same in black, with yellow and orange flames gracing the sides. Their features were distinct, but both had cherry cheeks, a ruddy complexion and dark eyes. It was easy to assume they were sisters. Only they weren't like any sisters he'd ever seen. A subtle glow surrounded their bodies, resembling the pictures in the cave.

"It's really you, I can't believe it!" The older girl exclaimed. "How in the world did you get here?"

"Yeah!" Lahcen said, feigning recollection, leaving Khalid and Qeriya dumbfounded and looking like guilty criminals. "That's right! It's us, we're back!"

Seeing the siblings' surprised faces and their hesitancy to answer her, the older girl restrained her excitement. "My sister and I are of the fire reaume."

"Fire reaume, of course you are!" Lahcen said, and a devious smile crossed his face. "Are you friendly? You look pretty scary."

"Of course we're friendly, unless you tick us off, that is." The younger girl smiled widely, showing a line of straight white teeth.

"Maria, stop!" The older girl scolded, jaw clenched. She stepped forward, gently pushing her companion back. "I realize this must be hard for you to believe, but we're your cousins. I'm Raquel and this is my sister, Maria. We've heard all about you. Our mother and your father are brother and sister."

"Our father, a fire reaume?" Lahcen asked in disbelief,

abandoning all pretense of recognition.

Qeriya glanced at Khalid and saw that he looked as unconvinced as she felt. He frowned. "Where we come from, there's no such thing as fire reaume. That being the case, we've recently discovered pictures of fire reaume, but that's it. I'm afraid our parents have never spoken of you before."

"Perhaps not, given your circumstances, but … well, you're reaume, too, at least in part," Raquel said, fiddling with her tunic.

"You mentioned that, but how do you know? And how do you know we're these cousins you think we are? We don't create fire," Khalid said.

"We know your names, and we've seen pictures of you in the games," Maria chimed in confidently.

Khalid squinted towards the girls. Just how many people outside of the desert were privy to pictures of their village? Were the images only of the games? Did any capture private moments inside people's homes, like the images they had seen on the screens at the border house? Thinking about such an invasion of privacy made Khalid sick, he wasn't sure he really wanted to know the answer.

Raquel took a deep breath. "There was a great war, many years ago, against the fire reaume," she explained. "The king's army killed many of our kind. Our parents told us that your family moved in with a village of rainforest humans living near our reaume. But the king attacked even the rainforest humans as well. That was a surprise to everyone. All of the rainforest humans were moved into the desert to join another settlement. We call them the desert dwellers. The king drew water away from the Wadi. He put up borders and locked everyone inside. This all happened before we were born, but we heard all about it."

"What are fire reaume exactly?" Qeriya probed, circling and scrutinizing the sisters.

Maria followed Qeriya's gaze with apparent distaste, the corners of her own mouth turning down.

Khalid watched the scene with apprehension. Qeriya sometimes had a knack for making a tricky situation even more so.

"Fire reaume shape the planet," Raquel continued with her explanation.

"What does that mean?" Qeriya asked.

"You don't know?" Maria asked, excited by their ignorance. She forgot about Qeriya's blunt inspection and began fidgeting with her hands, cracking each knuckle, one at a time.

"What do we know might be a better question at this point," Lahcen commented, rolling his neck to iron out a kink acquired from a long night on the ground without a descent pillow. Khalid could relate, he rolled his own neck.

"We fire reaume created this world," Maria announced.

Raquel quietly grabbed her sister's hands to stop her finger popping. Maria glowered back, but stopped nevertheless.

"We didn't create this world. The Spirit created the world," Raquel corrected, staring at Qeriya while maintaining a firm hold on her sister's hands.

Maria yanked herself free.

"But no one could live on it. The planet was mostly flat and covered by a shallow ocean, with only a little land. Centuries ago, fire reaume made it so that humans could live here, by stirring up volcanoes. This sparked earthquakes and other changes. It took years, but then, there were lots of different land environments ready to be settled. We wanted to keep as many natural plants and animals as possible, but most were killed over time as the planet became more like earth. We keep caring for the planet today, following the Spirit's instructions, given to us through Orchid Pond."

"You forgot to tell them the funniest part, Raquel!" Maria said, buzzing randomly about, reminding Khalid of a little bee. "Most native life died, except for cockroaches. It seems that cockroaches can exist on any planet and are able to survive just about anything. And they're nasty buggers, too, large and always getting into the food. I'm all for exterminating them personally."

"Cockroaches!" Lahcen exclaimed between fits of laughter. "They're here? I believe it! They even survived in the desert.

"Maria, that's awful!" Raquel exclaimed, extending a hand to catch Maria as she flew by and pulling her in to give her a hard stare. "We don't kill for convenience. All species were created by the Spirit and we're to care for them."

Maria lunged out of Raquel's grasp, but she wasn't fast enough and her sister caught hold of her again. She shot Raquel a defiant look. "Well, all the interesting species were killed, so why not kill off the annoying ones? Too bad they're not any good to eat. I think the Spirit must have made a mistake creating those things," she said, shuddering.

Raquel stared at her sister as if Maria had dropped unannounced out of the sky. Khalid, though, couldn't help but smile. He turned away trying to disguise the fact.

Lahcen continued laughing so hard that his belly shook. "You should see your face!" he told Raquel.

Qeriya had been silently observing, but Lahcen's laughter was infectious and she had soon joined him. But Raquel did not laugh and the two of them slowly gained control of their giggles.

Khalid found his own concentration wandering. The plant life was growing louder. Certainly plants didn't make much noise, but somehow, their slow movement and whisper soft sounds captured his eyes and ears as surely as if they were a host of people trying to talk to him all at once. He passed his hand through a cluster of leaves.

"How can a pond connect you with the Spirit, much less give instructions?" Qeriya asked. "And how can people create a world?"

"First of all, fire reaume are not people. We're not human,"

Maria began and flew over to Qeriya. "And second, I can see that you're a non-believer."

Raquel slapped her hand onto her own forehead. "Maria, you can be so exasperating sometimes. Don't be so rude!"

"A non-believer of what?" Qeriya placed her hands on her hips, squaring up to Maria. "I'm sure I don't believe a lot of things, is that a problem?"

"It is if you move back here with us," Maria asserted.

Raquel seemed to have given up. She stood, head in hands.

"Well, whatever it is that I don't believe in, I don't know what it is, nor do I know why it's so important. I pray every day, only the Spirit never gave me instructions on anything, much less how to create a planet."

"Our parents keep telling us they wish *we* came with instructions," Raquel said, trying to diffuse the tension, but her efforts met with blank stares. Only Khalid managed a smile, having witnessed and identified with Raquel's struggle to control her sister, lost cause though it was. In his experience, younger sisters were more dangerous governed than ungoverned.

"Anyhow," Raquel pressed on. "The pond isn't working at the moment."

"A rather fickle spirit if you ask me," Qeriya commented, folding her arms.

"Qe, shut it!" Lahcen said angrily, sending her a flat stare.

Khalid goggled back and forth between Maria and his sister. "I've no idea what you two are arguing about, or how it all got so inflamed in a matter of minutes, but one thing's certain, seeing you two together, I'm now thoroughly convinced that we are all, in fact, related." Qeriya and Maria examined the other momentarily. A smile crept first across Qeriya's face and was quickly picked up by Maria. Soon they were both laughing, and Khalid breathed a sigh of relief.

"Well then, since you're family, you should be allowed to see the pond for yourself," Raquel declared, elated by Khalid's tactful negotiation. "Your mom is human from what I understand, but your dad is reaume — a mix of reaume, just like our mother. I'm not so sure how that all works."

"Our dad is all fire reaume, and so are we. I just perfected my fire powers last week," Maria bragged. "Watch!" She raised her hands and fire streamed from an aura around her fingers. She curled the flame into a ball, shaping and smoothing it like a potter molds clay. The pressure changed the tender flame from orange to blue. She pulled her arm back to fling the fireball.

"No!" The three siblings yelled as one and Maria flipped backwards a few times, their shouts like gusts of air blowing at her.

Seeing Maria's shock, Khalid softened, "What we mean is, I think we saw your fire power already — when you trapped us in glass a moment ago."

Maria flipped forward, hiding a flicker of embarrassment and Khalid was struck by how much younger she appeared now than when she was acting tough. She obviously wanted to share all her knowledge with these cousins she'd heard about.

"Maria, your powers are getting stronger now," Raquel said. "It's important you don't use them without direction from me."

"You're only two years older, Raquel, you're not my mother."

Raquel pursed her lips and ignored Maria's snide outburst. "I let you use them just now because we didn't know if these people might be dangerous, but we know our cousins are safe."

"We are?" Lahcen surfed the air, racing down upon the sisters like a hawk descending on its prey.

Raquel flinched, whisking her spinning sister into her arms and somersaulting them both out of the way, their dark curls bouncing out of their braids and flying in every direction. Lahcen skidded to a halt at the last minute, sending a spray of water over everyone. Raquel's expression grew increasingly severe until, finally, she flung her hand in his direction and issued a puff of fire that singed the top of his hair. Lahcen's hand sprang to his head.

"Hey! My hair! What happened to my hair?"

"It serves you right, scaring fire reaume like that. You're just lucky they didn't turn you to steam," Khalid joked.

Maria wrestled free of her sister's grip and they guffawed, except for Raquel, whose silence resonated disapproval.

"Where are my manners? You must be hungry," Raquel said after composing herself. She searched around and found a Waree Palm to harvest. She removed a small knife from one of the scarf pouches dangling at her side and fiddled with a few of the branches, soon giving them each a white shoot. "Here's a snack for you. The flower doesn't taste like much of anything, but this white core is delicious. I'll get some more later on if you like it. And don't worry, Lahcen, our healers have a cream to regrow hair back at the village."

"Don't tell him that!" Qeriya taunted.

The three of them were pretty hungry and eagerly tasted the shoot, gazing around the forest at the potential food supply. Now that the sun was up, they could see trees and plants everywhere, in various shades of green and brown. Sunlight was muted to pale green after filtering through layers of plant life.

"Can you eat everything here?" Qeriya asked. Her dad had told her tales of houses made of food, but she had never thought there was any truth in them, until now.

"You don't want to eat the poisonous things," Maria said and pointed to a vine crawling up a nearby tree. "That curare will kill you."

"Actually," Raquel clarified, "That's true if you eat it, but the curare vine contains alkaloid chemicals that can be used in medicines. Our parents, your aunt and uncle, were trained as healers in their youth, and that's what I'd like to be some day."

"Actually ..." Maria stood cross armed and formal as she rolled her eyes and mocked her sister in the background. "I'm sure they really feel like getting a botany lecture right now,

Raquel."

"Maria!" Raquel ordered in a stage whisper. "Stop being rude."

"They were healers? What do you mean, were?" Lahcen asked.

Khalid's attention was drawn to a nearby tree whose blossom extended towards him.

"That's the Jippi Jappa palm," Raquel said. "We make baskets out of the fronds. You can eat its flower and shoots. The tree seems to be offering you a taste."

Khalid reached out his hand, plucked free one of the blossoms and tasted his gift.

"Thank you," he said, gently stroking a leaf. The branch returned to its position.

Raquel turned her attention to Lahcen, her skin exuding a blue hue. "Our parents were captured a week ago, at the volcano. All the adult reaume travel to the volcano annually, in order to gather information. The information determines our work for the following year. But this time the human king nabbed them for some reason."

"The royal family again," Lahcen said, exchanging seething looks with his brother.

Suddenly, the moist air around them was becoming thicker by the second. Khalid grew damp and limp at the abrupt change in atmosphere. He glanced around for the source of discomfort.

"Would you knock it off?" Qeriya finally shouted, punching Lahcen on the shoulder.

"Ouch, what was that for?" Lahcen exclaimed as the humidity shot even higher.

"You're making it unbearable," Qeriya said, wilting.

Lahcen lurched, bewildered, and as suddenly as it had begun, everything was back to a normal, sultry temperature. "How did you know it was me? I didn't know it was me. Wow! I'm just not used to all of this water responding to my every whim."

"Wait, do you know the royal family? Did … did you see the king?" Maria shuddered, backing into her sister and pulling Raquel's arm around her. Raquel added her other arm as well, holding her sister close, a mien of peace cascading over her, like a mother enjoying respite from an unruly child.

"No," Lahcen answered. "We just managed to avoid that … pleasure. His army was waiting for us at the border though, very insistent we take up his invitation."

"For some reason we're considered a threat to security and were lucky to survive our border crossing," Khalid said, walking slowly around them, his fingers extending an introduction to the multiple plants growing everywhere.

"How did you escape?" Maria asked, her eyes peeled.

"We surprised ourselves to be honest," Lahcen said. "We've always had abilities we couldn't explain. We–we don't understand them. None of us can touch fire, though."

"Fire or not, we saw you win the competition just yesterday, and you guys were seriously copacetic," Maria announced, holding her head high.

"Copa–what?" Raquel asked, putting hands on her hips.

"Copacetic," Maria repeated, as if that should explain everything.

"Do you know what copacetic means?" Raquel asked.

"It means cool!" Maria said, doing a funky dance move Khalid had never seen before. Raquel didn't bother to answer, shaking her head instead.

"I want to enter the fire reaume competition someday. I'm already working on a wicked fireball. I can usually hit the target. Watch!" Before anyone could intervene this time, Maria hustled to gather fire into what looked like a round bolt and whipped it at a giant bromeliad.

"Maria, no!" Raquel shouted and watched the distant flower take a hit that broke it off the tree. Maria recalled her fire before the plant burned.

"Nice one, Maria," Raquel said sarcastically, "you just demolished the toilet."

"The toilet!" Lahcen was the first to roar with laughter. Not even Raquel's pinched lips were enough to restrain him. "That giant flower's a toilet?"

"Yeah," Raquel answered in a clinical voice. "It digests feces."

"That's disgusting." Qeriya grimaced.

"Next topic," Khalid said.

"So can you pee in it, too?" Lahcen asked.

"Grow up, Lahcen," Khalid said as he socked his brother in the arm.

"What? It's a fair question. Quit treating me like a punching bag!" Lahcen rubbed the triceps on his sore arm.

"You can pee on any old plant. Just make sure it's a plant. It's hard to tell sometimes," Maria said.

"So, did your parents teach you how to use your powers, or did you just know?" Khalid asked in an effort to change the subject.

"We grew into them as you all did too, I'm sure. As we got older our parents gave us tips, and I suppose we just watched them."

"We had to figure our powers out for ourselves, and how to repress them. I suppose our parents caught them early," Khalid said. He heard a thumping noise and turned around to see Lahcen fiercely pounding the ground with a long stick. "What are you doing?"

"Khalid, I keep seeing something move, but when I look, the movement stops. There's something out there," he said, his voice sounding squeamish.

Khalid and the others searched around them for some sort of creature.

"Come over by us," Maria ordered and grabbed at their arms to pull them close. "It could be a boar. They move very fast and can be extremely dangerous."

"But if it's dangerous then we should protect you since you're the youngest," Qeriya said and looked to Raquel for support.

"Well, actually, Maria is our best hope if it's a boar," Raquel said with dubious conviction. "She hunts boar."

The others whipped their heads around to consider Maria's tiny frame. "Maria hunts?" Lahcen asked, noticeably aghast.

"Yes, of course I do." Maria held her chin high. "Do you get many boar in the desert?"

"Boar, meaning wild pig?" Qeriya asked. "I've heard about them in school."

"All right, you definitely need to listen to me," Maria advised. "These boar are nothing like pigs, wild or otherwise. They can be deadly, and they're very fast. You need to come close." She waved them all towards her and they obediently crowded around.

"I don't remember pigs being fast," Lahcen said.

"That's why I just said they're not wild pigs," Maria echoed. "Raquel, I'm going to need some help here. Get them in formation. There's no time for explanation. If it's a boar, there could be more of them. They usually travel in packs."

Raquel quickly replaced Maria in the middle of the circle, and addressed the others who stood at attention. "I'll need to lift you up fairly quickly, so don't be alarmed. And I'm sorry this had to be your introduction to our rainforest. It really is lovely here."

Maria glared at her sister and Raquel stopped talking. They all stood quietly, searching the ground close to them, their eyes darting repeatedly to Maria, who had lifted slightly into the air, surveying the area carefully.

"Usually they would have shown themselves by now. But they never approach unless they want to attack. Otherwise they avoid us."

"There it goes again," Lahcen said, his voice almost a squeal.

"Where?" Maria asked.

"There … and over there." Lahcen's hands darted in the direction of leaves rustling in sporadic places. "Don't you see the plants move? It's creepy!"

"Well, I see a little movement, that's all. But that's just the — oh, no, you're not scared of the geckos are you?" Maria chortled.

"What are geckos?" Khalid asked, already grinning widely at his brother, who was cowering in embarrassment. Whatever geckos were, they were obviously harmless, and so great fodder to tease Lahcen with.

"They're tiny lizards," Raquel explained. "They eat bugs."

"Little lizards once lived in the desert," Khalid said. "I wonder if they're the same ones we used to have?"

"Lizards?" Lahcen asked.

"Yep, lizards, and teeny tiny ones, too," Maria prodded. "You're waging war on harmless lizards. And you won't win, either. They're fast."

"Maria, be nice," Raquel quietly commanded her sister. She turned to the others. "Geckos are very fast. There's no way you can see them as they dart from plant to plant. I'm sure that can be scary if you aren't familiar with them."

"Just a little disconcerting," Lahcen said, trying to save face, tugging at his britches and shifting restlessly from one foot to the other. "So, do they ever crawl onto people?"

"They'll crawl on you, but only if you smell like food," Maria said and stuck her nose on his arm to sniff him. "Oh, yeah, you definitely smell like a bug. You'd better watch out for those little guys."

"Oh, Maria, sometimes you're insufferable," Raquel said. "Stop teasing our cousin!"

"But it's so fun!" She relented a little. "Oh, all right, sorry."

"I think you've met your match, Lahcen." Qeriya smiled.

"You look beautiful," Lourdes said. Lourdes's clear skin and deep brown hair added a look of youth to her age. "My son's a fortunate man." A flock of female attendants edged away and slipped outside, leaving the two women alone. Lourdes's gaze swept around the small hut, comfortably furnished with a bamboo hammock piled with soft cushions. A wooden desk stood opposite, with a side table in one corner. There was a row of hooks on the far end of the wall for clothes. Light leaked through small cracks in the side walls of the bamboo structure.

Clara smiled affectionately at her future mother-in-law; she had come to love this brave woman. Momentarily, she found herself blinded by tears as she thought of her parents. How she wished they could be here to share this day with them all.

Automatically, as whenever she was anxious or upset, her hand went to tug at her blonde hair, falling away again as she remembered that today, it had been woven in many braids, forming patterns she would scarcely have imagined were possible. Tendrils of the shining mass graced her pale skin. She wore a sleek azure dress that made her blue eyes shine like jewels.

Lourdes fumbled in one of her scarf pouches, pulling out a necklace and bracelet of deep blue sapphires. She placed the necklace around Clara's slim neck. "I want you to have these," she said, fastening the clasp.

"What a stunning gift!" Clara was overwhelmed.

Lourdes smiled, the corners of her mouth turning down as her joy slid into grief. "Only my mother and I are left. I wish Aedan's father and your parents could have seen this day."

They stepped outside into the faint glow of strings of tiny lights, illuminating the undergrowth of the rainforest.

"I'll walk with you down the aisle," Lourdes announced, fingering the wooden crown she wore, recently handed down by Aedan's grandmother. It was intricately carved into intertwining vines. Holes in the vines housed fresh blossoms. "My father made this. He was an earth reaume from the cold forest. He died many years ago. It may be yours someday."

"His carvings are magical." Clara stopped, taking Lourdes's hand in hers, she turned to face her. "Lourdes, you're so gracious. It means a lot to Aedan … and to me.

Chapter 12

Oracle

Anna knelt beside Orchid Pond at dawn and drew back her hip length brown hair with her hand so it would not disturb the water. The sound of birds cooing and cawing broke the silence. The temporary fire reaume leader stared at the black surface. It offered no reflection, but absorbed her image like a towel soaking liquid from her skin. It was time for the others to wake up.

Orchid Pond was supposed to be their connection to the Spirit, the author of all life, who gave them resources and instruction. That connection had directed her ancestors through every step of land formation when they first carved this planet. But now, when they needed it most, it had deserted them, leaving only an empty chill to replace her once unwavering faith.

Fire streamed through the aura surrounding her body, coalescing around the tips of her long fingers. She compacted the flame into a tight ball, soon blue with extreme heat, then thrust the blue flame at the water, where it burst into a cloud of steam. Once the cloud dissipated, Anna again looked for an image of some sort, anything at all that could help her. Nothing appeared. How was she supposed to lead the others without guidance and with no adults to help?

She knelt down to stir the pond with her fingers. That was something she'd been taught not to do, since children were forbidden from touching, but she was desperate. She tentatively felt the gleaming surface with the tip of her ring finger, half-afraid the water would bite it off. Nothing happened. Bolder now, she stirred the dark, obsidian depths in figure eight patterns and waited. Still nothing.

It had been five weeks since the adults were captured on their annual trip to the volcano, which lay beyond the far eastern end of the rainforest. They journeyed there every year to inspect the volcanic activity. The trip was supposed to last a week. Being chosen as a leader had been an honor for Anna, but now she knew there was no way this could end well. She raked her fingers through her hair in frustration. What did the human king want with the adults? When, as she was certain he must, would he come for the children under her care? Well, he wouldn't get them without a fight, but there was no way they could win a fight against humans.

She stood up again, sighing, having run out of ideas. What else could she do? Every option had been exhausted. She'd even tried spitting into the pond. She knelt down once more, this time in defeat.

This whole business with the king reminded her of stories about the Great War. She had still been very young when it ended. For some reason, the king had grown to believe the fire reaume were a threat to him. The attack was well planned and mercilessly carried out. When it was done, almost the entire clan had been wiped out. The handful of reaume still left disappeared into the rainforest, but when it came to the king's attention that the humans there sympathized with their plight, he herded them into the desert, over the Kipitaki mountain range. It was only a few weeks ago that she had learned what Kipitaki meant, "Old Woman," so named because it was one of the native features of the planet, formed without fire reaume intervention. She was a toddler at the time of the battle and didn't remember much, but her childhood years had certainly been shaped by it. She, in common with the few other survivors, had shared her home with many more children than those born to her parents. Every family in those early days swelled in numbers with orphaned children. The fire clan had lain low for many years afterwards, barely managing to rebuild, so why this act of hostility now? They were no threat to anyone. No one should even know the fire reaume existed; they took pains to ensure that, hiding in the forest and consuming little. So what was the reason for this unprovoked aggression?

The whooping sound of an orangutan in the distance broke her trance. She looked up from the pond. Figures stirred in the village a short distance away. She could see snatches of movement through a multitude of trees as the clan carried out their morning chores: fire tending, gathering food, making coffee and breakfast, doing laundry, and cleaning. Bamboo homes, fringed with thick thatch, lay in a subdued patchwork around a large fire pit. Somehow, all of these features blended into their environment, subtly woven into the fabric of the forest. Everything from homes to clothes providing a perfect camouflage, so that if someone stumbled down the path in passing, they could only identify the community by sound, and there was usually a lot of that.

It was almost time for the morning meeting, but Anna was in no hurry to see anyone or to relinquish her precious time alone. She desperately needed to be able to admit, at least to herself, that she was scared; to have the luxury of a private space to shed tears, each tear a tiny prayer disappearing into the black void before her.

"Spirit," she begged, her voice catching in her throat. "If you're in the water, show me. Prove that you care. Tell me what to do." She waited again, almost sure, given the force of her sending, that something would happen, that the Spirit would answer. But the pond's surface remained empty and still."

Anna forced herself to rise; wiping the tears from her face she donned a mask of self-assurance for the others. She smelled coffee. Glancing up, she saw a youth about her height and equally slender, with knobby knees and shoulders, carrying a hollow gourd from which trailed a wisp of steam.

"Thank you, Juan." Anna took the gourd gratefully and sipped at its contents.

Juan smiled, the smile dying away nervously as he stared at

the water, to be replaced by a frown.

"What is it?" she asked.

"Oh, nothing really," he began. "It's just ... I don't suppose you saw anything today?"

Anna stifled a sigh. "No, Juan, I'm afraid not."

Juan turned away, not meeting her gaze. "Well, I guess there's not much we can do about it. I mean, there's no way to force the Spirit to tell us anything, is there?" he probed cautiously.

"No. There's nothing we can do. I'm doing the same things our king and queen did when they were here. We're keeping the same routine, but the water gives us nothing. It's as if the Spirit disappeared along with our parents." She placed her hand on his bony shoulder. "I'm so sorry, Juan." Momentarily, his lips quivered, but he quickly straightened up, burying any flicker of concern and turned to join the throng of fire reaume youth, gathering on wooden benches stacked around the side of the pond.

Anna waited for everyone to settle before speaking. "Orchid Pond has yielded nothing in the five weeks since the grown ups were taken from us. I don't know why. This is a blow to say the least. That's all the more reason to band close together and stay quiet."

"Perhaps we should fight." A girl's voice called out and the speaker stood up. She looked solid and squat, with squared shoulders and strong muscles. "We could rescue those who are still alive."

"That's out of the question, Beta," Anna answered. "To be honest, I think we should consider moving the location of our village and going into hiding. Orchid Pond isn't yielding any information. I think they might attack us next."

"But why leave? We're more powerful than they are," Beta argued.

"We're more powerful, yes, but I guarantee you — we don't have what it takes to survive, much less win a conflict with the king. Your parents entrusted me with keeping you safe, and that's what I plan to do."

"Maybe we should hear what Raquel and Maria have to say," Beta pressed, sparking a murmur that ran through the assembled reaume.

"They're too young," Anna said.

"Still, they're our rightful leaders," Beta insisted. "We should at least hear them out." The rest of those present nodded their heads as if this was indeed a reasonable request.

"Fair enough," Anna said, relenting, looking around for the sisters, gradually beginning to realize, as no one moved to speak, that the girls were absent. The only sound was a slight rustle as some geckos darted through a mass of ferns.

A cold lump of fear settled in the pit of Anna's stomach. "Where are Raquel and Maria?" she asked. "Does anyone know why they're not here?"

"I haven't seen them since last night," a voice called.

"Has anyone heard from them this morning?" Anna asked again.

A young boy with dusty brown hair and eyebrows drawn in serious concentration got to his feet. "They went out extra early to gather firewood. It was still dark."

"Are you sure you saw them, Marco?"

Marco nodded. "I woke up early. I was thirsty and got a drink from the jug of water outside my door. I saw them walk by. They said we were running low on firewood and they were going to find more."

Anna fought her rising panic. She knew the sisters would never miss morning meeting unless there was a problem. Choking back her fear, she smoothed a calm mask over her worry.

"It's not like them to miss the meeting. Perhaps they got distracted," she said, her steady tone immediately reaching out to soothe the anxious group. She paused, thinking. "Maybe we'd better go and look for them." Her eyes searched the group.

"Those who are ten and under — you know the drill. Each of you take a younger child or two. Find a tree or large bush and mask yourselves within it. Stay quiet. The rest of you — come with me.

The assembly immediately split into two, the older clan members gathering closer to her, while the younger children scampered away, grabbing hold of even smaller hands as they hurried to find a hiding place.

Anna searched the faces of those close to her. "If you find them, and there's any sign they might be in trouble, alert me quietly," she told them, keeping her voice low. "When I give the signal, don't hesitate. Gather your fire and be ready to use it!"

It was a somber group that collected on a cliff overlooking the ocean. Waves crashed on the spired rocks below but the sound barely reached their ears. The sky was lined with a thin layer of grey clouds, and rain fell intermittently. It was as if the heavens, too, were grieving at the loss of this much loved woman.

Clara squeezed Aedan's hand. A group of dark skinned figures with hair like black wool, many of whom wore long braids, surrounded one side of the seaweed entwined casket, and Clara at last knew where Aedan's hair had come from. They were the ocean reaume, whose power her husband expressed. On the other side were a number of regal faces with strong features and skin like dark leather. They were layered in deerskin clothes and colorful robes, laced with brightly colored, beaded adornments. Supposedly they were air reaume, but were called the Eagle clan. They kept to themselves, even more so than the other reaume, but had come to mourn the passing of Aedan's grandmother, his father's mother; an ocean reaume who'd married into the Eagle Clan and spent her life with her husband's family. Someone on the latter side said a few words about her life, how she'd left her family and all that was familiar to live among the stars with strange reaume. They told of what a blessing she had been to her family.

Clara listened intently. What wonderful words, she wished she could have known Aedan's grandmother, Reina, they had called her. There was much she could have learned from Reina about living in a different clan. She did wish she had someone to talk with sometimes. It was hard to be singled out amongst those you would call your own, even if she would not have it any other way. She would be like Reina, she decided, because she would love her new family like Reina had loved hers, and they would come to rely on her in just the same way.

After the funeral she saw Reina's husband. He sat aside from the others; his large frame slumped forward on a wooden chair, his expression vacant. Clara's heart went out to him, he looked so lost, much like an abandoned child would look. She ladled a cup of huckleberry tea from a bowl carved out of wood that stood on a nearby table and carried it over to where he sat. "Here," she said, holding the cup out *to him, waiting as he took her offering with a weak smile on his lips and tears in his eyes. Clara laid her hand gently on his shoulder. "I'm so sorry," she said.*

Finally some life flowed back into his face. He nodded. "Thank you." He sighed, patting her soft hand with his rough one, dried and calloused by a life of hard work in a harsh climate. "You know," he said, his gaze fixed on another time and another place. "I still remember the first day I saw her, as clear as if it were only yesterday." He gave a lopsided grin. "Some days I have trouble remembering my own name, but I can remember that day as fresh and clear as mountain dew. I'd flown to the bay to fish. And I saw her, plunging in and out of the water among a group of dolphins." He laughed, a dry, hollow sound. "She looked as one of them, but so lovely. I came back many times to that place, to watch her frolic with the dolphins. Each time I flew lower and lower, until, one time, she rose up from the water and pulled me down with her into the waves." His gaze cleared and he looked at Clara. "She was beautiful," he said. "We had so much fun together..." his voice cracked as tears rolled down his face.

Chapter 13

Chameleons

"Look out!" Khalid called and yanked Lahcen to the ground. Less than a second later, a blue ball of flame streaked past where Lahcen had stood. Another flew at Qeriya, but she was ready and swiped the air to deflect it onto a nearby tree, leaving a blackened scar on its trunk. They were suddenly aware of aggressive stares closing in from every direction.

Khalid and his siblings quickly formed a loose circle, with their cousins at the center, like mother elephants protecting their young. Despite efforts to shove her back, Raquel forcefully nudged her way in between Khalid and Qeriya, leaving Maria to jump up and down behind them. Khalid felt fresh panic as, inspecting the forest, he saw not a few, but a sea of eyes.

"It's all right! We're all friends. These are our human cousins!" Raquel shouted. She and Maria waved their arms to signal everyone not to shoot.

"Raquel, don't believe them! It's got to be a trick, especially coming on the heels of the attack," a woman's voice called.

Khalid, tracking the voice back to its origin, could just make out the curve of a woman hidden within the vegetation.

"No ... no, don't you recognize them from the pictures in Orchid Pond?" Raquel pleaded. "And ... and they have powers, not fire, but still ... please don't be rash!"

Everyone paused as the strangers surveyed one another with guarded curiosity. Khalid strained to see more bodies to go with the disconcerting eyes. While fire reaume looked similar to humans, they appeared to have an innate ability to camouflage with their surroundings when still, and apparently moved so silently that not even their own kind could hear them approach; Raquel and Maria seemed as surprised as they had been at being ambushed.

"Who are these humans?" the same woman's voice asked. She stepped forward and her shape emerged from the undergrowth as if she was stepping out of a hidden picture. More reaume soon followed.

Khalid forced himself to stop gawping. The woman who had spoken from cover was a vision of loveliness. Her dark eyes shimmered and while her voice sounded wary, her tone was calm. Flawless cinnamon skin matched her aura. Each reaume, Khalid realized, exhibited a hue of a distinct tone. It was as if the heat that radiated off their bodies was tinted.

"They're not with the king, Anna," Raquel said. "They're our cousins, the ones from the desert. Remember seeing them win the competitions yesterday?"

Anna examined them, walking stiffly in a circle to assess each one. When she finally reached Khalid, her pupils noticeably dilated and her skin shone pale yellow. For all of their physical camouflage, fire reaume were obviously not good at hiding their emotions.

"Yes! I remember you, you're the climber."

Khalid struggled for something to say but he was dazzled by a smile gorgeous to behold.

She grasped his hand. "I hoped we'd meet. I'm Anna."

Khalid was acutely aware that his cheeks and ears were burning. He knew his brother must be smiling, accumulating more fodder for their unending war of words.

"I can't believe you're here," she said, tugging his hand to move him into a walk.

Everyone relaxed and more bodies emerged from the greenery as if stepping from a picture.

Khalid docilely allowed himself to be led, captivated by this nymph who, against all good sense, appeared to claim him as her own. It was the first time he'd held hands with a woman, other than his mother or sister. Such contact was suspect in the desert, but she was in charge here. Who was he to argue? He wondered if touching electricity would feel like this? Could it be a trap? It was possible, but all common sense had short-circuited.

Of course, it probably wasn't a trap. After all, his parents couldn't have told them about their heritage with things as they were. All they could do, he thought, with a sadness born out of new understanding, was discourage them from using their abilities. He remembered being small, walking with his mother, when a cactus flower bloomed. It called to him, but she wouldn't let him near it. He knew it had bloomed for him, he could sense it, and somehow he knew that she knew, but she deliberately guided him away. No, his parents would never have told him about all these relatives.

"I'm curious to know more about this Orchid Pond, your … majesty?" Anna smiled and Khalid felt his knees start to give way.

"I'm not a majesty. I've taken temporary charge until the king and queen return, or the heirs are old enough to rule. Your cousins, Raquel and Maria, are the princesses."

Khalid looked at his cousins. Raquel was walking, chatting with Qeriya, while Maria flipped in rapid circles, curls bouncing in front of her, entertaining Lahcen. Raquel saw that Khalid and Anna were looking back at them.

"Maria," she called, but her sister ignored her. "Maria, would you pay attention? Anna's looking." Raquel grabbed her sister in mid-flip to stop her, but she might as well try to tame an irritated python. The young princess flipped anyway and hurled her big sister into the mud.

"What did you say, Raquel?" Maria feigned ignorance, holding her hand to her ear.

Seeing all eyes on her, Raquel waved meekly to signal that she was all right and emitted a neon orange glow.

"Now that's my idea of a princess," Khalid said, breaking any lingering tension; the crowd laughed. As they made their way back through the forest, fire reaume surrounded Lahcen and Qeriya, laughing and asking questions, but none interfered with the temporary queen and her catch as they meandered down a trodden path. Everywhere he looked, Khalid saw trails branching off one another, like veins on a leaf.

"So will Raquel take the crown since she's the eldest?" he asked.

"In our community, sibling heirs rule together with whomever they marry. The first couple to bear children becomes the ruling family. But the leaders are the servants. Everyone is valuable, as opposed to the human kingdom. We don't acknowledge the human king's authority." Anna was silent for a while before adding, "Your coming to us is not an accident."

"What do you mean?" Khalid asked, reaching out his hand to examine an ornate orchid attached to a nearby palm.

"Our parents, all of the adults in our clan, have been captured by the king, and now you come. It can't be coincidence. The Spirit has answered us at last."

Khalid let go of the floral stem and considered how to answer. "I guess I'm surprised to hear you say that. We weren't aware we were expected here. We left suddenly because our parents are sick and we're trying to help them. We're on a search to find a flower that can heal them, the Paintbrush."

"Do they have an anomaly? People in our village have died from genetic anomalies, but unfortunately there's no cure." She lowered her eyes. "The king claims to have a treatment, but anyone who goes to the palace never returns."

"No one in our village can leave, so anyone with an anomaly dies at home. Our friend is a doctor, he said that anomalies are really a bunch of genetic disorders, but our parents don't have a genetic syndrome. They have a rare bacterial illness. It can be treated with the right antibiotic, and that grows on this particular flower. It's hard to explain all that's happened—" Khalid paused as the full weight of what had occurred in the past two days crashed down on him. He forced himself to continue. "But the king you don't acknowledge just poisoned our entire village. It happened right before we left. If Doctor Michael hadn't called us away from there, well, we'd be dead too." As Khalid said this he felt an injection of guilt penetrate his heart. How could he have doubted Doctor Michael after he saved them from genocide? He'd risked so much to protect them.

Anna's eyes, when she looked at him, were brimming with unshed tears. "You've been through a lot. We've lost our parents, but you've lost everyone. I've heard of this flower. It grows in the foothills of the mountains, a delicate bloom that resembles a paintbrush. But as we speak, the mountains are being covered with snow. It's winter there. You can't get the flower until it warms up," she said, troubled.

Khalid glanced back. Lahcen was blasting Maria's fireballs with water and making steam. Qeriya and Raquel raced in a loop to see who was faster. "I've heard of snow," he said.

"Wait with us for a few months," Anna suggested, "just until the snow melts in the mountains. Then we'll help you."

"It's just ... our parents need us to hurry. I don't know how long it'll take us to get to the mountains. It may be spring before we reach them. I don't think we can afford to wait."

Anna came to a stop beside a cluster of anthurium sporting pink blooms. She absently stroked a leaf. "Let's scan Orchid Pond and see if it holds any wisdom for you. It normally connects us with the Spirit. Ever since our parents were captured, though, it hasn't worked for us. I'm not sure it'll yield anything, but it's worth a try."

"So is this Orchid Pond an oracle? I've heard of oracles in legends and myths, but at this time it's hard to tell which of our legends and myths are true."

"An oracle? Yes, I suppose you could say that it's an oracle. It's one of only a few oracles where the Spirit communicates with us."

Khalid's eyes brightened. "Thank you, we'd appreciate any help we can get." As they walked on, Khalid felt as if his head were spinning. The wealth of greenery, endless water, and life blooming everywhere overwhelmed him. The plants and trees responded to his energy, parting to allow him to move through them unobstructed and caressing his arms and legs in gentle gestures of greeting and connection. He could feel their joy and he knew they could sense his. In the desert, he connected with grass shoots, cattails and flowering cacti, experiencing each one's unique character as a separate melody, but here, in this wealth of plant life, all he heard was orchestral. The plants were intensely curious, excited. Somehow, even they had been expecting him.

"Why do they respond to you like that?" Anna asked, noticing a Hog Plum bow its branches.

"I don't know why. I sense their consciousness and they mine. I'm never alone when plants are around."

She smiled curiously. "I've never seen a human like you."

"Well I've never seen a fire reaume at all," he replied and stopped to scoop some chicle out of a sapodilla tree. The tree extended a bough to meet his lips, offering up some of its sap on a leaf.

"We boil that down to make gum," she said. "We chew gum for enjoyment, but don't usually swallow it."

"What's the point of that?" he asked.

"Aren't you offending the tree? It seems to understand you somehow."

"No, it doesn't hear or speak or even think in language," he said as he licked the sap, but it was too much of a liquid to chew.

"Are your parents with the others?" he asked carefully.

Anna bowed her head. "I don't know if they were captured or … killed. We don't know what's happened. All we do know is that we haven't been able to find any bodies. I worry more that they're injured and suffering."

She offered him a small, painful smile. "There's our village, over there." She gestured to the right but, though his eyes searched the direction she pointed in, Khalid could see nothing. How was it he could sense plants and trees from far away, but he couldn't see a fire reaume five feet from his face?

Anna must have guessed some of what he was thinking from his expression. "Don't you see it?"

Khalid relaxed his gaze, as he did, outlines grew more prominent and he could see various pairs of eyes looking at him. No one moved, no one spoke. The longer he looked, the more detail appeared. Bamboo huts with open doors circled around a central area. His attention was drawn to one dwelling in particular, set to the side of the others and closest to the trail. He slowly waded through a clump of peace lilies and approached the hut entrance to see curtains pulled back, separating what he expected were sleeping quarters.

"That's Raquel and Maria's place," Anna said.

Khalid peered inside. The hut was a similar size to his salt-brick home. It was simple and sparse, with cushioned beds hung suspended from woven vines. A few clothes clung to wooden posts on the wall. The ceiling was strung with vines which circled and knotted around bottles of nameless creams, lotions and powders, leaving them dangling in midair. Two carved bowls straddled the midline of the floor. A leaf covered one bowl, while the other lay exposed, the leaf having slipped to the side. The uncovered bowl contained a toothbrush made from soft bristles. Along with the exposed toothbrush, a messy bed, scattered clothes and an assortment of small trinkets lay on the same side of the dwelling. The other side was well ordered and polished.

"Maria?" Khalid asked, gesturing to the messy side.

"That's right. How did you guess?"

"Even though I just met her, it's easy to see Maria's print on the place." Khalid smiled and Anna nodded in agreement.

As they continued through the village, a large iron pot resting on a wide fire pit piqued Khalid's interest. Tangential to the pot, a metal spit was braced by triangular wooden beams and hung over the rest the pit. Attached to one end was a crank. He had read about communal roasts in school, but of course, he hadn't experienced one, since meat never wandered into his part of the desert anymore. They soon came to the end of the village and continued on down the well-used path.

Within minutes he saw what could only be Orchid Pond, as still and dark as if it were black ice, it gleamed like liquid hematite. Cohane palm, fig and banana trees surrounded the stagnant water. Khalid could just make out the colors of a giant anaconda wound in the branches of one of the figs. Red-eyed tree frogs frolicked on a nearby bromeliad and he spotted a rusty spider perched on the bark of a neighboring palm.

Khalid and Anna approached the pond with cautious steps. Khalid could tell that Anna searched the cold depths for a sign, but, as he too stared into the forbidding waters, he could not even see his reflection. He bent down to stir it with his fingers, as if to wake it up, but Anna halted his moving hand. "Don't touch it," she said. "I don't know what it'll do to you. Just look into it; it yields when it's ready."

Khalid did as bid, fixing his gaze on the flat surface. Time inched by, but then, as he was about to give up and pull away, out of the corner of his eye, a glimmer snagged his attention. He stared hard … there was no change, and yet, there was a feeling, a sense of something immanent in the air. An image of a large room appeared, flashing across the still waters so suddenly that he blinked a few times, thinking he might be hallucinating. It flashed again; only this time the picture remained. Somehow he could see inside the room, as if the walls were invisible. In the picture, a group of adult fire reaume gathered around someone on a stretcher.

"I can see the light," Anna exclaimed, "it's showing you something!" Her eyes darted away from the water, coming to rest on him.

"I see figures," Khalid answered slowly. "They're rising out of the pond. Can you see them? Are they your parents?"

Beside him, he heard Anna draw in a sharp breath. "You found them!"

"I'm pregnant," Clara told Aedan as he prepared for bed.

"Di you thay pregant?" he asked, a lathered toothbrush filling his mouth.

"Yes, I said pregnant. We're going to have a baby," she answered, smiling wide, her skin glowing.

Aedan hurriedly spit out his toothpaste into a carved bowl and took a swig of water to rinse. Banging his bowl down carelessly, toothpaste smeared across his mouth, he stared at her. "But that's not possible, there must be some mistake!" he exclaimed, moving over to the bed where she was sitting, tucked beneath the covers.

Clara's joy disappeared as she saw the alarm in his expression. "It's not a mistake, Aedan. I'm already twelve weeks into the pregnancy. "I didn't think it could happen either, so I didn't think to check before, but it's certain. I saw the baby today, in Orchid Pond.

"But, how's this possible?"

"You were possible when everyone thought there was no way different reaume could conceive together. So why does this seem so strange to you?"

Aedan dry washed his face with his hands. "Because, well, you're human. Reaume at least share the same history. Human and reaume are so ... different." He paused, visibly collecting himself. "It's ... wonderful ... really, and I'm excited, it's just a surprise, that's all."

"Well." Clara wasn't convinced. "I hope it's a good one, because this baby's coming — like it or not."

"Of course, it's a wonderful surprise!" Aedan insisted. "I ... my mind just jumps ahead, that's all. We'll just have to be more careful, now that we have a baby. We'll have to try to keep it quiet."

"But why?" Clara's voice shook. Her wonderful news was turning to ashes. "What're you afraid will happen?"

Aedan's face instantly softened. He sat down beside her, looping his arm loosely about her shoulders. "Clara, you've seen how ruthless the old king was, both to your family and to mine. He was out to squash anyone who had the slightest ability to take away his power. Now there's a new king, and unless he's more just than his father, imagine *what he'd do if he found out that a human and a reaume had a child together?"*

A cold shiver went down Clara's spine, she stared at her knees, bent, under the covers. She felt as if she was doing something wrong, bringing a baby into a world where he would be marked for life. But why should she feel guilty? Despite the old queen's foretelling, up until it had been confirmed, she hadn't truly thought it possible for her to get pregnant. It had to be the will of the Spirit that he was to be born.

"Aedan, we can't worry about that now," she said as a strong conviction washed over her. She grabbed his hand reassuringly. "This is our calling, to parent this child, given to us in trust. This child is meant to be."

Chapter 14

Vengeance on a Stick

"Come on guys, you have to come with Raquel and me on the hunt," Maria ordered Qeriya and her brothers. The meeting had just finished and fresh morning light glowed around them, making colorful blooms pop into view as if illuminated from the inside. "Anna told us we could have a feast to celebrate your coming here, and we're providing the main course, the wild boar."

Qeriya wondered what meat might taste like. It had disappeared in the desert long before she could find out.

"But, Maria, you're so young. Are you allowed to hunt?" Lahcen asked in surprise.

"I'm not that young," Maria answered. "And yes, I love hunting — it's exciting!" She rubbed her hands together with malicious glee.

"I'm glad I'm not a boar!" Lahcen exclaimed. "I used to go hunting with our dad when I was young, but just when I reached the age to try it myself, the meat disappeared. So I've never hunted, unless you count the Geckos I tried to bash with a stick when we first met. The only meat we've had since is scorpion, if you can really call that meat. I'm guessing it's nothing like whatever this boar thing is."

"Who would ever want to hurt geckos? They eat all the mosquitos, although they can get pesky at times. Here, let me introduce you to Juan, he's the hunt honcho, and a great hunter, legendary if you ask me," Maria said, leading them to a group gathered nearby. The guy called Juan stood up and extended a hand. Qeriya thought he looked about her age although he was at least as tall as Khalid.

"Nice to meet you," he said warmly.

Qeriya could tell at once that Juan was a people person, well, would be if he was a person. He wore the typical tunic and leggings, which she was beginning to realize was a sort of fire reaume uniform, but he carried hand carved knives in holsters around his hips.

"I'm glad you've decided to come with us. This is Travis, Beta, Carl and Lucia," he said and the other hunters nodded their heads in greeting. "We're usually six, so you all make us nine. That means more arms to carry the meat."

"So, what are we hunting again?" Lahcen asked, his eyes twinkling. "I'm hungry already."

"Don't be," Lucia piped from behind. She didn't smile, her mouth moved as she chewed her gum. "It'll be a long time before we sink our teeth into anything. We're looking for a large, juicy boar."

"But you have fire power. Can't you just blast them like a blow torch or something?" Lahcen asked.

The others squirmed. "That's cruel!" Beta exclaimed.

"You're killing the animal ... aren't you?" Lahcen asked.

"We are," Juan agreed. "But what you suggest would be more painful than a quick, clean kill. We prefer the death to be instantaneous, which is tricky, because boar are fast and aggressive."

"Maria told us about them," Qeriya said. "She warned us that they're pretty dangerous," she added.

"That, they are." Juan nodded, his expression serious. "Suffice it to say that boar are cunning, but their meat is worth every ounce of energy spent in hunting them. The main thing to remember is for us to watch each other's back." He directed these instructions to the hunters. "Since there are nine of us, I'll watch two backs, Raquel and Qeriya. Maria, you and Lahcen team up.

Qeriya saw him glow yellow as he called her name. What did that mean? Did he like her? Flattered as she was by the thought, he would not find his attentions returned. She had allowed herself to be smitten once and it had backfired on her. No matter how worthy and good-looking Juan might be, it was a lost cause.

They filed through the forest, Lahcen and Qeriya tearing their way through plants and brush while the others dodged them. After a lifetime of growing up here the natives knew every inch of the wood, winding past large mango trees and around tangles of bamboo with precision.

Before long Juan lifted his arm, signaling the group to stop. "This will do. From here we need to move slowly," he ordered, "and keep your eyes peeled. They're somewhere close." He positioned himself beside Qeriya as they set off once more. "So, how do you like it here?" he asked, giving her a friendly smile.

"It's beautiful, full of water and life everywhere. I can hardly move it's so thick with plants. I keep thinking, if the desert had a fraction of the water in this place, the crop yield would be amazing."

"We don't need to plant many crops. We mostly harvest what's already here."

Qeriya shook her head. "Sometimes, I swear I'm in a dream," she said as she delicately floated over a patch of brush. "I keep thinking, soon I'll wake up, and that'll be the end of all this."

"Well, isn't that what happened to you? The world as you knew it ended. That's not a dream — it's your reality. I'm sure it's hard to trust that anything is real after something like that." Juan removed a long, curved sword from a sheath on his belt and walked in front of her to slice through the brush and break trail.

Qeriya gasped, recoiling. There was something intimidating about seeing him brandish such a weapon. "What do you do with that?" she asked nervously.

"It's a machete," Juan said. "I use it to clear brush on the forest floor and cut through produce."

"Oh, I see." She dropped back a few paces, but she could quickly see that her ploy had failed as he simply slowed down, matching his steps to hers.

"So, how are you doing now that everything's changed so

completely?"

Qeriya considered for a while. "It feels like every day, every hour, there's a new layer of truth I uncover that's so wholly different to anything I knew. It's hard to count on anything being true anymore."

A clump of peace lilies lay straight ahead and as she waded through them, Qeriya offered up a silent, wordless prayer to the Spirit. Peace was what she wanted most and yet it was furthest from her reach.

"That must be hard," Juan's voice was thick with sympathy. "Whatever we do involves counting on things. I mean, we're hunting boar, counting on there being some out there, and that our methods of catching them will work like they have in the past. We have to count on things or we get stuck."

"Stuck," Qeriya repeated, savoring the word. "Yeah, that's it. I feel stuck. We found out that what we thought was home is really a prison. And here it's so different from home it doesn't seem real. My parents aren't who we spent all our lives thinking they were, and I have relatives I never knew existed."

"You can count on your clan here," Juan said evenly. He met her gaze with his own. "And you can count on me."

Qeriya admired his chestnut eyes and graceful manner. Despite her determination to remain unmoved, she couldn't help but find him attractive. The feeling she got when she looked at him was all too familiar, and she didn't like it.

"Count on you? I just met you," she snapped. A moment later, seeing the hurt etched on his face, she would have called the words back if she could. He turned away from her, continuing to clear the way.

Qeriya followed after him, heavy with regret. He was such a good listener, so perceptive and caring; she hadn't meant to hurt him. She lightly touched his shoulder. "I'm sorry, really I am. You've all been good to us. We're very grateful. But as much as we want to get to know you, we need to move on. I don't know what's happened to our parents or our friend — Doctor Michael could even be dead because he helped us. I feel terrible having doubted him."

"Yes, I heard about what happened, but it seemed like leaving home and going the way you did was the only thing that made sense at the time. You had to act. You had to make a decision based on the information available," Juan said.

"But doesn't loyalty amount to anything? Sometimes we just need to trust!" Her ears started to heat up and she realized she was arguing with him as if he were Khalid and not Juan, a nice guy she met five minutes ago who was trying to offer his support.

"Yes, and trust him you did, despite the cautions you took. But you have to balance trust with thinking for yourself, Qeriya, especially when you live in a human world."

"What do you mean by human world?" She paused as something flashed past. It was so fast, she couldn't really be sure she had seen anything at all, but the brush rustled loudly, affirming her suspicions. "What was that?" Qeriya stared anxiously into the undergrowth.

"Did you see something?" Juan holstered his machete, scanning the ground.

It struck Qeriya as ironic that Juan would replace his weapon at the moment of attack, but he was fire reaume after all. "I don't know," she said, pointing. "I thought I saw something over there."

Juan raised his hand and blew a loud whistle through his fingers. The others swung around and gathered in a circle, their backs to one another.

"I don't think we should over react," Qeriya said. "I'm sure it's nothing. It's probably just a gecko. Heck, maybe I'm seeing things," she babbled.

Juan flew like an arrow into the air, trying to spot whatever it was that she had seen, and then shot downwards again, into the creature's path, sending it into reverse. The other fire reaume flew in obvious formation, spreading into a wide line, low to the ground, weaving in an almost choreographed pattern through one another; some speeding up and others slowing down in a predetermined sequence; a killing machine inching forward, seeking to catch the boar. The hunters did a wide sweep of the forest, heading right for it. A ripple went through the undergrowth as the beast charged, but instead of netting it, the wild animal nailed Carl, who had tipped off balance during flight. A tusk caught his tunic, sending him spiraling out of control. Beta raced to help.

Raquel, Maria, keep Qeriya and Lahcen off the ground and watch out," Juan ordered. "There's a whole pack of them out there. I spotted them when I was in the air."

Qeriya twisted this way and that, straining to catch sight of any of the animals. Abruptly, she was face to face with one, a huge thing, with mean little eyes. She leapt into the air seconds before the boar lunged for her, snorting loudly, its sharp tusks and teeth gouging at her ankles. Who exactly, she wondered, was hunting whom?

Raquel, already towing Lahcen, grabbed her, pushing them both higher into the air. Qeriya could see Maria hurrying towards them, trailing flames like a live rocket. She blasted the beasts with fireballs, singeing their noses and Qeriya watched as all but one fled.

Maria ran a small spear across the length of the lingering beast's skull, as if she was attempting to scalp it. Qeriya was impressed at Maria's ability to attack, as she herself felt paralyzed with fear. Snarling, the beast fought back, thrusting its bony jaw towards Maria. Qeriya didn't need to be told that a bite from those monstrous jaws would be cruel indeed, but Maria beat the boar down. Qeriya glanced at Raquel, who's eyes were nearly popping out of her head as she watched her sister battle. "It must be strange to see someone you've protected for so long protecting you," Qeriya said and Raquel nodded, open-mouthed. The others wove around one another, occasionally disappearing into the shadows as if they were balls of light being sucked into black holes, to chase another of the boar, reappearing minutes later.

The animal that had stood its ground finally ran off but Juan stayed apart and on lookout, against its return. The others gathered together in the long grass, in their characteristic circle, backs toward the center, waiting. "So," Qeriya asked, "what's the plan of attack?"

"The plan," Raquel explained, "is to trap one of them in a corner and make a kill before it or one of its clan kills us first."

"They'll hunt you?"

"Yeah. That's one reason we hunt them, that and because their meat is incredibly tasty."

"You risk your life and limb not to hurt them unnecessarily when they would dismember you without a thought? I wish I'd known this before I volunteered to come," Qeriya said.

"I can teach them about hunting, Raquel. I'm the hunter after all," Maria said with zeal, reaching an arm behind Qeriya standing between them, to poke Raquel derisively in the back. "You're just along for the fun."

"Suit yourself," Raquel said, stepping away from any more pokes.

"After trapping a boar, we make sure that it's adult size and slam its head with fire balls," Maria said, imitating the action with her arms.

"But I thought you didn't want to kill it with fire?" Qeriya asked, her eyes darting from one sister to the other in confusion.

"We don't light it on fire," Maria insisted. "We slam it with fire balls to knock it out and immediately withdraw the fire."

"Oh, yeah, that's much less cruel," Qeriya replied sarcastically, hearing Raquel giggle.

"It's less cruel than burning to death," Maria sneered.

"If your aim's good."

"Do you doubt it?" Maria said, forming a ball of flame. "See that orchid way over there?"

"You mean the one right next to Juan's head?" Qeriya asked pointedly.

"Yeah, that one," Maria confirmed, pulling her arm back to fire the ball.

The scene reminded Qeriya of the pictures of reaume shooting fireballs back in the desert cave.

"Watch me nail it."

"But you might hit Juan," Qeriya warned.

"Why do you care, you got a thing for him?" Maria challenged.

"Maria, don't play around like that, especially not now," Raquel said, turning towards her sister. The others didn't speak, they had casually widened the circle to give the sisters space to argue.

"I'm not playing." Maria slammed her fireball squarely at the target and the orchid fell limp off the tree.

"Why's it always the flowers? We're supposed to care for them. Why do you always destroy the epiphytes?" Raquel cried.

"Why not? They make the best targets," Maria replied, as if oblivious to any accusation.

"I care about Juan, but not the way you're insinuating," Qeriya said, shooting Maria a cold, hard stare. "I just met him!"

"Good, I'm glad we have an understanding, 'cause he's mine!" Maria snarled, her eyes flashing towards Juan to make sure he hadn't heard.

Qeriya bit back a roaring laugh that was about to erupt, and turned away.

Raquel stepped over to give her sister a quiet scolding, watching the other hunters for a reaction, but like well-trained giants, they did not divert their attention for a second. "Don't be silly, Maria, he's too old for you. He's fifteen and you're only ten. You're too young to have a boyfriend regardless. I can't believe you would even consider it."

"He's too old for now, maybe, but not in eight years."

"You can't hang on to him for eight years!" Raquel said. "That's just plain ridiculous."

"Just watch me!" Maria yelled, determination flaring in her face.

Qeriya and Lahcen stifled a laugh.

The noise of boar rampaging in their direction had an immediate sobering effect. The fire reaume swiftly reformed, weaving and battling the shrieking, grunting pack that came boiling out of the trees, stampeding directly at them. "Maria! I need you," Juan hollered. "Help me get this one. I can trap it!"

Maria darted over to where he stood and the two charged one of the beasts, forcing it into a natural corridor formed by overgrown fallen trees. Juan herded it under a rocky outcrop at the end of the passage, while Maria quickly formed a compact fireball in her hands, tending it until it glowed blue. She flew in sharply, a few paces ahead of Juan, whipping the ball at the boar, but the animal flung its head up at the last moment and cut through the arching fire with a sharp tusk, burning its tender jowls. With a scream of rage and pain, it charged at Maria before anyone had a chance to register what was happening.

Qeriya felt as if she were swimming in a vat of honey as she saw the catastrophe about to happen and knew she was powerless to act in time. Fortunately, Juan ran up and threw Maria into the air a fraction of a second before collision.

Moments later the tense silence was split with his agonized cry as the boar, maddened by pain and frustrated at being denied its victim, dug its ugly tusk into his thigh, flinging him high into the sky. Juan tore himself free of the boar's tusk and a mass of pulp sliced through the thick air, spraying them all with his blood. Qeriya froze.

Lahcen was first to gather his wits. He surfed over to Juan, pulling water from the air on his way. Condensing the water, he formed a liquid bandage that clung to the wound, curtailing the bleeding.

Raquel gathered the hunters into a new formation before the beasts, smelling blood, attacked again. "Lahcen's holding Juan. Let's finish what we came to do while Maria takes Lahcen and Juan back to the healers!" she called.

"How about that one over there?" Beta pointed to a smaller animal. "It should be easier to get. I think it's older. It won't put up such a fight."

"No!" Maria yelled to the stunned crowd. "We're getting the one that got Juan. I'm getting it!"

Raquel eyed her sister in disbelief. "Where did you come from? You're acting like a human."

"And what's wrong with being human?" Qeriya responded, offended. "You talk like it's an insult."

"Sorry, Qeriya, Lahcen. I know that sounds bad, but what she's talking about is vengeance. Fire reaume don't take revenge, only humans do that. Anyhow, it makes more sense to target this smaller one so we don't have any more injuries."

Maria shot away, charging the aggressive boar with unmatched ferocity. She drove the beast toward a clump of large tree roots, hurling bolts of fire at it, preventing it from changing course. Just as the boar reached the trap, Maria backed up, forming her ball. She waited for the exact moment it turned to look for her and slammed the fireball into the side of its head.

The beast was dead upon impact, collapsing in a large brown heap, while the other boar broke for cover, relinquishing their potential meal together with their dead and heading for safer territory. Qeriya saw flame in Maria's eyes, a flame she knew from experience, borne out of a drive to protect someone she loved. She would wear that expression too, if only she could find Prince Liam.

"Juan's all right, Maria," Raquel's voice betrayed her own fear as she tried to quell her sister's aggression. "He'll be fine, don't worry."

Maria moved silently to the head of the group, ignoring her sister and letting the others carry the meat back to the village.

As they walked, Qeriya spied Raquel studying her sister with new eyes, muttering in a quiet voice. "It's as if she were human."

Qeriya could hear a distinct note of panic.

"What's happened to my sister?"

"The council wanted to meet with me early this morning," Aedan told Clara as they gathered wood together.

"Oh, what about?" Clara asked, waddling along. She bent over carefully to pick up some small sticks for kindling.

Aedan glanced down at the bundle of wood he carried. *"Well, you know that, normally, it's the first offspring to have children that take over from the parents as the new royal family."*

"Yes," Clara said, searching his face for some hint of what was to come.

"Well, the council decided to strike this down in our case. They're not ready to recognize human leadership. It's not you in particular that concerns them — it's your humanity that's in question. They said to tell you that their decision took so long because they like you, but in the end they decided it was too risky to set a precedent."

"Oh, Aedan, I'm sorry!"

Aedan gave a slight shake of the head. *"Don't be sorry for me. I'm happy to let my sister take over. No, it's just that — I was hoping for more from them now that they've got to know you."* He glanced away from her. *"I suppose they'll never really get used to you being human."*

"Well," Clara said, more brightly than she felt, *"it would be nice if they could accept that. I do wish they could learn to trust me more, and yet, I feel welcome and accepted here, Aedan. Maybe this will be better for us in the end. We won't have the stress of leadership along with parenting. And they'll see that I'm not upset and clamoring for power, like they assume all humans do. If we ruled together, they'd always question my judgments. This way they can be friends with me and not worry.*

Aedan cupped her face in his hand. *"You're more gracious than I am,"* he said and tenderly kissed her forehead.

Chapter 15

Feast

"You should have been there, Khalid," Lahcen said as they gathered around a bonfire, fragrant smoke rising from the animal skewered over it. "I can't believe Maria likes to hunt. I thought ten years old might be a little young."

"My thoughts exactly," Khalid said as he took a shift revolving the pig slowly over the simmering fire, basking in the salty aroma of searing flesh.

"Boy were we proved wrong," Qeriya said, watching the spit turn. She might have felt sorry for the thing if it hadn't tried to shred her ankles, and then almost crippled Juan.

Lahcen gave a small shake of the head. "When I asked Juan if Maria wasn't a little young to be hunting dangerous animals, he said that he started hunting when he was five years old. Can you believe that? Isn't that insane? He said they have to be that young to start out, otherwise they wouldn't be able to do it at all."

"Why?" Khalid asked.

"I guess, emotionally, they have a difficult time killing animals."

"So," Khalid said. "I have a hard time killing animals, but I'd do it anyway if it meant feasting on this." He gestured to the roasting carcass.

"Maybe, but according to Lucia and Beta, most fire reaume would starve before killing an animal, so they have to train into it early."

Khalid lifted the corner of his lip, looking doubtful, rotating the lathe while Qeriya brushed sauce onto the meat.

Lahcen shrugged. "My thoughts exactly, but that's what they said. Anyhow, ten years old may be better than five, but it's still too young.

"I decided to stick by her today, just in case. Although, honestly, she protected me after all was said and done." He looked from Khalid to Qeriya. "Juan told me he's been gouged by a boar twice before. As it turned out, today was number three."

A youth about Raquel's age signaled for Khalid to stop turning the skewer. He handed each of them an engraved wooden platter and proceeded to carve pieces of meat onto them. Khalid thanked him, while the other two stared open mouthed at the ribbons of pork oozing clear juice. They moved to a table lined with other food.

"And Maria? How was she?" Khalid asked.

"Angry! There was no holding her back. Here's her revenge," Qeriya said, holding up her platter.

"Yikes!" Khalid quipped as he helped himself to a banana.

"I'm glad I was there to see it. She did it all by herself," Lahcen said as they finished piling their dishes and moved to sit at a table made of bamboo. It was one of many tables radiating from a giant mango tree trunk, like the spokes of a wheel.

"I'm not sure I wanted to see it," Qeriya said, scooping some breadfruit onto her plate. "That gruesome image will be forever imprinted in my head. It's enough to stop me eating meat ever again, except it was either them on our skewers or us on theirs. Did you see the size of those tusks, Lahcen?"

"They were scary," Lahcen agreed. "Juan's lucky to be alive, if you ask me. He's with the healer now. But get this — the healer says he'll be better by evening. Can you believe it? Think what a healer as experienced as Doctor Michael could do in this place, with all these different medicines and tools. The healer said they have thousands of treatments, and an endless supply of medicines." He blew on a steaming piece of meat and nibbled it with his lips, closing his eyes as he chewed.

Khalid took a deep breath, "I must say — the smell of this meat has me in a trance."

"No kidding. I can't believe this place. Mom and Dad used to tell us stories, but I never believed that every part of them was true," Qeriya said, lifting a portion of sweet potato to her mouth. "I thought they embellished things. Even though we learned about a lot of this in school, it's different actually experiencing it, like a dream." She took another bite of the tuber and closed her eyes, savoring its smoky, sweet flavor.

"Yeah, and Mom better not wake me up from this one," Lahcen chuckled, but his amusement was short lived.

Qeriya wondered how their mom and dad were doing, but even the thought of them seemed to turn her tasty morsels into clay. She could not picture them and still enjoy the feast, and this food was too precious to waste. She didn't want to think about parents right now. Neither, it seemed, did anyone else as they gobbled their food and engaged in animated conversation.

"Juan!" Lahcen called to his friend.

Juan, pale but undaunted, stumbled to the table with a bandaged leg, a platter in his hand loaded with pork and little else.

"You better already?"

"I will be once I eat the animal that gave me this," Juan said, pointing to his wound. He sat down beside them, leaning against the tree trunk. He stole a look at Qeriya and his aura glowed yellow, but she pretended not to see. He lowered his head and it changed to peach.

"The wound wasn't too bad really," he muttered. "So, do you like the meat?"

Lahcen and Khalid rolled their eyes in extreme pleasure.

"That good, huh?"

"Should we compare it with scorpions for you?" Lahcen asked, scrutinizing a bone he had almost picked clean to see if it would yield anything more.

"Sounds appetizing," Juan said, shredding his pile of meat and adding a pinch of crushed spices that were sitting in bowls on the table.

"They're delicious," Khalid said, biting off some heart of palm and crunching it between his teeth. "If only they were bigger. But I suppose you've been spoiled by this." He nodded to the mass of food that graced their platters.

"That's true," Juan answered, letting a chunk of hard-earned pork dangle from his fingers. "But we really don't eat this much very often, only on special occasions. We usually have a light dinner, with just greens, bananas and cocoa tea in the evening."

"What sorts of stories did your parents tell?" Lahcen asked.

"I can't think of them now without feeling sad." Juan drew in a long, slow breath and let it out again before he continued. "But we grew up hearing many stories, some of which came from Orchid Pond. Our parents received a lot of information from there. Although it doesn't give us kids much." Juan looked at Khalid. "You're the only one who seems to be able to access anything."

Qeriya fished a slippery avocado slice from a bowl and took a bite, entranced by its creamy texture and flavor.

"The absence of guidance from Orchid Pond has shaken everyone's faith around here. It's supposed to be our connection with the Spirit, who supposedly cares for us. But since our parents disappeared we've needed it most, and since then it's given us nothing. I speak for all of us when I say we feel betrayed." He sat, pensive, tipping his head from side to side as if weighing some thought, then shook his head. "I've given up hope on it now. We need to think for ourselves. I believe we need to attack."

"Attack, you mean like Beta suggested?" Qeriya asked, and this time Juan dampened his glow before she had a chance to wonder at it. She felt a surge of energy. She was tired of waiting.

"Yes, I think we need to attack the king and rescue our parents," he said, and took a bite of squash sprinkled with cinnamon.

They stared at him in disbelief. "But you heard what Anna

said," Lahcen began. "That's suicide. You don't know anything about the palace, or even if they're there. You'd be going in blind and handicapped without the adults. Better to fight them here, in your own element."

Juan gave Lahcen a long look before speaking. "You're right on the one hand, but if we wait, we'll lose the element of surprise, and surprise is our best strategy." He stared down at the table for a moment, ordering his thoughts. "Listen, I know it's dangerous, but I don't think it's as hopeless as it sounds. We just need a good plan. There isn't any hope for us without our parents and elders to teach us what they know, and show us how to access Orchid Pond. No one ever considered the possibility that the adults would all be imprisoned or killed while the children survived.

"I know that Anna and the others believe the king and his giants want to kill us, but I fear worse. I think they want to make us their slaves. They want to divide us from our parents so they can control us and we'll be forced to work for them. That, to me, is worse than death." He paused, running his finger along the grain of the table. "Plus," he said, looking at each of them in turn, "if we're successful, our parents might be able to help you with your quest."

Qeriya propped her chin on her hands, elbows firmly planted on the table, deliberating what Juan had said. If they could defeat the king at the palace, they could free the prisoners and be close enough to the mountains to harvest the medicinal flower.

"We need to look in that pond again, without Anna," Khalid said.

"Why without Anna?" Lahcen asked. "Isn't she your girlfriend?"

Khalid rolled his eyes in disdain and ignored his brother's taunt. "Juan, can you take us to the pond now? I know it's not morning. I just have to try."

After a moment Juan said, hesitantly, "I suppose."

Qeriya could almost see his internal debate as he struggled to decide the right thing to do.

"Are you up to it with your injury?" Lahcen asked.

"Yeah." He nodded, coming to his decision. "I'll be fine." They left their dishes and started down a nearby path. Juan lit a small candle, encasing it in a clear glass bubble, and with him hobbling gamely along, they made their way over the short distance to where the pond lay in wait.

As they left the feast behind them in the warm, velvet night, the sound of voices was soon replaced with the chatter of birds. Many times, since arriving here, Qeriya had awakened to their competing cries and calls. This was a place that never slept.

Qeriya stayed close to Juan's light, as if light itself had the power to protect her. Geckos scurried across the trail and under plant cover as she moved past them. What was she afraid of anyway, she wondered? Snakes! It had to be snakes; those giant tubes of terror whose jaws unhinged to swallow innocent victims whole, where they'd be immobilized in total darkness and slowly digested.

"Ouch! Qeriya, what are you doing to my arm?" Khalid asked, flinching.

Qeriya was suddenly aware that not only had she grasped his arm, she was pinching it with her fingernails. "Oh, sorry, Khalid," she said and then whispered so Lahcen wouldn't hear her — or she'd never hear the end of his teasing. "It's just, well, snakes."

"Oh," Khalid whispered back. He wrapped an arm around her shoulders. "Stay close to me," he said, keeping his voice low. "They won't be able to swallow two people at once — least not without a fight."

"Thanks," she said, shooting him a grateful smile.

By the time they arrived at Orchid Pond it was pitch black. Khalid went directly to the water and stirred it with his hands. Within moments a soft white glow appeared and they could all see. The light expanded and a picture came into focus.

Qeriya gasped, but swallowed hard to choke down any sound. The image projecting from the pond was a cross section of a rock-walled prison. The rock was tinged with the metallic blue of sapphire, edged by shades of purple and red. Juan stifled a soft cry as he saw that his parents, along with many others, were being held there. This time they all examined the scene more carefully. As before, the fire reaume were massed around something on the floor. Qeriya tried to make out faces, but there were too many people.

Khalid traced his finger along the water, where the image floated, and the figures were scooped to the side, as if they were tangible objects he had pushed out of the way. The three siblings stared uncomprehendingly at the figure the reaume had been clustered around. It was Doctor Michael, his face twisted in agony. Their parents, still unconscious, lay on beds beside him.

Qeriya scrabbled a short distance away, stumbling to her hands and knees, her stomach contents pouring onto the ground in heaving waves. As soon as she was done, she wiped herself clean with a nearby leaf, but she couldn't stop the flow of tears that followed.

It was less of a cry, more of an indignant squeal, as Clara and Aedan's baby boy slid from the protection of his mother's womb and took his first breath in the steamy tent. Clara fell back against the cushions, spent. It was over.

"I knew our child would be different, but a wild boar wasn't what I had in mind!" Aedan chuckled. "Don't let the hunters hear him!"

Clara and her husband would never look any more different than they did at this instant. Aedan, giddy and trembling with excitement, waited for the baby to be checked over before taking his son into his arms and carrying him to the bedside, where Clara lay sweating and breathless. She forced her eyes to open so that she could behold her newborn, but laughter was beyond her. Relief was all she felt. The pain was ended and her baby was healthy.

The fire attendants heated bamboo blankets in an oven and covered her with them. Once she was comfortable, Aedan placed their son into her arms and Clara held him for the first time. She stared, mesmerized by the cloudy dark-blue eyes and the rosebud mouth. She touched the tiny fist with a finger and smiled. "Hello, little one," she said softly. "It's me, it's your mama." She kissed his cheek, marveling at the softness of his skin. "They call you the miracle baby," she said. "I'm just so glad you're here, in my arms, at last."

Aedan stood transfixed, smiling, crying. Suddenly he remembered his scarf pouch and he pulled out a vial, twisting off the tight lid carefully.

Clara looked up. "What are you doing? What is that?"

"It's a serum made by your parents for their grandson."

"My parents? What do you know of my parents? Where are they?"

Aedan lowered himself down beside her, gently placing his hand on her thigh. "I'm afraid they're still imprisoned, but they're well. My mother went to see them again — they gave her this."

Clara felt her throat constrict. It was as if she'd been transported through time, back to the very moment she had been forced to leave them. Her grief was raw at the mention of them. How she wished they could be here to hold their grandson. "What's the serum for?"

"It's a special virus they created — to mask his genetic connection with reaume. It only takes a few drops on his tongue." He nodded at their newborn son. "This way, even if he hears about him, the king won't be able to find him.

Clara looked down at the tiny child now asleep in her arms: unable to recall when she'd ever felt so much sadness and joy, pain and relief all at the same time. If only her parents could be here with her, could hold their little grandson. A lone tear crawled down her cheek.

Chapter 16

Hallucination

"I realize the king took our parents prisoner four months ago, but I want to be certain we know where they are before we wage an attack," Anna announced at their morning meeting.

Qeriya sat with Beta, amongst a small group gathered on one end of the benches, listening as they muttered their discontent. Ever since the pond had revealed an image of Qeriya's parents and Doctor Michael, each morning began with an inspection of the water to see if anything had changed or if a new detail might catch their attention. To Qeriya, Beta and Beta's followers, which included Maria, this was intensely aggravating. The recurring image consistently yielded little information as to where the adults were being held, other than rock walls painted in a rainbow of colors, but according to Beta, they didn't need any more information, and sitting around waiting for confirmation that might never come was insufferable. Qeriya agreed. She had long gone past patience, her first glimpse of their parents, and Doctor Michael, suffering, had seen to that.

"They're in the palace. We need to strike," Beta argued, standing up, her aura swelling into a red cloud around her.

"We've been over this, Beta," Anna countered, closing her eyes for a moment to block out the conflict while she formed her reply. "We don't know where they're located for certain, and until we do, I'm not about to risk an attack."

"They have to be in the palace, where else could they be?" Beta said, her loud voice laced with frustration. "We need to do something while our parents are still alive." Many of the youth nodded, agreeing.

Anna eyed her charges, speaking slowly and purposefully to each of them. "We don't know where they are, and attacking the castle is a last resort since we are likely to fail."

"What if they kill them? We're running out of time! Anyhow, where else would they be?" Beta yelled.

Qeriya winced as she watched her stomping towards Anna. This could get ugly fast. But to her relief, Beta halted and turned towards the youth.

"Beta," Anna said, her voice calm though loud. "I was charged with keeping you all safe. Leading a group of you to fight the king on his own territory is a suicide mission. If indeed our parents are there, we have to go in as prepared as we can be. As it is, we need to be sure that's where they are before anything else, and we have to come up with a precise, detailed plan of action. I won't risk battle with a ruthless king without that."

To Qeriya's utter surprise, Beta's shoulders slumped forward as she and her followers conceded to Anna and stood down. It was obvious to Qeriya that they disagreed with Anna's decision, as did she, but they appeared to abide by it. Nevertheless, Qeriya wondered if there was a chance of rebellion, given such strong opposing opinions, and if she and Maria would be on opposite sides of a fight with Khalid and Raquel. That would be a disaster.

The meeting dispersed and the reaume began to gather into their work groups. Qeriya joined Lahcen and they started to walk across to Khalid, who was waiting for them, only to see Anna grasp his hand and pull him away. Qeriya tutted, irritated, Anna was always doing that. On the other hand, she had to admit that Khalid did not exactly resist, he just shrugged and let himself be led.

"Since when did he become so weak willed?" she grumbled.

"Since her, of course," Lahcen answered, pointing towards Anna. "I guess a doting beauty will do that to a man. 'Course, I wouldn't know myself," he complained.

"Well I hope you don't find out until we get back to Mom and Dad. I can't handle two love-struck brothers if it means all they do is disappear into a cloud of denial.

The reaume were drifting off to their separate tasks. Qeriya had elected to help Raquel organize games and races for the young children. Soon there were an alarming number of adolescent boys offering to help as well. She chuckled at the sight of teenage boys playing fire-dodge-ball with a bunch of preschoolers — and losing. That would be a good strategy if they were trying to impress Raquel. Of course, she herself had better be careful. She wasn't a fire reaume, and getting hit with a ball of fire would hurt.

Glancing around, she spotted Khalid and, carefully avoiding any stray fireballs, made her way over to him. Khalid, propped against the same fig tree that had hidden her from Qeriya's view, dreamily watched Anna giving instructions to a group of farmer-gathers. Qeriya ground her teeth, struggling against the need to do him some damage. Why didn't he feel the same urgency she did? They needed to get that flower! He would normally be the one to shuffle them along, but here he was, aimlessly following Anna as if he were hypnotized. Perhaps he was … what else could explain his blind contentment.

Qeriya's heart skipped a beat as she contemplated the idea. Terror tightened her chest, making her breathing shallow. That was it! The more she thought about it, the more obvious it became. Anna had done something to him, to all of them. It had to be that. There was no other explanation for Khalid's complete change of character. It wasn't like her brother to abandon all reason like this. He was normally disciplined, loyal, responsible; her brother, if he were himself, would show more concern for their parents.

Anna had finished. Smiling, she tugged Khalid to his feet. Qeriya bit her lip as she edged around the tree to follow them.

Their journey took them deep into the forest. Qeriya, moving quietly and keeping to the shadows where possible, cautiously leaving some distance between them, knowing that she did not have the gift of camouflage as her cousins did. Arriving in a small clearing, Anna slipped off her shoes and hugged a coconut tree. She gripped the trunk with her hands and feet, pushing and pulling her way up the entire length of the tree until she neared the top. Reaching for a nut, she knocked it free, letting it tumble its way to the ground. Khalid scooped it up and examined it. They had all eaten coconut and quenched their thirst with its water often since they had arrived, but none of them knew how to open the green, round nut. It was hard as a rock and covered in fibers. She saw Khalid feel for some way to get at the soft meat, without success. Just as Anna slid down the tree, he tried biting it. Anna snickered. If he had an aura, Qeriya thought, it would be glowing orange. She had to stop a chuckle; he looked like a guilty toddler.

"Watch your teeth. I'll help you with that in a moment," Anna said. "You need to break it without spilling the liquid."

Anna skillfully top and tailed the fibrous nut, scooping the milky gel into a bowl. Once it was emptied she sliced it open, handing half to Khalid.

"The water tastes better when the coconuts are still green, fresh off the tree," she said. "The jelly is the best part though, don't you think?"

Khalid sipped, savoring the nectar before swallowing. "It's all amazing," he said. "You're amazing. I've never felt so calm and happy. I don't know what could make this any better."

"How about if Mom and Dad were here?" Qeriya whispered. She could see Khalid gazing at Anna as if he'd just stumbled on paradise. Anna was gazing back equally intensely. Qeriya saw that her yellow aura had deepened to apricot.

"Oh, no, I really don't want to see this," she told herself, covering her eyes and peeking between her fingers every few seconds, to see if what she thought was going to happen was over yet.

Instead, Khalid turned away and Qeriya held her breath, glad she could stop squirming, but also hoping they wouldn't walk over to where she stood hidden.

Pulling another scarf out of her own, Anna handed it to Khalid. "Tie this around your neck and shoulders. We'll gather food for tonight."

Fortunately they moved away in the opposite direction, Khalid stroking each leaf and branch as he walked, in communication with the wordless forest world.

"What're we looking for?" Khalid asked. "I didn't really listen to your instructions. It's difficult to hear anything in this place," he said, nodding towards the surrounding plants and trees.

Anna laughed. "That's right, I keep forgetting, to you this place is a crowd, even though we're the only two here," she said, linking her arm through his. "Today we'll collect chilies, avocado, nuts, pineapple and acai fruit. Yes the scarves are that strong," she added, reading his mind as he pinched the thin material in his hand. "And we might even see some cloves, and vanilla bean to use as flavorings. I'll point them out to you as I see them."

"There's no need for that. I'll know."

Anna tilted her head, curious, but she didn't pursue it further.

They walked away quickly as Qeriya extricated herself from a clump of haleconias.

"What are you doing?" Lahcen asked from behind her.

Qeriya thought her heart would jump right out of her mouth. She aimed a solid whack at him which, to her displeasure, he just managed to avoid.

"Are you spying on Khalid?"

"Um, I was just — what makes you think that?"

"You can't fool me, Qeriya, Lahcen said, giving her a severe look. "I know you were spying."

"All right, yes, but I had to see what was going on, Lahcen. Anna's got Khalid under some sort of spell, I'm sure of it, and probably us too. Now she's all he cares about. He's lost his sense."

"Oh, come on, a spell? Are you implying that she's a witch? You're hallucinating, Qe. Don't you think you're taking things a little too far?" Lahcen ripped leaves off a nearby tree as he spoke, in stark contrast to his brother's gentleness with plant life. "You're getting paranoid."

"I'm totally serious. It's like they're Romeo and Juliette, acting as if they're the only two life forms on the planet. But we're supposed to be in a hurry to help Mom and Dad, and Doctor Michael seemed as if he was in agony. What's happening to him, while Kahild runs around all moon faced?"

For a few moments she was silent, then, "We need a plan to get him away from her. She's dangerous. She looks kind … but something's wrong here."

"Oh, come on," Lahcen said. "Let Khalid enjoy himself for a while. You heard, we can't leave until we have a plan. He's in love, that's the great spell he's under. We'll leave soon enough."

"He's 'enjoyed' himself long enough. And your complacency is just part of this weird magnet that seems to be holding us here. Supposedly Khalid's in charge of us, of our mission, but he isn't doing anything but following that girl around. We've been here a month already!" Qeriya said, frowning at the disturbing realization.

There was snow in the mountains, so she'd heard. But that wasn't true anymore. She knew these things in her head, but for some reason, even for her, getting from A to B felt like walking against a sand storm. Everything took so much effort, it was as if they were trapped in a dream, one of those where you keep trying to find your way out of somewhere, but you can't. She heaved her shoulders at Lahcen, like a bird trying to intimidate a predator. "It's her I tell you. I just know it, and if you won't do something about it then I will!"

"Yopo," Raquel said later that night as Qeriya pointed to a

powder suspended from the ceiling, along with other creams, powders and liquids. After a day of entertaining a brood of children, Raquel threw herself down on her bed and stretched in every direction. Even though it was still twilight, it had been an exhausting day and everyone had retired early. Maria wasn't back yet, but Raquel didn't seem to mind. "You blow it into a person's nose through that straw." She waved a limp hand at the short length of straw dangling beside the bottle. "It comes from a plant in the forest. There are other plants we use, too."

"What do you do with all of these powdered plants?"

"They give people visions, you know like realistic dreams," Raquel tucked her words within a long, slow yawn.

"Sounds like drugs. Drugs were a big problem on Old Earth. My history teacher talked about what a problem they were, but she didn't explain much more. What do they do?"

"Well." Raquel thought for a moment, her eyes roving the ceiling as if the answer might be hanging there. "They sort of take over your mind for a while. You see and hear things nobody else does. You don't know what's going on around you. It's pretty extreme."

A shadow crossed Qeriya's face as her cousin spoke, each word etching a blazing trail of suspicion onto her mind. Then the clattering started.

"Liquid sunshine," Raquel said, propping herself on one elbow. "I love thunderstorms. But this means Maria will probably be even later to bed. I don't think I can wait up for her."

"I just can't believe that you would use drugs here," Qeriya said, disappointment keen in her voice. "Drugs caused all sorts of problems on Old Earth. People couldn't stop using them once they started."

"We don't have drug problems. We have drug solutions." Raquel sat up, letting her legs dangle over the edge of her hammock. "Fire reaume don't abuse drugs like people do. Humans use drugs in dangerous ways, probably to escape being human. Who can blame them, as bad as they are to each other and the rest of the world? I'd probably abuse them, too, if I had to live with humans every day." Raquel casually flopped back down onto her hammock, causing it to rock back and forth. She turned to face the wall, curling herself into a ball and nestling her head on the pillow as if she'd just said goodnight.

Qeriya sat fuming; she had to bite her lips to stop herself telling Raquel exactly what she thought of her diagnosis of the human condition. "I don't think that's really fair. I mean, I don't know anybody who uses drugs."

"That's because nobody can get them where you grew up," Raquel spoke to the wall at first, then turned around again to face Qeriya. "They're a big problem with humans everywhere else, especially the palace. My grandmother, the queen, told my parents, and she would know. She snuck inside the palace once. People want drugs or doctors to 'fix' them. They don't understand that nothing can 'fix' them. A body isn't a thing, like a house or a tool. The body's alive and has to heal itself. Healers can only try and help that happen."

"I don't think it's fair to lump all people together like that!" Qeriya flared, leaping to her feet, one hand on her hip and the other making haphazard hand gestures at her cousin. "Okay, you're right — there are really bad human beings, but most people are just trying to make their way in the world. Some people start using drugs and end up making their problems worse. Anyhow, you have to remember that I'm human, too, and so are my brothers. We've never thought of ourselves as any different than the people in our village. It's a bit strange to hear you speak of humans as if you're so superior." Qeriya subsided, reigning in her irritation. It was all she could do to avoid pacing the floor like her mother did when she scolded her. It was odd too, as it wasn't like Raquel to go out of her way to be insulting.

Raquel sat up again, looking puzzled, which irritated Qeriya even further, but nothing more was said for the moment. After a period of mutual silence, Raquel smiled, as if she'd finally comprehended something. "Oh, no, I don't suppose we're superior at all! It's just that fire reaume would never hurt each other, or anyone, the way humans do. I can't imagine having to be human, and living among other humans, and still turn out to be a kind person like you. It's a total complement to you."

Qeriya did not smile back. She was wondering how Raquel's words could possibly be considered a complement, while at the same time, another, clinical aspect of her, was marveling at how sturdy a hammock it was not to spin her cousin onto the floor.

According to what Qeriya knew of the reaume, they were far from perfect. They certainly knew how to argue with one another. It seemed that Beta and her clan were an inch away from mutiny and Anna had put her and her brothers under some sort of weird spell. Qeriya shook her head. This wasn't worth arguing about. She had to remain focused.

"So, these powders cause visions?" she asked, slipping her legs into her temporary bed, a wooden platform with bamboo cushions and covers, squeezed between the hammocks.

"In a way. They take over the mind for a while, but the effects disappear within a few hours."

"Then the users go back to normal?"

"The patients go back the way they were, whether normal or not." Raquel smirked; her rare attempt at humor going unnoticed by her distracted cousin. "Over time, the powders can help whoever needs them." Raquel smiled with pride, pointing to herself. "That's what I study. I'm training to be a healer."

Qeriya stared at Raquel as if she were an alien. How could the same cousin, who didn't think her sister flipping in circles was appropriate, justify the use of drugs so casually?

Raquel must have seen something in her expression because she said, "I tell you, no one abuses drugs here like humans do. We design and use them so they're not addictive. They're medicines." Raquel lay back down. Her mouth stretched into a wide yawn.

"How do you do that?" Qeriya asked starting to yawn too, as if it was contagious. But she did not lie down.

"We only use the exact amount necessary, and only for certain conditions." Raquel stretched again and rolled onto her other side, facing the wall once more, signifying she was done talking.

Qeriya waited patiently as Raquel's breathing became deeper and slower, watching carefully for the convulsive twitching that would signal deep sleep. Raquel's shoulder twitched first, then her hands and legs shook. A series of small lurches later, the movement finally died down. Just as Raquel drifted to sleep the splattering of rain slowed to a gentle pitter-patter. It was such a short rain, as if a bucket of water had dumped from the sky, so unlike her rare experience of the torrential downpours in the desert. She quietly slipped out of her bed and tiptoed across the floor, checking for any sign of Maria outside the door. There was no one, throughout the village nothing stirred. Maria must have decided to stay at a friend's place.

Qeriya reached overhead, disentangling the yopo, and its accompanying straw, from its vine straps. Tucking both powder and straw into the folds of her tunic, she ducked out of the hut. Any lingering light had vanished with the rain. She knew Khalid and Lahcen were staying with Juan and thought of getting them first but decided not to. Khalid was too influenced by Anna's charm and might forbid what she was about to do, and getting Lahcen meant waking Khalid.

The camp was dark for the most part, but there were candles in enclosed glass luminaries, lining paths to the toilets, some distance from the huts, and some of the glittering globes were located at the base of each house. Other than that, the only sunshine left was the liquid kind, dripping from thatched roofs. Qeriya moved quickly.

Anna kept her own hut; as leader she did not share with anyone. Qeriya found it easily and felt her way to the door. A sliver of light from one of the candles outside cut into the darkened hut, the glow extending up to Anna's face as she lay on her back. It was only too perfect.

Qeriya arbitrarily packed powder into the bamboo straw, not knowing how much would be adequate. Somehow she managed to crookedly replace the top of the vial with shaking hands. Did she have too much? There was no time to second-guess. She needed to move fast in case Anna woke up.

Despite the urgency, she found herself hesitating. What she was doing was wrong. And yet, she didn't know what else to do. Qeriya carefully lined the straw up to Anna's nostrils, taking a deep breath, she waited for Anna to inhale. As she did, Qeriya blew the yopo as forcefully as she could into Anna's nose.

To her horror, Anna's eyes flew open, locking onto hers. In that split second, Anna recognized her and knew what she had done. She uttered a fierce scream that sliced Qeriya's ears; her eyes rolled up in her head and she slumped back on her bed, her body and limbs thrashing violently. Qeriya stared at her handiwork. She should flee — now — while she still could; get her brothers and escape. Instead she stood motionless, chained by remorse.

Anna's back arched until Qeriya thought she would surely break her spine. Her feet drummed a tattoo against her sheet "Sssh!" Qeriya whispered, making a feeble attempt to soothe her, as if doing so would erase her mistake. But there was no reaching the unconscious girl. Qeriya leaned over her, wanting, somehow, to ease the terrible stain on her back. She felt the pain burst through her head as Anna's fist connected with her temple, knocking her to the ground.

Qeriya, her wild eyes still fastened on Anna as she continued to spasm, contorting herself into impossible positions, edged herself into a corner. She was shaking so badly she couldn't have got to her feet if she had tried. But she didn't try. Anna was going to die! Tonight she had killed someone! Qeriya curled into a fetal position and howled with terror.

It was a few minutes before figures came running. More candles were lit. Then she heard a familiar voice.

"Qeriya!" Raquel cried. "What've you done!"

It was the same steamy tent as last time, but everything else was completely different. This time she was alone.

"Come here little one," she said and took the baby in her arms, "come to Mama." There was no one there to celebrate with her this time, only the attendants, and they had other patients to tend to, mostly casualties of the war raging nearby.

"Any news?" she asked, as her postpartum chills abated and she could think again. Her glance rested tenderly on her son, sleeping soundly beside her.

"I'm afraid none of it's good, are you sure you're ready?" the woman asked, her voice sounding uncertain.

"Yes," Clara said calmly. "I want to know what's happening."

The attendant seemed to crumple in on herself. "Your husband's all right," she said quickly, "but … Lourdes … the queen … the queen's dead," her voice quivered.

"Thank you for telling me," Clara said, holding onto her calm. "Please tell them to bring my other son here to meet his brother, and then you may leave us and help the others. We'll be all right."

The woman lowered her face in submission and left. Clara looked down at her tiny son, born the day Lourdes died, and wept.

Chapter 17

The King and his General

Rolph glanced at the woman with steel grey eyes standing in the doorway, his most capable lieutenant. Light emanated from the smooth black walls, as if they were luminescent. The woman waited patiently for a nod or any movement that might signify he was listening. The general cleared his throat and reluctantly pried his gaze away from the hologram on the table before him.

"King Seamus wants an update on the preparations," she announced briefly. A curt nod was her only answer and, having received it, she quickly departed.

He was almost ready, aside from the final check on prison cell B. The camera had to be perfectly positioned this time so that everything was captured in detail. The king was a detail-oriented man, as was Rolph. Attention to detail was why he had risen through the ranks so quickly. There were other guards who were smarter, but he knew how to anticipate the king, and that made all the difference. Unlike his son, Prince Liam, the king was predictable.

Rolph hadn't spoken with his highness since his arrival. The job he was taxed with was to determine cell placement in the most secure locations within the lava fields, and somehow restrain the natives. After all, lava was the domain of fire reaume. It was dangerous work. But now, on top of that, he had to orchestrate this particular cell, preparing it for high definition screening. He hoped the king would recognize and approve of his management so far.

He traced his fingers around an aqueous hologram of the newest rock cell and its features. He'd placed beds in the middle of the cell, forming a picture that was projected into Orchid Pond whenever Khalid's hand touched the water. The camera itself was unseen by the prisoners, an invisible membrane lining the obsidian walls. His colleagues would rush through such an assignment, thinking it a minuscule task, but he never rushed an order from the king, no matter how small it seemed.

As he touched the virtual hologram, the water rippled, but maintained its crisp image. He moved beds around the room in various formations, like a puzzle, until he got the effect he wanted. Everything had to be staged around that camera.

"General Rolph," a familiar voice sounded from the entrance. This was unusual. The king had come to him. His heart skipped a beat, but like a well-trained soldier he did not flinch. He rose and turned to greet the king.

"Your majesty." He bowed respectfully. "Welcome. It's been a while. I hope you've found your quarters comfortable."

"Of course. You're always prepared for me," King Seamus answered, coming into the room in his customary garb, a patterned robe of many hues and a headdress of feathers. His face was painted in a myriad of thick red and blue, the colors of war. The skin around his eyes was shaded with azure to match his stark blue hair. The monarch was never without paint in public, certainly Rolph had never seen him without it. Different color combinations represented the meaning of an occasion. A white base represented new life, black meant death, and purple signified marriage.

How fitting that the colors representing marriage should literally be a marriage of the war colors. Marriage was hard. While Rolph and his wife were technically still together, after their son died, their marriage had died too.

"I've been working on the latest cell design, with the beds placed before a camera as you requested," he said, showing the arrangement to the king, who studied the hologram for some time in silence. Rolph's apprehension grew with each second.

"Excellent work. The angle and lighting are perfect. You thought of everything, as usual. Your work never fails to impress." He smiled graciously, patting Rolph on the shoulder.

His monarch was appreciative and generous with praise, but the general was careful not to relax. He knew that maintaining the sovereign's favor meant never taking his approval for granted.

"Thank you, sire," he murmured, dipping his head respectfully. "You're certain the plan's not too dangerous? These fire reaume are powerful life forms. It's sure to stir a rebellion. Even though they're young, their power exceeds our own."

"Rebellion is what we want, Rolph." To the general's surprise, the king smiled. "Don't worry. Our scientists have developed weapons that work against them this time. They'll suffer the same painful burns they inflicted to defeat our army in the rainforest. And they'll remember their place in the end."

General Rolph found himself also wanting to smile, despite his resolve not to show emotion before the king. This information was indeed a relief. "Yes, that changes everything, doesn't it?"

"Fortune smiles on *us* now."

Rolph could no longer contain his exhilaration and, when his monarch began to laugh, he joined in. It was laughter mixed with pain as Rolph vividly recalled his own son's charred body, his hair singed. Even now, all this time later, he couldn't bear to think about how his son must have suffered. Well he would have revenge for what they did to his child, knowing that, working towards that, was all that kept him strong. He would do to their children what they had done to his son and let them watch, powerless, unable to help or fight back. They were too powerful now, too unpredictable. "We'll destroy them!" he ground out.

"No, no, Rolph, we won't destroy them, we'll use them." The king walked around the office, inspecting every inch of the space while they spoke. "They're to be our slaves."

"But—" Rolph hesitated, realizing he was about to argue with the king. This was completely out of character, but his son demanded justice.

"Yes?"

Instead of continuing, the general bit his tongue and bowed his head.

King Seamus must have seen something of the war raging inside him. "We can't win that war, yet. You must know that," he said. "Remember, there are reaume that wield weapons other than fire, and mass destruction will bring them all to war. We're not ready for that."

The general's face was pinched with repressed bitterness.

"Don't worry," the king added. "That time will come soon. One win, a little revenge, doesn't make for victory. We must be patient if we're to maintain control."

Rolph struggled to calm himself as he choked back the horrific memory of his son's death. The monarch was right. He was hurt and impetuous, a bad combination for good strategy. His ruler was a master of strategy. Rolph forced himself to detach from emotion and to view the situation from a less personal point of view; even though his son had died in battle with the fire reaume years before, the army had completed half of their mission. They had herded the rainforest people into the desert and successfully employed surveillance and border patrols without a hitch. The targets were identified as hoped. No, it was not bad leadership that left his son dead, it was a power that had grown way out of control and would soon take over. He had to trust his king, and he would trust him, with his life if need be, to secure the people of this planet. And yet, something was wrong. There was danger, he could sense it."

"Pardon me your majesty," he said, an uncharacteristic quiver in his voice, "it's just that not everything has gone according to plan."

The king's painted face grew grave under the shadow of his headdress. "Do you doubt me?" Cold replaced the warm glow that had been in his eyes only a moment before.

Rolph knew he'd overstepped his bounds. The sovereign

would never forget. Gracious as he was, the king never forgave doubt. "No, sire, I do not doubt you." The monarch's gaze pierced him and Rolph hoped his expression communicated an explanation he dare not voice. The plan had been to capture the three siblings before drawing the reaume into war, but the siblings had escaped.

"My plan has many levels, General Rolph."

Contrary to what he might have expected, the king placed a hand on his shoulder in a comforting gesture. Rolph's gaze shot up in delighted surprise.

"You should know I've thought of that. The first level didn't succeed, but that's no great loss. Much more has gone well. We'll face them all in battle soon enough."

"What's going on here? Why are there so many giants, why are you crying?" Aedan asked as he emerged from the forest, having negotiated a line of guards that surrounded the village.

Clara sat on a fallen, moss covered tree, sobbing aloud, hunched over in pain, the boys half-heartedly amusing themselves around her.

"Carlos and Laura are dead!" she cried, shaking her head from side to side like a mortally wounded animal.

"What! Why?"

"The king's army — they attacked. They're ordering everybody to march tomorrow morning. Carlos and Laura fought them, I think they wanted to provide a distraction and give me and the boys a chance to escape. But there were too many of them, they had us surrounded." She buried her head in his shoulder as he hugged her tightly.

"I thought the king was just at war with the reaume," he said. "Why would he attack a human village?"

Clara stared wildly at her husband through her tears. "It surprised everyone! No one knows why he attacked! There was no warning! Now, everyone left — we're all prisoners."

Chapter 18

The Siren

One day led to another in the forest. Khalid gently stirred the pond with a long stick, watching ripples pedal across the surface. It had been three months since he first saw his parents and Doctor Michael in Orchid Pond, just as he had this morning. He had made many friends during the time they'd lingered here. But it was decidedly time to go, so why couldn't he bring himself to leave?

He studied the water in detail. It seemed normal enough, according to the little he knew about ponds from school. Frogs were croaking and chirping, water striders raced along the surface at a fast clip, searching for fallen bugs to eat. But this wasn't a normal pond, it swallowed reflections and feasted on light, leaving a cold black chasm. Nothing was normal around here, he had come to realize, including the reaume, and especially Anna.

How Qeriya had born everyone's anger and distrust these past few weeks he could not fathom. He'd heard two words from her the entire time and spoken to her even less. He was not sympathetic, until now. Now his stomach contents churned when he thought of what she'd been through and how blind he'd been to her warnings. He stood up, took a few steps, debating whether to go do the morning harvesting, but the pond held him.

Again his thoughts turned to his sister and the way he had stood by, making no attempt to help her. Not that Qeriya was entirely the innocent. She'd come very near to killing Anna with her careless attempt to drug her. Anna's coma had lasted for weeks. Thankfully, she was all right now, and surprisingly understanding, even apologetic. What his sister had been thinking he couldn't guess, but he could no longer ignore what she had tried to say and he was sorry he'd alienated her.

He paused to savor the still, subtle movements around him, feeling fully alive, immersed in the present, with no voices to drown his consciousness. And yet, he couldn't stop thinking.

When he'd heard that Anna had awoken from her coma a week ago, he'd told himself it was time to leave. Then, once again, he had quickly become obsessed with her, like a dumbstruck puppy. He couldn't muster the strength of will necessary to leave without speaking with her. Some force attached him to this place, a spell of some sort. All he knew was that it was Anna. Even while she still lay in a coma, he had begun to realize there was something that drew him to her.

He crept slowly around the pond, scaling moss covered logs and thick brush. When they'd first arrived, Anna had said to wait until spring thaw to approach the mountains: that any flowers would not be visible before that. Back then, he'd wanted to leave despite her advice, but somewhere along the line, her words started to make sense, and kept making sense, even when they no longer did. And once she no longer made sense, the thought of leaving her didn't seem to make sense. If they left now, it would already be late summer before reaching the mountains; much later than planned, and yet leaving was simply not an option he was able to consider. Why?

He squatted down to thrust his hand into the water, and the same image appeared. Why did the pond only display to him? There were his parents, in the same room as Anna's, along with Doctor Michael. Khalid paused, drawing in a sharp breath. Something about the image was different this time. What was it? It was more distinct somehow. He sighed. His parents were most likely at the palace, which was also near the mountains, so there was no reason not to leave. His sister had tried to make him see every chance she got, until she'd finally taken matters into her own hands. She would have never done something like that unless she really believed they were in serious trouble. He stared moodily into the water again. By then she'd lost all hope in him. He shook his head, disgusted at himself. She was supposed to be his priority. She was supposed to be able to trust him, and the fact that she didn't was squarely down to his own failure.

Qeriya was right to take Anna's power seriously, he thought. After all, why could he not escape the fog in his head? He couldn't think straight, as if magic was holding him hostage, preventing him from taking action. Anna wanted to keep them there, he was sure, and somehow she was controlling his mind. He remembered now, too late, that Doctor Michael had warned them to stay away from the reaume. Perhaps the doctor had figured this might happen.

He stared hard at the image, hoping the oracle might show him something about Anna — it did not. Once more, his eye was caught by the differences in the image. Where they real? Or was his dulled brain just imagining them? He squinted at the obsidian surface, trying to pin down what exactly had changed. Instead of unreachable parents, trapped in a vague haze, the pond seemed to magnify the detail. He could see the walls more clearly, until, abruptly, they disappeared.

Khalid stood up slowly, suspicious of water that showed no reflection but supposedly offered a window to his parents' prison; a dark mystery that teased him with an image, only to snatch it away. If this was an oracle of the Spirit, it was fickle with its revelations.

"You didn't leave."

Behind him, a familiar voice, hitting his ears like a favorite song. Khalid whipped his head around. Anna had been recuperating since waking up; this was the first time he had seen her alone.

"No, I didn't leave. How could I leave without knowing if you'd be all right?"

Khalid's gaze locked onto hers, and the beginning of tears formed in both of their eyes. Suddenly a loud boom split the silence. It sounded like a weapon of some sort. Khalid grabbed Anna, pulling her close to him. His gaze darted around, scouring the undergrowth for some sign of what was happening. Nothing! Try though he might, he could see nothing strange, nothing that looked like some kind of weapon. He glanced down at Anna, surprised to see her wearing a playful, he'd even go so far as to say, flirtatious expression. It was all too clear that she was enjoying his protective affection. An invisible cord in his chest tightened, making him want to pull her even closer. He fought the temptation.

"What ... what was that noise?" he asked, releasing her.

"It's a cannon-ball tree," Anna said. "It keeps us alert around here."

Khalid backed away from her and her smile slowly slid from her face.

"Anna, why are you keeping us here?" he asked, donning his assigned scarf, tools nestled into a pouch that ballooned off it. He turned towards one of the many trails.

Anna tentatively followed him. "I admit I was influencing you to stay, but I'm not exerting any persuasion on you anymore. I just hope you can come to understand why I did it." Her voice quivered.

Khalid spun round. "I don't believe you. There's something about you that's still holding me prisoner." He turned back the way he had been heading. Everything in him screamed that he was being manipulated. And the depth of his feelings for Anna made the sting of betrayal even worse.

"I swear! I'm not, not anymore! It ended when I went into the coma. There's no way I can sway you unless I'm awake and alert. Please, you have to believe me."

Khalid paused, staring at her. He wanted so much to be able to trust her — but he couldn't. There was more at stake here than just his own future. He shook his head. "I don't buy it. There's some sort of weird magic that you're playing around with.

Whatever you think this Spirit is, it's not the Spirit I know. I don't get what sort of sorcery you're into, but I do know you're using it."

"Sorcery, magic? What're you talking about? This doesn't have anything to do with the Spirit, and it's not magic — there's no such thing as magic." Anna didn't attempt to disguise her frustration. "It's just like a human to assume anything they don't understand must be magic. If you don't understand something, it's simply a question, that's all."

Khalid could feel the anger and resentment boiling up in him. He turned away again, pushing his way through the forest. Finally, he couldn't stomach his curiosity any longer. He spun around. "Then what is it if it's not magic?"

Anna took a deep breath. "Listen," she said, speaking calmly and carefully, as if she was talking to her charges.

Her tone of voice made Khalid bristle, but, forcing himself to a composure he didn't feel, he listened.

"There's more to communication than the obvious, like talking, motioning or facial expression. Our bodies are constantly communicating with one another in ways we don't see. That's true of humans as well as reaume."

Khalid looked at her blankly.

"You don't know what I'm talking about?"

"No clue," he agreed.

"It happens through viruses, not the kind that make us sick, but a kind that carry information and emotion."

"You mean to say that you gave me a psychic flu?"

"No, of course not …" Anna gave him a small, strained smile. "It's subtler than that. In any case, these — viruses communicate and influence our unconscious."

"Okay," he drawled, his voice heavy with doubt. He folded his arms across his chest in an effort to knot his tongue.

"It's true, I'm telling you. Humans and reaume both have these viruses. The difference is that we fire reaume are able to control them, direct them purposely, as I've done with you. The viruses are like ..." she fumbled for words, her eyes searching the sky as if there might be a prompt in the canopy above. "I don't know, like subtle whispers to your subconscious, yeah, whispers ... whispers that coax you to stay and wait and not be anxious." Glancing at Khalid's thunderous expression she hurriedly added, "but I'm not doing that anymore, I swear! Anyhow, I may have influenced your subconscious, but I could never control you in any way, or even convince you to do something you wouldn't normally do. In the end, you were still able to make your own decisions.

"Qeriya's a perfect example. I influenced her as well, but she chose to fight it — or me."

Khalid froze momentarily, acknowledging the truth of Anna's words. "So," he said finally, "how do you know all this?"

"I learned it from my parents. But it was your grandfather who taught them, your dad's father. His mother, your great-grandmother, was water reaume. Anyhow, water reaume don't have the ability to influence others, but they're known for their intelligence. Nobody here considered what we were doing to be special in any way. Your grandfather's the one who taught us about viruses, and how fire reaume use them differently than other reaume or humans."

"Anna, do you know much about our parents?" Khalid asked, suddenly changing the subject. "They lived in this rainforest," he said, his voice wistful. He glanced around himself. "Even I lived here for a time, so you say, and yet I remember nothing about it."

Anna nodded slowly. "I'll tell you all I know," she said. "Your dad was born to Lourdes." As she spoke, her voice relaxed, becoming rich, sweet and smooth as chocolate. "She was queen of the fire reaume at the time. He was the firstborn of two children, Aedan and Arianna. My mother said that you and I used to play together as toddlers." Anna smiled and reached to cut some cinnamon bark off the tree, placing the wooden chunks in her scarf.

Khalid simply watched her work, listening intently. "Aedan, our dad's name was Aedan," he whispered under his breath.

"He took the name of Daniel in the desert. There were many people living there already, before the king forced the rainforest clan to join them, declared it a prison and restricted the water. The rainforest dwellers must have blended names with the desert dwellers for protection," Anna speculated, moving away to pick some Brazil nuts and tuck them into her scarf. "There was a war, when we were very young, between the king and fire reaume. We call it the Great War. Before the war, rainforest people and fire reaume got along. Your mother was a human, Clara, who lived among them."

"Clara, her name isn't Ruth?"

"No, it's not Ruth. Your mother's name is Clara. Somehow, during their time in the rainforest, Aedan and Clara met and fell in love. They married, had you, and then Lahcen. Your mother took you both to live with her human family to protect you during the war, but the king surprised everyone and captured the rainforest humans."

Khalid scoped the woods around him, trying to picture what his parents might have looked like here, years younger. He could easily see how his parents could fall in love in this place. The setting made him think of nothing but love, especially when Anna smiled at him as she was now. "Since you're such a good climber," she said, her lovely eyes boring into his own. "I thought you might climb up there." She pointed at a nearby tree, "and knock down the coconuts?"

Khalid scowled at her. "You're a good climber too. You just want to watch me climb," he accused, but an air of humor had crept back into his tone, and he obligingly scooted up the tree.

"How did you know?" Anna said, her voice sultry. She shot him a wide smile before continuing. "Anyhow, I don't know if this was the first time human and reaume ever married, but it was the first time children came out of such a match." She stepped back nimbly, away from the tree, as Khalid knocked a few coconuts to the ground before coming down to join her. Her eyes caught his and he moved towards her.

"I'm sorry that I have to be the one to tell you this. It must be hard to hear it all," she said, her voice soft with sympathy.

Khalid shook his head as if to clear it. Maybe hearing about his parents should have been difficult, painful even. But pain was the last thing on his mind. Really, he just wanted to kiss her, and to keep from kissing her, all at the same time.

Not only was he obsessed by her every move, he was so under her spell, he could no longer trust himself to make good decisions, and that was not like him at all. Normally, he knew his mission and was determined to fulfill it, and nothing ever stopped him once he was committed, not even an incredibly attractive woman. But with Anna, every time he considered leaving, she looked at him and his urgency dissolved into yearning. He cursed himself for a fool. The girl was a siren, distracting him, making him forget.

"You're doing it again," he said. "Even more than before."

"Doing what? Influencing you? I'm not doing anything at all anymore! Honest," she pleaded.

"Do you know why the king attacked in the first place?" he asked, not hiding his distrust.

Anna kept her glance on the forest floor. "Somehow, he'd discovered that children had been born to a human and a fire reaume couple. But he was also concerned that the fire reaume were getting stronger and more powerful. He felt threatened by us."

"Yeah, I can see why he would," Khalid said, his gaze raking her.

"What? Why do you look at me like that? Would you stop? I'm being straight with you!"

"You're a force to be reckoned with," Khalid threw at her.

Anna gave a curt smile and moved past him to continue with collecting food.

"So our dad was a fire reaume, born to Lourdes and who? Who was our grandfather?"

Anna glanced around, searching the greenery for anything edible. "To be honest, I'm a little unclear about him. He was half water reaume and half air."

"Do you know the other reaume?"

"By name only. I don't know much about them."

"That's what I'd like to find out someday." Khalid paused to examine a banana tree, but the fruit was not quite ripe so he moved on.

"Anyhow, I guess all of the reaume used to work together, but for many years now we've each found a place and remained in hiding."

"Do you know where the others live?"

"No, I don't. Your grandmother, Lourdes, was half earth reaume, but she died in the war, and I know nothing about her husband, your grandfather. He died long before her. I know that Lourdes only expressed fire reaume powers. She had no earth reaume qualities whatsoever, other than her fair complexion and bright red hair. She looked just like her father and even had his personality, so I'm told." Anna halted. "You remind me of some stories I've heard of him. They used to say that plants bowed to him."

Khalid examined Anna closely. She smiled as her hair dropped over half her face like a dark curtain and pulled the long silky strands over one shoulder, exposing a graceful neckline that sloped into a soft, strong shoulder.

Khalid fought the urge to reach out and stroke it. They were again uncomfortably close. He closed his eyes, shutting out her allure. They had only met a few months ago, and yet, if he were to spend his life with someone, he would want it to be her. How could he know that already, he asked himself, how could he, in so short a time, be so certain — unless he was trapped? Not only was Anna still exerting her power over him, but it was also decidedly stronger than ever, and there was no way he could hold out against it.

Khalid broke his trance and started moving again. "I wonder why Lahcen and Qeriya and I are all different, and not a combination of all reaume?"

"I don't know," Anna said. "It certainly is strange."

They entered a small clearing and Anna paused, grabbing a pointed arrowhead from her scarf. Removing the scarf, she tied the produce she had collected so far inside and rested it on a log. Kneeling before some plants on the ground she dug up a large tuber. "Sweet potatoes," she said, and handed one to Khalid. He knelt and took out his own pointed rock to help.

"All I know is that you all are a big deal to the king because reaume are not human," Anna explained. We're a separate species altogether, and yet, there's you," she paused a moment to let this sink in. "You were the first children born of a reaume and human union."

"I don't understand how you're not human," Khalid said, frustration lending an edge to his voice. "How can you be a separate species? He'd stopped digging and stood up in his agitation. "You look human and you talk like a human. Other than extra powers, you appear human. Why should it be such a surprise that reaume and humans could have children?"

Anna shook her head. "I know it seems that way, but reaume are not human. We're closer to the rest of the animal kingdom. Humans are … different." She brushed the dirt from her hands and stood up. Even without taking powers into account, we're still different. For example, reaume don't kill except to eat or in defense, like other animals. Only humans kill for revenge, or enjoy the suffering of others."

"Isn't that a little high and mighty of you, to claim that no reaume are prone to revenge? And believe me, not all humans enjoy watching suffering."

"I knew you'd react that way. That's why—"

"Why what? Why you wouldn't be honest with me? Why you'd rather mess with my mind? Somehow you're trying to tell me your motives for doing that are pure?" he snarled, agitation turning into irritation, at what he considered to be a serious case of denial on her part.

Anna closed her eyes, blocking out his anger. "Reaume are different," she said slowly. "We are never motivated by greed, only by what we believe is right."

"So none of what you've done has been motivated by greed," he pressed, not because he was curious, but to point out the ridiculousness in what she was saying. "But you strike me as being very much guided by emotion."

"I am guided by emotion, we reaume are very emotional and we have the same emotions as humans, except for greed and jealousy and malice ... we even argue and disagree like humans, but greed, retribution or any sort of 'harmful' emotion, for lack of a better description, does not govern us. We're not tempted by excess of any kind, and, by nature, we're highly empathic beings, more so than any other animal. To put it in simple terms, humans have the ability to choose good or evil — we do not. By nature we're good, ignorant and angry at times, but essentially good."

"You're never influenced by self-serving motives, you never deceive others for your own sake?"

Anna nodded.

"So you didn't — you aren't — keeping us here with you somehow, knowing we need to leave — for your own gain?"

Anna lowered her head.

"Even animals hurt and steal from each other, and they're considered basically good. How can you claim to live in the world and be so void of evil, especially given your treatment of us, of me?" Khalid spoke to Anna's bowed head, his anger spilling over into his words, his own skull throbbing, tears rolling down his face.

"I know you question my motives, but I'm not trying to hurt you, and certainly not for myself," Anna insisted, her voice almost a whisper.

"I can't begin to know your motives, but you are keeping us here against our will for some reason, despite the fact we need to act!" Khalid raged. He pulled in a long, deep breath to calm himself. "Look," he said, more in control now. "I care for you, but you've grown this care into an unnatural obsession to keep me here. I used to think it was this place, but I've come to know it's you. Why?"

Anna said nothing. Her head was still bowed, hair falling, like strands on a weeping willow, down either side of her head.

"We may be half reaume." Khalid sighed. But we're fully human by your definition and we're willing to admit it without this holier than thou facade. We're greedy, and even vengeful. I'm willing to admit that it's true, admitting it is what keeps it at bay. I wouldn't flinch before killing the prince after what he did to our village and to Qeriya."

Anna took a step back, as if his words were a verbal slap.

She passed a weary hand over her face. "Listen, I don't understand it, I don't know why, but humans can choose greed over generosity, power over service. Like I said before, reaume might disagree and argue with one another, we even get angry, but we never want to hurt another, no matter what injury we ourselves suffer."

"How can you possibly look at me after all that's happened and claim that reaume are essentially perfect?" Khalid demanded. "How incredibly biased!"

"Perfect you say, perfect? You can call us perfect if you wish, and you can think I'm biased, but you'll see in time that it's true, and it cripples us!" Anna had never before raised her voice to such an extent. "Because we can only be good, because we have no malice, we don't have the fight necessary to defeat a human king, especially one so ruthless. We can't confront a hate and greed we simply can't understand. Our powers can overwhelm any human." She nodded pointedly to him. "Yet even so, I wouldn't deceive you into doing something you're not inclined to do anyway, because it's not in my nature. I could, and yet I couldn't. Despite our incredible power, we have more flight than fight. We're unable to confront evil." She paused, collecting herself.

Khalid stood stock still, inviting her to continue with his rapt attention.

"The young fire reaume don't understand that fighting the king without human leadership is like walking into a trap! The challenge we're up against is more emotional than physical, and we can't win. We've allowed the king to grow in power, to consume in excess, to destroy the land we work to form, all just to avoid a fight. We may eventually fight to defend this world, and each other, out of some sense of justice, but just barely, and we'll do it knowing we will all die." She paused again and Khalid was about to speak, but she cut him off.

"If we're as good and perfect as you say, we would trade anything not to be, because it seems that good alone doesn't keep evil in check. It's the ability to meet evil with perfect understanding and somehow not be consumed by it that keeps evil down. We're incapable of this, and so are powerless to defeat it." Her eyes pleaded with him to understand.

If Khalid had a visible aura, it would have glowed pink with enlightenment as he turned her words over in his head. "So, that's why you're keeping us here, because you're not able to take offensive action against the king. You can't beat him, even if you're more powerful. You need us to help you fight when he attacks. Otherwise all the children—" He lifted her tearstained face, looking for confirmation, speaking gently. "You're afraid for your reaume."

Anna vigorously nodded her head. Hot tears streamed down

her cheeks. He gently wiped the wet drops from her face and slid his fingers through her hair, pulling her head to his chest, but she pulled away from him.

"I know Beta and the others believe we should attack, and that might be the best strategy if we were more like humans, but they're naive. Even if we know where they are, there's no way we could win this battle. I'm old enough to remember the aftermath of the Great War. Most of the others are not. Our population was decimated. It was awful! It's my job to protect the youth, Khalid, and I know that none of us could withstand a battle with the king, even here, in our own domain. We'd lose.

"But with you to lead us, it could be different. There's no hope for our reaume without you."

Khalid drew her towards his chest once again. He held her against him until he felt the tension ease out of her and she had stopped shaking. Then he gently stepped away, holding her at arms length as he wiped away fresh tears. When he spoke again his voice was gruff with tenderness. "Listen to me. We will help you, but you have to promise to release us first."

"Thank you." Anna's mahogany eyes shone with gratitude. "But I swear I'm not—"

Khalid interrupted her, placing two fingers over her mouth, his grip growing tighter around her waist.

"You really are the most beautiful woman I've ever seen," he said. Taking her hand, he drew it toward his mouth, and, eyes still locked on her face, placed a tender kiss in the center of her upturned palm. Immediately Anna's aura shone a warm apricot, and as she gazed up at him, Khalid saw a vulnerability and openness in her that was completely new. Gone was the self assured toughness he'd always detected previously. Slowly, he closed in on her, crushing her to him as their lips met. She melted into him, meeting his fierce hunger with her own burning need. A groan escaped Khalid. He could feel her heart, racing fast, matching the frantic beat of his own. He stared down into her face; his siren; keeping him prisoner, and he knew he was powerless to resist.

"Where are the boys?" Clara asked, her face ashen and sweaty.

"Don't worry about the boys, they're just fine," Aedan said abstractedly. Clara let his answer stand, she couldn't afford to worry right now. The pains were getting more intense and closer together. Aedan pushed the heel of his hand against her lower back once again. How many hours he'd massaged her and brushed the sand off her bedding, she couldn't begin to guess. For some reason the pain was in her back this time instead of round the front.

She was feeling an urge to push. Aedan read her cues and helped to bend her knees, coaching her to breathe and push. Clara bore down, using the power of each contraction to the full. Again and again she strained. Time blurred and her world narrowed to each cresting wave of pain. At last her shuddering body heaved one final time and as the child gulped her first breath, Clara heard a lusty wail.

Aedan swiftly moved into action. Wiping his daughter clean, wrapping her in his soft tunic, a relic from his home in the rainforest, he held the little bundle out to her mother. "Here," he spoke softly. "Here's your baby girl, Qeriya," he smiled tiredly.

Clara placed a kiss on her newborn daughter's downy head. "Hello, Qeriya," she said, her voice thick with exhaustion. "I'm so glad you're all right. Now, want to meet your brothers?

Chapter 19

Capture

Qeriya's eyelashes fluttered. Her mom was stroking her hair and it felt so good. Dad was singing one of his silly songs about bopping a desert mouse on the head, which of course they never actually did. Suddenly, it was all shaking, her mom and dad crumbling like fragile rock before her eyes. A piece of her mother landed on a miniature Doctor Michael. Qeriya looked up and saw Prince Liam. He was holding a glass sphere and shaking it. Although he was a distance from her, Qeriya could clearly see herself and her family encased inside the globe. He was talking to her, telling her, in his charming voice, how much he had enjoyed their time together. And all the while, he was shaking the glass ball, and destroying everything. Qeriya rolled off her platform bed and hit the floor.

For a moment, caught in that space between waking and sleep, she readied herself to meet the same coldness from everyone that she had endured since the night she'd almost killed Anna. Slowly, as she came round, she remembered that it was over, at least for now. Anna had awakened from her coma and had been released from healer care a few days ago. Thankfully, she'd checked out all right and had even apologized to her. She'd also explained Qeriya's motives to the reaume, so Qeriya was at last restored to good graces.

Raquel had been the one who was most hurt and horrified, and Qeriya knew it would take her the longest to come around, but she was already trying to build bridges with her cousin. During her time of informal exclusion, she had, of necessity, trod softly, often wishing she could blend into the background like the fire reaume. But now that Anna was awake, she could be as loud and outspoken as her nature demanded.

Qeriya pushed herself to her feet and started to get ready for the morning meeting. The other hammocks were empty. She took her time, then, pulling in a deep breath and unconsciously straightening her spine, she left the hut and walked tentatively through the thick vegetation to join the others. Seeing a sudden movement, she watched a bug that, an instant before, she would have sworn was part of a plant stem, and quickened her pace at the thought of so many hidden creatures around her. Every day there was something new. Somehow, the crazy dream she'd had seemed almost more real than the magical place in which she had awoken, even after her many months in the forest.

"Good morning," Juan said as he joined Qeriya on the trail, slowing down to let her go before him.

Qeriya thought that he looked altogether too cheerful for this time of the day.

"You look nice," he said. His aura radiated yellow and his eyes shifted to the ground.

Qeriya smiled. "Mornings are not my best time of day," she told him.

"Mornings are good when I get to walk with such pleasant company," he answered shyly, flashing her a quick glance before returning his eyes to the floor. His aura morphed into peach.

Qeriya turned red in contrast. "Well, thank you, Juan. It's, um, it's good to see you this morning, too," she stammered, hoping her brothers were safely out of range.

Up ahead, Maria and Raquel emerged onto the path from another trail. Qeriya hurried to catch up with Maria, only to see her glaring at the back of her sister's head.

"What's wrong?"

Maria aimed a kick at an unfortunate stray twig. "You're so lucky you don't have a sister."

"Oh, you don't mean that? Are you upset with Raquel about something?"

"Everything!" Maria crossed her arms over her chest and

crumpled her nose. "She's driving me crazy. I mean, don't get me wrong, I love her and all that, but she thinks she's the boss of me now that Mom and Dad are gone. I can't even collect firewood without getting a lecture — constant lectures! It's getting really annoying. She's only two years older than I am."

Qeriya laughed softly. "I hear you. I have two brothers to boss me around."

"Yeah, but they're fun." Maria shifted her sour gaze to Qeriya. "My sister acts like a mother. It's different."

Qeriya shook her head emphatically. "There's no difference, and my brothers aren't as sweet as your sister."

"Yeah, Raquel is sweet, sugar syrupy sweet, and that only drives me more crazy." Maria ripped a clump of leaves from a nearby cinnamon tree.

"She loves you, just like my brothers love me," Qeriya said. "I just wish they wouldn't love me quite so much sometimes."

Maria sighed. "Maybe, but it's making me more and more angry. I don't even want to come home at night."

"Hey." Qeriya halted, turning to face her cousin who likewise stopped. "Sometimes feelings are misplaced. They don't always tell the truth. Your parents being gone is making you angry, not your sister." Qeirya pointed to Raquel. "Remember that! And we need to do something about it." They resumed walking.

"What are you talking about? You're not making any sense," Maria said, glancing away.

"Don't I? Well, just keep this in mind, Raquel's lost her parents too." Despite Maria's avoidance, Qeriya knew that she was listening.

By the time they arrived at the pond for the daily morning meeting, Khalid and Lahcen were already in front with Anna.

"Orchid Pond has revealed more detailed information," Anna explained to the gathered youth. It appears that more parents were taken prisoner than we first realized. Many of us who believed our parents were dead may yet be mistaken. So far, we've assumed the king's motive is to wipe out fire reaume, but Juan has another perspective he'd like to share." Anna nodded for Juan to speak and he stepped forward.

"I keep thinking, if the king wanted to exterminate fire reaume, this would be the time — when we're at our weakest. Yet, he hasn't tried. I believe he's holding our parents in order to threaten us. He's waiting for us to plead with him, so that we'll be forced to work for him. I'm afraid there is no peaceful resolution." Juan addressed the crowd with confidence and Qeriya's spirits lifted. She scoped the crowd for interested faces, hoping that everyone would be listening to him.

"In that case, our laying low is what he wants. The alternative is for us to fight, but it's risky," Anna summarized gravely. "The king may assume we'll plead, but he'll be prepared for us to attack. We can't rush into this, especially since we're not strong. If we fail, they'll destroy us."

"Unless we make a bold move they don't expect. We need to plan an attack that doesn't rely so much on strength, more on nerve. Something he wouldn't expect from a young group of reaume," Qeriya said with new hope. It was about time the discussion went somewhere.

"Yes," Khalid echoed. "That's exactly what we need — bold and unexpected. But first we have to find out exactly where everyone's being held. We're assuming the palace, but we should re-examine the evidence now that we have more detailed pictures." He gestured toward the image in the water.

"The walls of the prison are made of stone which appears to have been painted a variety of bright colors. Perhaps some of you could identify the type of rock? That might help us place where it is."

"If the king succeeds in capturing us," Anna said, "Juan believes he'll keep us separated from our parents and force us to work for him."

"What I don't understand," Lahcen said, getting to his feet, "is, if fire reaume can create land, why are you at the mercy of the king? You're more powerful than humans, why are you not the dominant species?"

"We've discussed this," Anna said, eyeing Khalid. "And it's very difficult to understand. Domination is impossible for us. Offensive strategy is a foreign concept. Only the hunters manage it, and even then, only to eat. In warfare, we're limited to defense. Anything else is simply not in our nature." Anna glanced from Lahcen to Qeriya, searching for a hint of understanding, seeing none. "All life is capable of choice, but humans are capable of choosing hatred and greed in a way we're not. Humans can manipulate creation to serve them. Many people overcome this temptation — as I've heard it called by some — and yet evil is possible for you in a way it's not for us."

Lahcen and Qeriya glanced at one another, both as confused and insulted as the other. Qeriya had opened her mouth to speak, when, abruptly, Raquel stood up.

"That's volcanic!" she exclaimed, staring at the image. "The rock isn't painted at all, the colors are natural volcanic rock! I can't believe I didn't think of that before! My parents discovered those colored walls. The first eruption was super hot and spanned a wide area, more so than usual for a volcano, and it made those brightly colored caverns throughout the mound."

"But what volcano is it? " Anna asked.

Raquel clenched the hair on her head and concentrated as the memory spiraled its way out of the depths of her mind. "I think — I think they found these walls when they were exploring the rainforest volcano, the one closest to us!"

Everyone crowded around the pond to examine the picture closely and, one by one, they echoed her finding. Soon there was a flood of mass muttering and speculation as each reaume analyzed and interpreted his or her opinion. Agreement and arguments ensued and camps formed.

"What are you looking at?" Anna asked, noticing Khalid

studying a book in his lap. His finger traced a delicate page, gold embossed along the edges. It had drawings in faint relief that reflected elevation. The book was stiff at first, but the cover softened from the heat of his body and gently adapted to the shape of his lap.

"It's a journal Doctor Michael gave us," Khalid said. "You say your parents were taken at the volcano?"

Anna nodded. "That's right."

"You believe they're at that volcano?" Lahcen asked Khalid, pointing.

"Perhaps," Khalid answered.

"That would make some sense. After all, how could humans contain and transport the entire adult fire reaume to the palace without any escapees? Then again, how could they possibly contain fire reaume in their natural element?" Lahcen mused.

"I don't know, but look at this." Khalid turned the journal to face the crowd so everyone could see the page. He pointed to a sketch of a volcano beside a grove of trees. "See these bumps etched in gold relief? I'll wager that these are some of the molten rock caverns Raquel is talking about. I wonder if they've gained access to them somehow and are using them as prisons?"

Lahcen's eyes narrowed in thought. "Perhaps. They'd need a means of snaring and encasing the reaume, but this way they could then be kept on site without the risk of escape during transport."

"But how?" Juan asked. "They should be able to break out easily. It doesn't make sense."

Qeriya considered a number of ideas, hoping to create some clarity, but no matter how she stitched them together, there was no consistent explanation.

Suddenly, a young boy from the village burst into the gathering, panting, having run and flown as fast as his burgeoning firepower allowed. He was perhaps seven or eight years old at the most. His shock of short flaxen hair was twisted in knots while smudges covered his face. He stood, shivering, his mouth opening and closing as he struggled to form words.

"What is it Marco?" Anna asked, moving towards him.

"C-come! H-hurry!" he stuttered.

"They took everyone, Anna! The sick ... the healers ... my aunt!" His bronze skin drained of its color as he spoke, leaving behind an orange pallor. His words came hesitantly, as if the act of sharing what had happened made it all the more terrible.

"Who?" Anna asked. "Who took everyone, Marco?"

"Giants!" He turned his haunted eyes on them. "Huge giants came out of nowhere. Katia sent me to tell you." His small face crumpled as he fought back tears.

"They – they shot me! Katia threw fireballs at them so that I could get away, but I saw them catch her. They have some sort of strange fire. It hurts—" He winced and turned around, pulling up a blackened tunic. A gaping wound of charred skin and cauterized, raw flesh lay exposed underneath.

"Aedan," Clara whispered as she stole into their salt house after dark. He was cuddled on the blanketed floor with the children, who were fast asleep.

"What is it, Clara?" he asked, reaching an arm toward her, an invitation to join him on the ground.

Clara knelt down, whispering in his ear, "It seems that we're not alone."

"What do you mean?" he mumbled sleepily.

Clara took his hand in hers, using her fingers to sign the letters for 'Doctor Michael' into his palm.

A wide smile formed on his face as she signed and he pulled her close in a firm embrace. "What a relief."

Chapter 20

Tongue of Fire

"Where did they go, Marco? Where did they take your sister and the others?" Anna kept her voice steady.

It was so quiet that Qeriya could hear the plop of a frog entering the water as she waited. She brushed the back of her hand across her lips, tasting something bitter. It took her a moment or two to realize what that bitterness was — Fear! It was the taste of fear!

Marco pointed east. "T-that way! That's where they took Katia."

He twisted around to examine his bloody wound. "Their fire isn't like ours," he said, still trembling.

Lahcen approached Marco and gently lifted his tunic to expose the wound in full. "This shouldn't hurt, Marco," he said as the little boy stiffened apprehensively.

Lahcen drew liquid from around him, and just as he did so; Qeriya felt her skin grow taught. He positioned the layer of water over Marco's wound and, remarkably, the water remained in place as if it were a solid thing. "It's saline," Lahcen explained. "I drew it from everyone's skin. It won't hurt like plain water."

"They most likely went back to the volcano," Anna said, thinking aloud, hearing a swell of voices as the other reaume began to mutter quietly amongst themselves.

She placed a gentle arm around Marco, kneeling down so she could speak to him on a level. "You're a very brave boy, Marco," she told him. We're all very proud of you." She ruffled his hair. "Now, I know you've been through a lot, but there's something I need you to do for me, if you can?"

Marco swiped his arm across his tear stained face and nodded uncertainly.

Anna gave him a reassuring smile. "Good boy, Marco. I knew I could rely on you.

What I need you to do is, very carefully, go back to the camp. I want you to make sure the giants have really all gone. When you're certain, and only when you're absolutely certain that they have, I need you to check and see if any of our reaume managed to hide. If you find anyone, tell them we've gone to the volcano. Tell them to meet us there. Then I want you to come back here and help the children and healers. Okay, can you do that for me, Marco?"

This time when he nodded there was a little more determination in the young face and his shoulders were set as he limped away.

Qeriya's watched him go with tears in her eyes — brave, determined, wounded, and only a child. Abruptly, she fully appreciated the weight of responsibility Anna shouldered as the chosen leader.

Anna swung around to the gathered reaume. "The rest of you children and healers need to move the camp to our emergency location. Wait until Marco tells you it's safe and then help him organize it."

She gazed out, across the small assembly. "Are we ready?"

She was answered by an immediate transformation as fire spun through the reaume auras, encasing them in flame.

"Not Maria!" Qeriya pleaded, in a panic. "She's only ten. She can't fight! Let her help Marco!"

"She's the princess, she must fight," Anna's voice hovered in the air, like the multitude of female voices she'd once heard from the glass bubble. Then the living flames streaked away like burning meteorites, disappearing into the forest, leaving trails of singed leaves.

Khalid took one last look into the pond, just in case it yielded further wisdom, but nothing stirred the unbroken opaque surface. He reached for the limb of a banana tree, hoisted himself upward and fell back into the canopy. The full leaves cradled him like a slingshot, propelling him into the air, as he flung himself from branch to branch like a monkey. Lahcen stepped onto the water in the pond. Instead of engulfing him, the water puckered under his weight and then snapped taut like a piece of cloth yanked flat, flinging him in the direction of his brother. He gathered water from the humid air below, creating a path and riding the surf to join the others.

Qeriya glanced in the direction of the village. The thought of little Marco leading the young children into hiding made her heart skip a beat. She whispered a silent prayer to the Spirit and blew it gently towards them before swimming up into the air to join the others.

Once airborne, she could see a tower of billowing smoke drifting upward from a light blue mound that, she decided, must be the volcano in the distance.

She flew for what felt like an eternity, her heart pounded in her ears. Almost everyone who meant anything to her was heading toward a killer. But this was what she wanted, wasn't it, to fight for her parents? She arrived at the edge of the rainforest, where the trees had thinned, and found a skirmish already underway between the royal giants and the youth.

Anna was issuing orders in a crisp, commanding tone as she directed everyone into battle formation.

Qeriya watched as the reaume formed a series of circles, their backs to one another. Anna swiftly named the hunters as commanders, except for Maria, who was told to join a larger group led by Raquel. The look on Maria's face plainly said that she was not pleased with this arrangement, but she kept quiet. Qeriya, Lahcen and Khalid were left on their own to help in any way they saw fit. Qeriya decided to stick with Maria.

Enemy fireballs flew into the air and curved in their direction, coming from an army of giants who poured out of the volcano onto the vast plain between the rainforest and the mound. A large clear shield moved ahead of the giants, fortifying them as they marched. The fire reaume were forced to aim blindly over the top, hoping to hit as many as possible. Maria threw fast and far, her body pointing like an arrow with every toss.

"Wow!" Qeriya exclaimed. "You've got a powerful throw. You should be watching out for me instead of the other way around."

"I am," Maria said in a matter of fact tone as she whipped off another fireball.

Suddenly, Qeriya heard a loud scream and turned to see Raquel grab her leg in pain.

"Raquel! What happened?" Maria asked.

"They came from behind," Raquel winced. "It's their fireballs. Marco's right, they burn. I'll be all right in just a bit, it's minor." Lahcen rushed to Raquel's side to tend her wound as she lay on the ground, propped on her elbows, trembling.

"They've poisoned the fire!" Anna announced so everyone could hear. "Watch out for their weapons!"

Khalid moved deeper into the forest. Qeriya couldn't tell what he was doing until she saw a soldier, presumably part of a cadre that was hidden there. She assumed the enemy had planned to ambush them from behind.

Qeriya caught Beta's eye and Beta signaled to her group to follow Khalid, only to watch the giants turn tail and flee. Perhaps they knew that they were no match for the fire reaume at such close range. As they retreated to a few hovercrafts lingering back in the forest, Qeriya and the others pushed forward to overtake them. But they were not fast enough. The guards quickly boarded, and the craft sped towards the volcano with Qeriya in hot pursuit, only to realize that her companions had no intention of giving chase.

"Why are you stopping? Why don't you come? They're getting away!"

"That's right, they're running away, so they're not a threat anymore," Beta said.

"Yes they are a threat! They can tell the others about our position and our location and numbers ... everything! Not to mention, maybe we could learn something from them. We have to track them down!" Qeriya ordered. She glared at the group, but the reaume only stood there, motionless and, apparently, mystified.

What was wrong with them? Couldn't they see the danger in letting these giants go; trained men who had seen and could report everything to the king?

"It doesn't make sense, why would we imprison or kill them if they're running from us?" Beta asked, obviously, from the number of heads nodding in agreement, speaking on behalf of the group. Qeriya sighed, pushing down the urge to punch someone. She could see they were all genuinely bewildered.

"It's called taking offensive action," she tried to explain. "You know — in fireball — when a team intercepts the ball, they throw towards the goal? We've stolen the ball now and you just want to fling it out of bounds! You have to take the offensive to complete our mission. Defense will simply prolong the fighting, and that means more of us die. You want to win this battle, don't you?" She scrutinized one uncomprehending expression after another. This was going nowhere.

"But this isn't a game of fireball," Beta exclaimed. "They're alive."

"So are we, and that matters squat to them! Oh, never mind!" Qeriya muttered. The idiots just didn't get it, and she was so angry she thought steam might start coming out of her ears, and losing it wouldn't help matters at all. "C'mon," she said flatly. "Let's join the others."

Upon returning, Qeriya saw Khalid had cornered one of the giants, a straggler, in a thick patch of bamboo. The man was loaded with strange weaponry. Clutched to his chest was something resembling a thick tube and he used this to fire off random bursts into the forest around him. Khalid jerked his head at Anna who hurried over. He spoke into her ear and Anna nodded, immediately calling over a small group of reaume and issuing instructions in a low voice. Finished, she turned to Khalid and nodded once more.

Qeriya watched Khalid move off into the trees. The earlier incident with the band of reaume had left her wary and dispirited. She waited anxiously, wondering if the reaume would actually hold their ground if the soldier should decide to just up and walk away.

Whatever Khalid had in mind, Qeriya prayed for him to do it soon. A small movement at the edge of the bamboo caught her eye.

Khalid had taken a piece of twine from his backpack. He pulled it taught between his hands as he silently stole towards the giant from behind. At the last instant, the soldier's head whipped around — too late! Khalid's leap was well judged, carrying him into the air. Using the rope like a garrotte, he hauled on it, crushing his opponent's windpipe. The giant's hands clawed at his neck, desperately trying to dislodge the choke hold, but Khalid was ready. Leaping high once more, he looped the twine over the soldier's thick neck, pulling with all of his might. The huge figure crashed to the ground, narrowly missing him, but he hung on with grim determination as the creature thrashed to and fro, until, finally, it lay still.

Qeriya could see Khalid's hands trembling as the body finally went limp. It was the first time he had killed anything but scorpions. She could only imagine how he must be feeling, but there was no time to process anything. She had to get him out of there! Who knew what the thick vegetation might hide? Guards could be creeping up on her brother at this instant. Qeriya took to the air, flying over to Khalid. "Get moving!" she hissed, thrusting the pack back into his arms. Khalid obediently took it, his eyes, when she looked at them, were glazed with shock, but he followed her as they steered through the brush towards the crowd of fire reaume. Qeriya wasn't sure how focused he was, but it was urgent that she share what had happened on the chase, all of their lives might depend on the knowledge.

"That's why they need us, Qeriya," Khalid explained.

Qeriya breathed a sigh of relief as she saw he was coming back to himself.

"They literally don't understand—"

"Well they'd better learn fast!"

Qeriya saw the tension go out of Anna as they reappeared from the forest. She motioned the fire reaume together around her. "Listen," she announced, "I'm giving charge of this battle to Khalid. He'll lead us. Khalid, Lahcen and Qeriya are the only ones who can help us. Listen to them, even if what they say doesn't make sense to you. Obey them absolutely — as you obey me."

"I wish she'd announced that before I tried to get my group to go after the giants," Qeriya grumbled.

Everyone's eyes were on Khalid. For a moment he was silent, as he glanced around the youngsters whose attention he found himself suddenly the center of. Then he squared his shoulders. "Fire reaume," he said and his voice was edged with steel. "I'm only going to say this once, so you need to listen up." His gaze swept the crowd again, holding the look of each reaume for an instant before moving on. "This war is not going away. You're going to have to fight like you've never fought before. You're going to have to fight to kill!" A low, shocked murmur ran through the group. Khalid gave a sharp nod. "Yes, that's right — I said fight to kill.

"There is to be no mercy. Don't let them regroup. If they retreat, pursue and kill them, but don't follow them onto the plane. No," he said, hearing the gasps of disbelief, "it doesn't feel right — and I'm not going to justify it in any way. There's nothing right about it. But it's absolutely necessary if we want to survive. They won't be expecting this from you. The more aggressively we fight, the more we can surprise and overwhelm them, the faster we can win and stop this mess. I know this doesn't make sense to you, but it's an order. Just remember why you're fighting and what you want to accomplish!" Heads turned to look to Anna who nodded in agreement. A sea of frightened faces stared at Khalid and Anna.

"I know many of you are afraid," Khalid continued. "The idea of killing someone is completely foreign to you, but you're powerful! You can do this! And you're under orders. You *must* follow those orders, no matter what, because trust me, it's better to follow my orders than the king's orders."

Qeriya listened to her brother with growing admiration. She could see the sweat beading on his forehead; she knew that, inside, he must be scared too, but he didn't let his fear keep him from doing what he needed to and he spoke with a new authority.

Giants were amassing along the forest line. In one hand, each of them held a wide metal barrel from which fireballs shot forth, and in the other, a large container which they carried like a shield.

Anna pulled in a sharp breath. Inside her an alarm began to peal. Why would they be carrying containers into battle instead of custom made shields? The answer came to her in a staggering flash. "Get the containers if you can!" she yelled. "They hold our own!"

Lahcen gathered water from the forest mist, dividing it into sections. He threw the puddles, one at a time, with a flick of his hand, at those who carried the receptacles, covering each soldier's nose and mouth like a mask, depriving them of air until they fell.

Qeriya hurtled into action, flying over to the bodies, stripping them of their weapons and, together with a few other fire reaume, salvaging the containers and hauling them back to Anna at their temporary base, established further in from the forest border.

While the others fought, Anna opened the vessels and released the prisoners, who burst out of their prisons in fire form, then transformed and lay on the ground, relieved, but largely in a state of shock. One of them, Qeriya thought, was obviously Marco's aunt because, facially, she looked just like him. She struggled to her feet, immediately pinning Anna's attention with a wide eyed, silent plea for information.

"Marco's all right," Anna assured her. "He was wounded, but he'll be fine. He came to tell us what happened, just like you told him to do. I left him in charge."

Relief swept over the woman's face, she nodded a silent thanks before hurrying off to help the other prisoners who were being released.

Qeriya spotted Lahcen rounding up the kidnappers further north. He had fashioned the water into paddles that rained blows down on their attackers, forcing them into a small clearing. Once he had them all assembled, he formed a circle of spinning lassos out of the water, placing them around the giants.

Initially, Qeriya could see, the guards were not impressed by the idea of a bit of spinning water holding them prisoner but, as one of them found out when he gingerly poked the barrel of his weapon into it, the spinning lassos were lethal. The water knocked the weapon out of his hand, and, when he carefully retrieved it, he saw that it had been sheered off at the point of contact. Despite herself, Qeriya goggled. For a moment or two she was stumped by how it was possible to make water stronger than metal, then she grinned as she realized — it was the speed that provided the energetic force.

A volley of fireballs slashed through the air, skimming by so close to Lahcen's right side that he flinched, but he maintained the lasso. Qeriya tracked their source. Some of the guards who'd managed to avoid Lahcen's round up had circled around.

"Hang on, Lahcen!" she yelled, flying towards him, scooping

air into her arms as if gathering a load of blankets and shoving it towards Lahcen, blowing him out of the way as another volley of fire destroyed the tree he had stood in front of only seconds before.

Lahcen's power cut off like a snapped twig as his sister maneuvered him out of the way, and he could only watch helplessly as the freed giants scattered. "Gee, thanks for the help, sis," he said, not bothering to hide his irritation, "you're supposed to attack them, not me."

"You're welcome, you ungrateful brute." Qeriya scowled at him. "You're problem is, you just don't like that I saved your skin. You owe me one!"

Lahcen didn't respond, his eyes on something past her shoulder; he gathered water into his hand. Qeriya didn't need any warning, she hurriedly dropped low to the ground as Lahcen slammed a ball of water in her direction. It hit the fire ball streaking towards her back and exploded, leaving behind a cloud of searing steam hanging in the air.

"I think I just paid you back," he said, smirking.

New fireballs shot into view. Qeriya quickly compacted air in her hands. The pressurized air met the fireballs, causing an almighty explosion. As the smoke cleared, Qeriya stared, horrified, at the group of giants lying dead on the ground. She heard herself whimper as she went down on her knees, numb with terror at what she'd done: at what she'd been forced to do.

Lahcen squeezed her shoulder. "Take it easy, sis, I've got this." He was collecting and dividing water even as he spoke, his face grim.

Qeriya nodded weakly, trying hard not to throw up. She watched the men rushing toward them stop, clawing at the water that sealed them off from life giving air.

Qeriya willed herself to get to her feet and keep fighting. This was not something she could just sit out, leaving Lahcen alone to shoulder the burden of all the killing.

A loud whistle sounded, a call to regroup. Qeriya and Lahcen made a volte-face, melting into the forest to rejoin the others.

Khalid and Anna were stood in the middle of the gathered reaume and everyone's attention was fixed on something they were examining. Shouldering their way through, Lahcen and Qeriya saw that Anna had somehow managed to get one of the enemy weapons apart. Removing some of the fire, she had encased it in a globe containing some flame of her own. The silence in the clearing was absolute, everyone focused on the globe as her flame wrestled with the enemy fire like an animal, tossing and nipping the impostor, and eventually consuming it. A collective sigh of relief went up from the group.

Anna gave a satisfied nod. "Whatever this poison is, we can defeat it," she said. "Our flame is alive and it's stronger." She raked her hands through her hair, frustration washing across her face like a dark cloud. "Now if we only knew where they were keeping the prisoners, we could make a more precise plan."

Khalid looked at her. "I saw the rock caverns from the journal on the mound and in the lava streams. I imagine they're the prison cells," he added. "I'm afraid the only option we have is for you all to stir up the volcano and hope the king is forced out in the process. We need someone, or something, to annoy him, to distract him, like a mosquito, so some of us can get inside."

Qeriya glanced around, anxiously combing the trees for enemies. They were doing too much talking. If they didn't watch out, they'd be ambushed again.

Anna was shaking her head. "I agree we need a distraction, but stirring up the volcano's risky. What we need to do is find a way to distract them, so that a couple of us can get closer and look for chinks in their defenses. Then, when we attack, it'll be more effective.

"That's most risky for you guys," Khalid insisted. "It would lengthen the time you'd be fighting. Whereas a massive attack on the volcano will distract them more than anything else we could try and we can use the volcano itself as a weapon. The king won't expect you to risk your parents to mount a dangerous offensive. It'll give us the element of surprise, force them out, and provide a distraction, so you can figure out how best to release the prisoners."

Anna hesitated, her aura turning green. It was a shade Khalid was unfamiliar with, but her pallor told him all he needed to know.

"If we lead an attack on the volcano," she said, her voice shaking, "the prison cells may collapse — and with this poison fire—"

"That might happen, yes," Khalid said gently. "But I believe your parents would rather you defeat this monster and save what's left of your reaume than risk you all getting caught or killed. I know that's what my parents would want."

"Lahcen," Qeriya whispered, edging away from the group. "The escaped giants are taking their wounded back to the mound. If I follow them, they should lead me to the entrance. I can fly faster than they can run. There's still time to catch up. I'll stay low so they won't know I'm there. Finding the entrance will tell us where they're hiding inside the mound. We'll be able to mount a much more targeted attack without as much risk."

"Qeriya, that's insane!" Lahcen hissed. "There's no tree cover beyond the forest. That volcano mound must be at least a couple of miles away. You'll be spotted for sure. You wouldn't even make it back to tell us anything. And lava evaporates water. I wouldn't be any help if I went with you. Let's stick with the others."

"I can do it! I know I can! They won't see me if I hug the ground and I won't attack anyone unless they attack first. I won't go in, I won't even go close to the entrance. I'll just try to see where they're hiding, and come straight back." Qeriya edged away from Lahcen as she finished speaking. He lunged at her, but she was ready for him and slipped out of his grasp. Qeriya took off into the air with Lahcen hot on her tail, but as they scaled rocky terrain, his waterpower quickly weakened and he fell behind, leaving Qeriya on her own.

Qeriya flew close to the land. The air was drying out by the second. There's no way Lahcen could have made it this far. The giants were ahead, running en mass. They marched like machines, pulling a partial shield behind them. She rubbed her neck, remembering those large hands squeezing her, and kept her distance.

She wondered to herself how they could possibly fight a volcano. Khalid and Lahcen would be useless, since any water or plant life would evaporate. She was mildly helpful because she was able to fly. The fire reaume were the only ones capable of mounting an attack, and yet, even reaume power was limited, given the strange fire the king had produced.

Out of the corner of her eye, Qeriya saw a light coming up on her fast. Reaching her, it stopped, hovering by her side. "Juan!" she exclaimed. "What are you doing here?"

Juan grinned at her. "I could ask you the same. You left without instructions — or permission. But, I think gathering as much information as we can gives us our best chance. I want to help."

"But you're on fire. We'll be spotted for sure!"

Without answering, Juan blended the color of his fire into the black surface they flew over, as easily as he could meld with the hues of the forest.

"How do you guys do that?"

"I don't know. We just do."

"Well, let's stay close and keep our eyes peeled."

"Sure!" he said, and shot her another toothy grin.

They sailed over sheets of raw obsidian punctuated by large colorful blooms. Qeriya had a great respect for anything that could carve out a home here, in such an inhospitable place, and the blooms were some of the prettiest she'd ever seen. As they drew closer, below them, they saw the giants rush into a cavern leading directly into the mound, about two thirds of the way up the thick neck of the volcano.

"Look! The entrance! Quick!" They flew faster now, squinting to get a better sense of the precise location of where the guards had entered.

"Juan!" Qeriya yelled, but he didn't hear. Desperately she increased her speed, thrusting him out of the way just in time, as a thick stream of magma lashed out of the mound like the tongue of a frog, seeking to wrap itself around Juan and yank him into its hungry belly. Qeriya pushed him aside once again as more lava shot from the mound, reaching for him. Over and over the magma licked at them as they frantically dodged to stay ahead of its bite. They tried to fly back, but the lava just increased its stretch and the attacks came even faster. Qeriya rolled in every direction to escape the onslaught. They had split up to give each other some relief, but the blistering tongue was now intent only on her.

Juan rushed to help, shouldering her aside when she didn't recover in time from another assault. The next instant, she felt the sting of poisoned lava on her leg, as if a hot sword had sliced her flesh. Qeriya forced herself to keep moving. Freezing now, even for a second, would mean death. But how long could she keep this up? She was quickly tiring, and, judging from the wetness oozing into her shoe, she was losing blood.

Qeriya shook her head, her vision blurring as a heavy greyness blanketed her brain.

She could feel herself being jolted as Juan thrust her away from the unrelenting, endless onslaught from the tongue of fire. She fought to stay awake. Juan couldn't save them both without her at least trying to save herself. But it was as if she was wading through honey. Try though she might, the darkness was coming, eclipsing her vision, a great eyelid shutting down her consciousness. She barely felt strong arms enfold her as everything went black.

Clara concentrated on the letters her husband was forming in the palm of her hand, but it was hard, because she already knew what he was trying to communicate, and she didn't want to acknowledge it. He'd argued for a few years now that the kids should be allowed to race, that if they didn't give the boys more freedom, Khalid and Lahcen would take it for themselves. Clara had convinced herself that, somehow, she could preserve the bubble of protection she'd placed them in so carefully. But he was right; why did he have to be right? Already the boys were disobeying, and Qeriya was impulsive. There was no telling what she might do. Clara sighed. It was time to give her children some freedom, but she had a bad feeling ... a very bad feeling. And yet, what else could she do?

Chapter 21

Fire and Earth

"What happened?" Qeriya murmured. She opened her eyes to a plethora of long leaves, and, for a disorienting few seconds, she didn't know if she was lying on the ground seeing trees above or suspended in the air facing plants below. She had no idea how much time had passed or where she was, but she could hear voices in the distance. The battle was still raging. She tried to move, grimacing as her leg throbbed savagely. Looking down, she saw someone had bandaged it. Gritting her teeth, she fought through the pain and the waves of dizziness, forcing her aching body to obey, pushing to her feet from, what she had discovered, was the ground. Chaotic sounds of shouting and screaming cut through the forest, and Qeriya realized she was trembling, afraid those sounds heralded death and destruction for the fire reaume. She pulled herself together. There was nothing she could do about what was happening out there. Right now she had to concentrate on the immediate situation. She scanned the area for Juan, and found him lying on his side, tucked under a patch of tall, arching, lilies.

"Juan," she whispered. There was no answer. Bending down slowly, she placed the back of her hand above his mouth and held it there. He was breathing. Qeriya straightened up, examining their surroundings. Juan must have flown her here and bandaged her leg, only to collapse for some reason. He wasn't bleeding. Perhaps it was a head injury. She buoyed him up with air until he floated, then steered him in what she desperately hoped was the right direction. He had to get to the healers and she had to alert everyone to the location of the entrance.

Eventually, Qeriya found the reaume stronghold. The fighting was thick. The few guards who'd returned to the volcano seemed to have brought back reinforcements. Some of the reaume were on the field, randomly bombarding the volcano with fireballs, while others defended against bursts of poison fire attacks. The volcano, which had relentlessly lashed her moments ago, now appeared to be at rest.

"Nice shot, Maria," Qeriya called, as her cousin blasted a fireball at one of the enemy, who was about to fire at a fellow reaume.

Maria turned, staring at her in surprise.

"Hey, come here, I need you."

"I'm just warming up," Maria said, throwing more fireballs from her position, hidden amid a cluster of banana trees.

Qeriya marveled for a moment how Maria seemed to strike every target, whether it be poison fire or enemy insurgents.

"Maria, listen —" Qeriya persisted.

"So far, no one's died on our side, injured, yes, but none have died — because we fire reaume rock!" Maria grinned, letting loose some more fireballs. "Although, looked like you and Juan came close. That was scary. And the fighting's thicker now there's more giants."

"Maria, I need your attention, it's—"

"It was weird though. You were there — and then you were gone. Did you fly into the forest?"

"Maria! Listen to me! Where should I take Juan? He's injured."

"Injured! Juan?" Maria's jaw dropped open, she halted her pummeling. She couldn't have looked more shocked if she'd just been impaled from behind.

Qeriya was about to speak again, when Maria, trance broken, rushed to Juan's side.

"What happened?"

"I don't know. I was unconscious. I think he flew me out and bandaged my leg, but then, I don't know what happened. Anyhow, he needs the healers."

Maria looked back and forth between Juan and the battle.

"You probably won't be able to carry him. He's pretty heavy," Qeriya said, thinking out loud. "Shoot, I don't know where to take him, and I wouldn't see it if it were an inch away." Her eyes searched the ground cover as if it had an answer for her.

"I can carry him no problem, and I even know where the new camp is located. It's just—" She whipped some more fireballs at the enemy. "I can't leave the others."

"You can carry him? If you're sure, I can take over!"

"Of course I can carry him!" Maria huffed, annoyed by Qeriya's lack of confidence in her.

Qeriya slipped past to man the battle station Maria had established, watching as she ran over to where Juan lay. Grabbing a handful of sand from her pouch, fire pooling at the tips of her fingers, Maria raised her hand, spreading a weave of fast melting sand into the air around Juan, quickly forming a large glass bubble. Qeriya caught on and hurried over to lift Juan so that Maria could complete the sphere. Maria then towed an unconscious Juan deep into the forest to find the healer camp.

Seeing they were safely on their way, Qeriya turned to the task at hand, swiftly casting air to block a poison fire attack. Her volleys were fast, faster than the enemy, exploding their fire harmlessly before it ever came within reach of the reaume. She saw a giant targeting Beta and aimed her next strike at him. Beta's group manned the forest line, leaving them exposed; the other groups were deeper in the forest so better camouflaged.

None of the enemy forces had cover, but their sheer numbers were an overwhelming threat. Like the tongue of lava, no matter how many went down, they lashed at the reaume remorselessly. Qeriya frowned, she had to talk to the others, tell them about the entrance, as soon as possible. She had a strategy planned out in her mind. A small group could break off with her, circle north of the volcano, and ambush the entrance, catching the king off guard.

Just as she turned south, preparing to fly towards the heart of the battle, she saw a flash of hair and a knee pull back behind a tree. The figure was too small to be a giant. It had to be closer to her own size. Qeriya held her position, striving for a clearer sighting of the intruder. Again she caught a flash of something. Someone, Qeriya guessed no one friendly, was creeping towards her in the shadows. Whoever it was had somehow broken through their defenses unnoticed and was probably hoping to carry out a surprise attack.

Qeriya kept fighting, using air to detonate the enemy fire before it could get close enough to cause any damage, watching, with her peripheral vision, as the mystery person darted from tree to tree, closing in on her. She held her nerve, waiting for the figure to get close enough before swinging around and ... finding herself staring at a familiar face.

The green eyes that had sparked her affection not long ago, now incurred in her a resentment so strong, it pushed any fear she had into the background.

Prince Liam, his once handsome face marred with war paint and battle grime leveled his weapon at her.

Automatically, Qeriya gathered air to pummel him.

"Stop!" he said, the tone of his voice brooking no refusal.

"Is that supposed to be an order?" Qeriya spat. "I don't recognize your authority, prince!" Her heart pounded with rage as, without considering the consequences, she let fly with the air she had accumulated. It tore towards him, a cyclone, funneled and pressurized into a hot blast. It caught him off guard, but he was equally fast, meeting her weapon with a salvo of poison fire that exploded between them, sending them both reeling backwards.

Qeriya wrenched herself off the ground, spitting out a mouthful of dirt, quickly flying to where she had seen him fall. There was no sign of him, only the scuffed earth paid testament to the fact that she was in the right spot. Her ears registered a slight sound from behind and she whipped around, pushing outward with a wall of air, but Liam ducked behind a nearby tree, narrowly avoiding the blast.

Qeriya tore after him, plunging deeper into the undergrowth. It was useless, somehow, she had managed to lose him. Slowing to a stop, she stared wildly around her, hoping for some kind of sign, something to tell her which way he had gone. Abruptly, strong arms grabbed her, tugging her wrists behind her and pulling them, crisscrossed, up her back.

Qeriya screamed, more with fury than fear, flailing and kicking with every ounce of strength she could muster, but Liam merely tightened his grip. He was too big, too strong. She couldn't budge him.

"Stop struggling!" he ordered.

Qeriya could hear him gasping for air. Good, that told her he was at the edge of his strength.

"You're only hurting yourself," he said, beginning to drag her deeper into the forest. Qeriya drew in a lungful of air, ready to blow her breath into some kind of weapon. Crushing her wrists in one hand, the prince haphazardly covered most of her mouth and nose with a permeable, sticky substance that allowed her to breath, but left her unable to control the air, then he continued to pull her backwards. Qeriya lashed out, managing to land a kick squarely on his leg, but he only tightened his hold even more, until her hands began to go numb. She squealed through the sticky stuff as he lashed a thick cord around her wrists and legs, cinching it tight.

As he continued towing her further into the trees, Qeriya stopped fighting. She relaxed her arms and let herself be dragged along over the bumps and furrows of the forest floor. The cord was gradually loosening up and blood tingled painfully back into her hands.

"Where are you taking me?" She mumbled through what felt like a glob of tree sap.

"Somewhere," he said.

Qeriya thought his voice still sounded weak.

"Why did you do it?" she spluttered through the goo. Why did you pretend to be our friend when your heart was out for our blood? Do you even have a reason for killing everyone?"

"The sooner you learn to cooperate the sooner everything will be over," he said, straining, obviously irritated by the effort he was being forced to expend.

Qeriya did her best to make it as difficult for him as she could, digging her heels into the ground as deeply as she was able. Finally, he hoisted her over his broad shoulder. Qeriya squirmed, but any movement simply made his grip tighter.

"What is it you want?" she asked.

"What do you think I want?"

"You want to capture me."

He grunted. "I would think that was obvious."

"What do you want with us? Why are we such a threat to you? We're harmless."

"You think so?" he sneered, his words dripping sarcasm.

"Yes, of course! We don't want to rule, and we certainly don't want to hurt anyone. Why do you persist in killing reaume who are peaceful? They may be powerful but they're kind."

"D'you have it?" Liam asked.

"Have what?" Qeriya said, bewildered. Then she heard another, female voice.

"It's here, a covered one, like you said."

"Good! Give me some help here," he husked, "and watch out. You've no idea how much force those tiny muscles pack — she's got to be on steroids. You take her legs. I'll get her arms and open the hatch."

As the owner of the second voice swung into view, Qeriya shuddered. Standing before her was the woman with steel grey eyes, the same woman who'd come after her with a knife in the race

"This won't hurt a bit," the woman said, smiling.

Qeriya recoiled at what she saw. The woman's teeth had been filed into fangs, her face was painted white, dark grey circled her eyes. She wore a suit woven with silver strands of metal. Her dark hair was sectioned into thick chunks and twisted to stand straight out, like spikes, radiating from all over her head. She looked like the monster she was and Qeriya redoubled her struggles to get away. The prince and his companion mercilessly tightened their grip, forcing her to settle down. Beyond them, Qeriya could see a hovercraft. They carried her over and, opening it up, they shoved her, head first, inside. The woman stood back, waiting for the prince to slam the hatch. Qeriya held her breath, readying herself. As the door swung too, she thrust upward, slamming her feet into the metal, using the air in the cabin to strengthen her assault.

The door crashed open, knocking the prince off his feet. Qeriya heard the satisfying sound of bone splintering as his hand was impacted by the door. For an instant or two the woman stared stupidly from her to the prince. Qeriya knew she only had seconds, if they succeeded in trapping her inside the craft, she was lost. Yanking her arms free from the poorly tied wrist restraint, she threw herself forward, ramming her head into the woman's middle, hearing an 'oof' as the air was expelled out of her. The prince had staggered to his feet. He grabbed for her with his good hand, but all the fight had gone out of him and it was almost easy to shoulder him back off his feet. She rose into the air, putting some distance between them before stopping to rip her legs free and peel away the stuff smeared all over her mouth. That done, she turned to face her advisories again, only to see they were gone, hovercraft and all.

She weaved through the surrounding forest trying to pick up their trail, but it was as if they'd disappeared into thin air. The shame of her betrayal by the prince cut even deeper after this fresh assault. He had deceived her, and now she had been given an opportunity to best him and failed. Qeriya bit back tears.

Crying solved nothing. She had to get back and help the others. Taking to the sky, Qeriya set off to join the thick of the fighting once again.

Eyes narrowed, she surveyed the battle scene, searching for her brothers. Spotting Lahcen, Qeriya stepped out from behind the shelter of a fig tree just long enough to catch his eye before dodging back. He surfed over immediately. Seconds later, a poison fireball hit the space where he had stood. Qeriya blasted the enemy behemoth in return, while her brother remained oblivious to his near demise.

"You crazy nut!" he yelled, embracing her. "Don't do anything that stupid again. You're lucky to be alive. When you flew off there wasn't a thing any of us could do but start the battle. At one point, it looked as if both you and Juan were down." They ducked back behind tree cover.

"No," she said, "Juan got me out of there. Maybe you were right. Maybe I was a bit too hasty. I almost didn't get to share what I saw, but now I can tell you. The entrance is north of that notch." She peeled back leaves and pointed at the volcano. "Below the lip of the mound. There's a door. Do you see the discoloration in the face, two thirds of the way up?"

"Yeah, I see it," Lahcen replied, squinting.

"It's right there, a cave. That's where the giants disappeared. It was after they went inside that the lava tongue started lashing." She glanced at Lahcen. "I wonder why it stopped? Not that I'm complaining."

"I thought you and Juan did something to stop it."

Qeriya frowned. "No, we barely escaped. There was nothing we could do to stop it." They studied the volcano, Qeriya breaking the silence. "Lahcen — I was nearly captured just before I found you."

"What!"

"The prince, he dragged me into the forest." She shivered at the memory. At the time all she had wanted to do was fight him.

Now, reflecting on what had happened, she felt a lump of fear in her throat and quickly swallowed it.

Hearing a familiar, terrifying sound, Qeriya jerked her gaze toward the volcano. The magma tongue had reared its head again, like a Cobra aiming to strike.

"Anna!" Qeriya yelled as the lava targeted its next victim. Launching herself into action, Qeriya darted through the air, fast as lightening, thrusting Anna out of the way. Thwarted, the tongue struck the ground, leaving a trench of charred earth in its wake. Anna stared at Qeriya, dazed, but she quickly recovered, ordering the reaume to retreat.

They flew deep under tree cover once again as the blistering tongue probed the area, sensing for life forms as if it were itself alive. Perhaps the king was weighing whether or not to thrash the forest at random, Qeriya thought, or wondering if his objective was complete for the time being. After all, the young reaume had tasted his power. Maybe he figured they would be more cooperative now.

"Stop!" Raquel screamed, blasting through the forest, tailing what momentarily appeared to be a large bee, but which, Qeriya saw, was Maria returning to battle, having taken Juan to the healers. As Maria sped beyond the trees, into the battle zone, the magma lashed towards her before anyone could warn her.

"Maria!" Qeriya's scream pierced the chaos.

Instinctively, Qeriya, Raquel, Khalid and Lahcen raced to knock Maria out of the way. Qeriya got there an instant ahead of the others, scooping Maria up in her arms she flew forward. Suddenly walls of black rock appeared out of nowhere, surrounding them, rushing up toward them. Qeriya fought to slow their flight but she could see a collision was inevitable. Instinctively, she cushioned their impact with air, which bounced them backwards onto everyone else. They dropped to the ground, Raquel immediately reaching for Maria and gathering her up into a firm embrace. Qeriya heard the tongue striking at them over and over and steeled herself but, unbelievably, nothing more happened. She wasn't hurt — and, from the sound of it, neither was anyone else. A soft light came on, cutting through the darkness. Raquel held an illuminated globe in one hand and Maria with the other. Looking around, Qeriya saw they were enclosed in a black, rock dome; a shield that held fast against the attack from above. Try though it might, the lava couldn't penetrate the shelter.

"Raquel," Maria whispered shakily against her sister's shoulder, "just in case we die," her voice faltered for a moment. "In case we die, I'm sorry I got mad at you, I love you so much."

Raquel pushed Maria upright and stared her rattled sister in the eye. "Don't be silly, Maria," she said brusquely, "I already know all that. Pull yourself together. Dying's no excuse for losing your head." She brushed dirt from Maria's face and patted her on the cheek.

Maria eyeballed her sister in astonishment. Taking a deep breath, she struggled to calm down.

Qeriya didn't know what was more surprising, the protective dome coming out of nowhere, or her cousin showing such calm acceptance in the face of their brush with death. Hot on the heels of that thought came the sound of the magma attacking their fortress again. Qeriya held her breath, her heart galloping with fear, but it soon became clear that their shelter would hold.

"Where did the rock come from?" Qeriya asked Raquel and Maria. "Is this something all fire reaume can do?"

Both girls shook their heads, looking at each other in confusion. "Never," Raquel answered. "Fire reaume can direct lava to carve rock, and we can throw fire, but we can't wield rock. Rock is the domain of earth reaume."

"Who here is an earth reaume? Khalid?" Lahcen asked as the magma continued to strike at them overhead.

Before Khalid could answer, the noise stopped. For a long while they huddled together in silence and then, the rock disappeared as quickly as it had formed.

Free of the shield, they moved quickly, melting back into the safety of the forest.

"It must've been you, Khalid," Qeriya decided. "You're most like the earth reaume."

"It could be me, I guess." Khalid shrugged. "But I didn't feel anything," he said, trying to will the dome to appear again. Nothing happened. "If it's me then I need some practice." He jerked at the sound of a loud crack in the distance.

Qeriya stared in dread as the magma tongue prepared to strike at them again. Khalid lifted his arms and jagged rock erupted from the ground, rising, along with his arms, until it surrounded their heads like another dome.

"We need to fight back," Qeriya fretted, "before it goes after the others. But we can't see or move in here," she said, sliding the palm of her hand over the textured surface.

"We, or you all, really, since I'm useless out here," Lahcen said, pounding his fist into the other hand in frustration, "could work together to push the tongue back into the volcano's mouth. The pressure should force them out," he added.

"That might work if only we could see," Qeriya said. As she finished speaking her wish was granted and part of the top half of the shelter transformed, becoming thin and transparent, leaving open holes in the back to let air inside. "How did you do that?" Qeriya asked.

Khalid looked as surprised as she did. "I really don't know," he said, "when I need something to happen it ... just does. It's like the earth's reading my mind." His eyes, as he looked at her, were full of wonder and apprehension.

Qeriya smiled gently. "Yeah." She nodded. "I hear you. Anyhow, the entrance is located towards the top of the mound."

Khalid, who had been lost in thought, gave Qeriya a measuring look. "Can — could you fly this thing?" he asked, hands on hips, looking doubtful.

"W–ell, maybe if I circle a wind beneath us," she said, thinking aloud, scratching the back of her head, very unsure of herself. She couldn't reconcile how this would work. There was too much coordination involved. But then again, what else could they do?

"I'll try to maintain the shield while Qeriya flies us." Khalid dry washed his face before straightening and plastering on a smile. "How does that sound?"

"Don't try, just do it! Inspire us with some confidence why don't you!" Lahcen said tersely, pacing the small space back and forth. His lack of ability to help was making him antsy. "I just wish I could do something."

"You can." Khalid wiped his brow with his forearm. "You can keep us from getting thirsty. It's hot in here."

"Let's go!" Qeriya exclaimed. Mustering all her courage, she widened her stance to steady herself. "Ready?"

Moving to the back, she reached her arm through one of the openings Khalid had created, swirling the air into a funnel that lifted them, bumpily but steadily, off the ground. Khalid had been watching carefully, the instant the shelter rose, he quickly carved a rounded layer of rock underneath them, making their dome into a sphere. The wind caught the sphere, hauling it into the air, balanced on the crest of a spiraling tornado. Qeriya was pushed to the edge of her abilities, sustaining a cyclone while balancing the rock on the upward draft, careful to shift the storm as needed in order to catch them as they teetered one way or the other. Painstakingly, she aimed her funnel to allow her to place their fortress directly onto the magma tongue, predicting its frequent shifts, acting fast to compensate, and steadily squishing the snake like tongue back into its volcanic mouth.

The magma fought her at every turn, using its tremendous strength to push against the rock, thrashing about like a cornered animal in an attempt to whip them off, but just as Anna's fire had consumed the poisonous enemy fire, so the rock shield, powered by a storm, slowly and surely forced the lava into submission, until, at last, the mound was sealed. Qeriya dispersed the cushion of air between their sphere and the volcano opening, plugging it as effectively as a cork in a bottle. Khalid hastily sealed the holes of their safe haven and thickened the rock to add more protection from the extreme heat.

"The volcano won't be able to take the pressure for long," Khalid said. "It's going to blow. It's just a matter of time." He didn't say what they were all thinking: that they might end up crushing everyone, the prisoners along with the king.

"It's like that game we used to play," Lahcen said, trying to distract the others from their situation. "You know, the one where you run at the other person, and the first to swerve loses the game? Chicken, that's it, chicken, whatever a chicken is."

"You don't know what a chicken is?" Maria asked. "It's a bird. And it's really tasty, isn't it, Raquel?"

Raquel said nothing. Her face was green, whether with terror or motion sickness, Qeriya couldn't tell.

"Did you say you eat birds? That's awful!" Qeriya exclaimed in horror.

"We might not make it out of this, Qeriya, so eating birds won't matter one way or the other," Khalid said, face dripping with sweat. The heat had risen at an alarming rate and the dome was stifling.

"Raquel? Hello, is anyone there?" Maria waved a hand over her sister's face, but Raquel just lowered her gaze to the floor. Seconds later, she fell forward. Maria caught her before she hit the ground. "Raquel! Are you all right?" She turned her sister over, onto her back.

Lahcen knelt down, placing his ear close to her mouth. "She's breathing," he said. Don't worry. I think it's the heat." He lay Raquel down, making her as comfortable as possible. It's getting really hot in here. We should all sit down before we pass out."

Everyone slumped to the floor, along with Qeriya, her legs as heavy as a stack of salt bricks. She was completely exhausted, her breathing thick and labored. It felt as if there was no oxygen left in the air and, as when the tongue had bitten her, she could feel a greyness blanketing her brain.

Just as she was about to faint, Qeriya saw a host of hovercraft emerge from the entrance of the volcano as the king and his army fled from the caverns below. Khalid had carved a window of thin crystal to enable them to see outside. He opened it just long enough for Qeriya to tip the rock sphere off the top of the mound and let it somersault downhill, keeping herself and the others suspended in midair as it rolled. Lava blew into the sky like vomit, propelled by bubbles of gas, a shower of burning debris falling all around them as the rock rolled away from the mound. Finally, their domicile slowed to a halt, Qeriya relaxed her hold, gently lowering them all to the floor where they lay, spent. Finally, Khalid recuperated enough to carve a window once again.

Qeriya thought fresh air had never smelled or tasted so good. She could see from the other's faces that they shared similar thoughts.

Maria struggled upright. "The king escaped!" she husked.

"And we are not going after him!" Raquel said, her voice hoarse. Using the rock wall, she carefully climbed to her feet, turning to scan the rocky mound.

"You're all right!" Maria sighed, relieved. She gave her sister a firm squeeze. Raquel laid her head on Maria's shoulder, and this time it was Maria who offered comfort, stroking Raquel's hair and gently rubbing her back.

It reminded Qeriya of the times her mom had held her and comforted her in just the same way. She stared through the window at the volcano, at the trails of molten rock lying over everything, wishing now she had appreciated her mother more for what she did, instead of always chaffing against the restraints.

Fear cut into her like shards of glass, working its way up into her throat, making it hard to swallow. Would she, Qeriya wondered, ever have the chance again to tell her mom how very much she loved her.

Although the first, devastating blast was over, the volcano still spurted gasses, as if it were suffering a bad case of reflux. As they watched, glass globes began to emerge, popping out of the lava like bubbles, floating toward their rainforest home. Maria let out a cracked whoop, closely followed by a ragged cheer from Khalid. The adult fire reaume were free.

"It's Doctor Michael!" Qeriya exclaimed, seeing his limp form in one of the floating bubbles. "But where are Mom and Dad?" Around her, Khalid's shield was crumbling, like dough with too much flour in the mixture, sprinkling them with dirt. Finally free, Qeriya flew into the air.

"Where are you going?" Lahcen called, but she didn't answer. There was no time. She raced over to the globe that held Doctor Michael, directing the air currents, she steered him back towards where they had landed. Her eyes searched the globes filling the skies for a sign of her parents but she couldn't see them. Glancing at the glass containing Doctor Michael, Qeriya realized it was beginning to erode, turning into fine grains of sand that blew away. It didn't matter, she had him safely held on a cushion of air.

"It's Mom and Dad!" Maria exclaimed to Raquel excitedly.

Qeriya set down with Doctor Michael just as the sisters, becoming flames, streaked through the falling debris to meet their parents.

Overhead, the volcano rumbled again, the vibration causing Qeriya to stumble. Glancing up fearfully, she saw it no longer hiccupped spurts of flame. Instead, it vomited forth a massive column of lava, as if purging itself of the king's machinations. Every fire reaume in the area rushed to direct the lava flow and ash deposits, trying desperately to keep the deadly flood from overrunning them. A small sigh of relief escaped Qeriya; thank goodness the volcano was no longer poisoned. The thought was immediately followed by gut wrenching panic.

"Mom! Dad!" she screamed, bracing to fly into the center of the heat and chaos. Only to slam, face first, into Khalid's hastily erected barrier.

"No!" she screamed, clawing at the blockade imprisoning her. Blood streamed down from her forehead to mingle with the sweat on her brow. She had been too distraught to instinctively cushion her collision as she normally would.

Khalid was talking, she forced herself to focus. "Qeriya! Qeriya, we're all in danger and we've no idea where Mom and Dad are — or even if they're in there. We need you to roll us out of here."

"No!" She armed gore off her face. "I'm looking for Mom and Dad!"

Lahcen started to say something but Khalid signaled for him to be quiet. Gently, he placed a hand on her shoulder. "I know you want to get Mom and Dad, but if you leave, we'll all die. There's no way we can keep from getting buried alive by the volcano unless you move us."

Qeriya turned to face her brother, grabbing him, she hugged him tight, smudging blood onto his top. The pain of leaving her parents behind to be swallowed by rivers of boiling lava was a blade cutting through her heart, and yet, she couldn't abandon her brothers and Doctor Michael to certain death. She lifted her head and howled at the sky like a wounded animal. Around her the air stirred, twisting into a tornado that snatched the small group up in its teeth and careered off into the forest: away from lava, poison gasses, raining hot rocks and reams of volcanic ash falling like fine dust.

Qeriya strained with all her might to steer the storm while searching for a suitable place to put down. Finally, she spotted a clearing and carefully lowered them. Letting go of her control of the tornado, she collapsed in a heap. Covering her face with her hands, she gave way to the tears that threatened to choke her.

"Doctor Michael, Wake up!" Lahcen said, his voice insistent. Crouching, he examined the doctor's bloody and beaten frame.

"What's happening to us, Aedan?" Clara stared at her husband fearfully. "I can't feel my legs anymore. The numbness is inching up my body — it's happening to you too, isn't it?"

Aedan nodded as he slid down the wall of their house, joining Clara on the floor.

"Where are the children?" she fretted. "I'm scared, Aedan. I'm so scared," she cried, burying her head in her hands.

"Take my hand, Clara. We can't afford to be afraid," Aedan said steadily, reaching to firmly grasp her fingers in his. "I don't know what's happening to us, but I'm glad the children aren't here, in case it's something that could affect them. At least this way, when they come home, they'll see us and know straight away that something's wrong. They'll have the sense to be careful."

"What'll happen to them without us?" Clara mourned between sobs.

"They'll be fine," Aedan comforted. "They're smart, resourceful. We might not make it, but we don't need to be afraid, Clara, because the Spirit watches over us, and our children. You believe that, don't you?"

"Yes." Clara sighed deeply. "Yes, I believe."

"No matter what happens, all will be well," Aedan said. "Besides, they have Doctor Michael."

Chapter 22

Rebuild

The tent flap opened and Qeriya sneaked inside. She was carrying a gourd from which steam curled lazily upward. Carefully sitting down at the foot of Doctor Michael's wide cot she studied him as he slept. Dark circles hung heavy under his closed eyes and bandages created an unattractive patchwork of his skin. But he was alive, and fortunately his injuries were treatable.

These days, for her, every morning began in silent tears. She wiped them away, determined to enjoy her coffee. Her brothers still slept in the middle of the floor, around Doctor Michael, whose bed edged one side of the tent. They had been given the largest dwelling in the temporary camp. Cloth tents, covered with an oily wax, replaced the thatched homes of their former village.

"What about Orchid Pond? Will you travel back to use it?" she had asked earlier, only to receive a stony silence.

Finally Juan had explained, the king, he said, had control of the pond. Everything they had seen had been what the human king meant them to see. He had used their dependence on Orchid Pond to lure them into battle. They had been wrong, he said. The pond was not sacred at all.

Qeriya had been relieved to see that Juan was well again. He had sustained a concussion and had no memory of the fight, but had suffered no other damage.

Considering the numbers of giants who had died in battle, their own side had lost so few, and yet to reaume, any loss of life felt like defeat, especially in light of what they had discovered about their pond. The fire reaume carried this new awareness like a burden. While rejoicing in their reunion, they were left with gaping questions and a lot of heartache. They had believed in their oracle for centuries, faithfully following its instructions. Where had those instructions come from? Who had given them? What was this body of water they had once considered a medium for the divine? The mystery consumed them.

"Just because you were mistaken about the pond, doesn't mean the Spirit doesn't exist," Qeriya had told the disillusioned reaume. "I pray to the Spirit, but my faith doesn't depend on an oracle, it doesn't depend on a place or any sort of object. The Spirit you worship *is* real, it's alive and blows where it will, and nothing can contain it. Its house is just not what you thought it was, and it doesn't communicate as clearly as you imagined." She had tried to reassure them, because, somehow, in all the chaos she had experienced in the last few months, the Spirit had grown ever more real to her. There were times it had felt like the only reality in her life. Yet she also knew that when your paper house had been ripped apart, it was hard to rebuild, especially if you once thought the walls you had were solid. After something like that, it was difficult to believe that walls even existed capable of holding off a storm.

Qeriya sat by Doctor Michael's bed, watching his chest rise and fall. It was all that marked him as alive. If only she knew that her mom and dad were still breathing. A small, sad smile briefly twisted her lips — what she wouldn't have done to escape them a few months ago. She had taken them for granted, now their absence split her heart in two. How fragile were the ties that bound people together, so quickly dissolved by illness, betrayal, distance and ... she didn't want to think about the other. Despite her new family and her brothers, she felt alone in the world.

And yet, she wasn't really lonely. Everyone was alone, alone together; the Spirit of life that coursed through her, coursed through all life. The love she felt came from somewhere besides her. And even though her candle might extinguish, her light would live on, as would her parents, her friends and family. She felt that reality as keenly as she felt the gourd full of coconut coffee in her hands."

Anna, Juan, Maria and Raquel funneled through the door of the tent and tied the stiff curtain to the side. As the light outside brightened, it stole into the darkened space until a grey glow permeated the tent. Khalid and Lahcen awoke abruptly and propped themselves against sturdy posts on the other side of the tent from Doctor Michael, resting on their soft bamboo bedding.

Lahcen stretched his muscular frame and yawned, then rose to pull back a window flap at the other end of the tent. They all sat cross-legged on the floor, loosely gathered around Doctor Michael's bed. Anna scooted next to Khalid. Qeriya saw him clasp her offered hand and smile, lips pinched closed. He turned away to breathe into his other hand, checking his breath. His eyes grew big and he looked as if he was about to choke. Qeriya chuckled.

"What's so funny?" Juan asked as he folded his long frame next to her, smiling. Qeriya knew the appropriate response was to smile back and answer, but she was so embarrassed by his presence, that her smile grew much too large to be cordial and her attempt at hello sounded like a mouse squeak.

"How are your parents? Have they recovered?" Khalid asked Anna, avoiding breathing on her.

Qeriya listened hard, curious to hear about the experience of the imprisoned adults.

"Yes and no," Anna said, wagging her head from side to side. "Yes —they've physically recovered, but — no in the sense that it took a lot of assurance on my part before they'd let me out of their sight, despite my having led the youth without them for months now.

"Anyway, everyone says that the worst part of being in prison was being separated from their children, and not knowing if we were all right." She stifled a groan. "So now, they want us close by all the time. The youngsters are equally attached to their parents, even now, three weeks later, but for those of us who are older—"

"It's insufferable!" Maria exclaimed, collapsing onto a pile of meticulously folded blankets she had previously stacked in squares to form a cushion to sit on. "I'm ready for Mom and Dad to take a vacation without me, or else let me have one from them," she added.

"Maria, that's unkind!" Raquel chided, reaching over and shaking her sister's knee to emphasize her point. "They were imprisoned! Have a heart."

"Oh, I know all that. It just gets a bit overwhelming at times," Maria said, rolling her eyes.

"Those of us who are older and more independent are feeling a little stifled, that's all," Anna explained more gently. "I'm sure that'll change in time, especially when they realize how much we've grown."

"So, what comes next?" Juan asked, his eyes darting between Qeriya and her brothers. "Do you have a plan? We'd like to come with you and help."

Lahcen rubbed his chin with a thumb. "Thanks, Juan, that's nice of you to offer, but I don't know that we'll be going anywhere soon. Who offered to come?"

Qeriya nearly choked on the lump forming in her throat as the horrific thought entered her mind, the one she and her brothers had so far refused to give voice to, that their parents must be dead.

"Everyone you see here, Anna, Raquel, Maria and myself."

Qeriya kept her voice level by a sheer effort of will. "Didn't you just say how worried your parents were?"

"Yes, but they know we're determined to go, no matter what they think, and they're also grateful to you," Anna said, looking at Qeriya and her brothers with an expression of deep gratitude. "They know that you need help, and none of them have recovered their strength enough at this point to be able to. The giants kept them on the verge of starving the entire time."

"How awful!" Qeriya said, her eyebrows knitting with worry as her thoughts drifted to her parents and what they'd probably suffered. She just hoped they hadn't awakened from hibernation at any point during their imprisonment.

Qeriya heard a rustle beside her. Turning, she looked up to see a shock of Doctor Michael's disheveled hair lift off the pillow and move back and forth, as if the hair itself were the protruding antenna of some strange creature searching the room.

"Doctor Michael, you're awake!" she exclaimed.

The doctor flinched in surprise. "I am now," he croaked, pulling in a deep breath. He reached out a frail hand to Qeriya and smiled. Qeriya took it and gently squeezed back.

"Are you all right, are you feeling better?" Khalid asked.

"I'll put it this way. I don't feel all right, but I am all right. A few aches and pains, but from what I can tell, that's all." He groaned as he tried to lift himself into a sitting position.

"A few aches and pains? Yeah, right. Lie down and rest." Qeriya said, gently pressing him back down.

She was unable to contain her questions though. "We know you were captured, with our parents, but we didn't see them before the volcano blew." The lump that lingered in her throat made her voice ragged. "M-mom and Dad ... did ... were they—" Qeriya broke off, glancing up to the tent ceiling, struggling to dam the flow of her tears. The room grew silent.

"We believe our parents must've died when the volcano erupted," Khalid finished, a catch in his own voice.

"Died? No! Certainly not! No, they aren't dead!" Doctor Michael asserted, wincing as he spoke. "You didn't see them because they weren't there. They were imprisoned for a time, yes, but, eventually, they were taken away to the palace."

"How do you know they weren't just moved to another cell?" Qeriya asked, trying hard to squash the hope that had sprung to life at the doctor's words.

"I heard the giants talking, after they'd interrogated me." Doctor Michael closed his eyes, when he opened them again, they were full of pain. "There were three of them. They spoke as if I was invisible … Anyhow, I just know, and they're still in stasis."

Qeriya's heart beat a little faster, she could feel her hands shaking and her legs were suddenly weak; a mixture of fear and relief. They were not dead! They were not even suffering! And yet, they were still prisoners.

Doctor Michael looked around at them. "Could I … trouble you for some water?"

Lahcen smiled. "Coming straight up," he said, ducking out of the tent.

"This is an interesting place," the doctor said, propping himself firmly against the pillows, his eyes surveying the tent. He smiled abstractedly at the strange faces. "My goodness — quite a crowd."

"These are our friends," Lahcen said coming back in at that moment, carrying a gourd in each hand, gesturing to each as he introduced them.

"Water and fresh papaya juice," he said. "Which do you want first?"

Doctor Michael took them both off him, immediately taking a gulp of water. "It's certainly good to meet you all," he said before draining the rest of the bowl and handing it back to Lahcen. He tried some of the juice and a look of intense pleasure crossed his face. "Delicious!" He looked down at his wounds, covered with transparent bandages.

"How interesting," he said, sipping at the juice. "These bandages are clear and cool, like gel. They alleviate pain and itch, but don't smother the wound. They breathe somehow. I wish I had these back in the desert."

Qeriya smiled. Her parents might not be safe, but at least they were alive and not in any pain. A small glimmer of hope returned, and this time she made no attempt to stamp it out. Even so, there was a persistent, dull ache in her heart. Relieved though she was that her friends were now reunited with their families, in some ways, it made the constant ache that she carried more difficult to endure.

"The camp's coming along. Rebuilding will be tough, but at least they've got their priorities straight," she said, lifting her bowl in tribute. Coffee had tasted bitter when she'd first tried it, but then Juan had filled the rest of her gourd with a great deal of coconut cream and palm sugar. Now, morning coffee was her favorite part of the day.

"Where are we anyway?" Doctor Michael asked.

The three of them looked to the floor like shamed children. Qeriya knew that telling him where they were meant admitting they had disobeyed his orders to take the Eastern border and avoid contact with the reaume. But they would have to come clean sometime.

Lahcen spoke first, "We're in the rainforest, with the fire reaume. Remember them — from the pictures in the cave?"

The doctor nodded. "Yes, I remember. How did you get here?" he asked.

Khalid's head had sunk so far down he gave the impression that he was meditating on his knees.

Lahcen patted him gently on the arm.

"What's wrong? What happened?" Doctor Michael probed.

"Well, we didn't exactly go where you told us to," Khalid admitted reluctantly. "You said to go west, but we crossed the eastern border."

Doctor Michael tilted his head, as if trying to make sense out of this.

Khalid met his gaze squarely. "You have to understand," he said, "we didn't know about the surveillance. All we knew was that you followed us to the cave and saw us practice our powers. You were the *only* one who ever saw us. By the time we took part in the race, we were being hunted. Then our village was poisoned and something happened to our parents. I had to consider the facts. It was all too much of a coincidence at the time. It wasn't that I believed you were against us, it's just that I had to be cautious."

Doctor Michael's thick eyebrows crumpled into a tuft above his nose and he scrutinized his cream-colored bedcovers. "After all the time I've spent with your family, didn't you trust me?" he asked. He tried to pull himself into a full sitting position, but Qeriya gently pressed him back down against his pillows once again.

Khalid kept his voice level. "Doctor Michael, our parents were ill — our village was gone. We left like you told us to, and we took your journal. I have listened to you. But I'm the eldest, and that means I'm responsible for my brother and sister. I had to do what I thought was best."

Doctor Michael gave Khalid a long, searching look. He sighed. "I understand your predicament, but you need to trust me, Khalid." The wrinkles on his forehead deepened, making him look old and frail. "Your mission will fail unless you do."

Khalid looked at the floor, avoiding the doctor's stare. Anna stroked his arm. Qeriya sent him a quick, sympathetic smile. She had been furious over him not following the doctor's directions. But time and circumstance had matured her and now she knew that Khalid had been weighing his options, trying to do his best to lead them, and keep them safe.

Something else was worrying at her. Something she had to ask. "So," she said hesitantly, "does the king plan to kill our parents?"

The doctor gave a slight shake of the head. "No, they won't kill them," he said. "Your parents are too valuable right now. Remember, it's you they've been looking for all along."

"So all those people in our village, sick, dying, because of us?" Qeriya said, bile rising in her throat. She stared at the floor, momentarily blocking out the true horror of the implication. Her eyes spotted a spider walking across the bare tarp in the middle of the tent. It stopped when it encountered a moving blanket at someone's feet, scurrying first one way and then the other, surrounded on every side by obstacles and unsure of what to do next.

"It's not *because* of you that they're dying, it's as a *result* of you. There's a difference. The king wants you. The truth is, I'm afraid now that there's more to this illness your parents have than I realized. Frankly, it's an uncommon disease for a desert location." He paused. Glancing around at them, he said slowly, "I believe they've turned it into a biological weapon. Somehow, they infected your parents, banking on it being quick acting and virulent enough to spread from them to you. Only you didn't come home from school that day. You messed up their plan. Your parents were already unconscious by the time we returned from the cave."

The spider stood paralyzed in the middle of everyone, surrounded by enemies. Qeriya knew that a number of spiders in the rainforest were poisonous, and yet, why kill a spider because it may be poisonous and might bite someone? Why poison a village because three people in it may have powers and might be prepared to use them against you?

"The desert provided a situation of natural quarantine, so there'd be no risk of the infection spreading elsewhere if anyone else in the village contracted it. But, on the infinitesimal chance that it might, the feast in celebration of the games gave them an effective preventative." He sighed. "Poison the entire village, you stop the spread in its tracks, and maybe even get you guys in the process."

Doctor Michael shifted his position, favoring his right side, and giving his back some relief. Qeriya leapt to help him, but he held up a hand to halt her. He moved surprisingly well for someone so beaten, Qeriya noticed, encouraged.

"Your parents suspected all along that the king might attempt to search you out. It was their biggest and constant fear. So they had me watch you while they were at work. I've been keeping my eye on you for a while now. Although," he hesitated, frowning, "I didn't consider the possibility that they might be targeted to get to you." He shook his head again. "It makes sense now, though. They'd be weaker, easier to reach."

"Why do they want to kill us?" Qeriya asked, her attention still on the spider, which remained frozen in place.

"You three are the first children *ever* born of reaume and human parents. You've each inherited a different reaume power, except for fire. You're wild cards — a major threat to the king. Perhaps he wants to make an example of you to others who might want to intermarry and have children with unpredictable powers." He shrugged. "Perhaps he has reasons we don't know about yet."

"Do you know much about the other reaume?" Lahcen asked, hugging his knees to his chest.

"There are three other reaume, and they rarely have contact with one another, much less with humans. Intermarriage between reaume is, practically speaking, nonexistent. To have multiple intermarriages, especially in one family line, and then bear children with a human is rarer still. Science has clearly shown that this combination of DNA is almost impossible. The few children who've been born human and reaume — yes, I've found that there have been a few over the years," he said in response to the muttering that had arisen at his revelation. "The few children born have only possessed human characteristics, never reaume and yet, here you are, three children in one family, all exhibiting reaume power."

Silence spanned out in the tent as the doctor finished speaking and the three of them exchanged uncomfortable glances, very aware that their friends' eyes were on them. Qeriya felt like the poor spider, stuck, surrounded by obstacles on every side and weighed down by a hate so great, it ate her hope away. How could they ever help their parents or have a normal life with the king so vehemently against them?

"The king's afraid of your power," Dr. Michael continued. "He wants you dead. I'm pretty sure he planted people in the competitions whose job it was to kill or wound you. Either would've done. Then his 'medics' could've carried you off without suspicion. But you won instead, and the earnings meant you could escape and survive in the outside world."

"Why didn't the prince just kill us when we got the awards?" Khalid asked.

The doctor smiled grimly. "That would be easier said than done. You're more powerful than you realize. Plus, they would've had a war on their hands. And you three might just have slipped away in the midst of it. As it was, the way he played you, the prince almost got you all to eat the poisoned food before anyone else tasted it."

Qeriya bowed her head and clenched her teeth until her jaw hurt.

"Your parents are as safe as they can be for the time being. Only I know how to release them from stasis, so the king can't question them, and they won't kill them until they're certain they have you. Now," he said, suddenly brusque. "You need the flower, both to save your parents and in case they manage to infect you. Because of this, trust no one. You never know if there are spies about who'll hurt you, even among the reaume nowadays."

Raquel scooted forward on her hands and knees to the middle of the floor, while Qeriya watched without comment. Her cousin formed a small globe around the spider, gently sealing it underneath so it would not injure the little arachnid. Picking up the globe, she ducked outside.

"Which is it, Doctor Michael? Make up your mind, trust no one or trust you?" Lahcen teased to break the tension.

"Oh, you know what I mean," Doctor Michael grumbled,

waving a hand at him.

"So, they beat you for helping us?" Khalid asked, still avoiding the doctor's gaze.

"They figured there was probably a plan in the journal I gave you and wanted to know what it was, and they also wanted your parents out of stasis."

No one moved or spoke, feeling for him in his injured state, only able to imagine what he must have suffered at the hands of the enemy, and yet eager to know what he might have been forced to reveal. The doctor sent them a tight smile. "Don't worry, I told them the truth. I said that if I brought your parents out of stasis, they'd die and be of no use to them. I told them the infection they'd introduced was very advanced, that that's why I put them in stasis and under protection, which was true. They asked me why you escaped by way of the eastern route, and if you were in contact with the rainforest fire reaume. Again, I simply told them the truth, how I instructed you to cross the western border, knowing you'd be able to survive the desert. That if you'd taken another route, then you'd gone against my instructions, and that might mean you didn't trust me."

Qeriya sighed with relief.

Doctor Michael glanced at her. "They beat me bloody anyway, and continued to do so, frequently. They kept me in the cell with all the parents. I don't know why."

"That's where we first saw you — and our parents," Khalid said, "in the prison cell."

Just then, Raquel slipped back inside and sat on the floor. Qeriya smiled at her gratefully. Hopeless as its situation had appeared, the spider was all right now. Things were never as hopeless or impossible as they seemed when someone was looking out for you.

"How? Where did you see this?" the doctor asked.

Khalid shook his head. "I can't really explain how we saw you, or exactly why we did. The fire reaume have a pond that projects images and instructions. They believed it was some sort of oracle, but it wasn't. The king was showing them what he wanted them to see."

"We believed that it connected us with the Spirit," Anna added, "but then it stopped working when our parents were captured."

"A water library," Doctor Michael said. "I've only heard of them, I've never seen one. Amazing!"

The fire reaume looked from one to another to see if any of them recognized what a water library might be, but no one seemed to have heard of such a thing.

"What's a water library?" Lahcen asked. He was reclining on a mass of soft bedding, his ankles crossed, rocking his feet back and forth: the only thing moving in the room as everyone sat, stone faced, waiting for an explanation.

"A water library is a type of computer," the doctor told them. "It's a way of storing and accessing information, and an older means of communication. They were originally programed for the reaume with instructions on terraforming the planet, very sophisticated for their time. I'd thought they were obsolete. The king must have discovered that the water library existed and figured out how to hack into it. It recognizes users at the slightest touch and customizes information for them." He looked at Khalid. "You say it showed me and your parents in the prison cell?"

"Yeah, a few times. You were hurt, and Mom and Dad were unconscious, on stretchers."

"So that's why the giants beat me so much and kept me in there. That's why they put your parents in there. They were using us as bait! They filmed me in the cell with your parents and somehow fed the image onto the pond, hoping to draw you into battle. Fortunately you won."

"There's something I don't understand," Lahcen interjected. "Why didn't they just use our parents? Why hurt you?"

"You'd all seen your parents unconscious. They were probably banking on the fact that if you saw me in pain, it might push you into acting more quickly."

"Which it did, of course," Qeriya confirmed. She went to pat his leg, halting in midair. She didn't know which parts of him were uninjured and she certainly did not want to hurt him even more.

"They probably also thought you knew, even though you don't, that I'm not just your parent's friend. I'm also your uncle."

Qeriya sat up straight. Uncle? She would have never guessed such a thing could be true. Her mind raced through the years she had known him, hunting for some hint, some sign she had missed, but while they saw him frequently, there was nothing that could have made her think that he was anything but, well, Doctor Michael, a friend of the family, at least until just before they had been forced to leave. And yet, her parents had not been free to do and say as they might please. They were being watched. Of course they wouldn't advertise such a connection while under surveillance.

Lahcen's face mirrored her own shock. "Uncle? You're our uncle? How?"

Doctor Michael thirstily finished off the papaya juice. He closed his eyes for a few moments, tugging a thin bamboo blanket up to his chin before speaking again.

"I'm your mother's older brother. I was born when our parents," he nodded towards them, "your grandparents, were very young. It wasn't until I went off to a boarding school that your mother was born. I was eleven, I saw them as often as possible, but then it became too dangerous for me to come home. The king was growing wary, it had come to his attention that our parents were reaume sympathizers.

"After boarding school, I attended medical college at the palace, under a fake identity my father had managed to get for me, before they were imprisoned. It was then, before my first year in medical school, that they sent Clara away." He sighed heavily. "They didn't tell me — in order to protect both of us. Eventually I found out that she was living in the desert. I moved there in search of her.

"She'd grown up, but she still looked the same. I could see she had no idea who I was. She'd changed her name to Ruth to keep herself hidden. After a while, I confessed it all, who I was, that I'd come looking for her. We could only talk in code, an elaborate code your parents had developed."

"Uncle," Qeriya rolled the word around her tongue to see how it felt. She'd gone from no extended family, to having aunts, uncles and cousins, all in the space of a few months, but even so, she'd known this uncle for a long time.

"I never would have guessed. You and Mom don't look anything alike," Lahcen observed.

"Neither do you guys." Doctor Michael chuckled and Qeriya saw everyone shaking their heads in agreement.

"And here, we didn't think we had any family. Mom and Dad said they were only children," Qeriya told him.

"They didn't have a choice," Doctor Michael said.

"Oh, I know!" She struggled to speak despite the tension building in her chest. "Thank you." She took his hand firmly in her own. "I love you, Uncle."

The doctor stiffened. He patted her hand awkwardly. "You too, dear," he said and smiled.

"Do you know what happened to Mom's parents, your parents — our grandparents?" Khalid asked. "You said they were prisoners. Are they still alive?"

"They were alive and in good health when I left the palace. I'm assuming they're still alive. They're under house arrest, but they're treated very well. The king wants them alive. They're very knowledgeable, and experienced scientists, brilliant by any account." He suddenly looked very tired. "Their names are, Einar and Alexis."

Qeriya stared, as did her brothers, scarcely able to believe that they could have living grandparents. She had always been so envious of friends who had grandparents. Now she was discovering what a rich family of aunts, uncles, cousins and now grandparents she had, all of whom had cared for her over the years, even though she had been unaware of that.

"I hope we can meet them," Khalid said.

"Well of course you'll meet them, just as soon as you do what you set out to do. Listen, Khalid," Doctor Michael added, "obedience is your key to survival. I can help you, but I need you to trust me. Your wellbeing is what I care most about."

"Well, I think obedience is the best way to show love," Maria said. "So, Raquel, if you really love me, like you say you do, you'll obey me."

"I'll gladly obey you if you're queen, but until then—" Raquel let the rest hang.

"It's not if — it's when," Maria interrupted, "when I'm queen."

"Whatever you say, Maria." Raquel rolled her eyes, obviously not amused by the conversation.

"No way, Maria! We need you on the hunt! Let Raquel be queen," Juan teased.

"Why do you want to be queen so much anyway?" Raquel asked, irritated.

"Because, then I get the power!" Maria smiled hungrily, rubbing her hands together.

"I'd like to think that you're joking," Raquel said tightly, "but something tells me you're only joking in part. Do you really enjoy being in power that much? Why?"

Qeriya felt a nudge on her arm and saw that Khalid had inched closer.

"Listen, Qeriya," he said, keeping his voice low, speaking under Maria and Raquel's arguing. "I owe you an apology."

"Why?"

"For not being more supportive and available for you,

especially after what happened with Anna."

Qeriya stiffened.

He saw it and sighed. "I don't mean to bring it all up again. It's just that in trying to protect you, I've ended up hurting you. I should've listened. The truth is, you've had to grow up fast, and my not wanting to admit that has only made it harder for you. But you have grown up. We wouldn't have got this far if it wasn't for you."

Qeriya stared up to the sloped ceiling once again, stemming the tide of tears threatening to fall. She smiled, squeezing his hand in appreciation. She knew that if she spoke right then, tears would follow, and she was tired of crying.

Mustering his strength, Doctor Michael interrupted the arguing sisters. "Craving power for its own sake," he began, "that's why the king is more aggressive toward the fire reaume these days. The giants spoke about the Great War, how some reaume killed out of vengeance and how the fire reaume not only grew in power, but hungered for it."

"That's not true," Raquel countered, sounding panicked. She rose up on her knees. "Reaume are not tempted by power. We detest aggression."

"No? Are you certain of that?" Doctor Michael asked, propping himself up on his arm, dark hair standing on end. "Just right now, you said that your sister acted like a human."

He was staring at Raquel almost accusingly, but Qeriya knew that he was simply trying to emphasize the truth of his argument. The room had fallen uncomfortably quiet.

"That's just ... part of her nature," Raquel mumbled, darting a glance at her sister.

Qeriya also swiveled her attention to Maria, who sat quiet and still, huddled on the floor, chewing her fingernails and trying to appear oblivious.

Lahcen was looking at Doctor Michael. "What do you mean when you say that some fire reaume wanted power? That's not what we've seen at all."

The doctor frowned. "It isn't normally in their nature, but that's changing. Maria's an example of what's happening to the reaume as a whole."

"How? How can that happen?" Lahcen pressed, sitting upright and leaning against the sturdy fabric wall, stretched tight around a bamboo frame.

"It can happen for the same reason reaume and humans can now have children." All heads swiveled toward him. "It's happening because reaume are evolving, and doing so at an increasingly more rapid pace as time goes on. I've been wondering about this for a while now."

"Evolving?" Maria asked, getting to her feet, lips curling into a scowl. "You mean, like, changing into humans? I don't want to be a human. I'm not a human!"

"No, you're not," Doctor Michael agreed. "You're becoming something else altogether, something humanoid in the sense that you're developing moral choice, you look more human, and in some cases, you can procreate with humans, but you're still a different species. This is what frightens the king, especially since reaume are already more powerful by nature."

"So if all the reaume are a threat, why's the king so threatened by us three in particular?" Lahcen asked, gesturing at his siblings.

The doctor lay back against his pillows, exhaustion falling over him. When he spoke, his voice was scratchy and weak. "You three are already what he fears will come about; you're half human and half reaume and you have free will. When threatened, you can, and will, kill." Wearily, he looked from one to the other of them. "If you were in his place," he said softly, "what would you do if you could get your hands on the biggest threat to your survival?"

"Lahcen thought. "I–I'd lock us up."

"I'd study us," Khalid said flatly. "I'd poke and prod and —"

He looked away from Qeriya, "and ... I'd make sure I knew everything, every strength, every weakness."

Doctor Michael held Khalid's gaze. He nodded slowly. "More than anything, he wants to study you. He may even want to recreate something like you for himself, in his family, perhaps with the prince."

"That's horrible!" Qeriya exclaimed, shooting to her feet. "I'd rather he just kill us."

"Oh, he probably would, eventually. When he had what he wanted."

Qeriya could see the doctor had come to the end of his strength. He needed rest. She rearranged his pillows and helped ease him back down.

"You three are the ultimate product of evolution after all," he mumbled, eyes closed. Understanding you is the only way to redesign humanity and stay ahead of reaume power."

"Maybe," Lahcen said. But it sounds like the reaume's evolved nature isn't much different to us anyway."

"Maybe, maybe not," Doctor Michael countered. "But there's a big difference, you're part human, and your genetic makeup will reflect that combination." His eyes fluttered open and he turned towards Lahcen. "Nobody knows what the ramifications are yet. That's what the king wants to find out."

That the reaume were evolving made sense, given what Qeriya knew of Maria. She watched as her young cousin shaped a small fireball with her hands. Fireballs were forbidden in enclosed spaces, but nobody said anything, treading cautiously around Maria now, as if she were an alien. Maria might not understand everything; but it wasn't difficult to tell that what Doctor Michael had said about her sister had made Raquel tremble with fright.

"I guess that means that you and I have a lot more in common than we thought. Now, no fireballs in the tent," Qeriya ordered playfully, snuffing it out.

Maria grimaced in mock irritation, relieved by Qeriya's normalcy. She scrambled over on hands and knees, ready to wrestle, but Qeriya knelt down, grabbing her squirming cousin in a tight hug.

"Here, we'd better go and get packed. Doctor Michael needs to rest," Anna said. They dutifully rose from the tent floor and filed outside, Anna and Khalid holding hands. Lahcen picked up Maria and carried her out and Raquel followed Juan through the tent flap.

Qeriya brought up the rear. Just before ducking outside, she turned back to the doctor. "I'll bring you some soup later, so you can get strong for the trip ... Uncle. She heard an exhausted grunt behind her and caught one last glimpse of Doctor Michael's fierce eyes, appearing almost silver in the mild green light, as the door flap closed.

Glancing up, she saw before her a bee the size of her own head, sporting a furry black coat, accented with vibrant yellow. Instinctively, she stepped back, leaning into the tent as the insect flew by, seemingly oblivious to her. Everyone else had walked on, missing the creature's sudden appearance. Captivated, Qeriya followed as it twisted and turned through the wood for a short while, before joining a mass of others just like it. Startled at the sight of so many, Qeriya kept her distance, watching as the bee did a sort of dance for the others. Within moments, the mass, following the leader, lifted into the air and zoomed through the trees, reminding her of the flow of the Wadi as it navigated desert rock and scrub branches.

Qeriya did not dare follow, but she felt a kinship that she'd rarely experienced before. Their path was hers, she was certain of it, and along with that realization came an overwhelming sense of peace, as if there was someone or something that watched over her on her journey.

Lodestone Books is a new imprint, which offers a broad
spectrum of subjects in YA/NA literature. Compelling reading,
the Teen/Young/New Adult reader is sure to find something
edgy, enticing and innovative. From dystopian societies, through
a whole range of fantasy, horror, science fiction and paranormal
fiction, all the way to the other end of the sphere, historical
drama, steam-punk adventure, and everything in between.
You'll find stories of crime, coming of age and contemporary
romance. Whatever your preference you will discover it here.